THE BOOK OF FIRE

THE AZIMAR ARCHIVES BOOK THREE

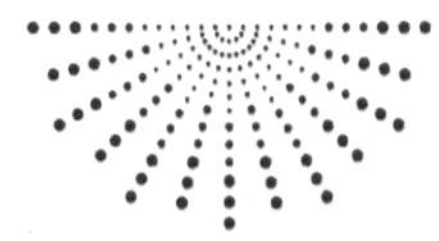

JACKLYN HENNION

DRAGON EYE
BOOKS

For Chansey and JiJi, the little lights of my life. And, as always, for Chase. You're my favorite.

PRONUNCIATION GUIDE

Alastor: Al-uhs-ter
Areanath: AIR-ee-uh-nath (*nath* sounds like *bath*)
Azimar: AS-ee-mar
Dars: DARZ
Doldural: dol-DURE-all (*dure* sounds like *lure*)
Eilonwy: eye-LON-way
Hasani: ha-SAN-ee
Mothlenor: MOTH-len-or
Nevara: nuh-VAR-uh
Nevina: nuh-VEEN-uh
Nunor: NEW-nor
Silvana: sil-VAWN-uh (*vawn* sounds like *yawn*)
Tathiel: TATH-ee-el (*tath* sounds like *bath*)
Tiryn: TEER-in
Vyris: VEER-is

ANNA

It wasn't the weight of him against her that always disgusted her, but the way his body had seemed to settle more closely against her own as the years passed. It was one thing to be the king's consort, and something slightly different to be his wife. But to realize that their bodies had changed to *fit together* … that was something else entirely.

Anna was silent as Mothlenor continued his "work", making no noise as his body continued to move against her own. This was not for her enjoyment, after all. And if she had the choice of doing it for her own pleasure, it certainly would not have been with *him*. It would have been with *her*.

And that singular thought helped Anna maintain her silence as Mothlenor panted and grunted away, his mouth close enough to her ear that she could feel his warm breath on her neck. And with one final thrust, Mothlenor's weight fell heavier against her. He stank faintly of sweat, and now there was the blossoming scent of his seed, and she felt the soft pulse of his blood as it returned from where it had swelled for the last few minutes or so.

And then, mercifully, his weight was gone.

Now Anna not only felt violated and disgusted, she also

felt cold. The cold she could live with. With a quiet sigh, she pulled the covers of the bed out from under her naked rear and draped them over herself, careful to hide as much of her flesh as she could. Not that it mattered. Over the years, Mothlenor had found plenty of opportunities to explore her body, and it was no longer the sacred thing it had once been.

The king was redressing, a quiet affair that often took him only slightly longer than the reason for his undressing in the first place. His hair was mussed, and he smoothed it straight with one long-fingered hand before slipping his usual dress robes over his head and torso.

"Why do we continue to do this?"

Mothlenor paused, turning to give her a surprised look.

Anna was just as surprised by the question, but it was already between them, and there was no retracting it.

His eyes narrowed slightly, the only sign of any offense before he turned his back to her again. "Because you're my wife, and that's what husbands and wives do."

"You can't enjoy it." Anna almost laughed, but held it in at the last possible second.

Mothlenor sighed, long and low. "There is a difference between enjoying something and not entirely disliking it." He turned to her again, one eyebrow raised. "I don't dislike it, though I know there are ways we can make it more enjoyable for me. But I also know that we can't always have what we would enjoy having." The muscle under one eye twitched almost imperceptibly, and Anna knew he was no longer speaking only of his own wants. "We must instead sometimes give those things up for what is better for Etritia, and learn to not dislike it."

Anna swallowed, realizing what he meant. "Better for Etritia?" But she knew the answer already, and when he turned towards her once again with those hawkish eyes of his, there was something like greed in them.

"A son, Anna. Etritia needs a prince." He fastened his

robes around him with a thick leather belt that he had carefully draped over a nearby chair, and the fearsome arcanist king stood before her once again, the look softened only by the fact that he was still barefoot. "And, if possible, a Gifted daughter."

"Trissa could be queen," Anna protested. "And she could be Gifted," she added, though she hoped not.

Mothlenor sighed again. "Etritia would be better served if left in the hands of a *male* heir. And my time is running out as—"

"You aren't that old." It was true. If anything, he looked younger than he had the day he had claimed her as his apprentice. There was almost no white to his long beard, and his hands were strong and sure as they laced his soft boots over the calves of his breeches.

Mothlenor gave her a look that might have been coy on anyone else. "You know as well as I do that looks can be deceiving, Anna. I don't know how much longer I can hold off the aging process, so procuring an heir sooner rather than later would be best."

Procuring. Like a child could be bought. Anna remained silent, the covers tucked carefully around her.

"As for Trissa being Gifted," Mothlenor continued, "I would have thought something would have shown by now. Five seems awfully old to begin showing signs of a Gift."

"It depends on the child," Anna said. "In the Coven, we—"

"The Coven is dead." Mothlenor's voice was a cold growl, and it startled her into quiet. "The Coven is dead, and Trissa is likely Ungifted." He stood, towering over her. "Keep her as your own, if you want her. Train her to be a witch, if it would please you. Or send her away to be raised as an orphan. But an Ungifted daughter is no child of mine."

Anna didn't argue. Why would she? If Mothlenor didn't want their daughter, that only meant Trissa would be safe from him. And if Mothlenor didn't want to hear that Coven girls weren't officially declared Ungifted until their sixth birthday, so be it.

But the thought of sending Trissa away from Etritia pained her. Would she be any safer, really? Would her life be any easier outside Etritia's walls? Anna didn't know.

"I thought you would be pleased," Mothlenor continued. "Knowing that your place in my kingdom is secure must give you some peace of mind. These are trying times." He tugged a wrinkle from his robes, smoothing the thick fabric over his chest and waist. "But those within Etritia's walls will be grateful they remained when my tasks are complete."

"There isn't enough within Etritia's walls to sustain those that remain," Anna blurted. Her face warmed immediately, knowing she had made an error. But the lack of food and water within Etritia while the castle and barracks never wanted for anything weighed heavily on her.

Ishta says there are dead and dying in the streets, and our population declines every year ...

Mothlenor's face was unreadable. The coldness in his voice told her she had angered him. "Then we will extend Etritia's walls."

"So you would make Etritia an empire rather than open the gates again?" She pulled the soiled covers of the bed more tightly around her. "Is that what you want? An empire, rather than a kingdom?"

"I want freedom for humanity."

The only freedom they need is from you and your men. And from this city.

"Do you doubt me, Anna?" There was ice in his voice.

Anna shook her head, thinking quickly. "I do not doubt your abilities, my lord. You can do all you wish."

His expression changed slightly, taking on the faintest look of pride. "Good."

"If I may have your leave, my lord, I'd like to return to my rooms."

Mothlenor waved a hand dismissively over his shoulder, stooping to read over a few pages of notes that lay on a nearby desk. "Go on. Return tomorrow morning—there is still much to be done."

Anna slipped from the bed, her eyes never leaving Mothlenor's back. There was always much to be done, and their work never seemed close to finishing. But it was better than the alternative had been. Anna gave an involuntary shudder, partly from the chill of Mothlenor's tower, and partly from the memory of her Coven sisters being locked away to rot in the dungeons.

She slipped her dress quickly over her head, bending to scoop her slippers up with one hand. Her underclothes she would leave behind. They would just slow down her retreat, and they would eventually be collected, cleaned, and returned to her. She was out of the bedroom and halfway through the study when Mothlenor called after her.

"Anna."

His voice came from the bedroom, but in the time it took for her to turn toward the sound, he had traversed the distance that separated them and stood just behind her. A gasp escaped through her gritted teeth. She would never grow accustomed to that particular trick.

He took her chin in one hand, gently, as though she might break if he held her too tightly. "I know that I am not to your … *taste*." He enunciated the last word carefully, holding her in place with nothing more than his gaze. "But I hope you can eventually grow to not dislike my companionship." His fingers tightened around her jaw, only just enough to notice. "Or to at least pretend as much." His grip loosened, and Anna thought his eyes might have softened. Perhaps it was only a trick of the light. "Have I not been compassionate, Anna?"

Anna swallowed; Mothlenor's fingers were warm and threatening on her skin. "Of course you have, my lord."

He leaned closer, the faint scent of sweat still clinging to him, mingled with the fresh scent of arcane energy. It would have been an attractive scent on anyone else, but on Mothlenor, it made Anna want to retch. "Have I not been kind to you over the years? Loved you, even?"

"O-of course you have, my lord."

He brought his lips to hers, and she did not fight him or pull away. He dropped his hand from her chin when they parted. "Perhaps you can one day grow to feel the same, Anna."

She said nothing, only dipping her head in quiet agreement. It would never happen, but she could never bring herself to tell him that.

Mothlenor waved her away. "Go on."

Anna fumbled behind her for the handle, opening the door without looking away from Mothlenor's retreating form. Only when the door was open and her bare feet were on the upper stair did she finally turn and flee from the tower. She didn't even bother to shut the door behind her. It would shut on its own. It always did.

Anna didn't look back until she was on the opposite side of the castle, close to the rooms she shared with her daughter. Even then, it was only the startling sound of a door shutting that drew her attention away from the stretch of hall in front of her. Her footsteps didn't slow until she heard the bright peal of Trissa's laughter, muffled but still easily recognizable. Hers was the only laugh Anna ever heard anymore.

When Anna opened the door to her suite of rooms, Trissa was not the first figure she saw. Her eyes instead fell on the slim shape of one of the few remaining servants who worked in the castle. The woman's hair was done up, as she usually kept it, and the more traditional simple shift dress had been long ago replaced with more sensible trousers and hard-soled boots. But they did little to conceal the curves of her hips, and when the woman turned at the sound of the opening door, Anna's breath caught at the sight of her face.

There was a fading bruise along one cheekbone, and her dark eyes had taken on a tired, forlorn look over the last few years, but she was still lovely.

"Lady Anna," Ishta said quietly, taking a hesitant step closer.

"Ishta." Anna took a quick step back, her shoulder blades pressing lightly against the closed door. Her fingers still lingered on the door handle, ready to open it once more if needed.

Ishta stepped away, arms dropping to her sides, chin drooping. "I'm only here to help Illa, then I'll be on my way."

As if the name had summoned her, another servant wafted in from the neighboring room, a basket of linens pressed against one hip. Her hair, a shade darker than Ishta's, was down, and she still wore the simple clothes all the servants once wore, though the black dye had faded some time ago. At the sight of Anna, Illa stopped, dipping her head elegantly. "Lady Anna." Her eyes shifted from Anna to her older sister, though Ishta hadn't moved. "I wasn't expecting you back so soon tonight. My apologies."

"It's alright, Illa. It was a long day, and I thought it best to go to bed early." Anna swallowed, stepping away from the door and walking quickly over to a nearby table, dropping her shoes against the wall as she went. She felt Ishta's eyes following her as she moved, but couldn't bring herself to look up. "Is Trissa alright?"

"Perfectly well," Illa answered. "She's been playing in her room since we returned from the baths, laughing up a storm."

Anna only nodded, keeping her back to the two women.

"I've got the fire in your room going, Lady Anna," Illa continued. "It looks like we'll have a cold night tonight."

"Thank you." Anna brushed a hand over the empty table-top, wishing there was something more she could do to keep her hands busy. *If only they would just leave ...* then she wouldn't have to struggle to keep herself from reaching out for the woman she loved.

"Trissa has already eaten, but I can return shortly with an evening meal for you, if you'd—"

"That won't be necessary." Even as she said it, a faint pang of hunger bit at her stomach. "If everything is in order here, I'd like to be alone with my daughter, please." The last word was almost a whine, but Anna couldn't hide it.

"Of course, Lady Anna. We'll be going now."

Anna waited until the door was shut before turning to face the room again.

It was empty, of course, but there was a lingering sensation of loss that pervaded the space around her. If it had just been Illa that had come to work in her rooms, it would have been fine. Illa was a nice woman, and Trissa was especially fond of her, and her presence didn't make Anna's stomach turn and twist on itself. But Illa had brought Ishta, not realizing tonight would be one of the nights Anna left Mothlenor's tower early. And with Ishta came guilt and heartache, and that damned sensation of loss that filled the room with its stifling stink.

Trissa's high-pitched, childish laughter rang out from a nearby room, and the sound of it brought some small relief to Anna's pain. She was talking, the words muffled and hard to catch, and Anna followed the sound, leaving behind the memories of Ishta's arms wrapped around her.

Trissa was already tucked into bed, an act she had taken to requesting from her "Auntie Illa" as often as possible. There was a new toy clutched in her arms, and though Anna couldn't see it clearly, she was sure that closer inspection would show her the familiar stitches and lovingly flourished "T" of the other gifts Ishta had made for Trissa over the years.

"Well," Anna said, and Trissa's round face lit up at the

sound of her voice, "you're already set for bed, aren't you? There's nothing left for me to do in here."

"I still need my sweet-dream kiss, and only you can do that!" Trissa's short arms shot up, and Anna crossed the room to sit on the edge of her daughter's bed and embrace her. "Did you see what Auntie Ishta brought me?" Trissa asked, her head pressed into Anna's chest. When she released Anna, she held up the misshapen toy for Anna to inspect. "It's a bear—Ishta said it will keep me safe while I sleep."

Anna took the toy, turning it over carefully in her hands. It was made from old clinic rags carefully steeped in old coffee, giving it a soft brown color. There was a small stain on the outside of one ear, too dark to be coffee, and Anna wondered how many Etritians had worn these rags before Ishta had decided to pull them out of circulation. It was almost shapeless, and only vaguely resembled any animal at all. Anna would not have guessed it was meant to be a bear at all if Trissa had not told her. And on the bottom of one foot was a small T, stitched in the same type of thread Anna had once used in her makeshift clinics.

"It's a lovely bear," Anna said, passing the toy back to Trissa. "How many of those do you have now?"

"Um ..." Trissa thought for a moment, searching the floor around her and counting. "Five!" she declared triumphantly, holding the newest addition to her menagerie aloft. "One for every birthday."

"That's right." Anna leaned to give Trissa a kiss on her cheek, not wanting to admit to her that there might not be a sixth one, if Ishta was almost half a year late with the fifth. Supplies for the clinics were extremely low, it seemed, and there was little Anna could do now to help. She straightened with a sigh. "I'm only sorry that you have to play with them all on your own."

Trissa shook her head. "I don't play on my own."

"Oh?" Anna asked, brushing Trissa's dark hair back from

her face. She'd inherited Anna's hair, and Anna's eyes, thank Imis, though her nose was slightly longer and thinner than Anna's own. "Does Auntie Illa play with you?"

Trissa shook her head harder. "No, but Nanny Cookie does."

Nanny Cookie. Anna sucked in a sharp breath, watching Trissa for any sign of deceit. The little girl didn't lie often, and never without reason, but Anna didn't want to believe that her daughter played with the old cook. Nanny Cookie, as Trissa liked to call her, had died the year before. She had been one of the lucky ones, dying of old age rather than of hunger, disease, hanging, or simply murdered by one of the King's Guard.

Trissa stared up at her, tucking her new toy under the covers next to her. Her eyes were innocent, and Anna didn't need to be Gifted to see that Trissa had meant what she'd said.

"Nanny Cookie plays with you? Are you sure it's her?"

Trissa nodded, brushing a lock of slightly curling hair from her face. "She makes faces and does silly voices."

Anna swallowed. "And what does she say?"

"That she loves me, and that she's sorry she can't always be around to play with me." Trissa wrapped an arm around Ishta's gift, promptly pulling it out from under the covers she had so carefully tucked it into and hugging it to her chest. "And that she's sad that you and Auntie Ishta can't be happy together." Trissa's head tilted. "What does she mean?"

Anna shook her head. Trissa was wrong. Cookie never learned about her daughter and Anna. They had been careful not to let her suspect that they were anything more than friends, and by the end of her life she was too confused to truly understand anything even if she had stumbled upon the pair of them mid-coitus. Not that Anna and Ishta had ever shared more than a few stolen moments together before Trissa's birth. And even less time after.

She never knew about Anna and Ishta.

Or did she?

Anna shook her head again. "I don't know what she means, darling." Anna gave Trissa a quick kiss on the forehead, pulling the covers up to her chin. "Can you keep Nanny Cookie's playtime with you a secret, Trissa? Can you not tell anyone else about it?"

Trissa frowned. "Not even Father?"

Gooseflesh prickled the back of Anna's neck. "Not even your father." *If Mothlenor found out that she might be Gifted after all ...* "Not Illa, not Ishta. No one." Anna swept a hand over Trissa's forehead. "Can you do that for me?"

Trissa hesitated, then nodded.

"Good." Anna gave her another kiss, this one on the cheek. "Now sleep."

Trissa obediently closed her eyes, clutching her new bear tightly to her chest. Anna stood, straightening the covers over her daughter's figure, then left the room, leaving the door slightly ajar. She waited, ear close to the door, not sure what she was listening for.

After a moment, Trissa whispered softly in the dark room. "Can you tell me a story, Nanny Cookie?"

In the silence that followed, Anna thought she might have felt the slightest shift in the still air, like a light breeze only barely adjusting course. She held her breath, tasting her surroundings for arcane energy and finding nothing.

Trissa was silent, perhaps listening to a spirit share a bedtime story, and Anna sent a wordless prayer to Imis that it was only the imaginative nature of a creative child that had her daughter speaking of playdates with the dead.

When she finally retreated to her room, after double-checking the lock on the door and pinning a chair beneath the knob, she smelled something distinctly feminine hanging in the air. The bed was made, the tops turned down in carefully even layers, and the fire gave off a warm red glow behind its grating. And Ishta had been here.

Anna curled beneath the covers, pulling her own gift from its hiding place beneath her pillows.

This one had also been made from discarded rags, though it was a shapeless doll, not a bear. And where Trissa's bear had a stylized letter T on the bottom of one foot, this doll had a small, rather plain A stitched into the center of its chest, over where the heart might have been. Whether the tiny monogram was supposed to indicate that this doll represented Anna herself, or if it was instead Ishta, with Anna always in her heart, Anna had never asked. It had simply appeared in her room one evening, when Anna still carried Trissa in her womb, and the two women had never spoken of it since.

The doll was worn in spots, but as Anna cupped it loosely in her hands she could see that someone had taken the time to mend the worst parts. Anna lifted the doll to her nose, inhaling gently, and was not surprised to find Ishta's scent lingering on the thin cloth.

When Anna eventually fell asleep, it was with Ishta's doll curled to her chest and a few errant tears drying on her cheeks.

NUNOR

Darlyth's jowled face was paler than Nunor remembered, surely as a result of the great king finding himself nearly trapped within his own realm and unable to see the sun for some considerable length of time. But Nunor sat silently as Tiryn told Darlyth all they had come to learn in the last year, leading up to their latest information on the possible location of the gold dragon needed to reclaim the Amulet of Fire.

Tiryn was mid-sentence when Darlyth raised a hand to stop him. "What of the Earth Amulet, Tiryn? What do you know about it?"

Tiryn frowned. "Nothing more than what I have already shared with you, Lord Darlyth."

Darlyth sighed, his broad chest sagging slightly. "I had hoped that your news would be more promising, but progress is progress."

Beside Nunor, Darmon smashed a fist against the table. "Progress is not enough!" Darmon's heated gaze fell first on Nunor, then across to Tiryn, and finally onto Darlyth. "If our Earth Amulet cannot be returned to us, then we should be going out to destroy the men that stole it from us!"

"The man that stole it from us is already dead, Darmon," Nunor growled. "He died to spirit the damned thing away, and to keep Doldural safe from Mothlenor for as long as possible."

"And he broke the treaty between our people to do so!" Darmon shouted, rising to his feet. "Which means there is nothing to stop us from ravaging their cities until it is returned to us."

"Darmon, you fucking idiot," Nunor started, standing to face Darmon, no more than a hand's breadth away from his cousin. "No one knows where the Earth Amulet is. We have nothing more than a shitty little bit of poetic drivel to guide our way, and we are doing our best. *On our own.*" Nunor bared his teeth in a smile. "If you want to get the amulet back sooner, then perhaps you can get off of your fucking ass and—"

"Stop it, both of you!" Darlyth's voice thundered.

Silence fell in the room, but both Nunor and Darmon remained where they stood, glowering at each other.

"Grinor, please," Darlyth said quietly, motioning towards the older dwarf who sat on his opposite side, next to Tiryn.

Grinor cleared his throat, his eyes darting about the room. "Well, we've already established some time ago that Areanath's actions did in fact break the letter of the treaties between mankind and the dwarfs and elves. But with the alternative—"

Darmon snorted loudly, crossing his arms over his chest, but said nothing.

"The alternative," Grinor continued with a look at Darmon, "coupled with the letters that Areanath sent before his death to both King Darlyth and the Vyrisian king that begged us to keep the treaties in our hearts and minds, we can conclude that Areanath's actions did *not* infringe upon the *spirit* of the treaties." Grinor swallowed audibly. "He was only trying to protect us, and we owe him more respect than he's been recently receiving from this council."

"Owe him?" Darmon asked, face twisting. "Owe the man that stole from us, then let his murderous brother take the throne? Owe the man that has caused the deaths of countless dwarfs all across Azimar, at the hands of his own people, no less?" Darmon sneered across at Grinor, who paled against the look. "We owe him *nothing*."

"Darmon, please," Darlyth started.

"We continue to meet here, year after year, and we continue to listen to this *elf*." Darmon accented the last word with a finger pointed at Tiryn. "This elf, who continues to bring us nothing new, nothing useful. And Grinor sits there, begging for peace, begging for patience, and you do *nothing*, Father." Darmon glared down the table at Darlyth. "If I didn't know any better, I would say that you are afraid. That you are a coward."

Nunor growled wordlessly, reaching for the knife on his belt. He wasn't sure if he meant to kill his cousin or only threaten him, but the movement of his hand to his waist drew Darmon's attention, and the dwarf drew his own blade nearly as quickly as Nunor did. It was only Darlyth's voice behind him that paused Nunor's hand.

"Get out, all of you!"

Darmon and Nunor both stared at Darlyth, and across from them Grinor did the same. Only Tiryn seemed unmoved, his lithe hands carefully draped over one another on the table, head bowed slightly to stare at them.

Darlyth stood, waving one jeweled hand towards the door. "I said get out!" Grinor jumped, then stood quickly. Tiryn followed suit, though it took him a second to disentangle his knees from the underside of the table. Grinor led the way, and Darmon followed behind, staring daggers at nothing at all. Nunor made to follow his cousin, but Darlyth dropped a heavy hand on his arm. "Except you, Nunor."

Nunor thought there might have been something dark and ugly in his voice, but he couldn't place it if there was.

Darlyth and Nunor waited, still on their feet, until the heavy stone door echoed shut behind the others. At the sound, Darlyth released a sigh, turning away from Nunor.

"My lord?" Nunor asked, his voice gruff. He cleared his throat, following with a softer, "Uncle?"

"Darmon is right." Darlyth placed a steadying hand on the back of his chair, looking over his shoulder at Nunor. "I am afraid."

The simple admission left Nunor's throat dry. Dwarfs never admitted fear. Their king especially.

"I am afraid that if I take our people to war against Mothlenor, we might lose. And that it would mean the end of all of dwarf kind." Darlyth turned and fell into his seat again, motioning for Nunor to do the same.

He did, but slowly, carefully, imagining that at any moment the floor might give way and swallow him whole.

"I am also afraid that war is inevitable if the Earth Amulet is not found very soon."

"War is not inevitable," Nunor protested. "We just need a little more time. We're close to finding the second amulet, and the others will surely come close behind."

Darlyth snorted. "You are not close to finding the second amulet. I heard Tiryn. He said you had a promising lead on the location of the golden dragon. The amulet itself has not been spotted, and your lead may prove as useless as each one before it."

"We just need more time," Nunor repeated. "If I could have more dwarfs, we could—"

"I am dying, Nunor." Darlyth shook his head slowly. "There is not much time left."

There was a quiet moment, during which they could only stare at each other. Nunor's mouth worked silently; Darlyth's jaws were fixed tightly together.

"How? Why?"

Darlyth sighed. "You might as well ask the sun how it rises, or the stars why they shine." Darlyth fixed him with a look, not unkind, and said softly. "I am old, Nunor."

Nunor could only shake his head.

"Twenty years ago, before this mess all started, I could have died happily. I had lived a long life, longer than most, and it had been filled with mostly good things." Darlyth leaned back, crossing his hands over his long beard. "But now, I have been holding on to what little life force the gods have seen fit to give me, and the longer I hold on to it, the harder it becomes to keep it in my grasp."

Nunor sighed, his knuckles white as his hands pressed against the stone table before them. "How long?"

Darlyth considered for a second, his head tilting. "Two years. Perhaps three, if we are lucky. Less, if we are not."

"And then?"

Darlyth snorted again. "And then I will die, and Darmon will take the throne after me."

"Not Darmon." Nunor grimaced. "Anyone but Darmon."

Darlyth chuckled, the sound deep and somehow sad. "Grinor feels the same way. He is not my first choice, though he is my son." Darlyth's mouth twisted in the thick foliage of his dark beard. "I would much prefer that you follow my path. But, as a Halfhelm …"

Nunor Halfhelm, last surviving descendant of a dwarf whose foolishness cursed his family with a damning name, fell against the back of his chair with a groan. He didn't want to be king, but … *Anyone but Darmon*. "What if I earn a new name?"

Darlyth nodded. "I hope you do. If any Halfhelm could, it would be you."

"What do I have to do?"

Darlyth straightened. "Find the Earth Amulet. Before my time is up." His eyes narrowed, staring at Nunor. "Find it and save Doldural from war. Then you will have earned a new name and will be made king after me."

Nunor wanted to protest, but shouting and the sound of the great stone door to the council room opening once more halted his words.

"—the time for war!" Only the last of Darmon's cry was heard in the council room, but Nunor could guess the sentiment easily enough.

"What is the meaning of this?" Darlyth hissed. "Grinor, Darmon, I told you to leave me."

Grinor dipped his head as he entered behind Darmon, both anxious and hesitant to enter. "My apologies, my lord, but—"

"We've had news from one of the mining colonies to the south," Darmon growled, reaching through the open doorway and pulling a younger dwarf through. "They've been attacked. By the *King's Guard*."

Nunor stared at the young dwarf in front of him. She was petite, even by dwarf standards, with her bright hair braided and pinned up. It had surely been lovely when fresh, but now it hung in angry tatters around her head like one of the halos often seen adorning the oldest statues of the gods. Dirt and ash smeared her cheeks and clothing, and even from a distance Nunor could smell the heavy scent of blood and death on her.

"Go on, have a listen, Father." Darmon gave the woman a shove, sending her stumbling closer to the council table. She hesitated, then gave a dreadful bow.

Darlyth waved her on. "Please, if my son thinks that what you have to say is important enough to interrupt a private council, then you're free to dispose of the pleasantries, miss …"

"Alain, my lord. Of the Obsidian Order." She gave another bow, despite Darlyth's words, though this second one was more prim and less rushed.

"The Obsidian Order?" Darlyth turned to Nunor, his eyebrows raised.

Nunor understood his surprise. The Obsidian Order was one of Doldural's best companies, comprised of both excellent miners and capable swordsmen, housed within a single underground city to the southeast. Only the best members of the best families joined the Obsidian Order, and were sent to work the richest mines. Nunor himself would have been in the Obsidian Order, if not for his family name.

"I take it that your city is no more?" Darlyth asked, his jaw set.

Darmon stepped forward. "They set fire to the entire complex, Father."

Alain bowed again. "But we were able to seal the exits behind us as we escaped. They won't be able to follow us to Doldural, my lord."

"Unless they dig through the rubble," Nunor muttered.

Alain turned, giving him a glare. "I knew what I was doing, Master Halfhelm. The tunnels collapsed for miles. No one will get through." Her jaw worked. "Human or dwarf."

"How many escaped before the tunnels were collapsed?" Darlyth asked.

"Twenty-six," Alain whispered.

A collective gasp stilled the room. Twenty-six survivors. From a colony of nearly ten times the size.

"This …" Darmon began, his voice low. "This is why it is time for action, Father. It is time for war." Grinor opened his mouth to protest, but Darmon cut him off with a sharp motion of one hand. "This is not the time for cowardice. Your people need you to *do something*, Father."

Nunor watched as Darlyth's jaw worked for a moment. Finally, he spoke. "Have all the remaining Orders retreat into Doldural."

"What?"

Nunor was surprised to hear his voice echo with Darmon's.

"Grinor, send the notice out. All families and Orders are to return to Doldural." Darlyth turned to Alain, and she straightened as he addressed her. "The remaining Obsidian Order members will join the Emeralds for the time being, and patrol the tunnels for any sign of King's Guard intruders."

Alain bowed her head again, but her words of acknowledgment were covered by Darmon's protests. "You can't be serious? You want us to flee into our den like rats?" Darmon advanced on his father, stopping short when Nunor stepped between them. "We are dwarfs, dammit! We do not run away from conflict and bloodshed. We run *into* it!"

"King Darlyth is only doing what he thinks is best for all of dwarf kind," Nunor said, glaring at his cousin. "The answer does not always have to be war."

Darmon sneered, his eyes shifting from his father to Nunor. "What do you know of war, Halfhelm?"

Nunor sucked in a breath in one sharp hiss, settling his shoulders. "I know that my forefather was eager for bloodshed, and it was to his detriment." His hand dropped once more to the knife on his hip, but only out of habit. "I would listen to our king, Darmon, unless you would like to doom your family line to a name such as mine."

Darlyth stood, and Nunor turned as he addressed them all. "My mind is made. Doldural will shut herself off from the rest of the world, and await the return of our Earth Amulet. We will protect ourselves, should the need arise, but we will not go out into Azimar and seek vengeance for ourselves." He gestured at Alain and Grinor. "Please make arrangements for the lady, Grinor, and I expect a full account of this latest tragedy as soon as possible." He waved one hand towards the door, dismissive and tired. "Now get out."

Darmon turned on his heel in a huff and stormed from the room. Grinor went more slowly, taking Alain by the arm and speaking to her in low, hushed tones.

Nunor waited until the others were nearly gone before turning back to Darlyth. "I promise you, my lord, I will bring the amulet back."

Darlyth sighed. "Just remember my words, Nunor. Time is running short. Grinor knows it. Darmon suspects it. And I need you to make sure that what little time is left is not wasted."

Nunor nodded, bowing to Darlyth. Then, in an uncharacteristically gentle gesture that unnerved him as much as it pleased him, he hugged Darlyth, pulling the large dwarf into a tight embrace. When they parted, Darlyth's eyes were wide, but a smile stretched across his lips. Nunor straightened with a grunt. "I hope you go gently, Uncle."

Darlyth's smile deepened. "I don't intend to go anywhere just yet, Nephew."

Tiryn was waiting for him just outside the council room. Other than the tall elf, standing slightly stooped in the dwarf-sized hall, there was no one else in sight.

"I take it Darmon stormed off somewhere, eh?" Nunor asked.

"Cursing under his breath, yes." Tiryn's face was drawn. "I heard the initial report from the dwarf woman, but Grinor insisted I wait out here while it was delivered to the king."

Nunor shrugged, leading the way down the hall toward the nearest exit that would take them to the surface. "The loss of a mining colony is a great thing, and not easy for any of us to discuss even among ourselves."

"How many were lost?"

Nunor turned, realizing Tiryn had not followed and was still rooted to his spot just outside the door. Nunor sighed, staring at his friend. "Over two hundred."

Tiryn's breath released in a low curse, and Nunor grunted in surprise. The elf closed his eyes, his head tilted back, and he took a moment for himself. Nunor waited, accustomed now to Tiryn's calming ritual, even if Tiryn himself was not wholly aware of it. The swearing had been a shock. Tiryn usually left that sort of language to Nunor.

"You asked me once," Tiryn said, leveling his eyes to Nunor once more, "if I would curse Mothlenor, given the chance."

Nunor snorted. "You said no. Some shit about curses causing more pain than the cursed deserves."

"Actually, I didn't answer."

"Sounds like you." Nunor crossed his arms over his chest, taking a few steps closer to Tiryn.

"I didn't answer because I didn't know my answer," Tiryn said. "I didn't know what I would do if I ever found myself facing him."

Nunor gave his friend a look over. Something had changed in Tiryn, and he was only just beginning to understand it. Whether the change had come on gradually or was a response to the latest news of non-human deaths at the hands of Mothlenor's men, Nunor couldn't be sure. But Tiryn was different.

"You know now?"

"I do," Tiryn said. "Though I don't like what it says of my character."

Nunor snorted again, turning his back on Tiryn even as he waved him on. "Let's go then. I think it's time you and I did our own investigating."

Tiryn's soft footsteps padded behind Nunor, the elf catching up to him in no time with his long stride. "Investigating what?"

"First," Nunor held up one finger, "we find the Earth Amulet before Darmon takes the dwarfs to war." Another finger lifted. "Second, we figure out the perfect curse for you to slap on that maniac in Etritia."

"Third," Tiryn said, dipping his head as they walked beneath a slight deformity in the ceiling of the hall, "we celebrate our impending victory."

"With a lot of ale, and a lot of ladies."

3

ROLAND

When Roland and Alastor stopped each night, it was always Roland who saw to their horses, while Alastor set up their small tent, started a fire, and put together some sort of dinner. But they had been on the road for several weeks now, their last stop in a town almost a distant memory, and their supplies showed it.

So while Alastor carefully stacked an armful of dried twigs and small limbs and magicked a fire over the ensemble, Roland pulled bags and saddles and blankets off their tired mounts. The bags were emptier than they had been at the start of this latest trek, and the horses were thinner. Perhaps they were all a little thinner and emptier than they had been before. As Alastor started work on the tent, Roland fed the horses the last few scoops of grain from the bottom of the feed bag, giving each of them a handful at a time.

"Sorry, boys," Roland murmured as Alastor's dark horse lipped at the palm of his hand, searching for more food. "That's the last of the good stuff."

"There's still the apples. A few of them, at least." Alastor motioned in the direction of the packs Roland had set aside. His dark hair fell into his face, and he brushed it out of his eyes with the familiar sweep of one hand across his brow. "We're not far from Emery. We can stop there tomorrow for a few things before we reach Larten."

Roland scooped up a second feed bag, this one heavy with half-dried crab apples that he and Alastor had spent an hour or more collecting from the ground and lower branches of half a dozen stunted trees. *When had that been? Two weeks ago?*

He lifted a few pairs of ugly fruits from the bag, then set it between his feet and held out both hands for the horses to nibble and munch on the small treats. "I'm not sure we have the funds for much, but a bag of feed will get us from there to Larten with no trouble."

"Perhaps we should ask Mathius to procure a new tent for us as well." Alastor fingered a worn spot in one corner, where the thick hide had rubbed itself thin against the stake that held it down. "This old thing has just about had enough."

"We'll be able to mend it. Don't give up on it yet. I've had worse tents serve me for longer than we've had that one." Roland rubbed affectionately at the necks of both horses, and one lifted its head to lip at his ear.

"If you say so. It's just …"

"What?"

Alastor sighed. "It gets difficult, sometimes. You know? Always riding, always searching. Scraping by until we can stagger back to the only place we can call home."

"We're not exactly doing the king's work, Alastor. We're trying to stop everything from falling apart, and that means we have to be fine with being uncomfortable from time to time." Roland set to brushing the horses, starting with his own. "We'll stay in Larten for a bit. Let our asses and thighs recover from the saddles. Sleep in a soft bed."

"Have warm meals with fresh meats," Alastor grumbled, bending over the bags and rummaging around inside. "Maybe have a warm woman or two after the warm meal."

Roland snorted. "Being on the road has never stopped

you from finding a warm woman, Alastor." He looked over the wide back of his mount at his nephew. "How many farmer's daughters have you snuck off to the barn with in the middle of the night?"

Alastor snorted. "I have a gift, and gifts should not be wasted." He straightened, brushing his hair from his eyes once more. "I think it's the hair."

Roland shook his head, trying not to smile. "Your mother would be mortified."

Alastor pointed at the feed bag partially filled with apples that still sat on the ground. "That last one gave us a few extra handfuls of feed in the top of our bags, I'll remind you."

"Your mother would still be mortified."

Alastor laughed, and they continued their work in silence. It wasn't until both horses had been brushed and led off to a nearby stretch of tall grass to eat their fill and Roland and Alastor themselves sat by the fire to have their own meal that either of them spoke again.

"Do you think this next one might be the real thing?"

Roland sighed, staring down at the chunk of dried salted beef he held. It was always the same question, every time they heard even the smallest whisper of a dragon sighting. "I don't know."

"This one feels … different, though," Alastor said, tearing a bite from his own dried beef. "Doesn't it?" He chewed and waited, staring across the fire at Roland.

"You've said that before." But Roland knew what Alastor meant. Rumors of dragon sightings always turned out to be dead ends—Melonya's case being the sole exception—but this one had left a strange feeling in Roland's heart since the moment Tiryn had shared the news. It was almost a hopeful feeling, and though it had faded some during their trip south, it had not entirely gone.

Roland sighed. "It does feel different, but I don't know what that means." He stood, holding out the small wooden bowl that held his measly dinner for Alastor. "Here. I'm not so hungry anymore."

Alastor took the bowl, giving Roland a hard look. "You hardly touched your dinner last night. You have to eat something."

"I'll eat when we get to Emery." Roland patted Alastor on the shoulder. "I just need some sleep tonight."

"You haven't been doing much of that lately either," Alastor called after him.

Roland stopped, turning to look at his nephew. "What do you mean?"

Alastor shrugged, tearing another bite of his food. "You've been talking in your sleep a lot," he said around a mouthful. "Tossing and turning all night." He shrugged again. "I'm surprised you feel rested at all when you get into that saddle every morning."

Roland stared at the fire for a moment, thinking. Had something been keeping him up? He couldn't remember. He shook himself and turned back to the tent. "Probably nothing important. Just time for one of those soft beds Mathius has."

He and Alastor exchanged good nights, and Roland kicked off his shoes and stretched out across the top of his saddle blanket, not even bothering to pull it over himself, and he was already drifting before his eyes had even fully closed.

Nevina was waiting for him when he fell asleep. Or when he awoke. He was never quite sure.

She sat in an ornate chair that he half recognized, legs draped over the side, wineglass in hand. Her legs and feet were bare, the rest of her covered in a robe made of some smooth and thin material. And, as it usually was when he saw her now, her veil was gone. Piercing blue eyes stared at him from her thin face.

"Well, this explains it."

Her lips quirked. "Explains what?"

Roland fell into the chair beside her, taking her free hand in one of his. "Alastor just told me I've been talking in my sleep." Her skin was soft beneath his fingers, and when he inhaled, the scent of roses filled his nose. "I guess we've been seeing a bit of each other lately?"

"A bit." Her lips quirked again. "I wouldn't need to disturb your sleep so much if you would just remember what I've been trying to tell you."

Roland looked around him. "I think I remember a little. We're in Areanath's rooms. The way they used to be, anyway."

Nevina nodded, taking a sip of her wine.

Roland smiled at her. "You're drinking Vyrisian." He chuckled when she nodded again, this time with a slight roll of her eyes. "No one's had Vyrisian in—"

"Twenty years," Nevina said. "So you've said." She dropped his hand, sitting up and tucking her legs beneath her. "Come on now, there must be more you remember."

Roland looked around the room once more, trying to recall their previous conversations there. The sensation was tantalizing, like a half-recalled word. Or seeing a face and not remembering the name.

His gaze fell on the open door across from him, through which a bed could be seen. The covers were rumpled, and he thought he could see a pile of white cloth on the floor nearby. He raised an eyebrow, looking across to Nevina again. Had they used that bed in another waking dream like this one? *Could* they use that bed?

Nevina's eyes rolled again, and the door shut of its own accord with a soft thud. "Try again, Ajax."

Ajax ...

The sound of her voice using his old name stirred a nearly forgotten memory. Roland thought on it for a moment, watching Nevina's expression shift from amused annoyance to patient interest. Roland sighed, rubbing at his temple. "Something about the Coven. That's all I remember."

Nevina frowned slightly, taking another sip of wine.

"You could just tell me again."

"I guess I'll have to. But it does nothing if you can't remember when you awake."

"How many times have we done this?" Roland asked, sitting upright and reaching for her hand again.

"Half a dozen, perhaps more." Her voice was flat, almost tired. "It's hard for me to keep track myself." She dropped her hand into Roland's and he squeezed her fingers gently. "I need you to try to remember, Ajax."

He pulled on her hand until she leaned across the distance between their chairs. "Kiss me, and I'll remember."

She laughed, the sound low and soft. "That's what you always say." But she kissed him, both of them leaning together until their lips touched.

"You haven't aged at all," Roland said, tracing the line of her jaw with a finger.

"Well, I'm dead. And the dead don't age." Nevina took his hand again, pulling it away from her face. "More importantly, you haven't aged at all either. And you are still very much alive." Her touch found a small marred spot on the inside of his wrist, where the flesh was whiter than the surrounding skin. "You have some new scars, but I imagine your nephew's hair will start to grey before yours does."

"What is this, Nevina?" Roland asked. "A dream? A memory? Something in between?"

Nevina's eyebrow raised, and her gaze became distant for a moment. "I don't know."

Roland tightened his hold on her hand, and she shook herself slightly, taking a sharp breath. "Now," she said, sitting upright and folding her hands into her lap, wineglass cradled between interlaced fingers. "I need you to concentrate. Try to

keep what I'm about to tell you close to your heart, so that
you might remember when you wake up."

Roland nodded, straightening and turning to face her.
The room felt colder without her hands to hold, but Roland
ignored the discomfort and focused on Nevina's eyes. "About
the Coven? But the Coven is dead."

Nevina's mouth curled into a smile. "The Coven is not
dead."

Roland's breath caught, but then he shook his head. "You
mean Layle, right?"

Nevina nodded. "Layle, yes. But she's not the only one."

Roland tried to remember the young girl he had found
out in the farmlands of Etritia. She had been angry, and
powerful, and very alone. And she had been pregnant.

"Layle had a daughter?" He asked.

"Layle had a son," Nevina said. "But the son had a
daughter."

Roland tried to think it through. Layle's son would be
how old now? A little younger than Alastor? And could he
imagine Alastor fathering children? Roland grimaced,
recalling his joke about his nephew sleeping with farmer's
daughters. It was technically possible …

"How old is she?"

Nevina took a careful sip of wine. "She's six."

So young … "And she's Gifted?"

Nevina only nodded.

Roland sighed, falling back against his chair. "So there are
two Gifted women somewhere in Azimar. That does not
make a Coven."

"There are three."

"Three?" Roland sat up again. "Who is the third?"

Nevina traced a finger around the rim of her wineglass,
making it hum slightly. She stared down at her hands, and
when she spoke, her voice was flat again. "She's the daughter
of an Ungifted Coven sister. Someone Mothlenor spared,

apparently." Nevina looked up at him. "You might know her better as the current queen, Lady Anna."

Roland took a slow breath. "The queen is from the Coven?"

Nevina nodded.

"And she has a Gifted daughter?" Roland knew that Etritia had celebrated the birth of a daughter a few years ago, but to know that someone so close to Mothlenor could also be descended from the Coven … "How did you find out about this other girl?"

Nevina shifted in her chair, her gaze not quite meeting his. "She can see me. Speak to me. She's Gifted with more than just the usual kind of Sight the Coven women possess, it seems."

"What do you mean she can see you?"

She swallowed, tracing her finger around her glass once more. "When I died, my spirit did not fade away as it should have. Mothlenor kept me." She looked up at him, and Roland could see her eyes shining slightly with the threat of tears. "My soul is trapped in this world, and the princess can see the imprint of my old self and communicate with me."

"Like we are now?"

Nevina nodded, smiling slightly. "Yes, though she does not need to be asleep to do so."

Roland waited, thinking. Heat flashed over him, settling into his stomach and writhing there. How many times had she shared that her soul had been made prisoner? And how could he not have remembered that look in her eyes when he awoke? How could he forget with every sunrise what Mothlenor was doing to her?

"I know what you're thinking, Ajax," Nevina said. "You're angry that I've been made to suffer even in death."

"Angry doesn't quite do it justice."

Nevina nodded. "I've said it before, but Mothlenor's actions will be his undoing eventually. Keeping me in this world has given me the chance to tell you everything I can learn. And it has helped me to learn about my family. I'm glad for it."

"Your family? You mean Layle and—"

"Arella." Nevina smiled again, the motion causing a few errant tears to streak down her cheeks. "She named her granddaughter after the sister she lost down in that dungeon."

Roland was silent, his own throat thick. He remembered Arella. Her voice was almost lost to him, but her face was still clear in his mind's eye, and the way that she had clung to Layle's hand …

"The Coven is not dead, Ajax," Nevina said, her voice firm. "And they need you."

"Me?" He laughed, shaking his head. "I've already failed them once, Nevina."

"You're the only one I can trust to find Layle. And the only one outside Etritia I can guide."

Roland shook his head. "No, I can't be the one to find her. I promised myself that I would never seek her out, never try to reconnect. Not after what happened to her Coven sisters."

"Then break that promise," Nevina said. "For my sake."

Roland was beginning to understand why his mind might have chosen to forget his previous conversations with Nevina. "Why find her at all? Why not let her and her grand-daughter be?"

"I don't think her part in the future of Azimar is quite over." Nevina stood, reaching for him. "I think you'll need her before the end. And she will need you."

Roland stood, dizziness making him stumble, but Nevina's hand was there to catch him. "What do you mean? What's going on?"

"No more time for talking, I'm afraid. You're waking up." Nevina's hand held his, but he could hardly feel it. "Promise me you'll remember this time."

Her form was fading, or perhaps it was his. He leaned close to her, reaching for her. When she stepped into his arms, there was almost no weight to her body. "Kiss me, and I'll remember."

Her lips quirked into that smile again, and she brought her mouth to his. He felt the warmth of her face, so close to his, but could not feel her press against him. She stepped back, and the warmth of her ebbed. "Promise me, Ajax."

Nevina was little more than air now, just bright blue eyes and the lingering scent of rose oil.

"I promise I'll remember. I promise I'll find her."

"Find who, Roland?"

Roland opened his eyes, Alastor's face swimming into focus. It was dark, the smell of woodsmoke heavy in the air. Woodsmoke and roses. "What?" His voice was thick, and Roland was surprised to realize that tears were running out of the corners of his eyes and into his ears and hairline.

"You were mumbling in your sleep again," Alastor said, settling down to sit beside him. "Then you said, clear as a summer day, 'I promise I'll find her.' Find who?"

"I-I don't remember." But he had known only a moment before. The woodsmoke stung his eyes, and he pressed them shut as he sat up. His mind's eye conjured the image of piercing blue eyes, and he thought he could hear a gentle humming sound—like a finger tracing the edge of a wine-glass. "I need to remember."

"Great Ones, are you *crying*?"

"Shut up, Alastor. I need to think." He almost had it. He'd promised he wouldn't forget. Something about the Coven, but what was it?

"And here I thought I would just settle in for a nice night, maybe dream of kissing some tiny-titted farmer's daughter, but then I have you crying in the corner like a child." Alastor sighed, rubbing his eyes.

Roland's stomach lurched. "Kiss me and I'll remember."

"No thank you, Roland." Alastor grimaced, his face only inches from Roland's. "What's gotten into you?"

"I remember," Roland groaned. "Dammit, I remember, and I can't believe she's sending me off on such a fool's errand."

"What are you talking about?" Alastor asked. "Who is *she?*"

"Nevina wants me to find her daughter."

Roland explained everything to Alastor, and they sat together until the sky lightened into grey.

"How do you think you'll find her? The dragon's eye?" Alastor asked.

Roland pulled the fist-sized stone from the inner pocket of his vest. He always kept it on him, as he had for years, though it had been some time since he had looked into its depths. "It would help, sure. But I think I'll need Nevina's help to find her." He stared at the stone briefly, thinking about the young girl he had met so long ago. But when the colors of the stone shifted, he quickly looked away, palming the stone and hiding the image it had begun to conjure. He was not ready to see the woman that girl had become just yet.

Alastor slept as Roland packed their camp together and saddled the horses as well as he could. When Alastor awoke, and the rest of their belongings were safely stowed away, they made off for Emery.

In Emery, they purchased more feed, as they had already planned. But the feed bag and tent went to Roland, while Alastor left the town with almost nothing.

"Are you sure you don't want me to come with you?" Alastor asked for perhaps the dozenth time. "I can take notes of your mutterings. Keep you safe and sane out there?"

"No," Roland said. "The others need you to stay on course. Go to Larten. See what Mathius knows and tell him what I'm up to. Hopefully the others can join you if this latest dragon sighting turns out to be the real thing."

Alastor squinted up at him, and for a moment he looked once more like the young man Roland had first known, looking up at him from the deck of a merchant ship, some five-odd years ago. "You sure you'll be alright?"

Roland nodded. "I'm sure." He gave Alastor a hard pat on the back. "Besides, I've got all the goods. You're the one that might not make it," he joked.

"Larten isn't far." Alastor smiled slyly. "And I can always charm my way into sharing a barn with a farmer's daughter."

Roland shook his head. "We're not in farmland anymore, Alastor. You should know that better than I do."

Alastor shrugged. "A fisherman's daughter, then. And what could be more romantic than looking up at the night sky from a sandy beach?"

Roland snorted. "I fear what your mother would do if she could hear you talking like that. She'd take me to the tanners, I'm sure."

Alastor laughed, pulling Roland into an embrace. His arms were strong, and Roland couldn't help but remember Hasani holding him in much the same way. "Take care, Uncle," Alastor said, releasing him.

"And you, Alastor. Don't do anything too stupid."

They both pulled themselves into the saddles of their horses, and with a final farewell, they went their separate ways.

4

LAYLE

Layle knelt in the cold morning dew, tugging at weeds. The knees of her pants were soaked through, and dirt was caked under her fingernails from digging the most stubborn roots out. The sun was hardly over the horizon, but sweat was already beading along her forehead and trickling down her spine.

It would be a warm day. Perfect for planting her silkleaf seedlings. *If only I can get this damned bed cleared out.* She swore at a deeply rooted dandelion shoot, wiping her hand across her brow. *Can't you stay in your designated corner? Why must you stray so far from home?*

A bright peal of laughter echoed through the still air of the garden, and her head came up. Arella stood not too far away, bent over to examine something in the grass. Then, with a carefully timed pounce, she fell to the ground, hands cupped together. Layle watched her bring her hands up to peer into the gap between her fingers, another giggle escaping her lips. She spoke, but Layle was too far away to hear the words.

"What have you got there, Arella?" Layle called, and the girl jumped at the sound of her voice.

"A grasshopper," Arella answered, clambering to her feet. "You want to see?"

"I know what grasshoppers look like." Layle sat back on her heels, brushing dirt from her palms. "Why don't you let him go, and come give me a hand here?"

Arella made a mumbled reply, bending at the waist to open her hands and let the insect loose. Layle watched her granddaughter stare at the fleeing grasshopper, a childish pout on her round face.

"Come on now," Layle said, waving Arella over. "That's not a very nice face to be making when your grandmother asks for your help."

Arella made her way over, her footsteps intentionally dragging and her slightly chubby arms crossed over her chest. "I'm coming."

"Why are you chasing grasshoppers? I thought you hated bugs?"

Arella dropped to her knees in the grass across from Layle, and Layle pointed at a clump of spiderweed topped with cream-colored blossoms; Arella obediently began tugging at the roots. "I was trying to catch one for Trissa. She's never seen a grasshopper."

"Trissa?" Layle asked, pinching off a dandelion flower and offering it to Arella. "Is that one of the girls in town?" The name sounded vaguely familiar, but she couldn't match a face to it.

Arella shook her head, bending to let Layle tuck the flower behind her ear. It stuck through her hair, the yellow petals accenting the blonde curls nicely. "No, she lives in Etritia. In the castle."

"Ah." Layle bent again to pull at the stubborn clump of weeds in front of her. "Is Trissa here now? Can I see her?" How many imaginary friends had Arella conjured up over the years? The most recent had been an old cook by the name of Cookie, of all things. She had not stayed for very long, but then none of them had.

Arella made a face. "No, she's not here. She's in the castle. With her mother and the king."

The weed finally tore from the ground with a satisfying ripping sound, and Layle tossed it aside with a sigh.

The king.

Thinking of Mothlenor made her skin crawl.

"What does Trissa do in the castle?" Layle glanced up at her granddaughter, stretching slightly to reach another clump of spiderweed. "Does she work there?"

Arella shook her head, the scowl on her face deepening. "No, she's the princess. Princesses don't work."

Layle smiled at that. "This princess works," she said, tickling Arella's ribs.

Arella's scowl melted and she squealed, squirming away from Layle's fingers. When the two of them settled again, Arella shook her head once more, sending the dandelion in her hair falling to the torn ground. "I'm not a real princess. But Trissa says I can be queen, since I'm the older cousin."

"Cousin?" And there was that name again, the name that Layle could almost recall. "You don't have any cousins, Arella."

Arella frowned, her brows pinching together. "Trissa *is* my cousin. She told me so."

With that last utterance of the name, Layle remembered where she had heard it. It had been in another town, one closer to Etritia, when Arella was still just a wailing child. Trissa had been the name given to the king's daughter. The first royal child in decades.

Layle felt a sudden chill stir the warming air of the garden. "Who told you about the princess? Was it one of your little friends from town?"

"No." Arella's frown deepened. "They don't know her. Trissa told me. She talks to me, from the castle."

Layle closed her eyes, trying to still the shaking in her hands. "Arella, I need you to tell me the truth. Who told you about the princess?"

When she opened her eyes again, Layle could see that Arella was holding back tears. "I am telling the truth. Trissa talks to me. She says that her Auntie Nevina—"

"Don't say that name," Layle hissed. Her voice had been louder than she meant it to be, and Arella burst into tears. "Don't ever say that name again, Arella!" Layle fought down a wave of nausea. Arella might have found out about the princess from some gossip in town, but no one would dare to mention the name of the woman who supposedly killed their last king. There was no way for Arella to learn her great grandmother's name.

Except ...

"Why?" Arella cried. "Why do you hate Trissa? Why do we have to live here?" She wiped at her face, smearing dirt across her cheek. Snot dribbled from her nose, and her cheeks were a ruddy red color. "Why can't we go live in the castle with the rest of our family?"

"Arella." Layle reached for her granddaughter, but Arella smacked her hand away, stumbling to her feet.

"I want to go home!" Arella yelled.

Layle's voice hardened again. "We are home."

"I want to go home to the Coven!"

The Coven.

Layle's heart skipped a beat. And in the tear-streaked face of her son's child, she could see the scared face of another little girl, also named Arella, as she told Layle about a nightmare full of dragons.

Layle swallowed. Arella stared at her, waiting for an answer.

"The Coven is dead."

Arella stamped one foot, choking out a sob. "No, it isn't. Nevina says the Coven is alive."

"Nevina is dead." Arella let out another sob, and Layle's voice shook as she continued. "Nevina is dead, and the Coven died with her. There is nothing left out there in the world for us."

"You're lying," Arella said between sobs. "You're lying, and you know it."

Layle was surprised to realize that she was on the verge of tears herself. Had she known this day might come, when she took that tiny infant from her son's lover? Had she known that her granddaughter might find a way to pull her back into her old life when she gave that baby the name of her dead sister? "I would not lie to you, Arella. The Coven is dead. They died a long time ago."

Arella lifted her chin stubbornly, though her bottom lip still trembled. "They didn't all die. We're still here. And Trissa. And her mother. We are the Coven, and the Coven is still alive."

With that, Arella turned and fled back towards the house. Layle watched her go for a quiet second, Arella's sobs punctuating the quiet garden. Layle pushed herself back to her feet, standing to chase after her. "Arella, wait!"

Arella was only a few steps ahead of her when Layle stepped into the house. The interior of the house was darker and cooler than outdoors, but Layle hardly noticed it as Arella crossed the living space and stormed into the room the two of them shared. The door shut behind her with a slam just as Layle reached it.

On the nearby mantle, a white dragon's egg wobbled dangerously, and Layle barely managed to traverse the distance to catch it before it fell. "Great Ones take it," Layle swore. She tucked the egg into the crook of one arm and tried the handle to the bedroom.

The door remained shut, as if it had been locked.

But the door had not been made with a lock.

Layle stared first at the metal door handle in her hand,

then at the metal cuff around the same wrist. *I could open it. I could break her magic down. She has no control. She has no idea what she's doing.*

But Layle let her hand drop from the door handle.

"Arella, would you please open the door?"

"No!"

"Arella, please," Layle said. "I'm sorry. I'm just not ready to talk about the Coven." She sighed, resting her free hand against the wooden door. "Clearly you are."

"Go away!"

"I'll go." Layle took a step back from the door. "I'll be out in the garden. Those silkleaf seedlings won't plant themselves." She tried to laugh, but it sounded like a dry sob. Layle took a breath, then released it in a slow exhale. "And when you're ready to come out, I'll tell you everything I can about the Coven. And about Nevina. And about the first Arella."

There was silence on the other side of the door for a moment. Layle stood, waiting, hoping her granddaughter might say something in return. At last, there was the smallest sound of movement, and Arella spoke up.

"You promise?"

"I promise."

It was quiet for another moment. Then Arella's muffled voice came through the door once more. "Alright. I'll go back to the garden in a little while."

Layle sighed, taking another step away from the door. "Alright."

She returned to the mantle, lifting the dragon's egg up to place it back into its designated place. It was only then that she realized the stony shell was warm to the touch.

Layle hesitated, staring at the white egg. She traced a finger over one of the blue lines spiderwebbed across the surface.

The egg was just as cold as it normally was.

Layle replaced the egg on the mantle with a quiet huff. *It was only my imagination.*

Still, Layle could not find it in her to turn away from the cold stone orb. She stood in the center of the room, hands on her hips, staring at the egg as it sat above the fireplace.

After a few moments, she turned away with a shake of the head, and stepped out through the door and back into the sunshine.

B ehind her, Arella's soft voice filtered through the door as she spoke to a little girl who was not there. And the white egg gave a single shuddering twitch and was still.

5

ALASTOR

Jaimes was studying when Alastor found him. He'd taken up residence in Mathius's inn, once his own father's inn, and had become reclusive as he aged into full adulthood. The room was both neat and cluttered, depending on where one looked. The bed had been tucked into one corner, taking up as little space as possible, and one half of the room looked like Azimar's smallest library. There were shelves taller than Alastor, packed full of books, and a small reading nook had been formed against the wall closest to the door, complete with a lantern to read by in the darker hours. The other half of the room was less tidy, with a high-top table and an assortment of instruments and various ingredients, many of which Alastor couldn't name, and a few that looked slightly revolting.

Alastor watched his brother for a moment as Jaimes made a short notation in a heavy-looking book, head turning every few seconds to check on the small cauldron simmering over the benchtop fire he'd ordered custom made from Cusch. His hair had grown longer, and Alastor had half a mind to comment that someone might mistake him for a woman if he didn't get it trimmed. But Alastor's own hair was wild and unkempt, and easily just as long as the sandy-headed alchemist's in front of him.

"Jaimes," Alastor called, stepping just inside the room. "Mathius tells me that you hardly eat. He's not sure you've been sleeping much, either."

Jaimes looked up, a smile lighting his face. "Alastor!" He nearly set the quill he held down, taking half a step away from whatever experiment he was working through. But he hesitated, glancing once more at the simmering metal pot, and instead waved Alastor over. "I'm glad you're back in town. Come on in, I'll just be another moment or two."

Alastor sat on the bed, frowning when a small cloud of dust and ash flew off the covers as he settled against them. *Mathius was at least right about the not sleeping bit.*

He waited, watching Jaimes move slowly from one end of his makeshift workbench to the other. The limp in his leg was still prominent, but Alastor was sure it had improved since the last time he had wandered through Larten. Jaimes was thinner, though. Alastor could see it in the way his shirt hung from his shoulders, and in his hands when Jaimes reached for a fat jar of leafy greens, plucking out a few and dropping them into the cauldron with a hiss.

Jaimes muttered to himself, making another note in the book. He seemed to have already forgotten Alastor was there.

"Jaimes," Alastor called again. "I've come to ask a favor from you."

Jaimes waved a hand over his shoulder. "Sure, sure. Ask away. I'm listening."

"Roland and I had to part ways for a bit. And Nunor and Tiryn still haven't returned from Doldural."

"Uh huh." Jaimes walked to the opposite end of the table, misshapen leg dragging slightly as he went, and plucked another jar from the haphazard collection that waited there.

"I want you to come with me to find the gold dragon."

"Uh huh."

"You're not even listening to me, are you?" Alastor sighed, waiting for Jaimes to answer.

Jaimes said nothing, only watched the cauldron and took notes, one hand reaching for the burner underneath and making a slight adjustment. The flame thinned slightly, growing brighter.

Alastor crossed his arms over his chest. "I'm getting married. She's a great bear of a woman."

"That sounds great."

"She's literally a bear," Alastor continued, staring at the back of Jaimes's head as he walked the length of the work-table again. "Myra introduced me. You remember Myra, right? Roland's old friend?" Jaimes made a sound of acknowl-edgment, and Alastor pressed on. "Apparently she has a friend in another wyre family, and we met, and one thing led to another, and …" Alastor trailed, waiting for Jaimes to speak.

Jaimes continued his work, bending to sniff at the liquid now letting off thick, gurgling bubbles.

"Great Ones take it, it's not even fun to pick on you when you're like this." Alastor sighed, raised an arm and extin-guished the small flame on Jaimes's workbench with a half-hearted wave of the hand.

"What?" Jaimes stiffened, then rounded on Alastor, his brow furrowed. "Dammit, what was that for? Do you know how much work you just ruined?"

"Judging by those circles under your eyes and the ash collecting on the bed, I'd say about five days. Maybe a week." Alastor stood, reaching around Jaimes to take the notebook from the table. "Mathius is worried about you. He thinks you've gone a bit mad with this medicine business."

"Mathius doesn't know what he's talking about." Jaimes reached for the book as Alastor stepped away with it, but

Alastor jerked it out of reach. "Sometimes it's necessary to make sacrifices for the good of the world."

Alastor gave him a look. "I think we both know that well enough."

"One of us more than the other, perhaps." Jaimes lurched forward on his twisted leg, but stopped after only a single step. He held out his hand, reaching for the book again. "Give it back."

"Not unless you promise to listen to what I have to say." Alastor flipped through the last few pages, trying to make sense of the tiny scribblings and the half-finished sketches.

"Good luck trying to read it," Jaimes said with a snort. "I've written it in my own kind of shorthand. Makes it easier to take notes during experiments."

Alastor grimaced. "I think Mathius was right about you being a bit mad."

"Give it back, Alastor." Jaimes's voice was firmer, almost angry. "That's years of work you're waving around."

"Not until you promise to listen," Alastor said. He gave Jaimes another look over. "And to eat something. Gods, you look like you might fall over dead any moment."

Jaimes sighed, running his hands through his hair. It made the unruly mess even worse, and it did nothing to make him look less like a madman and more like a tired alchemist. "We're not children, Alastor. This isn't a game of Keep-Away we're playing."

"Well, one of us is writing little notes in a secret script, so who does that make the child?" Alastor held the book out, but pulled it back as Jaimes reached for it. His brother glared at him, but Alastor did not offer it out again. "Promise you'll eat something and listen to what I have to say." Alastor's nose wrinkled. "And take a bath."

Jaimes's glare deepened. "Are you saying I smell?"

"No, but you look like shit."

Jaimes's mouth worked wordlessly for a few amusing

seconds, then his jaw tightened and he gritted his teeth, still glaring at Alastor. "Fine," he grumbled, waving the extended hand. "Now give me the damn book."

Alastor thought of pressing him, of making him actually say the words "I promise", but he had been childish enough already, and Jaimes was nearing the point of screaming profanities, though he hid it well.

Alastor passed the book over. "What are you working on, anyway?"

Jaimes snorted, turning and setting the notebook next to the burner and rapidly cooling cauldron. "Same thing I'm always working on."

"The restoration potion?" Alastor leaned against the table of Jaimes's little reading corner. "Still? It's been years—why are you still beating your head against that same problem?"

Jaimes shrugged, falling onto the edge of the bed in a small cloud of ash. He grimaced, waving a few floating grey particles away from his face. "I just know the answer is still out there. And I want to be the one to find it."

"The answer to immortality?"

"Not to immortality," Jaimes said with another grimace, this one directed at Alastor. "But to restoring what the body has lost. Eyesight, hearing, or … or memory." Jaimes motioned weakly at the cooling mixture on his workbench. "Restoring lost limbs. Healing scars." He rubbed at his calf absently. "Untwisting broken legs."

"And from there, the secrets to immortality are surely only a few alterations away." Alastor crossed his arms over his chest. "I don't want to talk you out of your work, but we've had this discussion before. And you remember what Tiryn said, that all things made for the good of the world can be twisted to become her undoing?"

Jaimes rolled his eyes. "Tiryn doesn't understand."

Alastor frowned. "He does. I think we all understand."

Jaimes stood, reaching for a slim tinderbox at the far end

of the worktable. "No, you don't." He worked at the burner, bent over slightly, trying to light it again. His bad leg stuck out beside him at an odd angle, and it pained Alastor to see it. "You all think you can understand what it's like to live with something so broken, but you don't really get it. I can't run. I can hardly walk. I have to live the rest of my days knowing I'll never be able to fight again, like we did back on the *Kingfisher*." He bent lower, making some small adjustment that Alastor couldn't see. "That I'll never be with a woman."

"You can be with a woman, Jaimes," Alastor said, leaning against the workbench. "You don't need a fully mobile leg to do that. I'm sure there are a lot of women in Larten or Hythe that would be happy to show you, especially after that bath."

Jaimes slammed the tinderbox down onto the top of the table. "That's not what I meant, dammit!" He paused, taking a breath, and set to work on the burner again. "I meant having a life with a woman. I meant love, Alastor. Not just sex."

Alastor sighed. "You also mean with Eilonwy, not just any woman."

Jaimes harrumphed, peering at Alastor from around his alchemical setup. "She wouldn't have me. Not like this."

"I think you underestimate how she feels about you." Jaimes only snorted, and Alastor bent to look his brother in the eyes as best as possible with the contraption between them. "She liked you before your leg was ruined. She liked the way you saw everything so differently from anyone else. But after that day—"

"Don't talk to me about *that day*." Jaimes sneered.

"After that day," Alastor repeated, "she started to really care about you, and how much you sacrificed for her."

"Did you come here for a reason?" Jaimes asked, his tone biting. "Or just to try to give me more of your rubbish advice?" He cursed as the burner finally caught, only to have the delicate flame blown out by his own breath.

Alastor gave Jaimes's shoulder a gentle push until his brother straightened with a glare. Then, with a second lazy wave of the hand, the burner was lit. Jaimes's glare only grew harder, but Alastor took a step back and motioned at the cauldron. "You're welcome."

"I hate it when you do that."

"You mean magic?" Alastor asked, eyebrow raised. "You used to love it. You were better suited to it than I'll ever be."

"Not anymore." Jaimes fiddled with the settings on the burner again, and the flame shifted shape slightly. Heat was already rising off the top of the cauldron as the liquid inside warmed. "Now what do you want?"

"I want you to come with me to find the golden dragon. Roland is off on his own task, and Tiryn and Nunor are still in Doldural."

"No." Jaimes's voice was flat.

Alastor laughed. "Oh, come on, Jaimes. Great Ones know you could use some time out of your little workshop here."

"What I'm working on is too important to leave sitting around for months on end." Jaimes turned his back to Alastor, searching through the jars on his table. "I'm sorry, Alastor, but I won't go."

"You can't be serious."

Jaimes did a half turn, as much as he could without moving his bad leg. "I'm very serious. What I'm working on could be just as important as finding the amulets, and I won't leave it behind." He gave Alastor a small shrug before turning back to his work.

Alastor stood for a moment, too stunned to speak. Jaimes continued in silence, making small changes to his burner and writing out a note in his odd script. "So that's it, then?" Alastor asked quietly. "That's the end of the tale of Harlan and Silvana's boys? Always together, always on some adventure, now just one stupid sod going off on his own, and one brother staying firmly put like the weeds he grows for his experiments."

Jaimes bent over the warming cauldron. "It's time for us to grow up, Alastor. This isn't some grand adventure. We're not on the *Kingfisher* anymore. Those days are behind us."

"For one of us, perhaps." Alastor retreated towards the door. "I haven't given up just yet."

"Alastor, wait."

Alastor turned, surprised to see Jaimes staggering after him. Jaimes held out a hand, and when Alastor took it, he was pulled into a hug.

"It is good to see you. I meant that." Jaimes's voice was softer and kinder than it had been a moment before, but there was still enough firmness to it to tell Alastor that his brother couldn't be swayed. "This isn't how I wanted our story to end, either. But this is how it needs to be." Jaimes released Alastor, shifting his weight on his leg as he did.

"They say every end is just a new beginning." Alastor shrugged. "Perhaps this story will be just as good as the last one."

Jaimes nodded, then narrowed his eyes, his face twisted in confusion. "Did you say you were marrying a bear?"

Alastor laughed, and Jaimes's own chuckle joined it. "You really need to step away from your work every once in a while. Go out and talk to someone." Alastor gave Jaimes's shoulder a gentle pat. "Make sure you eat something. And bathe."

Jaimes nodded again. "I will. And …" Jaimes hesitated, his cheeks flushing slightly. "If you see Eilonwy, will you give her my regards?"

Alastor smiled. "Sure, I can do that."

"Good luck. I hope you find what you're looking for."

"I hope you do, too."

6

SYRANI

Gentle tapping on her brow woke her, and when Syrani opened her eyes it was to see a narrow masculine face with thick brows and a sharp jawline. And rounded ears.

"Are you ready to go?" her oath brother asked, his words thick and slow in the elven tongue.

Syrani sat up, shoving her brother aside and dropping her feet to the floor. "Just a moment. Is everything prepared?"

"Everything is prepared." His eyes followed her in the dark as she slipped on some worn boots. "Your father is downstairs."

"Of course he's already ready," Syrani said with a snort.

"Your father is …" Her brother hesitated, and when she caught his face, it wore a frustrated scowl.

"Common is fine, Hasani," Syrani said, switching to his native tongue.

"He's a stubborn old elf. He wouldn't let any of us get the jump on him. Especially not today, of all days." His words were rushed, and he let them out with a sigh.

Syrani laughed, motioning for him to take the lead through the dark Hometree. "You're not wrong."

"Sorry," Hasani said, his voice a whisper in the dark. "I'm trying to get better at speaking elven, but—"

"You're doing fine." Syrani gave him a hard pat on the shoulder. "You're a credit to your race for even trying, Hasani."

"Syrani." From the dimly lit floor below them, Syrani's father stepped forward. A hunting bow rested under one arm, unstrung and plain looking. "There is little time for chatter," he said in the elven tongue. "We should be going. The Hunt will not wait for us."

Syrani muttered an apology, which Hasani echoed in the elven tongue, and they followed her father out of their Hometree and into the Vyrisian woods.

The sun was up, and beside her, Hasani was panting and sweating. Humans did not do so well in heat, and although Hasani had grown more accustomed to the Vyrisian climate, they were still forced to stop every few hours for him to eat and drink and relieve himself. Syrani and her father could have continued without half as many breaks, but they wanted Hasani there with them as much as he wanted to be there. So they did not complain at the slow progress, and they ate and drank and laughed with him during those pauses in their hunt.

And when they finally tracked the black elk to a small glen far outside their Homewood, it was Hasani's shot that dropped the beast. And it was Hasani that carried the cleaned carcass for the first hour, though he did not get a chance to carry their Hunt prize again.

During one of their pauses on the trip back to their Homewood they were attacked. Her father fell first, and Syrani stood, paralyzed, as four shadows emerged silently from the trees and advanced on her and her oath brother.

Hasani grabbed her upper arm, tugged her to her feet and they fled, leaving her father's corpse behind.

They ran, both of them panting.

Syrani was faster. She could make it back to the safety of their Homewood in no time. *But Hasani ...*

Hasani pulled her to a stop. His face was red, his breathing labored. He pressed one of their bags to her chest, almost sending her falling. "This is what they're after. Your father and I were going to destroy it, so he could never get it back. You have to keep it from them."

"Hasani, we can keep going. We're almost there." But they were still several hours away at his pace, and Syrani knew he could not keep at it for that much longer.

"Go, Syrani," Hasani said. In the elven tongue, his words were more command than plea, and Syrani took one involuntary step back. But he reached for her, and she stepped into his embrace. A screech echoed from the woods behind him. "Goodbye, Syrani."

Syrani ran, listening for the sound of her brother's footfalls behind her. But he did not follow. Tears stung her eyes, and she did not stop running until she passed through the protective barrier that surrounded her Homewood.

She stood on the other side, watching the trees for any sign of her family. But it was the four demons that emerged from the woods. There were shouts from the other elves of her Homewood, and after a barrage of fiery arrows, the demons fled. But her father and brother did not return that night. And when they were brought back the next day, it was in the arms of other members of the Homewood, their bodies covered in soft white cloth.

And all the while, Syrani held her brother's pack to her chest, unwilling to let it go.

Gentle tapping on her brow woke her, and when she opened her eyes, Nieve was leaning over her. "You were dreaming again, weren't you?"

Syrani brushed Nieve's hand away and sat up. "I was."

"The same one as always?"

Syrani nodded. "The same one."

Nieve sighed, sitting on the foot of Syrani's bed. "I'm sorry."

Syrani sat up, dropping her bare feet to the floor. "Is it time?"

"Yes." Nieve remained where she sat, her dark hair spilling over both shoulders. "My father is already waiting."

Syrani grimaced. "He doesn't plan on coming with me, does he?"

"No," Nieve said with a soft laugh. "I think everyone here knows how you feel about doing the Hunt with others. And they respect that, though they might not all understand it."

"I don't need them to understand it." Syrani stepped into her hunting boots and got to her feet. "I just need them to let me work in peace."

"They will."

Nieve followed her out and into the rest of the small house they shared with Nieve's father. It was no Hometree, but then Syrani wasn't sure she could stand to spend another night of her life within the protective warmth of living wood.

"Syrani."

The sound of her name, today of all days, brought her to a stop. But it was Nieve's father, the village Elder, who called for her. His voice was thinner and shallower than her own father's had been, but it was no less warm.

He crossed his thin arms over his narrow chest and took a low bow. "Good questing, Hunter."

Syrani repeated the motion, their bowed heads almost touching. "Thank you, Elder. I will not disappoint you."

Nieve's father laughed, a dry raspy sound. "You haven't yet. This will be your fifth Hunt with us, and you've never returned empty-handed." He gave her a sly look, one eyebrow raised and just the barest hint of a smile to his mouth. "The younger men could learn a lot from you, if you had the patience for teaching."

Syrani sighed. "It's not my place as an outsider, Elder. We've discussed this."

"We have also discussed," the Elder said with gentle stubbornness, "that you are no longer an outsider to us. You are Vyrisian, yes. And all but I were born here in Azimar. But you have been welcomed into our family, Syrani. You are no more an outsider than Nieve."

Syrani turned to catch Nieve's eye, but the young elf woman only shrugged, giving her a look that told Syrani that she once more sided with the Elder in this particular argument.

Syrani sighed again, sidestepping the Elder and heading for the door. "I will repay your continued hospitality by bringing you the finest deer I can find in the surrounding wood." She picked up her bow and a bag of gear that was already waiting for her by the front door.

"Do you know the one you want?" Nieve asked.

"There's one I've had my eye on, yes." Syrani tucked her bow under her arm. "He likes to feed in a glen about two days' hike from here. He would be a good Hunt prize."

"Two days?" Nieve hid the concern in her voice well, but not quite well enough. "Are you sure that you don't want one of the others to go with you? I'm sure any of them would love the chance—"

"No." Syrani turned back to Nieve, giving her a sharp look. "Do you think I can't handle a few nights in the woods on my own? Hunts in my Homewood lasted easily three times as long."

"But this isn't your Homewood, Syrani," Nieve protested. "It's more dangerous here."

A vision of four demons sliding their way from dense woodland crossed her mind's eye. Her skin broke out in gooseflesh, and Syrani had to suppress a shudder. "I don't think that's true." She sighed, opening the door at her back. "Besides, I'll have Halcia with me."

Nieve looked like she might argue more, but a raised hand from her father stopped her. The Elder gave Syrani a small bow. "Go on then, Hunter. We will await your return."

Syrani returned the bow and left before Nieve could protest again. The door shut with a hollow snap behind her, and Syrani began the brisk walk through the grey morning fog.

There were only a few others awake at such an early hour. A pair of elven farmers, one young and one old, stood on the edge of their field, arms raised and voices singing out across their crops. Syrani could feel the arcane energy that they wove into their words like a light breeze across her skin. But it was simple magic, nothing like what was sung in Vyris to keep the Hometrees alive and well. Syrani could have taught them, if she had the patience for it. But as much as they wanted to be, these people were not her people, and they had fallen too far from the old Vyrisian ways to come back now.

"Good questing, Hunter!" a small voice piped.

Syrani came to an abrupt halt, narrowly avoiding knocking over the elf child that had jumped out to greet her. "Thank you, Eysa," Syrani said through gritted teeth. "It's a bit early for you, isn't it?"

"I wanted to make sure I could see you off." The young girl fastened her hands behind her back, standing with all the confidence a twenty-something elven child could muster. "This might be the last hunt you do on your own, you know." Eysa wagged a finger in Syrani's direction. "I plan on being there beside you next year."

"Not going to happen," Syrani snapped. The faint hurt expression that flashed across Eysa's face softened Syrani's next words. "You're still too young. And not good enough a hunter to take on the Hunt."

"I've been hunting," Eysa protested. "And I'm the best of all the children."

"But you've never been Hunting." Syrani emphasized the last word, and Eysa's face fell.

"Then maybe you should teach me."

There it was again. The plea to share what she knew with people who were not a part of her family. Not that there were rules against it, not really. But … "It's not my place. Your elders should be teaching you. Not me."

Eysa groaned. "I will never be the hunter you are unless you are the one to teach me."

Syrani needed to leave, but Eysa would follow her all the way to the ends of Vyris if she did not satisfy her enough to make her stay behind. Syrani tapped a foot against the ground, staring at the small child in front of her. "I will teach you when I decide you are a good enough hunter for my lessons to stick."

That seemed to work, and Eysa's eyes widened and a smile stretched across her face. "You promise?"

Syrani nodded. "I promise." Though the promise meant almost nothing. Syrani could easily make it nearly impossible for the young girl to prove herself a worthy enough hunter. But Syrani somehow doubted that Eysa would prove to be a troublesome student.

And teaching one elf child to properly perform the Hunt would stop the Elder from pestering me as well.

Eysa beamed, and the warmth of it touched Syrani, though she did not want to admit it. "Then good questing, Hunter," Eysa said again, "and I'll begin preparing for our first Hunt together."

The young elf stepped aside, allowing Syrani to pass with little more than a roll of her eyes. Syrani left the stone and wood structures of the elven village behind, slipped through the thin arcane veneer that protected them from human eyes, and stepped into the dark and cool surroundings of the

Felgar woods. She looked to the sky, cloudy and bright blue through the heavy treetops. *"Halcia? Are you out there?"*

The voice that answered her call was deep and feminine. *"Of course I'm out here. Where else would I go?"*

The gentle connection their minds made as they found each other comforted Syrani, and her shoulders relaxed. On this side of the barrier, they could know each other's mind nearly as well as they knew their own. But inside the village, within the protection of the barrier, they were cut off. And that separation made Syrani feel lonely and vulnerable, despite the arcane shield that surrounded the elven settlement. And despite the company of others of her kind.

Syrani set to walking, her strides long and sure. *"How are you?"*

"Fine enough. Did Eysa stop you on your way out?"

Syrani let out an involuntary snort. *"Yes. She wants to do next year's Hunt with me."*

A glum sense of acknowledgment rolled from Halcia's mind to Syrani. *"I thought she might say something. I overheard her discussing it with Nieve."*

Syrani stepped over a thick root, her foot coming down harder than she had wanted. *"And you didn't think to tell me?"*

Halcia gave an annoyed snort, wherever she was, and both the sound and the emotions behind it rocked gently against Syrani's own annoyance. *"This is the first time you've been beyond the veil since then."* Doubt crept into the dragon's next words. *"Besides, I thought Nieve had convinced her not to bother you about it. She knows how you feel about helping them."*

Though she surely hadn't meant them to, Halcia's words stung. *"I do the Hunt every year. Is that not help enough?"*

"I wouldn't know," Halcia said.

But Syrani knew, though she didn't want to admit it. She quickened her pace, almost jogging through the trees. *"Will you stay with me, Halcia?"*

"Of course. Where else would I go?"

They traveled for the rest of the day that way, Syrani on foot, Halcia on her wings. And as evening fell, Halcia guided Syrani towards a large valley tucked between two gently sloping and tree-covered hills, where they could both rest for the night.

Syrani started a fire with a tired wave and a small burst of arcane energy. She brought down a hare with a quick shot from her bow, then cleaned it in silence, waiting for Halcia to join her. The hare was almost ready to eat before Syrani heard the great beat of wings on the night air.

Halcia came to land with a crash, and Syrani had to lock her knees to keep from falling over. The hare jumped dangerously on its spit, and the fire wavered. Syrani raised an outstretched hand to the flame, steadying it with a second burst of arcane power.

"Careful there, you almost knocked my dinner into the fire."

"My legs are asleep," the great dragon said as an apology. *"It's not often I fly for so long."* She lumbered into the firelight on unsteady legs, each foot hitting the earth with a soft thud.

"You could have rested."

"And let you out of my sight?"

Syrani smiled, opening her arms to embrace Halcia around her great neck. "You've gotten bigger."

"It has been some time."

"It can't have been that long."

Halcia seemed to consider for a moment, a sense of resigned resentment washing over Syrani's mind like water over river stones. *"We've only seen each other twice since last year's Hunt."*

That couldn't be right. Could it? But Halcia would know better than her; Syrani was the only companion the great dragon had ever had. Syrani closed her arms tighter around Halcia's long neck. "I'm sorry. We won't always have to live like this. One day, we can both be free."

Halcia bent one great wing around Syrani's body, the thick webbing rubbing against Syrani's back, until the elf was cocooned against the beast's chest. *"May the Great Ones bring us that day sooner rather than later. I don't want to wait another year to embrace the only friend I have."*

Syrani ran a hand over the hard golden scales of Halcia's shoulder. They were warm from the heat of the fire, but the heat was superficial. Beneath the campfire's touch, Halcia's scales were deeply cold. Syrani always imagined that it was the chill of clouds and higher heights than Syrani herself had ever experienced that kept Halcia's armored body so icy to the touch, but she had never asked. "What if I talked to the Elder again? What if I promised to share more of my knowledge with them, in exchange for you being allowed to stay within the village? You wouldn't have to hide away then, and we could see each other whenever we wanted."

Halcia unfurled the wing that covered Syrani, and the two of them parted. *"You know I'm too large to stay within the village. It wouldn't work."*

"We could build a space for you. It wouldn't take much time at all." But even with Syrani's help, it could take a year or more to finish a stone building large enough to house the great dragon. And how long would it last her before she outgrew it? Two years? Five?

"You would build a stable for me, like one of the horses you pet and feed and ride?" Halcia asked, a bitter note of sarcasm coloring her words. *"How kind."*

"I'm only trying to offer a solution." Syrani turned the spit, glaring at the skinned and skewered hare. "I don't hear you doing the same, Halcia."

"We could just leave."

Her words were said with such finality that it startled Syrani. "Leave?"

"Why not? What reason is there to stay?" Halcia lumbered closer to the fire, finding a comfortable position to lie in

before collapsing to the earth in a rumbling yet graceful way. *"You have made it very clear to them that you've chosen to maintain yourself as an outsider. You do not want them close to you. You do not want to care for them."*

"Just leave?" The idea had some appeal to it. It would certainly make her life with Halcia easier to enjoy. *But ...* Syrani recalled the excitement that lit up Eysa's face when she heard Syrani's promise to teach her when she was ready. And although they could be annoying at times, both Nieve and the Elder had done nothing but care for her over the years.

"You're not sure you can leave them behind." Halcia's voice was not unkind, but Syrani thought she could sense displeasure in the dragon's words.

"I may not want them close. And I may not want to care. But what I want and what has happened are two different things."

"I see." Halcia's words were even and toneless.

But Syrani knew she had upset her. She poked at the roasting hare, watching the juices that ran from it fall into the fire with spits and hisses. "I'm sorry."

They said nothing for a long time. Syrani ate in silence, staring at the edges of the fire. In the corner of her eye she could see Halcia lying nearby. Firelight glinted off her golden scales, bouncing and shifting with each breath the dragon took. Her long tail, barbed slightly at the end, was curled until its pointed tip rested behind the enormous claws of her rear legs. Her head lay between her front legs; her eyes were shut. Syrani could almost envision her as a large cat, warming itself by the fire. The tip of Halcia's tail even swept and twitched along the ground every few moments, digging shallow gouges into the dirt. If the dragon had been purring, the vision would have been nearly perfect.

Halcia's tail gave one annoyed flick. *"I am still angry with you. No little imaginings of me as some oversized pet will change that."*

"Better a cat than a horse," Syrani said with a smile. "Cats have more freedom to go and do as they please."

Halcia's eyes opened, the pupils narrowing against the light. Even they looked like a cat's, though each eye was nearly the size of one of Syrani's hands. *"I am not a pet. I am a dragon."*

"I would never dare say you were a pet." Syrani shifted slightly, turning until she faced Halcia. "And I know that I have upset you, but I'm afraid there is little I can do to undo what I have said."

"We can still leave." Halcia blinked slowly, her tail making another agitated sweep across the ground.

Syrani sighed, wiping grease from the fingers of one hand along her pant leg. "I'm not sure that I want to leave. Perhaps I have been too hard on them, Halcia. Perhaps we can find a way to live together, all of us—"

"Stop." Halcia lifted her head, her nostrils flaring.

Syrani shook her head. "No, you stop. If you would stop fighting me long enough to—"

"Stop talking, Syrani. Someone is coming."

Only then did Syrani notice the way Halcia's head was tilted, her nose sniffing at the air. Unease and fear settled over Syrani, and she couldn't be sure if they came from her own mind or from Halcia's.

"Eysa? Or someone else we know?"

Halcia rose to her haunches, head lowered to stare across the fire, deeper into the valley. *"No. A human."*

Syrani heard a horse's whinny, loud on the gentle breeze that carried the sound through the valley to them. "Go," Syrani said in a hoarse whisper. "Get out of here."

"What about you?" Halcia stood, wings spread, ready to flee.

"They've seen the fire. I'll wait. I can protect myself, if

needed." Syrani closed her eyes, concentrating. Her palms and fingertips warmed and tingled as she funneled arcane energy to them. "Just get yourself out."

Halcia obediently turned into the wind and took a few lumbering steps before leaping into the air. The sound was deafening to Syrani's sensitive ears, and she could only hope that the human headed her way was far enough away to have not heard it.

Syrani waited until she could see the shape of the horse moving through the dark before activating her spell and rising to her feet.

"Great Ones' blessings, friend!" The voice that called from the saddle of the horse was masculine, with a northern accent. His face was hidden in the hood of his cloak, but Syrani could see a pale chin and the ends of dark hair peeking behind the fabric. "May I share your fire for a bit of rest? I don't have much to offer, but I have some bread I would be happy to break with you."

Syrani motioned to the opposite side of the campfire. "My fire is your fire, friend." Her voice came out as a low and gruff man's voice, and in the light she could see thick and dark hairs scattered across the back of her outstretched hand.

The man stopped his horse and jumped down from the saddle. He did not remove any of the gear from the horse's back, which Syrani took as a good sign that he would not stay too long. "I appreciate your hospitality. I can honestly say I was surprised to see a campfire so far down the valley."

"We are not too far from Cardyn," Syrani said, her eyes on the stranger as he fumbled through one of the saddlebags his horse carried. The tip of a sheathed sword flashed from beneath the hem of the man's cloak. "And the weather is nice for the journey."

The man turned. "On foot?"

"Sorry?"

He waved an arm, indicating the darkness around them. "You have no horse."

Syrani shrugged a shoulder, trying to make the motion seem uncaring. "As I said, the weather is nice, and it's an easy enough journey through the valley."

The man returned the shrug. "Fair enough. I can't be one to judge another man's habits." He held out a loaf of hard bread, the end closest to her unwrapped. "Bread?"

Syrani nodded her thanks and together they snapped the loaf in half, each taking their share and retreating to opposite sides of the fire.

"I have hare, if you would like some," Syrani said slowly. "I was not expecting company, but there is still a good bit of meat left."

"It would be rude to refuse such an offer, and it has been a long time since I've had fresh rabbit."

Syrani held out the spit for him to take, hoping he might show his face as he leaned for it. But instead he stood and came to a stop little more than an arm's length from her and resumed sitting. He tore a fat chunk of meat from the small animal, smashed it into the hard lump of bread, and wolfed it down in a few bites. Syrani tried to hide her disgust as he finished his fast meal with a loud belch.

"Apologies," the man said, wiping his mouth. "But, as I said, it's been a long time since I've had fresh rabbit." From beneath his hood, Syrani caught the barest hint of a smile.

"I cannot be one to judge another man's habits," Syrani said.

He laughed. "Lucky for me that I not only ran into another traveler, but one with a sense of humor as well."

Syrani forced a smile, then tore a small piece of bread and slipped it into her mouth. "Are you traveling far?"

The man shook his head, his face still hidden in shadow. "Not much further, I don't think. I'm looking for someone, and I think I'm close." He leaned towards her, and Syrani fought the urge to shirk away. "What about you? You're headed to Cardyn, but where are you from?"

Syrani shrugged. "South."

"You don't sound like a southerner."

Syrani smiled. "I wasn't always from the south." Syrani felt herself beginning to tire, the effort of keeping her disguising spell active wearing on her. If the man did not leave soon, she would have to make some excuse to leave herself, before the disguise fell completely.

The man only nodded at her reply, then tore another small strip of fatty rabbit meat from the remains. "Where did you find the rabbit? I didn't see many in the valley. And none this large." The meat disappeared into the shadow of his cloak, and he made a small and oddly disgusting slurping sound, followed by an equally disgusting sigh of contentment.

"I shot it in the woods." Syrani's words were terse, and they were losing their rough edge.

"The woods?" The man hesitated, his head tilted in her direction. "You know there are elves in the woods, don't you? Aren't you worried?"

"Not particularly," Syrani said, irritated now. She pitched her voice lower, trying to hide the fact that it was sounding more and more like her natural voice. "Will you be staying long, friend?"

The man shook his head. "No, actually, I won't be." He stood, getting to his feet with a grunt. Syrani followed his example, though without the unnecessary noises. "I have someone to find, and I hope I can get to where I need to be soon." He rolled his shoulders, the tip of his sword once more showing from beneath the edge of his cloak. "Thank you for your hospitality, and an extra thank you for the rabbit."

Syrani sighed, her own shoulders relaxing. "Thank you for the bread, and for the company." The bread was still held half forgotten in her hand, and the company, well … *He will be gone soon, and he will be easy enough to forget.*

The man brought the first three fingers of one hand up to tap lightly against his collarbone. "Good questing, Hunter."

"Thank y—" The words were nearly out of her mouth before she realized the man had spoken in her native tongue.

Syrani swore she saw him smile beneath his hood.

"How did you know?"

He snorted. "Oh, please. I've been around elves long enough to know how to spot one, even when they're trying to hide themselves." He offered out his right forearm, tugging the sleeve up to expose the flesh beneath. "I'm Marked. I mean you no harm. But I could use your help, if you're willing to give it."

Syrani shook her head. "Not until you tell me how you knew I'm an elf."

The man sighed, dropping his arm back to his side. "You're camped just outside what is fairly well known to be an elven section of woodland. You're carrying a bow, but you have no horse, and it is Hunting season, after all." He laughed, his head shaking beneath the heavy cloth that covered his face. "And most damning of all, your fire has no firewood." He pointed back to the campfire, and Syrani cast a glare over her shoulder. "Which tells me that it was cast using magic. And, given where we are, that would once again point to an elf."

Syrani cursed, but the man raised a hand.

"Stop me if I go on too long, because there's more." He pointed down at her feet. "You said you're traveling from the south, but the nearest human settlement to the south is a stinking little shithole on the coast, and we are a good five or six days ride from it. And those shoes look far too nice and far too new to have been worn long enough to make that same distance on foot."

Syrani rolled her eyes, crossing her arms over her chest.

He sighed, crossing his arms over his own chest. "And last, but certainly not least, you make a really terrible human. My guess is that you only had a moment or two before activating that disguise spell, but come on. That look is just … bad."

Syrani glared at him. "What's wrong with the way I look?"

He laughed. "You've got the face of a man that was dropped as an infant a few too many times, with the clothing of a particularly fastidious hunter, and the mannerisms of a merchant with a huge stick shoved so far up his own ass that when he sneezes, leaves come out." He shook his head again. "What's not wrong with it?"

Syrani's jaw worked for a moment before she could reply. "Your point has been made."

The man held out his arm again. "I'll show you mine if you show me yours."

Syrani weighed her options for a moment, but her energy was failing too quickly for her to have much choice in the matter. She let the disguise spell go, glaring at the man as its effects faded.

He straightened as it fell away. "A woman?" He shook his head. "Well, aren't I a fool for eating like a pig."

Syrani held out her hand. "Your arm, please."

He held out his arm, palm up, and she squeezed his wrist between her thumb and forefinger. "My name is Alastor."

"Good for you." She sent a slow trickle of energy from her hand into his wrist. If it hurt him, he did not show it.

"And yours is?"

"No."

"Your name is No?"

Syrani sighed. "No, I won't be telling you my name."

"That's a shame. I would love to know what to call someone so perfectly beautiful."

Syrani rolled her eyes, suppressing a gag. A bright rune blazed against his skin, activated by the energy she sent searching for it. She raised an eyebrow, looking up at him. "You don't look much like a savior."

"Looks can be deceiving, my lady."

With his wrist still held between her fingers, she sent a jolt of energy down her arm and into his. He leapt back with a startled cry, shaking his hand and cursing. Syrani couldn't help the smile that came to her.

He laughed. "I see the Great Ones have given us a sign. They've sensed a spark between the two of us."

Syrani groaned, taking a step away from him. "I'll set you on fire if you don't shut up."

"You already have, my lady."

Syrani shook her head, fighting the urge to knock the man to the ground and leave him where he fell. "What do you want?"

He straightened, his hood falling deeper over his face. "I'm looking for an elven village near here. I'd like to meet with their Elder."

A muscle in Syrani's hand twitched as the arcane energy she had spent slowly returned to her, and she flexed her fingers experimentally. "What is the name of their Elder?" It was possible that he meant Nieve's father, but it was just as likely that it was another village this stranger searched for.

"I don't know."

"Then what's the name of the village?"

The man shook his head. "I don't know that either."

Syrani let out a laugh. "Then how will you know that you've found the right village?"

The man did not laugh. Instead his voice grew very serious. "Because someone in the village I'm looking for has a dragon."

Syrani tried her hardest to suppress the shock his words gave her. She shook her head. "The dragons have been gone for centuries."

"You know as well as I do that isn't true. Just five years ago, not one but *two* dragons made their presence known."

Syrani nodded reluctantly. "Neria and Melonya. A sea dragon and a land dragon. One young, one impossibly ancient."

"And there will be others. The one I hope is close is supposed to be 'bright as the noon sun'. So yellow in color, or red. Perhaps gold."

"*Syrani.*" Halcia's voice came with a quiet growl, but Syrani ignored her.

"What would you do, if you found this dragon?"

The man sidestepped several paces, giving her a shrug as he squatted to bring his hands up to the fire's warmth. "The same as my uncle did when he found Melonya and her Riders. Ask them for their help."

"Their help? With what, exactly?"

"*Syrani, stop talking to him.*" The warning in Halcia's voice was stronger, but Syrani was watching the human in front of her.

The man sighed, the sound equal parts irritated and exhausted. "I'd much rather save this conversation until after I've had a better rest." He found a gouge in the dirt at his feet, and ran a pair of fingers through the fresh-cut earth. "Are you sure you don't want to just tell me ..." He faltered, his fingers finding a second tear in the earth before him, then a third. He touched each one for the briefest of moments, then his head shot up to her. "These are claw marks."

"*Syrani, do something!*"

But Syrani was already acting. Her hand raised, and beyond the flames Syrani watched the stranger bring his hand up in a defensive gesture. But it would be useless.

Her attack hissed through the fire, a red-orange ball of pure arcane energy. It wouldn't be enough to kill him, but that hadn't been her intent. She only wanted to knock him out and give herself the chance to run.

But the attack collided with an arcane shield the man had cast to protect himself. He had been nearly as quick as Syrani, and her arcane blast collided with his shield in a shower of red and gold sparks. Both fizzled away, leaving nothing between Syrani and the stranger but empty ground and a small campfire.

"Not many humans can do magic," Syrani said, flexing her hands once more as arcane energy continued to return to her emptied reserves.

"I told you I've spent a lot of time among elves." The man's head tilted. "The dragon, is it yours?"

"Syrani, I am coming."

Worry and fear hit Syrani with Halcia's words, and the eerie sensation of wind flowing over her skin brought up gooseflesh. *"No. Stay away. We don't know what he wants with you."*

Syrani refocused her attention on the human, who stood waiting for her answer. "What do you want?"

"I only want to ask for your help," the man said, raising both hands in a placating gesture.

"No! We won't go!"

Halcia's words were directed not only to Syrani, but to the human as well. His head jerked up towards the sky, and his hood fell back enough to expose pale flesh and a thin jawline.

Syrani saw her chance, and with what little energy she had managed to summon, she sent another arcane blast straight for him. Even if he had seen the attack coming, there wouldn't be enough time for him to react. The reddish ball of energy hit him square in the chest, knocking him off his feet and sending him sprawling to the ground with a grunt.

She watched him, one arm still raised, though she knew there was little in her left for another hit. The man did not move, though his chest rose and fell with smooth, even breaths.

Heavy wing beats stirred the still air around her, and Halcia once more landed with a heavy crash. Her claws dug more fresh rends into the earth and she slowed her momentum with large loping steps. The sight of her, or perhaps the smell of her, caused the stranger's horse to let out a shrieking whinny and bolt away. When Halcia finally came to a rest, it was with her legs spread wide, tail raised defensively, and her teeth bared in a snarl.

"Kill him. Kill him now and be done with it."

"What?" Syrani let out a startled laugh, shocked by the ferocity in Halcia's words. "We cannot kill him—he has a Mark. He's a friend to elven kind."

"So you have no issue attacking him, but you won't kill him?" Halcia's words had a sardonic twist to them, but Syrani found herself wondering the same thing.

Why had she attacked him? She thought back to the moment she sent the first orb of energy hurtling toward the stranger. She had been frightened by the man's realization. She had been worried, both for herself and for Halcia. And she had been angry.

No.

She had not been angry.

Halcia had been angry. Furious enough that the dragon's emotions had overcome Syrani's own.

"If you will not kill him, I will."

Halcia snarled, a sound Syrani had never heard her make before, and cut the distance separating her from the prone figure with the calculated steps of a beast stalking prey.

"Halcia, no!" Syrani dashed between them, raising her arms even as Halcia raised one great clawed forearm to tear at the stranger.

Halcia retreated with a growl, golden eyes fixed on Syrani. *"Move."*

"Why are you so angry? What has he ever done to deserve death at our hands?"

"I want no part of the madness he brings us."

Syrani sighed and dropped her arms to her sides. "You have no idea what he planned to ask."

Halcia growled again. *"I do know. And I want nothing to do with it."* She lifted her head, turning away from Syrani. *"If you won't kill him, then at least leave him there. We still have time before he awakes."*

Syrani almost argued, but thought better of it. If Halcia truly knew what the man planned to request from them, and if she was so upset by the idea that she was prepared to kill him rather than hear him out, then perhaps it was for good reason. "Fine. But at least let me fetch his horse."

Halcia made no answer, but the large eye closest to Syrani narrowed slightly.

Syrani turned, glancing over the man before searching the darkness for his horse. His hood had fallen away from his face, and in that smallest look Syrani saw an impossibly familiar face.

Hasani.

The thought was her own, but it caught Halcia's attention. *"Who?"*

Syrani knelt for a closer look. The hair was longer and the face younger, but the features were nearly identical. Pale skin, thin chin, slightly heavy brows and a prominent jawline. If she lifted one eyelid to see the irises beneath, Syrani was sure they would be the color of midnight in summer.

Syrani turned back to her companion. "We cannot leave him."

"What?" Halcia's head dipped once more, upper lip pulled back to expose the tips of her largest fangs.

"I knew this man's father." Syrani looked down again at the stranger's face, sure it had been an illusion. But his face had not changed. The man lying at her feet was clearly the son of her oath brother. "His father gave his life to save mine.

And yours." Syrani flexed her hands again. The fingers were nearly numb from arcane energy returning to her through them. "We owe him for his loss."

When she answered, Halcia's voice was even toned, a sure sign she was hiding her emotions. *What do you plan to do with him?*

"I'm going to take him home."

7

ANNA

Anna walked the long hallways to the baths alone. The castle was quiet, as it had been nearly every day since she had come here. She had been told stories of the laughter and joy that once filled the cold halls and the empty rooms, but she had never heard or seen much of it herself. Even the stories had stopped after Cookie's death.

Anna wrapped her arms around her chest, shivering slightly in the chill, and remembered the old cook's face. Not as it had been in the last year or so of her life, but as it had been shortly after Anna first met her. Her face had been plump and rosy cheeked, and though her eyes were often red rimmed with large circles beneath them, they had been kind eyes. And Cookie had been kind to her until her death.

And is it possible that she is really still here? Still wandering these very halls? With Trissa as the only one who can sense her presence?

Another shiver shook her, and she quickened her pace. The baths were warm, and the water would help her forget the nonsense that had plagued her since the night Trissa had brought up the old cook.

Nearly a week had passed, and it seemed all was as it

should be. Trissa had made no mention of conversing with the dead again, and Anna did not ask her daughter any more on the matter. The less talk there was about it, the less likely it was that such gossip would find its way to Mothlenor. And that, without a doubt, would be better for Anna and Trissa both.

If Mothlenor was content to let Anna raise Trissa away from his oversight, then Trissa might have the chance to lead something of a normal life. And Trissa was more than worth the occasional trip from Mothlenor's study to his bed, even if it risked carrying another one of his children for him.

Trissa was here now, and needed her protection. Anna could worry about another child if another one ever came.

The entrance to the baths was marked by a set of heavy double doors, beyond which was a small room, little more than an alcove, for dressing and undressing, though it was hardly used. At the opposite end of the dressing room was a second set of double doors, these ones smaller and heavier than the first. Anna passed through the alcove and opened the second set of doors, the handles slick with condensed steam. It was hot inside, almost suffocatingly so, but she knew it would only take a moment for her to adjust. It would take much longer to scrub the king's scent from her body, and the touch of his lips from her own.

Mothlenor almost never kissed her, perhaps aware of how much it disgusted her, but there had been little holding him back this time. And rather than fight him, Anna had consented, though it made her stomach roil with every brush of his lips against her skin.

And now his smell lingered in her hair and in her clothing, and his seed in her loins. And there was little to do about it now, except to scour herself in the hot waters of the bath. And perhaps to cry about how the world should have been, though tears and soaps would do nothing to change the way things had come to pass.

There was a servant in the bath room when she entered. The air was too hazy to make the woman out clearly, but Anna saw a plain black smock. That alone was enough to tell her it likely wasn't Ishta, so Anna did not hesitate to strip off her clothing as quickly as possible and step down into the bathing pool set in the center of the room. The water was pleasantly warm and clean, and the sight of so much of it when there was little clean water to be had in the city made her sick. But Mothlenor had not let her leave the castle in years, and there was little to be done for the people of Etritia from within its walls.

"I'd like something to drink, please. And get rid of the clothes. Sell them, burn them, I don't care. I just don't want to ever see them again."

The woman nodded and backed out of the room, leaving without a word. Anna went immediately to the collection of soaps that sat along one wall of the bath. There was a good number of them, some new and unused, a few older, all nestled together in a little basket. She wasn't sure how Illa and Ishta did it, but that basket had never gone empty, despite the poverty and need that ravaged the Etritians just outside the walls of the castle. And her favorite ones had not once disappeared, which Anna took as a sign that the few servants they had left tried their hardest to show Anna as much care as they could.

Anna picked an old bar from the assortment, trying to ignore the hot guilt she felt at no longer having the power to do anything to help the Etritians in the same way.

She scrubbed at her upper arms and shoulders, letting the foam work up until it trickled down to the faint scars on her wrists, then she set to work on her hair. Her back was to the door, and her mind too focused on thinking of anything other than what had occurred in Mothlenor's bedroom. Anna didn't notice the servant returning until she heard the clink of a metal platter on the stone floor.

Anna jumped slightly, startled out of her anxious cleansing ritual, and tilted her head just enough to see a glass of chilled white wine and a small bunch of green grapes waiting nearby.

"Thank you."

"Of course, Lady Anna."

Anna jumped again, covering her breasts with both arms. She turned just as the black smock and underdress that Ishta wore fell to the floor. "Ishta, please, you can't be here with me."

Ishta stepped out of the neat pile of clothing, leaving the tiny black slippers she wore behind. "Are you really going to tell me to go?" She didn't wait for Anna to answer before descending the steps into the water.

"If someone saw …" Anna began. But she couldn't finish the thought.

"There's no one to see. And if someone were to come in right now, it would only look like a servant helping her queen bathe. Because that's all I'm doing." Ishta waded towards her, her arms lifting, and Anna instinctively stepped back. A pained look crossed Ishta's face, but she kept moving, her hands reaching only to pull out the comb that held her hair up. Ishta's hair, darker than Anna's by only a few shades, fell and uncurled to cover her shoulders. "I won't do anything to put you or Trissa in danger, I swear it." Ishta fingered the teeth of the comb and frowned. "I just want to be here for you, Anna. Please don't send me away."

Anna cast a quick glance around the room. The air was still steaming, but her eyes had adjusted to the haze. The room was empty and still, and she and Ishta were the only ones present. How long had it been since they had spent even a single moment alone together? How long had it been since Anna had been able to speak freely with another, without fear of her words reaching Mothlenor?

She could never truly be with Ishta, not as she wanted to,

but a few moments of peace and comfort in the company of a friend could be enough.

Anna bit her lip and gave Ishta a quick nod. She couldn't trust herself to speak, but the gesture was enough to ease the tension in Ishta's shoulders. Ishta approached with caution, arms raised slightly as if she were approaching a skittish animal that might flee at the slightest provocation. Anna wasn't entirely convinced that wasn't the case.

When they were little more than a pace apart, Ishta held out her hand and Anna dropped the floral-scented block of soap into her palm. "Turn around."

Anna quietly turned, keeping her arms crossed over her chest.

Ishta started where Anna had stopped, running her fingers through the tangles in Anna's hair with gentle tugs. "Do you want to talk about it?"

"No."

"Not even with me?"

"Especially not with you." Anna sighed, watching the bubbles resting on the surface of the water as they floated away from her. "None of this is what I wanted."

Ishta made a soft sound, and Anna tried to ignore the warmth of her fingertips where they brushed against the nape of her neck. "I'm not sure any of us wanted this."

"Do you think I can change it, somehow? Do you think I can do more?"

Ishta flipped Anna's wet hair over one shoulder, bringing the soap to the damp skin between her shoulder blades. "Do you think you can?"

Anna bit her lip. "I don't know." She turned to look over her shoulder at Ishta. "How are the people out in the city? How are the clinics?"

Ishta was silent for a moment, and Anna wondered if she would answer the questions at all. She set the soap aside, stretching to reach for a lacquered wooden bowl that rested on the lip of the pool. Anna watched the muscles of Ishta's back flex as she moved, startled to see a long dark scar that ran around the curve of one hip. "The people are strong," Ishta said. "But their strength is fading. They are hungry and afraid, and there are fewer left within the city every year."

Ishta's words weren't a surprise. Things had changed little since Trissa's birth, it seemed. "They're starving to death? Or being killed by Ferrand and his men?"

"No," Ishta said. She poured water down Anna's back and over her hair, and goosebumps broke out across Anna's forearms. "Most are leaving. They find ways to save up enough gold to bribe a King's Guard into letting them slip through the gates. They go south, many of them. Or west, to seek asylum in Vyris."

"Do they make it into Vyris?"

"I don't know. We never hear from them again."

Another splash of water ran down her back, and Anna shivered in the sudden chill the hot water left on her skin as it rolled down her spine. "At least they aren't dying."

"Not here, anyway."

Anna turned to look over her shoulder again, and this time Ishta met her gaze. "You haven't left Etritia yet. Why?"

Ishta shrugged. "I would think it's obvious."

Anna's stomach turned unpleasantly. "And Illa?"

Ishta nodded. "Illa stays for Trissa."

"And the others? Do they also stay for us?" Anna almost didn't want Ishta to answer. It was hard enough to know that Ishta and Illa remained in Etritia to care for her and her daughter.

"Some of them might have their own reasons for staying behind. But I think most are just trying to save up enough to get themselves and their families out. I would expect the city to be nearly empty in another five years."

"And you?" Anna asked. "Would you leave then?"

Ishta's hand closed around Anna's shoulder. Her palm

was calloused, but the touch itself was gentle. "I would never leave. Not unless you and Trissa could come with me."

Anna's stomach turned again. "Ishta—"

The door to the baths slammed open, and Trissa's pealing laughter echoed through the steaming room. Ishta's hand was gone from Anna's shoulder in an instant, and they both turned as Trissa's bare feet slapped against the stone floor.

Illa followed the young girl in, the child's clothes already off and draped over one arm. "Trissa, stop running! You'll slip and bust your head open." But Trissa ignored her, already leaping inelegantly into the water.

Anna and Ishta both gave startled gasps as water splashed and sprayed them, and Illa's gaze instantly swept from Trissa to them. Illa's eyes narrowed as she spotted Ishta, naked and standing intimately close to Anna.

"Wait, Illa, it's not—" Anna started, but Ishta cut her off.

"It's alright, I was just about to leave anyway." Ishta made for the edge of the pool, pulling herself out of the water with ease. Once on her feet, water dripping to the floor, she took the towel Illa hastily offered her and made for the exit, scooping up her clothing and shoes as she went.

Illa waited until her sister was in the dressing room, the doors shut behind her, before speaking. "I'll return in just a few moments with a fresh set of clothing for you, my lady." And then she disappeared after her sister.

Trissa's head broke the surface of the water, and the young girl let out a gasping breath. "I did it longer this time, Auntie Illa!" Trissa blinked rapidly, brushing wet hair from her face and searching for Illa. "I did it for … twelve seconds." Trissa spun awkwardly in the water until she caught sight of Anna. "Where did Illa go? And why are you here?"

"Well, hello to you too, Trissa." Anna waved towards the door, where raised voices could be heard. "Illa had to leave for a moment. She'll be back."

Trissa sighed, pulling her face into an exaggerated frown

as the voices on the other side of the door grew louder. "Are Illa and Ishta fighting again?"

Anna nodded. "Yes." She thought of sealing the door, keeping the sounds of their arguing confined to the small room the two sisters were in. But would Mothlenor know if magic was used within the castle? Would he come to investigate?

Trissa groaned. "They always fight. Illa gets so angry with Ishta. She'll never get back in time to help me clean up."

"Can I help, instead of Illa?"

Trissa gave Anna a skeptical look. "I guess. But you have to do it quickly, and then leave. I like to play in the bath for a long time." Trissa paddled over to the stairs and sat on one of the lowest ones.

"You play in here?"

Trissa nodded. "Illa has to stay in the next room. And I have to stay by the stairs. Those are the rules."

"Alright." Anna grabbed the soap Ishta had left nearby, making a note to ask Illa about Trissa's strange arrangement.

"Not that one!"

Anna jumped, then looked down at the soap in her hand. "What's wrong with this one?"

"It's not the right one." Trissa pointed to the basket. "Get the other nice smelling one."

Anna sighed, then returned to the soap basket and picked up each bar and sniffed it. Most smelled like almost nothing, but one had a familiar scent. *Roses ...*

"That one," Trissa said. "I want that one!"

"Alright, alright, calm down." Anna waded over to the stairs, holding the soap under her nose and inhaling gently. When was the last time she had inhaled the unmistakable scent of roses? The last time she and Ishta had met in the gardens? Cookie had said Areanath grew roses in the garden when he was king. Had the scent been as important to him as it was to her?

"Hurry, hurry!"

Anna clicked her tongue at Trissa, sitting on the step above hers, and taking her tangled and damp hair in hand. "You must be the only child in all Etritia this desperate to bathe."

Trissa fidgeted where she sat, crossing her arms over her chest and kicking up small splashes of water. "It's not the bathing I like, it's the playing after."

"Why? You like playing in the pool by yourself?"

"I don't play by myself," Trissa said, her voice carrying a sarcastic lilt.

"You don't?"

Trissa froze and her splashing stopped. "You told me not to talk about it."

Anna sighed, her hands dropping to her lap. "Are you sure it's the same sort of thing?"

Trissa turned, giving Anna a faintly ill look and a slow nod.

Anna groaned. *If Mothlenor found out ...*

"I'm sorry. I haven't told anyone. I make Illa leave so she doesn't hear me talking to her."

"To Cookie?"

Trissa shook her head. "No, not Nanny Cookie."

"Who then?" Who else would choose to remain behind in this terrible place, when their soul was finally given the chance to flee?

Trissa's expression grew pained. "I promised I wouldn't say."

"You promised me. But now I'm saying it's okay to tell me." Anna leaned forward, giving Trissa what she hoped was a reassuring smile. "Illa and Ishta are still gone—no one will hear if you whisper in my ear."

Trissa shook her head again. "I promised her, too. I said I would never tell anyone that she was still here."

Anna inhaled a slow breath. "You shouldn't make promises with the dead, Trissa."

A cool breeze stirred across the hot water, making gooseflesh break out on Anna's skin once again. Trissa's gaze snapped to focus on a spot only a few feet away from where the two of them sat.

"Trissa …" Anna wanted to warn her daughter, but against what, she didn't know. She couldn't see whatever threat Trissa could.

"Are you sure?" Trissa asked the empty spot along the pool wall. There was a quiet span of perhaps a second or two, then Trissa turned back to Anna and motioned for her to lean closer.

Trissa's breath was hot against Anna's skin, and Anna kept her eyes focused on the spot along the pool wall that she was sure was not truly unoccupied.

"Her name is Nanny Nevina."

Anna didn't remember getting to her feet, and she only vaguely heard the pleas from Trissa for her to stay. When Illa opened the door to find out what the commotion was, Anna grabbed the damp towel from her hands and had barely managed to get it around her body before shoving open the second set of doors. She could still hear Trissa calling for her, but her daughter's cries were quiet compared to the name that echoed in her mind.

Nevina.

Nevina.

Nevina.

Anna only made it a few steps down the hall before falling to her knees and vomiting across the stones.

8

ALASTOR

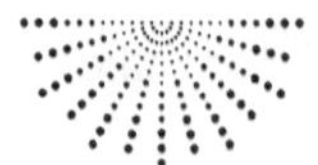

Murmured voices woke Alastor. He shifted, feeling soft bedding and comfortable covers surrounding him. How long had he been asleep? His back and hips ached from riding in a saddle for days on end, but there was no general fatigue or road weariness to his body, which told him had slept for several hours.

The murmuring continued, and Alastor opened his eyes to unfamiliar surroundings. The elf woman he had met in the valley had not killed him, that much was clear. She had instead brought him to a cozy home. The room he was in was sparsely decorated and tidy, and the voices he heard came from an adjacent room.

"… don't understand why she brought him here. Why not just leave him?" a woman's voice asked. She spoke Vyrisian, though it was with a delicate and informal slurring of the language.

"You should not question her motives, Nieve. She could have just killed him," an older male voice said.

"She *should* have killed him," the woman, Nieve, responded. "It would have made my life a lot easier."

"Nieve." The man's voice took on a gently stern tone. "Such things are better left unsaid."

Nieve grumbled something inaudible, and there was a clattering sound like wood knocking together.

"I believe our guest is awake," the man said, switching to the common tongue.

"A simple enough thing to fix," Nieve said, still in Vyrisian. "Just say the word, and I can make sure he sleeps for a very long time."

"Nieve," the man snapped. His tone softened. "Some refreshments might do us all some good."

Nieve sighed, then said in the common tongue, "Of course, Father."

The two elves that came through the doorway from the adjacent room were similar in appearance, but only enough to suggest a familial relationship. The woman was dark haired and slim, with features that suggested both Vyrisian and Azimarian elven heritage. She carried a wooden tray with an assortment of mugs and cups carefully arranged across the surface. The man was silver haired and also slim, but he stood much taller than Nieve, and the shape of his ears and the prominence of his cheeks and brows suggested purely Vyrisian birth.

"Where am I?" Alastor asked, sitting up from the bed he rested on. "And where is the woman who attacked me?"

Both elves knelt at the side of his bed. Nieve set the tray on the floor between them and set to work pouring a thick green liquid from the large mug in the center of the tray into three separate glasses. A fourth glass remained untouched.

"You are in our home. My daughter and I have been caring for you for the last two days now."

Two days? No wonder he felt rested. "And the woman?"

"Our ... friend will be joining us shortly. She had a task she did not want to leave unfinished."

"The Hunt, you mean?"

Nieve exchanged a look with her father. "Are you sure I shouldn't just poison him?" She asked in Vyrisian. "The tea is foul enough to hide the taste."

"Nieve," the man said. His Vyrisian was crisp and authoritative. "Do not make a fool of us. This man is here for a reason, and I would like to know it." He took two glasses in his hands, holding one out for Alastor. "Would you like some tea? The taste is not something that you might enjoy, but it will give you plenty of energy for your journey."

Alastor took the cup with a murmur of thanks, but did not drink it right away. "It was the Hunt she was doing, wasn't it?"

The man sighed. "Yes, it was." He took a small sip of the thick liquid. "Syrani said you were able to tell she was an elf, despite her disguise."

Alastor's raised an eyebrow. *Syrani. A very nice name for an elf.* He brought the cup to his lips. "It was not a good disguise, and I have a few elven friends that have shown me the easiest ways to avoid notice in Azimar." He took a sip of the tea. The liquid was almost thick enough to chew, and it had a bitter, earthy taste to it. He grimaced, fighting down a gag. He turned to Nieve, speaking in the clearest Vyrisian he could muster. "You are correct. It is foul enough to hide the taste of poison."

The man let out a snort, but Nieve glowered at him. "Do us all a favor, will you?" Nieve asked, switching once more to the common tongue of Azimar. "Don't try to speak in Vyrisian again. Your tongue is much too fat and sluggish for it." She stood with a final glare and took her cup of tea with her to the far end of the room, turning her back on them.

"Forgive my daughter," the man said. "Her words may be sharp, but her heart is kind."

"I know a few like her," Alastor said, taking another sip of the tea. "There was no harm done."

The man set his cup on the wooden tray and folded his

arms across his midsection, his palms cradling his elbows. "Syrani told us that you were searching for a nearby elven village. That you had business to discuss with their Elder. Is this true?"

Alastor nodded. "Yes, though I think my journey may have ended a bit sooner than intended."

"Oh?"

"I am searching for a dragon in this area. I believe it and its Rider may be the ones to help us find the Amulet of Fire."

"Dragon?" The man asked.

Nieve turned to say, "Us?"

Alastor sighed. "I would much rather prefer to have this conversation with the Elder of the village. I appreciate your hospitality, but if you could point me in the direction—"

"You *are* having this conversation with the Elder of the village," Nieve said, giving Alastor a glare. "My father has been Elder for decades. Anything you need to discuss about Syrani and the rest of the village should be discussed with him."

"Nieve," the Elder said with a soft groan. "Please, mind your tongue."

"So, Syrani *is* the Rider?" Alastor straightened, looking from Nieve to the Elder. "I suspected as much after our encounter in the valley. There were claw marks similar to the ones Melonya makes."

"So you *do* know the dragon Melonya," a voice said from the adjacent room.

The Elder stood as the elf Alastor had first met in the valley entered the room.

"Syrani, we didn't hear you enter." The Elder bowed to her, crossing his arms over his chest and touching his fingertips to the opposite shoulders. "This man was just beginning to explain his reasoning for being so close to our home."

Nieve quietly returned to the wooden tray at her father's feet and poured the remains of the thick tea into the last of the four cups. She ignored Alastor, refusing to even look his way.

Syrani returned the Elder's bow. "I only just returned, Elder. The Hunt was a good one. I have taken the prize to Eysa and her father for them to prepare for the Harvest Feast." She took the offered cup from Nieve and murmured a small thanks in Vyrisian. Syrani turned to Alastor, looking at him over the rim of her cup. "Continue."

Alastor hesitated. He had meant to discuss the situation with the Elder alone, in the hope that he might at least guide Alastor in the right direction. But the Rider was already here, and she and the Elder acted as if they were almost equals. They both stared at him expectantly, the Elder with kinder eyes than Syrani. And though Nieve had returned to the opposite end of the room and stood with her back to them, Alastor was sure she was listening just as intently as her father and the Rider.

"So," Alastor began with a sigh, "you know the tale of Melonya and her twin Riders."

"It has traveled well through the few remaining elven settlements, yes," the Elder said. "I am more surprised that you know about it, young man."

"I know about it because I was there."

Nieve snorted from where she stood, but the others made no such sound.

"If you were there, then you would know the names of all who traveled on that ship, and what became of the vessel they were on," Syrani said.

"The *Kingfisher* was destroyed by the sea dragon Neria." Alastor set his cup aside and got to his feet. "As for the names of those who were on the *Kingfisher*, I know them. But I will not share them." He smirked at Syrani, repeating what Roland had said not too long ago. "We're not exactly doing the king's work. And our names and faces must be as unknown as possible."

Nieve turned to face him again. "Then how are we to know you can be trusted? That Syrani didn't bring a King's Guard spy into our midst?"

Syrani gave Nieve an irritated glare. "He's been Marked."

The Elder's brows lifted and he made an interested murmur. Alastor held his forearm out obediently, and the Elder gripped it in gentle hands.

Nieve snorted again. "And where did *you* get a Mark?"

"From Tathiel. After we retrieved the Amulet of Water." Nieve seemed momentarily satisfied with the answer, perhaps even surprised. Her eyes widened slightly before she turned away from them once more with a huff. Alastor's arm burned uncomfortably as the Elder examined the Mark, but he tried to show no sign of discomfort.

"Savior, hmm," the Elder muttered, releasing Alastor's arm. "It's a good Mark."

Alastor tugged his sleeve down into place once more. "I hear that a lot."

"I am sorry, young man." The Elder folded his arms in his strange way once more, the fingertips of each hand gently cupping the opposite elbow. "We have interrogated you and doubted you, and we have not even taken the time to learn your name."

Alastor brought his own hands up to cross his chest, his fingertips tapping lightly against his collarbone as his mother had taught him long ago. It wasn't exactly the same as the elven motion, but it was similar enough to suggest the greetings shared the same history. "I take no offense, Elder. My name is Alastor."

"Alastor, son of?" Syrani asked. Her expression was neutral, but her eyes were bright and watching him.

Alastor frowned. No one had ever asked him that before. "Son of Hasani. Though I never knew him."

Syrani nodded, but said nothing further.

The Elder addressed Syrani, though his eyes did not stray from Alastor's. "Do you trust him, Syrani?"

Syrani hesitated, and Alastor briefly imagined all the ways in which he might be killed if she answered in the negative. But she gave a brief nod. "I do."

"I don't," Nieve muttered from the opposite side of the room.

The Elder sighed, giving Alastor an apologetic look. "Unfortunately, my dear, your opinion does not weigh quite so heavily on my mind on this particular matter."

Nieve made another comment, this one quieter than the first. Alastor could not quite pick up the words, but the way the Elder's brows furrowed slightly suggested they were not kind.

"What is your plan then, Alastor, son of Hasani?" Syrani asked. "You have found the Rider you seek. What next?"

Alastor shrugged as he searched for the best words to soften Syrani's hard stare. "Next we begin our search for the Amulet of Fire."

Syrani's head tilted. "You mean you don't already know where it is?"

"We have an idea of where it might be." Alastor sighed, reaching into the inner pocket of his vest and removing a small book bound in dark leather. He opened it to one of the first pages and held it out for Syrani. "Take a look."

Syrani gave him a narrow-eyed glance as she pulled the book from his hand. She was very careful not to touch him, and Alastor was keenly aware that she did not trust him, regardless of what she had told the Elder.

Syrani held the opened book out for the Elder to read along with her. Nieve's curiosity must have gotten the better of her, as she too peered over her father's shoulder to read the text beneath.

"Bright as the noon sun,
With heart and wings of Fire;

To see the deed done,
Find the Beast of Flame inspired.
A guiding light will resolve the path
To a mislaid star far overhead.
While the demon's Fiery wrath
Signals Azimar's greatest dread."

"Ah," the Elder said, a slight tone of amusement to his voice. "It's a poem."

Nieve snorted. "It's nonsense."

Alastor gave Nieve a hard look, which she returned. "It's all we have."

Syrani carefully shut the book and tossed it to Alastor. "It's in Vyris."

Alastor fumbled with the book as it hit him square in the chest. "Wh-what?"

Syrani fixed him with her hard gaze again. "The Amulet of Fire is in Vyris. I know the place the poem mentions."

Alastor's heart raced. "That's great. That's excellent! Let's go!"

"Not so fast, Alastor, son of Hasani." Syrani stepped in front of him, blocking the path to the door she had come through moments before. "It will not be an easy place to get to. There is the small matter of getting into Vyris to begin with. And the amulet's location cannot be reached on foot."

Alastor laughed. "So? You have a dragon. He can take us."

"*She* could, yes." Syrani smirked, the first true expression she had made since entering the room. "If you can convince her to help you. And not to kill you on sight, of course."

Alastor frowned. "You're not serious, are you? If you are the dragon's Rider, then surely she will go where you go?"

Syrani's smirked softened into a sad smile. "Unfortunately, our bond is not so close as that." Syrani swept a hand, indicating the space they shared. "Look around you, Alastor. Do you see a dragon? Do you sense her presence?"

"No." Alastor shook his head, then concentrated his mind.

It had been easy for him and Melonya to make their first mental connection. He had felt Melonya's mind before he had seen her. He sensed the closed and disconnected consciousnesses of the elves in front of him. But there was nothing so deep and powerful as Melonya's mind out beyond the house they stood in. "No," Alastor repeated. "I can't sense her."

Syrani nodded. "There is a shielding spell around the village. It protects us from anyone who may come looking. I helped the Elder craft it shortly after I arrived here." She gave the Elder a respectful nod, which he returned. "But it keeps Halcia and I separated." She turned back to Alastor. Her shoulders were slumped slightly, and her mouth was turned down at the corners. "As long as I am within the village, I can't feel her presence or hear her voice. And the time apart has had its toll on us."

Nieve and the Elder both looked at Syrani in alarm.

"My child …" the Elder said, touching Syrani's arm briefly.

"You should have told us, you stubborn ass." Nieve's words were harsh, but her voice was gentle and the gaze that fell on Syrani was uneasy.

Syrani shrugged. "I didn't realize that we were falling apart until it was already happening." She fixed Alastor with another neutral stare. "Which is why, if you want her help, you will have to convince her to come with us."

"Us?" Alastor asked. "So you will come, at least?"

"I will." Syrani gave him a curt nod. "How else will you be able to find the amulet, if you don't have my help?"

"I'm coming too." Nieve glanced back and forth between Alastor and Syrani with narrowed eyes before settling her gaze on Alastor. "I don't like you, and I don't trust you." She crossed her arms and shouldered her way between her father and Syrani to stand before him threateningly. It might have worked, if she hadn't been several inches shorter than him.

"Our people need Syrani, and I won't let you drag her across all of Azimar just so the two of you can be killed by the first band of King's Guards you meet."

"Nieve," the Elder said tiredly, "I think we can trust Syrani to care for herself."

Syrani raised a hand to pacify the Elder. "Actually, I think I would enjoy the extra company, Elder."

Both Nieve and her father turned to Syrani in surprise.

"You want someone else to join you?" Nieve asked, smirking. "I'm glad to see that our affection for you is starting to wear you down at last. We'll finally make you feel welcome here after all."

"I just want the extra sword arm, Nieve," Syrani said, exasperated. "If it's alright with the Elder, anyway."

The Elder bowed to Syrani. "I would be honored to have my daughter join you on your quest, Rider."

Alastor shrugged. "I'm fine with it as well."

Syrani's neutral gaze pinned him again. "I wasn't planning on asking you."

"The Harvest Feast is tomorrow night. Should we wait until after it to leave?" Nieve asked Syrani, ignoring Alastor altogether.

"It would give us time to prepare." Syrani tucked her chin into the palm of her hand, her expression thoughtful. "And give the human time to convince Halcia to come with us."

"The human can start on that right away, if someone wouldn't mind showing me the way," Alastor said forcefully. He was already beginning to see how this journey would wear on him. *Damn Jaimes for refusing to come along!*

Syrani looked up at him, giving him a brief glare. "No one knows you're here. I would prefer to keep it that way. We will wait until nightfall." Syrani turned for the door, motioning for Nieve to follow her. "Stay with the Elder until I return for you." She disappeared through the doorway, Nieve close on her heels.

Alastor stared after them in bewilderment for a moment.

The Elder knelt to retrieve the platter and the remains of the tea. "You will get used to her, I am sure."

Alastor took the tray from his hands, balancing it easily with one hand. "You mean she's always like that? So … demanding and cold?"

"Demanding, yes. Insistent and stubborn, too." The Elder led Alastor through the same doorway Syrani and Nieve had gone through only a moment before. The room beyond was a small kitchen, not unlike what he could find in human towns throughout Azimar. Syrani and Nieve were already gone. "But not cold, no." The Elder waved Alastor through to the adjoining room, this one a sleeping area with low beds and a warm fire in the center of the room. "Distant. Careful. Slow to trust. But never cold."

"What is this place, Elder?" Alastor counted the double rows of beds. There were a dozen in all, but only one had been dressed for sleeping.

"Not long ago, this place was a place of healing and rest." The Elder folded his arms once more, his back straight and chin high. "But now it is only my home. And a home for Nieve and Syrani. And that will have to be enough for an old man like me." He motioned to the furnished bed. "You can rest here. I am sure you could do with a bit more sleep, despite the rest you have already found here."

Alastor bowed to the Elder, resting his fingertips to his collarbones once more. "Thank you, Elder."

Syrani came for him as evening faded into night. Nieve was with her again, and she stared at him with a glower as Syrani passed his weapons to him.

"I wondered where these had gone," Alastor said as he belted his sword around his waist. His familiar old dagger he slipped down into his boot, where it fit snugly into a worn hollow in the leather.

"Not that you needed them. You've already shown

some skill with the arcane." Syrani turned her back on him, leading him to the only exterior door Alastor had noticed. "We will head out of the village. Halcia should be close by. I can call for her once we are outside the shield."

Alastor walked with his head down low, though there was no one out and about to see them. Syrani led the way, her strides long and purposeful. Nieve followed behind, and Alastor was distinctly aware of how closely she watched him. There would be no time to defend himself if she felt threatened enough to strike him.

They were nearing the gateway out of town when a young voice called out from the shadows of the building closest to the gate. "It's true then. There is a human here."

Nieve hissed a low curse in Vyrisian as Syrani pulled them to a stop.

A young elf girl showed herself, one hand fastened angrily on her hip while the other held a short bow in a loose grip. "Why did you bring a human here, Syrani?"

"Go home, Eysa," Syrani said. "This does not concern you."

"Not until you tell me why there is a human in our village."

Alastor stepped around Syrani, his arms raised in placation. "I mean you no harm."

Nieve grabbed the back of his collar and pulled him back as the elf girl sprang into action. Her bow went up and an arrow was strung and pulled taught before Alastor could take a breath. "Don't move, human," the girl said. "Or I will kill you."

"Eysa," Syrani snapped. "Go home. I will deal with the human."

Eysa released the tension on the bowstring, glowering at Alastor. "I would never doubt you, Syrani. But I hope you know what you're doing." And with those words, the elf girl slipped into the shadows and disappeared from Alastor's sight.

Syrani tracked the girl's movements, evidently able to see her without trouble. "She will tell her father about you. And by morning most of the village will know that you were here."

"Then maybe we should leave sooner?" Alastor asked.

Syrani considered for only a second before shaking her head. "No. They deserve an explanation. Disappearing will only make matters worse."

"Then perhaps we should keep moving. Before we are stopped again," Nieve said quietly.

Syrani led them on again with nothing more than a stiff nod.

They left the village without further incident. Alastor felt the shield as they passed through it. It was like walking through a thin curtain, but the air on the other side felt oddly cooler and cleaner.

Syrani's head almost immediately tilted as if she were listening to something. "She's sensed my presence. She is coming."

Suddenly Alastor felt very nervous. His palms were sweating slightly, and he rubbed them along the heavy fabric of his trousers. "You weren't being serious about her killing me on sight, were you?"

Behind him, Nieve snorted. "It's a bit late to be asking that now, isn't it?"

"Have you ever spoken with a dragon, Alastor?" Syrani asked, ignoring his question.

"I've learned to speak with Melonya. And though we didn't converse back and forth, I have also heard the voice of Neria."

Syrani lifted a single eyebrow. "So you know how it works then?"

Alastor heard the heavy pulsing on the air of wing beats.

Syrani's dragon companion would arrive at any moment. "I do." Alastor braced himself for the dragon's consciousness to meet his own.

But the dragon did not immediately bring her mind to connect with his. Alastor felt it as she drew closer, like sensing a storm approaching over the horizon. But she did not introduce herself or even acknowledge him.

When the dragon landed, it was with a shuddering crash that shook Alastor. He nearly stumbled to his knees. Syrani and Nieve had both braced for the impact, bending their knees slightly to absorb the shock wave they seemed to know would come. But Alastor was not so well prepared, and his arms thrashed as he tried to maintain his balance. He thought he might have heard Nieve chuckle at him over the sounds of the dragon coming to rest on the ground, but it may have been his imagination.

"Halcia," Syrani said as she reached both hands up to caress the dragon's snout. "Thank you for coming to meet with the stranger and me."

Alastor felt a heavy chill come over him as he stared up at the great dragon. She was huge, nearly twice the size of Melonya, though Melonya was over a decade old now. And her scales were a magnificent golden hue that left him in awe. Even in the darkness of late evening, he could see how her massive body caught every glint of light, from stars to the faint glow of the setting sun. Her scales reflected some of the light back as a deep crimson, shifting slightly with each small movement.

Bright as the noon sun, Alastor thought. *The Beast of Flame inspired.*

There was a whisper of power in the air, and the dragon dipped her head and snaked it around Syrani's shoulders in an imitation of an embrace. Syrani's entire body relaxed as the great dragon held her. "Please, Halcia. Speak so the human may hear you."

Only then did Halcia turn her gaze on Alastor and address him. *"So, this is the human Syrani has chosen to spare."* Her eyes were huge and yellow, with red flecked throughout the irises. They were both unsettling and beautiful. *"Why should I spare your life as well?"*

9

EILONWY

The inn looked different in the full light of day. Happier, in a way. Or perhaps it was only the time and the affection its new owner had given it over the last few years. Eilonwy and Tathiel had made it an annual tradition to check in on the former captain of the *Kingfisher*, and every year Larten's inn and tavern looked busier and busier.

"Are you ready?" Tathiel asked, wrapping an arm around her waist.

Eilonwy forced a smile as someone passed within a foot of them. The stranger gave them no notice, which Eilonwy took as a good sign. "Do I look ready?" she muttered.

"You look perfect." Tathiel flicked the end of her nose affectionately. She must have made a face, because Tathiel rolled his eyes and sighed. "Really, you look fine. Now let's get in there and get this charade over with."

The bell over the door chimed as they entered. It made Eilonwy's skin crawl, but Tathiel kept a firm hand around her waist as they crossed the threshold.

Behind the reception desk was a man Eilonwy remembered easily enough, though there was more grey to his beard than there had been the year before. He straightened as they entered, and gave them a warm and welcoming smile. But his eyes did not seem to recognize them as they brushed over their faces. "Good afternoon, and welcome to Larten's one and only inn."

"Hello, Mathius," Eilonwy said as they neared the desk.

Mathius gave her a more careful look, his eyes narrowing slightly. She waited, hands folded over one another and resting on the top of the reception table as he tried to recall where he might have seen her face before.

Eventually, he smiled, and Eilonwy's shoulders relaxed. "It's a very good job this time. It looks so perfectly natural." He tapped his cheekbone. "Only the eyes are the same."

"I have to keep something the same, or I would scare myself silly every time I looked in the mirror." Eilonwy tucked a strand of hair behind her ear, now much smaller and rounded at the top. "I don't like doing this all the time."

"It's better than the alternative," Tathiel reminded her.

Mathius nodded, one eyebrow raised. "Your brother has you there."

"Husband, this time," Tathiel said with a wave of his left hand. A silver band was wrapped around the third finger. An identical one on Eilonwy's own hand caught the inn's light and glinted brightly.

"And the names?" Mathius asked, pulling a heavy ledger towards him.

"Eileen and …" Eilonwy frowned, trying to recall what they had decided only moments before.

"Travis," Tathiel said, giving her a soft squeeze. "But there's no need to register us. We won't be staying overnight."

Mathius paused, a quill hovering over a blank spot on his ledger. "Oh?"

"She just wanted to check on Jaimes," Tathiel said.

"How is he? And where?" Eilonwy looked over Mathius's shoulder, where she knew the kitchen could be found.

"He's up in his room, same as always." Mathius sighed. "As for how he's doing … Not so well, I'm afraid."

"Alastor sent us a note. It said he refused to leave the inn." Eilonwy stretched her hands across the table, trying to force herself not to twist them around each other anxiously. "But it can't be all that bad, right?"

Mathius nodded. "He was fine for a few days after Alastor came to see him. But he's right back to not eating most days and not sleeping most nights."

Great Ones damn you, Jaimes, Eilonwy thought bitterly. *We need you.*

"I'm going to go up to see him." Eilonwy slipped from Tathiel's protective embrace and lifted the heavy skirts of her dress to head clumsily for the stairs. She hated dressing like a human. Her strange outfit was burdensome and unfamiliar, and she longed for the chance to rip the tight slippers from her feet and replace them with her hunting boots once more. But it was necessary, and it was temporary.

"Wait, Ei— Eileen," Tathiel said, stumbling over her assumed name. "I'm right behind you."

"Actually, I have something you might want to hear about," Mathius said. "Let her go on her own. Jaimes will be happy to see her, I'm sure."

Eilonwy didn't wait for Tathiel to make up his mind, but she was oddly grateful when he didn't follow her.

She found Jaimes's room without a second guess. It was the same room he always stayed in, ever since his leg had healed enough for him to climb the stairs. And it was the only one with a tray of uneaten food still sitting outside the door. Eilonwy sighed at the sight. Half of a baked potato and a mug of ale. She knelt to touch a fingertip to the mug. It was warm. And judging by the congealed goat's cheese coating the surface of the potato's fluffed insides, the food had gone cold.

Eilonwy rapped a knuckle against the door, biting back a

cough at the acrid tang of burned herbs that hung around the doorway.

"I said I'm not hungry, Mathius. Just let me be, dammit."

Eilonwy's heart twisted at the voice within. She opened the door and let herself in. It shut behind her with a soft click.

Jaimes stood with his back to her, hunched over a table with one hand scribbling madly into a notebook as he shuffled through amber bottles of herbs and liquids and checked labels with the ease of a practiced herbalist. He seemed taller than she remembered. And thinner.

"Jaimes?"

He straightened and turned towards her. "Eilonwy?" His face was slimmer, and there was a short sort of beard growing on his chin, though it was still thin and patchy. "Eilonwy, is that really you?" He limped towards her, his bad leg dragging a little with each step.

She held her arms out to embrace him. "It's really me. Though I don't look much like it, I know."

He pulled her close, leaning some of his weight against her. She took it gladly. Her head fit nicely into the hollow of his shoulder; it hadn't when she had seen him last. He really had grown. "I would recognize that voice anywhere. I will always know it's you, Eilonwy." His breath was warm on her neck, and a strange shiver coursed its way over her. Jaimes pulled away, fingering a lock of her hair and giving her a quirky smile. "Even if you've decided to go brunette for a bit."

Eilonwy shook her head. "What are you doing?"

Jaimes's eyes widened and he pulled further away. "I'm sorry, it's been so long …"

Eilonwy didn't want to release him. There was a strange comfort in his arms that grounded the anxiety she felt. "What are you doing here, Jaimes? You should be with Alastor."

Jaimes tilted his head and let out a huff. "Alastor? Why?"

"Why?" She glared at him. "What do you mean, why? He's looking for the golden dragon."

Jaimes rolled his eyes and turned his back on her. "Ah, yes. The golden dragon. I remember. How many times has he thought he was on its trail?"

"It doesn't matter. You should be there for him."

"Again, why?"

"Because he's your brother."

Jaimes snorted. "Eilonwy, look at me." He turned, gesturing towards his twisted leg as it bent awkwardly just below the knee of his trousers. "I would be useless to him. Why don't you and Tathiel go with him?"

"We've been scouring Vyris for any signs of the other amulets," Eilonwy said softly. She brushed a hand against the half of the Water Amulet she wore around her neck. Even tucked beneath the collar of her dress, she still felt the warmth of it. "We only came here to see you."

Jaimes smiled at her. "I'm fine, really." He motioned towards the mess on the table behind him. "I have my work to keep me busy."

Eilonwy nodded. "I've heard." She couldn't help the angry bite that sank into her words. "Your work does seem to keep you busy. Too busy to eat or sleep, I understand."

Jaimes rolled his eyes again. "I take it you've been talking to Mathius."

"And Alastor."

"I'm fine," Jaimes repeated with added force. "And my work is very important."

Eilonwy reached for him. "I understand that. But your brother needs you. We all need you." *And I need you too, you stubborn idiot.*

Jaimes held up a hand, and she withdrew the arm she had extended for another embrace. "I'm needed here in my workshop more." Jaimes sighed, running a hand over his patchy beard. "If I can figure this out, I can fix my leg. And then I promise I will be right there beside Alastor."

"Magic can fix your leg, Jaimes."

"I don't want magic." His voice was firm, and she could see a small muscle in his jaw twitching as he clenched his teeth. "Arcane energy would only be a superficial and temporary fix. I want a permanent solution."

"Jaimes ..."

"Don't you want to be fixed too?"

Eilonwy was taken aback. "I'm sorry?"

Jaimes raised an eyebrow. "Don't you want to fix your scar?"

"No." She frowned. "There's nothing to fix about my scar. It's a part of me, just like everything else."

"You mean like that brown hair and those rounded ears are a part of you?" Jaimes asked with a smirk.

"What?"

"I suppose it's easy to not worry so much about something as superficial as a scar. Not when you can just cover it up with a bit of glamour magic."

"I cover it up, Jaimes," Eilonwy said, her fists balling together at her sides, "because it is too easily recognizable."

Jaimes nodded. "Right. But it's just a scar. Easy to hide." He turned his back on her again, once more bending over the notebook that rested on his table. "It's not like it's a disfigured leg or anything."

Eilonwy scoffed. "Tiryn said that your leg is fine. That you're holding yourself back."

Jaimes's shoulders tensed, but he did not turn to face her. "Tiryn doesn't know what he's talking about."

"You don't need fixing, Jaimes." She tried to make her voice softer, despite the annoyance and anger that steeped inside her. "You're perfectly fine the way you are."

"Ah. 'Perfectly fine.' Excellent praise from a girl with a scar she is too ashamed to be seen with."

His words stunned her into silence. She could only stare at his back, trying to untangle the emotions whirling within her. *Wasn't he the one who said I would still be beautiful, even with a scar? And now he wants to "fix" me.*

"What has gotten into you, Jaimes?"

"Nothing," Jaimes snapped. "I am just very busy, and I am tired of being interrupted from my work." He gave her one last look over his shoulder. It was just a glance, and Eilonwy couldn't read the expression on his face. "Go on with your life, Eilonwy. And leave me here."

Eilonwy hesitated for only a moment. The threat of tears was what finally drove her out of the room. She slammed the door behind her with unnecessary force and stumbled for the stairs, almost tripping over the skirts of her dress. She cursed when she heard the thin fabric tear.

A door further down the hall opened. "Havin' a turn of trouble there, girl?"

Eilonwy looked up at the overweight and sweaty man that leaned against the doorway of an adjacent room. "I'm fine."

"I heard you in there, exchanging words with that strange little boy." The man staggered out into the hall, a bottle of mead in one hand. He stank of drink and stale piss, and his eyes were glazed over in an alcoholic fog. He blocked her retreat to the stairs, his bulk taking up the majority of the hall. "Fine thing like you needs someone a little bigger than that tiny cripple."

Eilonwy glared at him as he stumbled closer. As he teetered dangerously close to an oil lantern hanging from the wall, she let out a little pent-up anger in the form of a small burst of arcane energy. The lantern flared, and the man leapt back a stumbling step. Dark smoke lazed up to the ceiling as Eilonwy fed another trickle of arcane energy into the flame. "Careful there," she said. "You might just catch fire, soaked as you are in your bottles."

Instead of turning away and letting her pass, the drunk only laughed. His huge belly bounced and the air between them filled with the grotesque stench of his foul breath.

The door to Jaimes's room opened, and he stepped out into the hall, his damaged leg dragging slightly. Eilonwy tried to ignore the gaze he cast her way, but to no avail. Her cheeks warmed and her anger flared again as Jaimes stood stupidly in the hall.

"And there he is!" the drunk exclaimed. "Your lady and I were just getting acquainted. Since you seem to be on the outs and all."

"Get out of my way," Eilonwy said.

"Or what?" the drunk asked with a sloppy sneer. He pressed his free hand against the opposite wall and leaned his weight against it, further blocking the way down. "You gonna get the broken boy there to do something about it?"

A long thin hand hooked under the drunk's outstretched arm. Within a second, Tathiel had appeared from the stairs and had the drunk's arm pinned uncomfortably in a locked hold. "She won't need to get him to do anything. If you don't get out of the lady's way, I'll shove that bottle so far up your ass that you'll have to eat the cork to recap it." Tathiel twisted his grip slightly, and the drunk let out a pained yelp. "Do you understand?"

"I understand, you sneaky little whelp," the drunk whined. "Now let go of me! Before I get the innkeeper to toss you out."

"I happen to know Mathius very well," Tathiel said softly. He released the man with a disgusted huff. "And I also happen to know that he doesn't take kindly to his guests being assaulted by drunks such as yourself."

The man rubbed at his shoulder, turning to give Tathiel and Eilonwy a shared glare before skulking back to his room.

Jaimes still stood in the doorway, a pained expression on

his face. Tathiel gave him a nod. "Jaimes. Good to see you again."

Jaimes returned the nod. "And you."

"We're done here." Eilonwy made for the stairs, pulling the shoes pinching her feet off as she went. "Let's go."

"Eilonwy, wait!" Jaimes called after her.

Eilonwy ignored him. If he wanted to chase her, he would have to leave his precious workshop. And Eilonwy was sure he would choose his work over her. The thought only made her angrier, and she increased her pace until she was nearly running down the stairs.

Tathiel caught up to her just outside the inn. "What happened between the two of you back there?"

"I don't want to talk about it." Eilonwy kept walking, not sure where she was leading them. She just needed to get away from Jaimes, from the inn, from all of Larten. "What did Mathius want to talk to you about?"

"There's a band of elf traders heading east. They came through two nights ago." Tathiel kept his voice low, tilting his head to speak close to her ear as they continued their brisk walk away from the inn. "He thinks they may have come from Vyris."

"So he wants us to hunt them down, kill the traders, and free the elves?"

"He doesn't want us to do anything," Tathiel said. "He just thought we might want to know about it." Tathiel paused. "And he said nothing about killing anyone."

"Are you opposed to the idea of killing those who would sneak into our homeland and steal our kin to sell into slavery?" Eilonwy asked. They were nearing the gate out of Larten. Their belongings were stashed away out in the stubby grasslands just beyond. She couldn't wait to be out of her disguise and once more feeling like herself.

"Not necessarily."

"Then let's go."

10

JAIMES

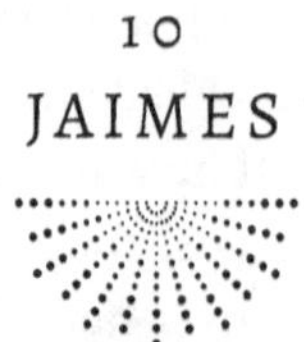

Jaimes watched Eilonwy rush down the stairs and out of sight. He wanted to follow her, but what was the point to it?

"Goodbye then, I guess," Tathiel said. "I'm not sure what you did, but thank you for leaving her in that mood for me." Jaimes caught a brief roll of Tathiel's eyes before he too turned for the stairs.

"I'm sorry," Jaimes said. "I-I didn't think …"

Tathiel peered over his shoulder, giving him a slight shake of his head. "When it comes to Eilonwy, perhaps you should start thinking."

Jaimes blinked. "What?"

Tathiel sighed. "None of us are children any longer, Jaimes."

"I know that," Jaimes scoffed.

"Do you now?" Tathiel turned, giving Jaimes a scrutinizing look over. "Then perhaps you should do a better job of remembering that. Especially when it comes to my sister."

Jaimes had no idea what Tathiel was talking about. But he shrugged his shoulders. "Alright. I'll try."

Tathiel shook his head again before heading down the stairs.

Jaimes retreated to his room, shutting the door softly behind him. "What was that about?"

It was easy to understand what he had done to upset Eilonwy. He had let his emotions get the better of him. And when she slammed the door, it had hit him like a slap to the face. No matter his frustrations with himself, he couldn't just let her walk away like that.

But that drunk bastard in the next room had to say just the right words to bring all those insecurities flooding back.

He called me a broken cripple boy.

Jaimes leaned his head against the door, shutting his eyes.

And when she looked at me … That look in her eyes said everything. I really am just a broken cripple boy to her.

"Great Ones take it." Jaimes stumbled across his room, his leg aching and flaring painfully with each step. He stopped in front of his open notebook. "Years of work for nothing."

Would things have ended any differently between him and Eilonwy if he had not let his anger and frustration show?

But seeing that wedding band …

Jaimes rested his hands against the tabletop, letting his head hang.

Eilonwy had almost flaunted it, but had never said a word about her husband or marriage. Had she been trying to let him down easy? To tell him that he had never had a chance to be hers?

"Dammit!" Jaimes slammed a fist down on the table, knocking a small number of amber bottles over.

Had he really been foolish enough to think that Eilonwy might wait for him to find a cure for his twisted leg?

Jaimes snapped the notebook shut and hefted it with one hand.

Was that what Tathiel was trying to tell him? That they

were all trying to move on with their separate lives, Eilonwy included?

Jaimes wanted so badly to throw the notebook into the fireplace on the adjacent wall. All his work had been in vain. Eilonwy had found another to share her life with. And Jaimes could guess that he had full use of both legs.

There was no reason to continue. And yet …

Jaimes set the notebook back onto the table. He opened it, shuffling through the pages until he came across the most recent one.

There was also no reason not to continue.

The pressure of time had been alleviated. He was no longer racing against an invisible foe in an effort to earn Eilonwy's heart. That was long gone, apparently.

But it didn't mean he should not continue his work.

And he was close to finding an answer. He could feel it.

Jaimes righted the fallen bottles, arranging them carefully so that their labels could be read easily. And then he picked up his quill once more and dated the top of the next fresh page.

"I'm sorry, Eilonwy," he muttered as he wrote. "But if I can't finish this for you, I can at least still finish it for myself."

11

ALASTOR

"*Tell me why I should also spare your life,*" Halcia repeated. "*I do not have the same sense of indebtedness that Syrani feels towards you. And your presence here threatens us all.*"

Indebtedness? Alastor swallowed, trying to form a coherent thought. The sheer size of the dragon before him was intimidating enough, but the strength and power in her words was more than he had expected. "I mean you no harm, great Halcia," Alastor began.

But Halcia laughed at him, the sound rich and wonderfully feminine. "*You are no threat to me, even if you had come here with the sole intent to kill me, human.*" Halcia sat back on her haunches, her huge clawed feet digging into the soft earth as she settled herself. "*Answer the question.*"

"I have only come to ask for your help. And to offer my own in return."

"*So you have come to burden us? That is certainly not in your favor.*"

"Halcia, please listen to what he says," Syrani interjected. "He has come to ask for our help in retrieving the Amulet of Fire. He wants to correct the imbalance in Azimar."

Halcia's great head tilted as she looked Syrani over. "*And do you plan on giving this stranger your assistance?"*

"I do, yes." Syrani nodded. "I know where the Amulet of Fire might be. And if I can help restore peace in Azimar, I will do so."

Halcia's lips curled back, revealing huge teeth. *"Why do you care so much for Azimar?"*

"Azimar is our home." Syrani frowned. "Why would I not care for it?"

A low growl emanated from Halcia's chest, and Alastor took an involuntary step back. Beside him, Nieve did the same, muttering a low curse in Vyrisian. But Syrani remained where she stood, her back to them as she stared up at the dragon.

"Azimar is not our home!" Halcia shouted. *"Your home was in Vyris, before you ran away from it like a coward. And I have no home."* Halcia's jaws snapped dangerously. *"Do you think I enjoy living in this land? Where I cannot be free to roam as I want? Where the only companion I have has locked herself behind a shield where I cannot reach her?"* Halcia stood, stamping one forefoot against the earth and sending a second tremble through the ground. *"Azimar has never shown me the slightest affection. It is dangerous for me. For all of us. And that is not a home I am willing to protect."*

"Halcia …" Syrani began, reaching for the dragon's snout again.

"The answer is no, stranger." Halcia turned her gaze on Alastor. *"I will not harm you, out of respect for Syrani. But neither will I join you on this fool's errand. If Azimar is going to fall, then let it fall."* Halcia stood on all fours, her legs bent and her head lifting to sniff at the air. She gave one last look to Syrani, who stood before her with upraised arms, reaching for another embrace.

"Decide now, Syrani. Will you leave with me, as I have asked before? Or will you stay with these people, in this land that does not care if you live or die?"

"Halcia…" Syrani said slowly. There was a pleading tone to her voice that sent an ache through Alastor's chest. "Halcia, I cannot make that choice." Syrani's arms were still extended, her head tilted back and fingers stretching to reach the great dragon's neck. "Please, don't make me choose."

Halcia let out another low growl. *"Then I will choose for you."* And with a few lumbering steps and a leap, Halcia was airborne, her wings flapping heavily and sending concussions of air down to tousle their hair and stir their clothing.

Syrani turned, pushing her way between Alastor and Nieve to chase after the dragon, wide eyed and pale faced. "Halcia, wait—please come back!"

If Halcia answered, it was to Syrani alone.

Alastor reached out a hand to reassure the dark-haired elf, but Nieve batted his hand away and put an arm around Syrani's shoulders. "She'll come back, Syrani. She just needs some time to cool down and think things over a bit. This isn't the first time you've fought, right? And she's always come back."

Syrani shook her head. "She's never left. We've fought, but she always stayed until we worked it out."

Nieve cast a look at Alastor behind Syrani's back. It was something like a glare, but with a pained and helpless mix to it that Alastor recognized with mild surprise as an expression of annoyed desperation.

"Come on, Syrani," Alastor said, giving her arm a gentle squeeze as he stepped around the two women to take the lead on the way back into the village. "Let's see if the Elder might make us some more tea, and we can sit and try to think this through."

"No," Syrani said firmly, and Alastor turned to face her. "No, you two go on. I want to stay here. She can still hear me, even if she won't answer. I don't want to leave her alone again."

"Are you sure you'll be alright?" Nieve asked.

"I'll be fine." Syrani's voice was calmer, regaining some of the hardness Alastor had heard in it before. "I'll come for you if she returns."

She said if. Not when, Alastor thought. *If Halcia returns.*

"Alright," Nieve said with a slow nod. "I'll bring you some food in a bit. And we can talk then."

Nieve led them back to the village, though she kept glancing back at Syrani every moment or so. When they made it through the barrier once more, Nieve paused just inside to stare at her friend.

"She'll be fine," Alastor said, though he had no way of knowing for sure.

"You know nothing about her, human," Nieve said. "She is not as cold and distant as she wants others to believe. And she is hurting."

"Then why leave her out there?"

Nieve sighed. "Because she does not want others to know that she can be as weak as the rest of us. She wants to be alone, even when she is hurting. Especially when she is hurting."

Alastor waited for a moment, then gave Nieve a gentle tap on her shoulder. "Come on then. Let her be alone. We can go back to the Elder and tell him what's happened. And then we'll go see her later."

Nieve nodded, turning away from Syrani's distant figure with one final glance back. "Alright. Just don't ask for any of that damned tea. I hate the stuff."

The night passed fitfully. Alastor lay awake for several hours on his borrowed bed in the front of the Elder's house of healing. He thought of Syrani, and listened for her to return to the home she shared with Nieve and the Elder. He thought of calling out for Halcia and asking her to return home, but then he remembered that the shield around the village would prevent his message from reaching the great dragon. And he had no idea where she might have gone or if she was still close enough to hear him.

He awoke at mid-morning. Sunlight was streaming through the slats in the shutters, and he heard singing coming from the roads and fields beyond. There were many voices, rich and beautiful, and though Alastor could not understand the words they sang, he felt the power their song produced. It was that buzzing arcane energy that woke him more than the light or the sounds of the elves of the village going about their day.

He sat up, seeing the Elder standing at the shuttered window as he did. The Elder held a wooden cup in one hand, and from the tangy smell of wet earth that wafted towards him, Alastor suspected it contained more of the foul tea the Elder seemed so fond of.

"Did she come home?"

The Elder didn't jump or even turn at the sound of Alastor's voice. "She did not." He continued to stare at the window, though the shutters were not open. Alastor made no comment on it.

Instead, Alastor nodded his head towards the singing villagers. "What are they doing?"

The Elder turned, giving him a single raised brow. "Harvesting. Tonight is the Harvest Feast."

Alastor frowned. "And the singing? The arcane energy?"

"Our way of preparing the soil for winter." The Elder brought his cup to his lips, blowing lightly across the top. "You don't know much about the elven way of life, do you?"

"I guess not."

The Elder nodded, more to himself than to Alastor. "We sing when we work the fields. A song for seeding. A song for caring. A song for reaping. And a song for healing the earth before she rests."

"Hm," Alastor murmured. "The words. They aren't Vyrisian."

The Elder smiled slightly. "They are not. The words are from an even older tongue. It's the speech of the Great Ones."

"Ah," Alastor said slowly. "The language of the gods."

"You don't believe me," the Elder stated.

"I believe that a lot of the races have their own idea of what the Great Ones were. And that we have no way of knowing who is right and who is wrong."

The Elder smiled again. "Perhaps you are right. But we few here hold our own beliefs. Right or wrong."

The front door slammed, causing Alastor to jump. The only reaction the Elder gave was to bring his cup to his lips and sip from the concoction within.

"Is that stupid human awake yet, Father?" Nieve called from the adjacent room.

Alastor stood with a sigh as Nieve entered the room. "I'm awake. Is Syrani with you?"

"No." Nieve's voice had a hint of venom to it. "She's still waiting outside the shield."

"Can you take me to her?"

Nieve held out an arm to stop him as Alastor made for the front door. "No. That little brat Eysa has told the whole town about the dark-haired human Syrani is hiding here." She motioned back the way she had come, scowling. "People have been pounding on that damned door all morning long. They won't let my father rest. They ask for your head. Or for your help." Nieve glared at him, the expression already all too familiar. "You have caused enough trouble while you slept. I won't let you go out there and cause any more."

"Nieve," the Elder began, but Nieve cut him off.

"No, Father. This is for his own good and for yours. He stays here until nightfall. And I will see to Syrani."

The Elder considered for a moment, his face expressionless. Then he answered. "Alastor will be my guest for the day.

And when the Harvest Feast begins, I will introduce my guest to the rest of the village."

Nieve cursed, but the Elder continued.

"I will explain his presence in our home. And that he will accompany you and Syrani on a mission to help save Azimar. If my people still trust in me, they will accept that."

Nieve grimaced, but said nothing for a long moment. Finally, she sighed and gave her father a respectful bow. "Of course, Elder."

Nieve disappeared shortly afterward. Alastor assumed it was to keep Syrani company. She said nothing to either Alastor or the Elder as she left, but the door slammed hard behind her.

The Elder continued to stare at the shuttered window, and after a short time the sight of it began to unnerve Alastor. He took to pacing, then to snooping around the rest of the house. Most of the doors were shut, and he dared not open them. In fact, he hardly touched anything, only observed what was out and plainly visible, which was very little. He retreated to the room he had slept in and continued pacing.

When the Elder eventually moved, it was to stand at the front door. Alastor was about to ask if he planned on going out when there was a hesitant knock against the heavy wood.

The Elder opened the door only wide enough to make his profile visible. "Yes?"

Alastor heard the low rumble of a male's voice, speaking in Vyrisian. By the intonation and inflection, Alastor assumed a question was asked.

The Elder smiled, letting his voice carry further than necessary to address only the elf that stood on his stoop. "All will be explained in due time. Please, continue your preparations for tonight's feast. I will bring my guest, and all will be made clear then."

Another low phrase was uttered in Vyrisian, and the

Elder politely waited for a moment before shutting the door. He returned to the adjacent room, giving Alastor a tired smile. "That should keep them away for a while." He folded his arms in his odd way again, one hand cupping the bottom of his teacup. "I have my own preparation to see to, young man. I hope you can forgive me for leaving you unattended for a few hours."

"Will I be safe here?" Alastor asked. He was sure he already knew the answer, but it had never hurt him before to ask such a question. "Will they respect your wishes?"

The Elder nodded gravely. "No harm will come to you while you are in here. This is a place of healing. Not of butchery."

Alastor returned the nod. "Thank you, Elder."

The intervening hours between morning and night passed slowly. Syrani did not return to the house, though Nieve showed herself long enough to shove a plate of fresh bruit into Alastor's hands. "Eat," she demanded. "The feast will not be until after sundown, and humans are so pathetic when it comes to fasting."

Alastor took the plate, which held a huge bundle of fat grapes and a crumbling hunk of goat cheese. His stomach rumbled appreciatively. "Is the village fasting?"

Nieve rolled her eyes. "It is customary for us to do so before a Sowing Feast and a Harvest Feast, yes."

Alastor returned the plate, though he knew his empty stomach would hate him for it. "Then I will also fast, out of respect for your people."

Nieve arched an eyebrow, clearly impressed. "I will tell the Elder of your desire to adhere to our traditions. Perhaps he will share it with the rest of the village, and they will also come to have a little respect for you."

"Ah," Alastor said, giving Nieve what he hoped was a sly smile. "Then you do respect me. You've just admitted it."

Nieve glared. "Every time you open your mouth it ebbs a

little more. I would keep that tongue of yours still if I were you, human."

Alastor slept more, enjoying the relative comfort of the Elder's healing house while there was something resembling a soft bed for him to lie on. Syrani had not told them where their journey might take them, but if the Amulet of Fire was indeed in Vyris, then the road would be long. And long roads did not make for comfortable journeys.

He awoke long before the sun set. The singing of the elves out in the streets had grown louder, and he could smell incense and ash burning. There was also the delicious scent of roasting meat wafting through the air, and Alastor's stomach continued to rumble as the minutes stretched on.

Perhaps Nieve had been right. Maybe humans were pathetic when it came to fasting.

The Elder came to collect him as the last light of the setting sun cut strange shadows across the floor of the healing house. Alastor stared out of one of the windows through a thin gap in the shutters, his witch light hovering just behind one shoulder.

"It is time, Alastor. Our people are eager to see your face and to learn of your reasons for coming to our village."

The Elder was dressed in a fresh set of robes in a faint green, trimmed in gold. They were old. Alastor could see spots where the fabric was beginning to thin slightly. Elven fabrics were supposed to be incredibly resilient, especially ceremonial garbs like those the Elder wore. Tiryn had told him once that elven craftsmen wove magic into nearly every-thing they wore. If the arcane energy in his robes was already faded enough for the elbows of his sleeves to thin, how old would that make the garments?

Alastor pushed thoughts of ancient clothing out of his mind as the Elder waved him forward and opened the door that led out into the village. He followed closely behind the Elder, trying painfully not to make his staring too obvious.

Everywhere there were lanterns and lights. Some were hanging from wooden stakes driven into the earth, and the light within was mundane and yellow. Others danced and floated above their heads, much like his own witch light that bounced against his shoulder. These were multicolored and magnificent, clearly more for festive decoration than practical use.

The smells that assailed his nose as they left the quiet solitude of the healing house made Alastor groan in hunger. He had already caught whiffs of meats, but in the open air of the Harvest Festival he could smell the mouthwatering scents of sweet breads and warmed wines and countless other dishes that mingled together and made his empty stomach howl in torture.

As the Elder's presence was noticed, and therefore Alastor's presence, those elves closest to them paused momentarily in their chatting and revelry to offer the Elder a respectful bow. Alastor received a few bows himself. He also received just as many scowls and more than a handful of curious stares. Evidently not all had chosen to believe that the Elder was harboring a human in their midst, and the sight of him shocked a small number of elves into open-mouthed surprise.

The elves of the village were all Azimarian elves, save the Elder. They all had the same medium-toned skin, and their hair ranged in color from light brown to darkest black. None had the incredibly fair skin and silver hair and extra elongated features that Tathiel and Eilonwy shared and that the Elder also possessed.

"You are the only Vyrisian, Elder," Alastor whispered to the elf who led him through the streets.

"I am," the Elder replied. "Not many have made the journey from Vyris to Azimar since the Great War."

"But you did?" Alastor sidestepped as a pair of very young elf children ran past him, giggling madly. They had apparently already broken their fast on some hard candies shaped like rods, and they now chased each other and brandished them like swords.

"I had good reason to, young man."

Nieve appeared from the shadows just beyond the brightly lit path that led from the healing house to the center of the village. The two children dashed around her legs, using her body as cover in their imagined sword fight. Nieve shouted lightheartedly, tossing her hands up in mock surrender. Unlike the rest of the village, her skin tone was fairer and the points of her ears slightly longer.

"I think I understand, Elder."

The children circled Nieve one last time, the upper hand in their candied sword fight evidently shifting from one to the other. Then they dashed back the way they had come, weaving their way between the Elder and Alastor without a glance at either adult. Alastor was more interested in Nieve's expression, which was a delightfully affectionate and warm smile that made her eyes shine in the bright lanterns floating around them

As soon as she noticed his staring, however, Nieve's smile vanished and her eyes fell flat and dulled into a more neutral visage.

She fell into step beside her father as they continued their slow journey down the main thoroughfare.

"Syrani?" the Elder asked her.

Nieve only shook her head.

When they sat, it was at a large and plainly made wooden table weighed down with platters and dishes heavy with food. And while it was the largest table, it was not the only one. The entire center of town had been converted into an open-air dining hall, complete with a large grassy space where a handful of agile elves were dancing to an energetic melody playing somewhere Alastor could not quite see.

The Elder took the centermost seat, though the chair was

no different from any of the others, and Nieve took the place just to his right. The Elder motioned to the seat to his other side. "Please, Alastor. You are my guest, after all."

The wooden seat beneath him had hardly begun to warm before a slim and attractive elf offered him a sweet-smelling liquid from a clay pitcher she held with both hands.

"Thank you." Alastor held the cup in front of him out for the elf to fill. She did, carefully and with an ease Alastor recognized from his own youth spent pouring ales in the inn in Larten. She waited for him to try it, leaning slightly and in a not unintentionally provocative way that accentuated the slight curves of her breasts. Alastor tasted the beverage, his eyes lingering in a similarly not unintentional way.

The liquid was warm and not overly sweet, with a cooling effect that left his tongue tingling. Alastor made a surprised sound, which seemed to please the elf. Her large eyes squinted slightly as she smiled deeply.

"What is it?"

"Sweet water," the elf replied in a slightly accented voice. "A liquor made from fruits and sugar cane. My family makes it for the whole village." She held his cup steady, her thin fingers wrapping around his, and topped it off with more of the concoction. "Here, have some more." She flashed him a sly smile. "And I'll be back around later to see if there's anything else you might like to try."

She was already leaving before Alastor could get another word in, her hips swaying seductively.

The Elder did not stifle the loud chuckle that escaped him. Alastor turned to catch the cheerful elf's gaze. On his other side, Nieve was grimacing.

"Are the other women of the village always so much more … polite than your daughter and Syrani?" Alastor asked with a grin.

The Elder shook his head. "Not in the least. But Verelyn …" The Elder hesitated, eyeing the disappearing back of the young elf. "Well, Verelyn has always been far more polite with the younger men of the village. And evidently you are no exception."

"Disgusting," Nieve muttered.

Alastor and the Elder talked at length, occasionally interrupted by an elf coming to pay respects to the Elder. Most of them ignored Alastor entirely. Those that didn't, exchanged nothing more than pleasant and generalized greetings. Absolutely no one offered a name or their hand to shake. And after the first few greetings, Alastor stopped offering his as well. And at no point did anyone choose to take the empty seat beside Alastor.

They spoke of mostly nothing. Alastor ate what was offered to him, and only when the Elder ate. He was not suspicious of the food, but only trying to be respectful of his hosts. He could feel enough eyes on him as it was; he did not need to invite more by eating like a starved piglet.

The Harvest Festival was slowing down—Alastor felt it more than saw it. There was a lively energy in the air that made Alastor's heart dance to the rhythm of the lutist's strings, though he had still not been able to spot the elusive musician. But as the first few hours passed, the energy in the air changed. The music grew softer and quieter, and he could hear melodic singing accompanying it. A male's voice, as well as a female's, and they sang in overlapping verses. The words were not entirely Vyrisian, but something Alastor could not understand.

The tone of the conversations around him shifted, though they were still just as loud. There was less laughter. Less dancing. And Alastor soon noticed a distinct lack of elven children, though there had been easily half a dozen when the festivities began. There were fewer women present, too, though he could still occasionally spot the lovely Verelyn through the crowd.

The Elder sighed, setting his cup of sweet water aside. "I

think it is time, Alastor." He stood, raising both hands to gather the attention of the elves still present. They fell silent almost immediately. Beside him, Nieve also stood. Alastor began to rise to his feet as well, but a quiet snarling hiss from Nieve and a gentle shake of the head from the Elder kept him in his seat.

The elves still present for the festival gathered closer. There were perhaps twenty of them, all grown well into adulthood. There were no children left, having apparently been sent home before the hour grew too late. Some still held drinks in their hands. Others stood close to their partners, though if it was for protection and comfort or merely out of affectionate habit, Alastor did not guess.

"My friends," the Elder began, lowering his hands. He smiled. "My family."

Alastor could nearly feel the warmth his words produced in the gathered crowd.

"Another year has passed in our loving town." The Elder lifted a hand, now holding a cup full of the clear sweet water. "The goddess Ymis has seen to give us a bountiful harvest, and the god Ilir has granted our people the strength to reap what we have grown, and to hunt what we still lacked." He raised the cup higher. "Tonight we honor the Great Ones, and ask that they give us their favor in the years to come."

There was a murmur of assent throughout the gathered crowd, and cups were lifted to mimic the Elder's respects.

"Now, to other matters," the Elder said, turning slightly to give Alastor a nod. "I have no doubt that you have all heard about my guest by now." Alastor stood, and the Elder motioned towards him with one hand. "This man has come to our village to ask for our aid in a mission to protect all of Azimar. And I have decided to accept his request."

Another murmur echoed through the crowd, this one louder. The elves remaining under the witch lights and lanterns exchanged worried glances and low words with their neighbors. Alastor shifted uncomfortably, and the Elder raised his hand again to call for silence.

"I will not ask any of you to risk yourselves by going beyond the shield and into Azimar. Syrani and Nieve have already agreed to go with the traveler, and they do so with my blessing. They will set out at midday tomorrow, and I hope we can all be here to wish them well."

Another wave of muttering went through the crowd, and a male elf stepped forward and addressed the table in Vyrisian. "How can you be sure that what the human says is true? That he is not deceiving you?"

Alastor opened his mouth to answer, but Nieve beat him to it, also answering in Vyrisian. "We can't be sure, Rhyrso. But Syrani believes him. And I trust Syrani's judgment."

"And where is Syrani?" a familiar voice piped up. The question was posed in the common language, and all heads turned as the young elf child from the night before stepped from the many shadows cast by the witch lights and made her presence known.

"Eysa," the male elf, Rhyrso, hissed. "What are you doing here? I told you to go home."

"Relax, Rhyrso." Nieve beckoned Eysa forward. "Your daughter was the first outside the Elder's home to learn of the human. There is no secret here to keep from her."

"Where is Syrani?" Eysa repeated. "No one has seen her since last night. Our Hunter has disappeared."

Again Nieve answered first, keeping her voice level. "She is scouting the roads ahead," she lied. "We expect her to return shortly."

"Why Syrani?" Eysa asked. She pointed at Alastor. "Why not send the human? It is his quest you are endangering yourselves for."

"Because Syrani is our Hunter, Eysa. Who would be better for the task?" Nieve crossed her arms over her chest, giving the young girl a stern look.

Eysa sighed. "I don't understand why she would agree to help a human. What has he done that we have not? What has he offered her that we can't also offer?" Eysa stamped a foot, her small hands balled into fists and her lower lip trembling. "Why does she want to leave us so badly?"

This time Nieve did not answer immediately. She exchanged a glance with her father, her expression unreadable.

Alastor cleared his throat, and Eysa's angry gaze shot to him. The eyes of everyone else also shifted to him. "As someone who has also left their home behind for this quest, I think I can answer on Syrani's behalf."

"Speak, honored guest," the Elder said. "And we will listen."

Alastor took a breath, and when he spoke he aimed his words directly at Eysa. "Syrani isn't leaving because she doesn't want to stay here. She is leaving so that she can help to ensure that this village will continue to survive in the years to come. She is not leaving because she does not care for you. It is because she cares for you that she is leaving." Alastor paused, then quickly added, "And I will do everything in my power to make sure that she returns to her home."

Eysa sneered. "Who are you to make a promise like that one, human?"

Alastor tugged up his sleeve, exposing the pale flesh of his inner arm. "I am a savior. I am a fighter. And I am a sorcerer, though admittedly not a great one." Alastor gave the young girl a small smile. "And I will repeat my promise: I will do everything in my power to make sure that Syrani returns to her home."

There was a moment of silence following Alastor's words. Finally, the Elder broke it. "Are there any further questions, or have you been satisfied?"

Eysa gave the Elder a respectful bow. "I have been satisfied. I apologize for doubting your decision, Elder."

"If Syrani were here, Eysa, I think she would be pleased to know that she will be dearly missed. I have spent many hours trying to convince her that she is no longer an outsider in our midst, but if she had heard your passionate words, I have no doubt she would finally understand that she is a part of this family here." The Elder lifted his cup again. "To Syrani and Nieve, good luck and good fortune in the times ahead."

The crowd's response was much louder than before. It was almost a cheer. Rhyrso pressed a cup into his daughter's hand, and he and Eysa clinked their glasses together before drinking in unison. Nieve sipped delicately at hers, her cheeks and ears glowing a slight red in the witch light hovering above her head.

"Thank you, Alastor," a quiet voice behind him said.

Alastor almost jumped out of his skin, but instead only spluttered his drink all down his chin. The elf made a shushing noise, and Alastor's nerves settled as he recognized the figure hiding behind him. "S-Syrani," he stammered, wiping his face with the back of his hand. "How long have you been standing there?"

Syrani did not step away from the bushes she had hidden herself in. "Just a moment. I don't want my presence to be noticed." Her voice faltered. "I'm not sure I could endure the company."

"I understand." Alastor returned his attention to the Elder as he announced that the celebrations should continue. Almost immediately the lute music began to play again, and Alastor wondered if perhaps there was no musician at all, and if the Elder was conjuring the music himself.

"When did the Elder say we would be leaving the village?"

Alastor watched as the elves resumed their drinking and cheerful dancing. "Midday tomorrow. Why?"

"Pack your things tonight. We will be leaving before dawn. I hope you find some time to rest."

"Why so early? Why not midday?"

Syrani's tone took on an irritated note. "Because before dawn there will be no one to waste our time with fond farewells and tears and other nonsense. We can leave in peace."

"If you insist. You will get no objection from me." He spotted Verelyn dancing, her hips moving delightfully. She must have felt his eyes on her, because she looked up almost immediately.

"Get some rest, Alastor," Syrani said.

Verelyn crooked a finger at him, beckoning him towards her. Alastor smiled. "We'll see how the rest of the night goes, Syrani. But I will be ready before dawn." He set his empty cup of sweet water aside and made for the dancing elf. Syrani made an exasperated sound behind him but said nothing.

Alastor reached Verelyn easily enough. No one wanted to get too close to the strange human, so there had been little need to weave through the crowd.

"I told you I would ask if there was anything else you would like to try," Verelyn asked in her slightly accented voice.

"You did," Alastor said.

"And is there?" She stood close to him, though there was no need. Alastor wasn't about to comment on it. He was enjoying the scent of her far too much. She smelled like rain-dampened leaves mixed with a light weedy scent.

He smiled at her, and she returned it with a rather coy one of her own.

"I think there is one thing."

1 2

ISHTA

Anna refused to leave her bedroom for nearly three days. All Ishta could do was bring her some food every now and again and leave it outside the door. Each time she did, Ishta spoke soft words through the door, hoping Anna might hear her. The door did not have a lock, but when Ishta tried the handle, it would not open. And the metal handle buzzed unpleasantly in her hand if she held it for too long. The meals were hardly eaten, though it was clear someone had pushed the food around, and Ishta never once heard the door open or close to collect or return the dishes.

Even Trissa was moody and out of sorts, though it fell to Illa to care for her. Ishta loved the girl, but Illa had a better way with her. Yet even Illa's charms did nothing to soothe the child. Trissa cried well into the first night after whatever the incident had been that taken place in the baths. By the next morning, when it became clear that her mother would not leave her bedroom, Trissa slammed the door to her own room shut and only left for meals with Illa and Ishta.

What either woman or child did in their seclusion, neither Ishta nor her sister ever learned. It was obvious something had happened that upset mother and daughter both, but Trissa would not answer their questions and Anna would not open her door.

Not until the third night.

Illa had just finished taking Trissa to bed. The girl's mood had improved somewhat throughout the day, and Illa shared Trissa's hopes that things would return to normal in the queen's quarters soon enough. Ishta had her doubts, but she didn't share them with her little sister. The two women were clearing the common area, more out of habit than out of necessity, when a door opened softly behind them. Ishta was sure it would be Trissa, perhaps coming to ask for one more kiss goodnight. But when Ishta turned, it was Anna who stood in the doorway of the common room.

She looked like she had been recovering from an illness, not merely seeking some sort of refuge in her bedroom. Her hair was dirty and stringy, and her bed clothes hung strangely around her shoulders. Ishta was sure she'd lost weight, and it showed in the hollow of her cheeks and in the curves of her neck. Mostly Anna looked defeated and exhausted, eyes swollen and red with dark circles under the lower lids and slumped shoulders.

"Is Trissa in bed?" Anna's voice was hoarse, and Ishta realized with a pang of sadness that those were probably the first words she had spoken in three days.

Illa nodded, glancing between Anna and Ishta. "I just put her to bed. She'll be asleep shortly, I think."

"Do I need to leave?" Ishta asked, her own voice cracking.

"No." Anna raised a hand, taking a step forward. Then she stopped, pulling her outstretched hand in and tucking it in to her chest. "No, please stay. I need to talk to you." Anna looked from Ishta to Illa and back again. "Alone."

Illa sucked in a breath, giving Ishta a look that clearly suggested she didn't like the idea.

"I just need to talk," Anna emphasized, giving both of them a pleading look.

Illa let her held breath out in a sigh. "Are you hungry? I can bring you something."

Anna shook her head, her lips curling into a small smile. "I'm not sure I can handle much food at the moment."

"Something to drink, then?" Illa was already retreating towards the door, but she cast another warning look over her shoulder at Ishta. Ishta fought the urge to glare at her.

"Something to drink might be nice." Anna wrung her hands together, shifting her bare feet slightly. "And you can take your time. Ishta and I will behave ourselves."

Illa frowned, but gave Anna a dainty bow. "Of course, Lady Anna."

Ishta waited until the door closed behind Illa. "Are you alright?"

Anna shrugged a shoulder. "I'll be fine. You? Did Illa give you much trouble after what happened in the baths?"

Ishta crossed her arms over her chest, not sure what else to do with them. "She did. But I think she knows nothing serious happened between us." Ishta smiled. "And Illa's bark has always been worse than her bite."

Anna only nodded, and a heavy silence fell between them.

Ishta broke it first. "What did you want to talk about?"

Anna took a slow breath. Her eyes seemed distant and not entirely focused when she answered. "I think I need your help." She motioned back towards her bedroom. "Let's talk in there."

"Are you sure?" Ishta asked, hesitant. "If the king finds out—"

"I've just spent the last few days in that room, and he never came to ask about me. I'm sure he won't notice if someone else is in there with me for half an hour." Anna's voice had taken on an irritated tone.

"Alright. As you wish."

They settled on the bed together, an arm's length between them. Anna was silent for a long while, hands draped between her knees. Ishta waited, letting Anna collect her thoughts, just grateful to be in the same room with her without feeling shame and hurt.

"You know what I used to be," Anna said.

Ishta nodded. "I do." Neither said it, but Ishta knew they were both thinking it.

Coven.

"And Trissa, she doesn't know?"

"No." Ishta crossed her legs under her with a groan. "No, Mother made Illa and I promise to never tell her. Before she was ever born, even."

Anna's shoulders relaxed. "I made Cookie promise me, as soon as she said I'd had a little girl. There she was, holding Trissa, still pink and screaming, and I made her swear to me that she would never tell my daughter what she was."

Ishta rubbed her face with her hands. She suddenly felt so tired, as if the weight of all the years before her and behind her were suddenly pressing down on her. "Illa and I have heard Trissa talking about our mother. Talking *with* our mother."

Anna made a sound that might have been a whimper or a laugh. "I had hoped it was just imaginative play. But in the baths ..."

"What happened in there?"

Anna covered her face with her hands and let out an anguished wail. "She told me that Nevina was in there. That she could talk to her." She dropped her hands from her face, tilted her head back to stare at the ceiling. "I have never once said that name, in all the years I've lived here. And yet she said it, clear as day."

Ishta held out a hand, halving the distance between them. Anna took it, pressing her palm against Ishta's. "Trissa is Gifted," Ishta said.

Anna nodded. "I have been trying so hard to forget my past. To focus on Trissa, focus on keeping both of us safe here. And now I have a Gifted daughter, and everything is rushing back to me." Anna turned to face Ishta, her eyes wide and glossy with tears. "What do I do now?"

"I don't know."

Anna sobbed, tilting her head back to stare at the ceiling again. "I am the last of the Coven. I betrayed my sisters when I took Mothlenor's offer. When I chose my own life over the future of Azimar." Anna's hand left Ishta's, and she wiped her eyes. "And now that choice has come back to haunt me."

"I …" Ishta started, her cheeks hot and her stomach churning. "I don't think you are the last of the Coven, Anna."

Anna sniffed, turning back to Ishta. "What?"

"I think one of Nevina's children found a way out." Ishta pulled her legs tighter under her, wringing her hands in her lap. "She has to be out in Azimar somewhere, if she survived."

Anna's face contorted, confusion knitting her brows together. "How could you know that?"

"You have to understand, Anna," Ishta said. She closed her eyes, making it easier to ignore the hurt she was sure Anna's eyes would betray. "We loved Areanath. My mother especially, but he was kind and caring and sweet with all of us. And when he died …" Ishta sighed, chancing a look at Anna. Anna's expression hadn't changed. *Yet.*

"When Areanath died, it was like a part of Etritia died with him. Etritia was in mourning, all of us. And we were so angry."

"I remember," Anna murmured. "I came here with the former Matriarch. We had to disguise ourselves." Anna shook her head slowly, her eyes unfocused. "I was so scared. I thought we would be discovered and killed. But Nevara was so sure that Nevina and the girls she'd taken from the Coven were still alive." Anna wiped at her eyes again, blinking away more tears. "I begged her to go back. Told her that Nevina was gone. That she had been hanged."

"That's not how she died."

Anna's voice was quiet. "What happened to her?"

Ishta took a deep breath. "My mother and I went to see her the day after Mothlenor announced she had been captured by the King's Guard. Ferrand had *visited* her first." Beside her, Anna stiffened, and Ishta swallowed. "My mother knew what had likely been done to her, but Cookie was so angry …" Ishta turned, taking Anna's hand again. "We all believed Mothlenor when he said it was Nevina. You should have seen him when he came in from the Last Hunt. He was disheveled and bleeding, and he seemed so distraught. We all believed him, Anna."

Anna wouldn't meet her eyes, but neither did she pull her hand away from Ishta's. "What did Cookie do to her?"

Ishta shook her head fiercely. "She wasn't overly cruel. But she wasn't kind, either. We only did what Mothlenor told us to, and we didn't know about the girls until later. By the time we were let down to care for them, half of them had already died." A lump formed in her throat. "There was so much blood. You could smell it from down the hall." Ishta suppressed a shudder at the memory, and Anna covered her mouth with her free hand. "They were just children. I was just a child myself."

"How did I not know any of this?" Anna asked, her words muffled slightly by fingers that still pressed lightly against her lips. "Why did no one tell me?"

"We were forbidden to speak of anything that happened down in the dungeons. And when you came, Mothlenor himself told us never to tell you." Ishta shrugged a shoulder. "Even Illa doesn't know the whole truth. Mother didn't want her to see any of it. Illa was too young, she thought."

Anna sighed, her whole body sagging with it. "You still haven't told me how Nevina died."

"I don't know. All I know is that first one of the girls went missing from the dungeons, and Mothlenor nearly killed my mother over it. Then Nevina went missing from the dungeons, and Mothlenor made no mention of her ever again."

"You think Mothlenor killed Nevina?"

Ishta nodded. "I think so. But there's no way of knowing."

Anna's head lifted, her gaze leveling with the door. "There is a way to know."

Trissa.

"No, Anna." Ishta stood, stepping between Anna and the door. "You can't do that."

Anna blinked, surprised. "Why not? If Nevina's soul is somewhere in this castle, I intend to try to find a way to communicate with her myself." Her eyes grew vacant as she stared past Ishta to the door beyond. "She's the only one who can tell me how to protect Trissa."

Hot guilt bit at Ishta. She had assumed Anna meant to use Trissa to speak with Nevina. *But her only thoughts of Trissa were how to keep her safe.*

"What can I do to help, Anna?" Ishta returned to her seat on the bed, reaching for Anna's hand once more. "If there's something you need from me, some potion ingredient or what have you, I'll do my best to get it for you."

"I want you to find a way to get Trissa out of Etritia, if need be."

Ishta's heart leapt. "You want to leave the castle? For good?"

Anna shook her head, her dirty hair falling into her face. She gave Ishta a pained expression. "No, I want you to leave the castle. And to take Trissa with you."

"What?" Ishta choked out. Her mouth worked silently for a few seconds as she struggled to make sense of Anna's request. "Why me? Why not Illa?"

"I would feel better knowing Trissa's gone with you. That both of you would be safe." Anna shrugged, sighing a little. "Illa can go as well, if she feels she must. I don't expect a lot of good will come to Eritia any time soon, and there's no point in so many of us staying behind out of nothing more than a silly sense of duty."

"Anna—"

Anna raised a quieting hand. "I'm not saying that it is going to happen. I'm only asking you to prepare and plan for that possibility."

"I can't leave you behind."

"And I can't go with you."

Ishta snorted. "Why not? What's keeping you here, if Trissa and I are both gone? A silly sense of duty?"

"No, something far more lasting, I'm afraid." Anna shook her head again, tracing the thin white scar on the inside of one wrist with the opposite thumb.

"Mothlenor," Ishta breathed. "Mothlenor and his magic."

"I can't leave unless he lets me go."

Ishta chewed her lip. If Anna was desperate enough to protect Trissa and the girl's Gift from being used by Mothlenor that she was willing to send her only child and the woman she loved away, then who was Ishta to refuse? *But a lifetime without Anna ...* Not that she and Anna could ever truly be together. Mothlenor had seen to that.

"Alright."

Anna smiled, weak and thin. "Thank you." She started to lean forward, as if for an embrace, but she had hardly crossed the distance separating them before seeming to think better of it. Instead she stood, and Ishta followed, a significant part of her aching for that small brush of affection, however brief it would have been. "I suppose Illa has been kept waiting long enough. And I think it's time I took another bath. Alone this time."

"Do you think you can do it? Figure out a way to speak with Nevina's soul?"

Standing in little more than an open robe and a thin bedding gown, with bare feet and dirty hair, Anna looked more like a frightened child than a queen. "I don't know." She absently tugged a wrinkle free from the front of her robe. "I want to try. I have a lot to explain." Anna sighed, meeting Ishta's eyes briefly. "And to apologize for."

When they reentered the common room, Illa was waiting for them. There was an empty glass and an unstoppered bottle in a bowl of ice sitting on a towel on the small dining table, and Illa sat in the chair closest to it, arms crossed and foot jigging up and down irritably. Anna's dinner, long cold and uneaten, sat at the far end, waiting to be taken down to the kitchens for disposal.

When Illa caught sight of Anna and Ishta, she jumped to her feet. "Lady Anna. I've brought the wine, as requested. Can I pour you a glass?"

Anna shook her head. "I can do it, Illa. I have somewhere I want to go anyway." Anna reached for the glass and pulled the bottle from its ice bath, shaking free the water and ice that clung to it. "I'll be gone a while, I think."

"My duties are nearly done for the day," Illa said hesitantly. "I can come back and stay with Trissa until you return."

Anna smiled. "I had hoped you might suggest it. If you're sure it won't cause trouble for you, I'm sure Trissa would be glad to know her Auntie Illa will be staying the night to watch over her as she sleeps."

Illa bowed, failing to hide the smile that flashed across her lips at Anna's use of the familial term. "Of course, Lady Anna. It would be no trouble." When she straightened, Illa made for the far end of the table, reaching for the dishes and uneaten food. "I just need a few moments to rush this down to the kitchens and—"

"I'll take it, Illa," Ishta interjected. "I need to head that way anyway." *And I know a stubborn old bastard that could use that meal a little more than the kitchen waifs Illa collects from the city.*

Anna ignored Illa's words, as well as Ishta's for that matter. She was already halfway to the door, the damp of the wine bottle tucked into the crook of her arm making the side of her robe cling to her pale skin. "Goodnight, ladies. I'll return before morning, I'm sure."

Illa and Ishta watched as she left, letting the door shut on its own behind her. Ishta thought of following her, offering to escort her to the baths. Ferrand was gone, as he often was in recent years, but his men still prowled the castle at times. But if anyone could protect themselves against a King's Guard, it was Anna. And any King's Guard foolish enough to attack the queen would not live long enough to regret it.

"Does she look ill to you?" Illa asked. "Sickly, and paler than usual?"

Ishta snorted, taking the plate and silverware from Illa's hands. "She just spent three days locked in her bedroom, eating nearly nothing and worrying her heart out." Ishta stared at the door, wondering if it was too late to run after Anna. *But if someone saw us together ...* Ishta sighed. "She looks like someone who has carried a heavy heart for far too long, and it has finally broken."

Ishta made it down to the kitchens without incident. She was even able to pack away Anna's unwanted meal without being noticed. It wasn't tidy, but then the old coot that would receive it had never complained about the mess before. Ishta dropped the bundle and a few scraps of fruit into her market bag, worn thin and barely keeping itself together after so long, and carefully concealed both bag and face in a hooded cloak before slipping out of the side door and into the gardens.

The gardens were close to the barracks, but in an ironic twist of fate, the barracks were almost always deserted at this time of night. What would a King's Guard do inside, when there was whoring and beating and swindling to be done out in the rest of the city? And perhaps it was that same logic that kept her dirty friend holed up so close to what any reasonable person would assume was the most dangerous place to be in the dark of night.

Ishta slipped from shadow to shadow, tracing her way through alleys and deserted houses in silence. Twice passersby came within easy reach of her, but they took no notice of her. The first, a drunk King's Guard on his way to bed, was easy enough to avoid. Ishta heard him stumbling up the road long before she saw him. Second was a pair of young men speaking to each other in hushed whispers as they hurried through an adjacent alley. Ishta caught a flash of gold and an excited murmur before the two passed out of sight around a corner.

Either thieves splitting their gains, Ishta thought as she peered down the alley after them, *or fools looking to lose what little earnings they have on the night's vices.*

When Ishta reached the worn-out old barn that sat evenly between Etritia's main gate and the southernmost gate, she lifted a broken bit of wooden siding and wriggled in as quietly as possible. Setting the bag down on the ground nearby, Ishta took two long steps inside, then gave a long, low whistle.

The air inside the abandoned barn was still, but Ishta's muscles were tense and her senses poised. The air stank faintly of piss and stale ale, and Ishta held her breath as she took another slow step deeper into the shadowed building.

Ishta sensed movement out of the corner of her eye, and she ducked and rolled instinctively. Once she found her feet again, she spun on one heel and kicked out with the opposite foot. It made no contact, and she realized her error only when a thick arm curled under her chin and pressed threateningly against her throat.

"Too predictable," a sour voice breathed in her ear. "No more threatening than a spoiled little house cat."

"Even house cats have claws." Ishta grunted, ramming an elbow into the bony man who held her. She could have injured him if she'd wanted, but a half-hearted prod into the ribs was enough to bring her point home. And for good measure, she stomped a foot down on one of his own, only noticing when her boot came down that he was barefoot. He'd had shoes when Ishta had last seen him.

He grunted, more from surprise than pain, and the loose arm around her neck disappeared. "So I see."

Ishta turned, her eyes still adjusting to the darkness. The man before her was once well built and sturdy, but now he looked like one of the many starving and hopeless vagrants of Etritia. "What happened to your shoes?"

He shrugged. "I don't remember. Fucking lost 'em, didn't I?"

Ishta sighed. "Seems so. Do your feet hurt?"

He shrugged again. "No more than yesterday. No more than they will tomorrow."

Ishta wanted to press him, but he would only become more irritated and agitated. So she gathered the discarded bag, reaching inside to pull everything out. "I brought you some food. When was the last time you ate?"

"I don't remember." He reached for the package, giving her a stare with narrowed eyes. "From the castle?"

"Straight from the queen's own dinner," Ishta said with a nod.

He made a grumbling sound, shoveling a small wad of food into his mouth with his fingers. "Nice of her to share." There was a bitter edge to his words, but he shoveled another bite of food into his mouth before the first had been swallowed.

Ishta bit her lip, not wanting to anger him by defending Anna. "How have you been, Dars?"

"I'm alive," Dars grumbled around a mouthful of food. "Can't say the same for the rest of the Old Guard. Not sure if that's good or bad." He gave her another look; one eye was still narrowed.

"Is that a black eye?" Ishta reached for him, but he snarled at her and retreated a few steps away, squatting and holding the food she had brought him close to his chest. Ishta raised her hands in submission. "I'm sorry. I just want to look at your eye."

"It's fine," Dars snapped. "I can take care of myself."

He didn't retreat again as Ishta approached and gently prodded at the swollen flesh around his eye.

"How did it happen?"

"I don't remember."

Ishta sighed. "Were you down in the fights again?"

Dars grunted. "Only good way to earn some money."

Ishta couldn't deny the truth in that. "Did you win at least?"

Dars nodded, shoveling more food in his mouth. "Won more than I lost."

"What did you do with the money?"

Dars laughed at that. "Didn't buy myself some new boots, did I?"

"Dars …" Ishta sighed. "I worry about you, you know that."

"I can take care of myself," Dars insisted. He tapped his temple with one long and dirty fingernail. "I've still got a little bit going on up here."

Ishta sat in the dirt a few feet away from him, cradling her bag in her lap. "I might be leaving Etritia."

"Oh?" Dars wiped his mouth with the back of his hand. "About fucking time."

"Come with me."

Dars shook his head. "No. I've been here this long. Might as well stick it all out."

"Who will take care of you, if I'm not here?"

"I can take care of myself," Dars said bitterly, but there was a hint of insecurity in his words.

"Where are your shoes? When was the last time you ate?"

Dars growled, tossing the rest of his dinner at her. It missed, splashing against the dirt inches from her knee. "I don't remember!"

"Then please come with me. I can help you remember things like that."

Dars balled his fists, his face twisting into a terrifying grimace. "No! I can't leave."

Ishta shook her head. "Stubborn old man."

Dars's face fell, and he brought one hand up to beat against the side of his head. "I'm sorry, I shouldn't have yelled."

"It's alright." Ishta reached for him, and Dars dropped his hand into hers. "We can talk about this again later. I don't even know if it's going to happen."

Dars nodded. "You have to find someone who will let you out."

"Do you know someone?"

Dars's head tilted. "Maybe. A King's Guard by the name of Gallant."

"Gallant?"

Dars laughed again. "Don't let the name fool you. He's Ferrand's man through and through."

"What does he look like?"

"Big guy, bald head and bushy beard. Likes to pick his teeth with his pinky nail." Dars demonstrated, and Ishta suppressed a shudder of disgust at the image the description conjured. "Might find him at the southern gate tonight, actually."

"Then I should get going." Ishta reached into her bag once more, pulling out a small piece of fabric. "But I brought you something else."

Dars's eyes widened as she held out the small scrap towards him. "You got one on your own?" He held the emblem up, fingering the white stitching depicting a tower crossed with a pair of blades. The tower was topped with a six-pointed crown, a new addition that Mothlenor had added to all King's Guard uniforms.

"Stumbled across a King's Guard with his hands down a little girl's bottoms. Gave him a good whack over the head and helped her get home." Ishta crossed her arms over her chest, suddenly ill at the memory. "Ripped it off as a token. But I don't want to keep it."

"Did you kill him?"

Ishta chuckled, but the look in Dars's eyes cut it off. "No, no I couldn't kill him. I'm not a killer."

Dars shrugged, tucking the King's Guard emblem into a pocket somewhere. "You might have to next time."

Ishta found Gallant at the southern gate. He looked just as Dars had described him, tooth picking and all.

"Sir Gallant?" Ishta pitched her voice low, feeling ridiculous both using the name and adopting the masculine pitch to her words.

"Who the fuck's asking?"

"I heard you might be able to arrange passage out of Etritia."

Gallant spat a wad of phlegm into the dirt and gave Ishta once over. "For a price."

Ishta fought the urge to pull her cloak tighter around her. Not all the King's Guard were all that bright, but it was too soon to tell where this one stood. And even the subtlest motion might tip him off to the fact that she was a woman, and women wandering alone at night were not safe in Etritia. "Name the price."

Gallant sneered. "How many need passage?"

"Two."

"Then it's two hundred gold marks."

Ishta almost fainted. She hadn't seen more than ten gold marks at a time since Areanath was alive. "That's impossible."

"You haven't been the first to say it, but others have managed it. Two hundred."

"Fifty." Even fifty would be hard for her to save up, but it was an easier goal than two hundred.

"Two hundred." Gallant rolled his eyes, sticking his pinky nail back in his mouth and digging into his gum line.

"You don't seem to understand how negotiation works."

"You don't seem to understand that I ain't negotiating."

Ishta's heart was beating hard enough for her to hear it. "One hundred."

Gallant sighed. "If you say one more number that is anything lower than two hundred, I will personally see to it that you hang from the gallows in the morning."

"You can't be the only one I ask."

Gallant sneered. "I'm not. But they'll ask for more than two hundred, I can guarantee you."

"Two hundred it is."

"That's what I thought. You have two weeks, then I forget your face, and we'll have to begin our 'negotiations' again. And I won't be saying two hundred then, either."

Ishta retreated through the alleys of Etritia, listening for the jeers and yells of the night's vices. If she could find one of the underground organized fights that dotted Etritia, she could perhaps find a way to save up two hundred marks of gold. After all, there was only one good way to earn money.

13

JAIMES

The letters swam before his tired eyes as he penned them, but Jaimes kept writing. His work was going well, unburdened as it was now that his efforts were for his own interests. He had made good progress, but the final tests were still a long way off at the rate he was working.

"Doesn't matter," he mumbled, dropping his quill to make an adjustment to the flame under his cauldron. The flame intensified, the core growing brighter and the flame thinning into a cone no wider than his forefinger. "Got all the time I need now, haven't I?"

His speech was slurred from exhaustion, and he read the last two fresh lines over again, trying to pick up the thought he had set aside with his quill.

"Simmer the decantation of wormwood and frosted pine slurry over low heat, adding three dried petals of sweet tansy and a single belladonna fruit after five minutes have elapsed. Crush the fruit for increased juice extraction, and …"

And what?

Jaimes stared at his notes, trying to recall.

Beside him, the light of the flame shifted slightly. It wasn't much, but it was enough to draw his attention back to the cauldron.

"Damned thing," Jaimes muttered, adjusting the flame again. His tabletop burner had been acting up all day, and he could find no reason for it. The fuel was still good, though the jar was now a little less than half full. The wick was still strong and useable. But his flame would not remain as he set it. This time it had gone cooler, but there had been an instance not even an hour ago that it had suddenly flared white hot, bringing his liquid to a boil in less than a minute. He had been lucky that time because the mixture was boiling just as he needed it to. He had mist-imed his steps, an error he attributed to an ill-timed knock at the door and the confused stupor it put him in. He could have lost the entire batch if it hadn't decided to boil when it did.

Jaimes turned to the notes again. He needed to get some sleep, but it would have to wait until he finished this last test. And if the test went well, he might try the next steps. And if the test went poorly, he may begin all over again.

He sighed. He could sleep when he reached a long cool-ing-down period for the brew. There would be one eventu-ally. And then he could get a quick nap in before getting back to work.

"Simmer the decantation … low heat. Three sweet tansy petals, one belladonna fruit … Dammit all!"

The flame shifted again, once more cooling to a solid red cone with only a small orange center.

Jaimes slammed the book down, upsetting the burner slightly, and turned the fuel nozzle until it was fully opened. Except it was nearly opened already. By all rights, the flame should have been hot enough and high enough to singe his brows where he sat.

But the flame did not change. It remained a stubby two-inch cone with a cool orange core.

"Great Ones take it, what's going on with you?" Jaimes asked the burner.

The burner replied in a smoky, feminine voice. "You just said the decantation should be simmered over low heat. But you have the flame set high enough to burn the whole place down."

Jaimes's first instinct should have been to shout in startled horror. Or perhaps to shut his experiment down and take a long rest, and hope his hallucinations faded with sleep.

Instead he laughed, resting his weary head in the palms of his hands. "Mathius warned me that I might start to lose my mind if I kept working as I have been. I'm not sure I want to see the look on his face when he learns that he was right."

The flame under his sample shifted again, this time curling and undulating until a small face could be made out. The eyes were tiny red pinpricks in the orange core, the mouth a similar smudge of red fire. When the flame spoke, the mouth moved as a normal mouth would, and thin black smoke issued from between the lips.

"You're not seeing anything that isn't actually here," the flame said to him. "I am a spirit of fire."

Jaimes blinked, then rubbed his dry and cracking hands over his face. The face in the flame was still staring expectantly up at him when he uncovered his eyes. "Alright," Jaimes said, addressing the flame of his bench top burner and feeling ridiculous. "What are you doing in my lab, oh great spirit of fire?"

"Helping you with your little project, apparently," the flame said. There was more than a hint of derision in her voice, and Jaimes felt his neck warm in annoyance. "You've nearly ruined two samples today alone, do you realize that?"

Only I would hallucinate a creature with such a cheeky mouth.

"I don't need help," Jaimes insisted. "I don't know what you are—fire spirit, hallucination, whatever. But you can leave now."

The flame shifted again, and Jaimes instantly sighed in relief as the face within the fire disappeared. But the smoke curling from the burner changed direction and darkened, and a tiny female form emerged from the sooty vapor. It drifted towards his notebook, which he instinctively covered with his spread hands, giving an involuntary angry shout as he obscured the notes within.

"Get your petals and fruit ready, it's nearly time to add them," the figure said.

"Hey, get away from my notes! Do you want to catch them on fire?" Jaimes snapped the book shut and tucked it close to his chest, giving the smoky illusion a glare. "What are you? And why are you still here?"

The figure sighed, her arms going akimbo, and Jaimes had the distinct impression that she was fixing him with a glare that was just as annoyed as his own. The problem was that she was too small for it to have any effect.

"I told you," the figure said, "I am a spirit of fire. And I'm still here because you've got a rather interesting setup going on, and I'm not keen on leaving just yet." The spirit pointed at a jar and repeated her earlier order. "Get your petals ready, your five minutes have nearly passed."

Jaimes reached for the indicated jar and unstopped it. "How did you end up in my lab, fire spirit?"

"Vash."

"Sorry?" Jaimes dropped three dried sweet tansy petals on the workbench, pressed the cork back into the jar and set it aside.

"My name is Vash," the fire spirit said. "Now the belladonna fruit. Don't forget to crush it."

Jaimes waved a hand irritably. "Yes, yes, I remember." He pulled another jar across the table towards him, careful not to bring any part of his body too close to the smoky spirit. "I didn't realize fire spirits had names."

"You have a name, don't you?"

"I do," Jaimes said, pressing the flat of a nearby blade against the hard rounded fruit until the skin split. "Mine is Jaimes."

"I knew that." The spirit, Vash, drifted closer, until Jaimes could almost make out the features of her tiny face. "And if you can have a name, why can't I?"

Jaimes considered the question for a moment, obediently dropping the prepared petals and fruit into the cauldron at Vash's indication. "I suppose that's fair." He shook his head. "But you didn't answer the question. What are you doing in my lab?"

"Well, that should be obvious, if you knew anything about fire spirits."

Jaimes thought back to his time on the *Kingfisher*. Tiryn had told him about the various elemental spirits, and he was sure he had listened attentively. But that had been years ago …

"Let's assume I don't," he said finally, leaning back in his chair and staring at the small figure floating through the air in front of him. He realized then, looking more closely at her, that her form was still connected to the flame that burned beneath his cauldron. Her head, torso, and upper legs were defined and easy to make out in the black that issued from the burner. But from the knees down, her figure melted into nothing more than typical smoke. Her hair, which drifted languidly, dissipated as normal vapor would. Her entire self was contained in a space that took up no more than three inches in length of inky mist.

"Someone used magic to conjure fire, and I came with it."

Jaimes snorted. "Magic fire, here? I can't recall the last time that's happened."

Vash's form darkened. "It happened right here. Some crude and poorly mannered human lit the burner with arcane fire."

"Alastor," Jaimes said with a sigh, recalling the incident now. "My brother."

"I've been here since."

Jaimes tried not to consider what Vash may have witnessed in the time since Alastor's visit. Had he done anything he might be embarrassed by? He couldn't remember, and yet he was sure he'd likely done something. His face warmed. "Why are you still here?"

Vash snorted. "You have enough fires lit in here that I could stay indefinitely, if I wanted."

"Why here, though?" Jaimes asked. His voice cracked audibly, and he cleared his throat, fixing Vash with a stare that he hoped was authoritative. "Why are you here, in my lab? Why not go somewhere else?"

"I've already said why," Vash answered. "I find you interesting and your work intriguing. And besides," she added, crossing her tiny arms across her thin and nearly formless chest, "I can't just pack up and go. I can only go as far as my little tether allows me."

"Why, what happens?" Jaimes drummed his fingertips against the top of the workbench, already contemplating whether it would be worth the hassle of beginning his experiment anew if he put out every single fire in the room and rid himself of the sassy spirit.

"Have you ever stopped existing?"

The question startled Jaimes, and he straightened. "No, of course not." He hesitated. "At least, I don't think I have. Unless you count before I was born, but then that wasn't really 'stopping existing' … more 'beginning to exist', and really—"

"You would know if you had," Vash interrupted. "It's not a pleasant experience. One moment you're existing perfectly, and then the next someone whips their manhood out and pisses on the campfire or a candle gets blown out or a fireplace doused. And then it's nothing." Her tone was very flat, and Jaimes was sure that if he could see her eyes clearly, they would be wide and afraid. "Nothing but endless dark and cold." Her head cocked. "Do you know what it's like for a spirit of fire to be cold?"

Jaimes opened his mouth to answer and say that he did not, but he could imagine it was not ideal, but Vash cut him off again. "It's antithetical, is what it is. It's impossible, and yet it happens all the time. And it's enough to drive some of us mad." Her voice hardened again, and Jaimes suddenly felt very uneasy in the presence of the tiny spirit. "So you wander through the dark and the cold, and if you get lucky some half brained arcanist casts a tiny spell and you're back in the light and the warmth. And no matter how much some pale little apothecary may find your presence annoying, all you can do is hope that he decides to discard the thoughts running through his head and let you exist in this place for just a little longer."

Jaimes swallowed. "Alright."

"Thank you." Vash sighed. "Now. Your decantation has been simmering nicely for a good while now. What's the next step?"

Jaimes opened his notebook, flipping to the last page as quickly as his fingers would let him. "Oh," he said glumly. "I don't know. I didn't get that far in my planning."

Vash snorted again. "Figures. You've been nodding off all morning." She drifted closer, and Jaimes fought the urge to shut the book again. "If I understand your notes correctly, this is a repetition of the previous experiment, correct? With a slight variation in the initial extraction process, which you've already done."

"Y-yes," Jaimes stammered, hoping she was correct. He honestly couldn't remember what he'd had in mind for this test.

"Then you're in luck," Vash said. "Now we let it cool to room temperature and filter the liquid through a copper sieve." She pointed to the bed. "Which means you can rest. You haven't slept in two days, you idiot, and you're going to cause a disaster if you keep working like this."

Jaimes waved her off, then grew alarmed when the air current his movement created buffeted Vash's small form enough to break it apart. But she reformed instantly and with seemingly little effort, and he let out a low sigh masked as a groan. "I'm fine."

"Are you, really?" Vash asked. There was marked sarcasm in her rich voice. "Have you managed to entirely convince yourself that I am in fact what I claim to be, and not a hallucination brought on by lack of sleep and poor diet?"

Jaimes considered for a moment, watching the way Vash's hair drifted and dissipated like the smoke from the nearby candle. "No, I guess I haven't."

"Then go to sleep!" Vash ordered, pointing at the bed once more. "You've been playing in here all alone for long enough, Jaimes. Now it's time you had someone to act the part of your doting assistant. Someone to make sure you eat and rest enough."

Jaimes wanted to argue, but he saw there was no point to it. He had been planning on resting when he reached the next cooling period for his sample anyway. What harm would there be in letting Vash keep an eye on his work while he slept? She had evidently been watching him work for days now anyway.

"Fine," he muttered glumly. "But don't touch anything." He reached for the burner, intent on turning it off, but hesitated. Instead, he pulled the nearest candle a little closer, then gave the tiny smoke figure hovering over his workbench a cautious glance as he closed the valve connecting the burner to the small supply of lantern oil it used for fuel.

Vash's form shifted slightly, her lower smoke trail drifting from the unlit burner to the candle just an inch or so from

her. She nodded at him, the motion so small that it was difficult for him to see. "Thank you."

Jaimes grunted a reply and slid into bed, clothes and all.
He didn't want Vash to see him undress, though there was a
very good chance she had already seen him do so before. The
bed smelled faintly of freshly laundered linens with a heavy
scent of his various experiments clouding it. He wondered if
Mathius had his bedding washed separately from the rest of
the inn's linens.

"Vash?"

"Yes?" Her voice was quiet enough that it was difficult for
him to pick up even from a few feet away.

"Are you a hallucination?"

She laughed. It was a pleasant laugh, and Jaimes liked the
sound of it very much. "You'll have to wait and see when you
wake up."

14

EILONWY

S he could feel her brother's warm breath on her neck. His breathing was slow, as was hers. It was easier to focus on the task at hand if they took a moment to steady their heart rates and slow their breathing. It was harder to defeat a focused elf. And easier to be defeated by one. But it still annoyed her.

"Can you please be a little quieter?" Eilonwy asked, directing the question through the mental connection that tied her to her brother.

Tathiel put a gentle hand on her hip, leaning further over her shoulder to peer through the bushes they crouched behind. *"Relax, sister. They can't hear us."*

Eilonwy exhaled hard. *"But I can, and it's getting under my skin."*

"You've had that issue a lot since we left Larten." Tathiel leaned away from her, and the heat of his breath no longer brushed against her flesh. *"Do you want to tell me about what happened between you and Jaimes?"*

"Now?" She turned, giving him a hard look. *"You really ought to work on your timing."*

"Not now." Tathiel rolled his eyes, motioning back towards

the heavy brush that concealed them from the road with a slight jerk of his chin. *"After."*

Eilonwy did not answer, but she turned and once more watched the road that stretched out before them. The caravan Mathius had told Tathiel of was coming up the road right towards them. It had been easy enough to find, and even easier to maneuver around the scouts and find an ambush position further along the road they traveled. Now all that was needed was to wait.

"I count seven men, three on horseback and two in the wagon box. Last ones in the wagon with the ..." Eilonwy hesitated. *"With the prisoners."* She let out a slow breath, willing the hot anger that flooded her to dissipate. *"Counting the three scouts we spotted on the way here, that means a total of ten men."*

"Should be fine enough." Tathiel slipped closer to her, gesturing towards the trap they had laid for the slavers. A heavy tree lay across the road, blocking the caravan from continuing further. *"Can you hold the illusion until they reach it?"*

Eilonwy answered with a nod.

"Then we start with the ones that go to remove the barricade. Take them by surprise. Then finish off the others." Tathiel removed a pair of short blades with near silent motions as the caravan drew closer. *"And the scouts? We should have taken them when we had the chance."*

"No," Eilonwy said. *"The scouts we leave. Let their fallen allies serve as a warning."*

"And if they hear us and come running?"

"We kill them." Eilonwy shrugged. *"Ten dead men will serve as a better warning than only seven."*

"Or ..." Tathiel's projected voice took on a hesitant and worried tone. *"We kill the others silently."*

Eilonwy considered for a moment. The caravan was halting as the illusionary barrier was spotted. One of the men on horseback barked a command, and the two men in the wagon's box and the two in the back jumped down to head for the downed tree. *"Like death descending from above."*

Tathiel set his blades carefully on the ground and laced his fingers together, forming a stirrup. *"You want a boost?"*

Eilonwy turned to face him, placing one booted foot in the hollow formed by his interwoven fingers. *"Wait until they're trying to lift it."* She crouched awkwardly, every muscle in her body ready to move, poised like a snake waiting for the chance to strike. The brush was to her back, and she relied on Tathiel's judgment. But his judgment was never wrong in matters like this one.

He watched the approaching men through a gap in the leaves of the bushes, and she watched him for any flicker of motion.

A muscle in his neck twitched slightly, giving her just enough advanced warning to deepen the flex in the muscles of her thighs.

"Now!" Tathiel barely rose from his squat, but his arms launched her high upwards. The tension in her legs released like a stretched bowstring letting loose an arrow, and she arched her back as her own added force took her higher into the air. The summersault brought the four men below her into view, and she angled her hips slightly as she descended, making sure she would land in their midst.

They hadn't even noticed her, though she sailed right over the heads of two of them.

She landed in a half crouch, eyes level with the navel of the closest of the four men.

Her hands were quick, the blades pulled from the sheathes on the small of her back flashing.

The man closest to her didn't even have time for his mind to register the presence of a fifth body before his throat was slit. The unfortunate man at his side had long enough to blink stupidly before a blade was dug deeply into his chest, through ribs and into his heart.

The last two jumped, startled, but they too did not have enough time to react sensibly. One fell back against the illusionary tree, and Eilonwy brought him down with a stab to the bobbing apple of his throat. The illusion broke, and the dead man crumpled to the ground. Her blade hadn't even come free of the third man before the other weapon was stabbing into the side of the fourth man's neck. Eilonwy freed this knife with a sharp tug and a spray of blood as his neck was opened deep enough for the head to fall back against his shoulder blades and he collapsed to the dirt.

Eilonwy turned on her heel, sighting down the stretch of road in an instant, and threw the dagger she held in her left hand. It was the weaker hand, but her aim was true. The blade lodged itself into the forehead of the only remaining horseman with enough force to knock him from the saddle.

Eilonwy let out the breath she'd been holding in a long exhale.

The startled horses gave a chorus of whinnies, but their masters were in no condition to soothe their startled nerves.

Tathiel pulled one of his blades from the side of a second horseman. "Five to two. You always seem to get the better odds."

"I always seem to get the head start." Eilonwy bent to retrieve her blade from the last horseman's skull, tugging it free with some effort. The metal was covered in gore and bits of hair and bone. She wiped both of her weapons carefully on the shoulder of the dead man's wool shirt. "And this isn't a game, Tathiel."

"Hel-hello?" a frightened voice called. They spoke in the common tongue of Azimar, though Eilonwy noted the heavy Vyrisian accent that made even the single word sound almost melodious.

Tathiel and Eilonwy both went to the rear of the covered wagon, lifting the oiled tarpaulin that draped over the back simultaneously.

Three blinking elves stared at them from the dark interior of the wagon, hunkered together in the far end. A fourth elf lay on his back, his head cradled in the lap of one of the others. Eilonwy noted the dirty and bloodied bandage that was wrapped around his head and the way his face and eyes did not even twitch in the sudden light of the lifted wagon flap.

Eilonwy leaned her head in, dropping the tarpaulin until it rested against her shoulder and reduced the light filtering in. "It's alright. We're here to help."

The three that stared at her sighed in relief, and one gave a low muttering of praise to the Great Ones. Eilonwy noted that one of the three was female, and all three had heavy bangles on their wrists. No chain connected the shackles to one another.

Eilonwy cursed.

"How did they capture you?" Tathiel asked.

Eilonwy lifted herself up and into the wagon, careful not to disturb the wounded elf lying on the wooden slats of the wagon.

"They just caught us by surprise, is all. Not all at once, mind you," the elf to the female's left said. His accent had far less of the Vyrisian lilt to it, and Eilonwy suspected that he was an Azimarian wood elf. "Got us one by one."

"They took Mirith and I together," the woman said coolly, motioning to the unresponsive elf. It was her lap his head was cradled in, and she stroked his dark hair as she answered. "They almost killed him. I didn't want him to die alone, so I went willingly with them."

"He might not make it much longer, as it is," the first elf said. "The fever has gotten worse, and I don't know the first damned thing about healing. Not that the humans would have cared to help. What's another dead elf, but a small loss to their profits?"

"And you?" Eilonwy asked, motioning towards the final elf, who had still not spoken. He was dark skinned, not an uncommon thing among Vyrisian elves, but his close-cropped hair was not the usual style worn among any elves. The careless cuts where the tips of his ears should have been were easy to see, and Eilonwy felt a brief wave of nausea at the sight of them.

"He doesn't speak," the male elf said.

"They took his tongue when they took his ears," the female added. "Poor boy can't even tell us his name. Just garbles nonsense that we can't understand."

The boy, as the female elf had called him, nodded slowly and made a strange gurgling noise that might have been a few words. To Eilonwy, they sounded like nothing comprehensible.

Eilonwy turned to Tathiel. "Get us out of here. Before the scouts notice something is wrong."

"Go?" Tathiel snorted. "Go where? Why not just turn them loose?"

"Because one of them is dying," Eilonwy hissed. "And they all have those damned arcane traps around their wrists. They would be defenseless."

"I was never much good with magic, anyway," the male elf said lamely. "Always kept buggering it up."

Tathiel cursed, eyeing the heavy metal cuffs on each of the captured elf's wrists. "Go where, Eilonwy?"

"Back to Larten?"

"Larten? Why?" Tathiel's face screwed up.

"Jaimes will help us." She nodded towards the elves. "Will help them."

Tathiel made a sour face, but he nodded. "Help me tie the horses to the wagon. We can always use fresh mounts."

When Eilonwy and Tathiel were both out of the wagon, Tathiel rested a hand against her shoulder. *"Will he make it that far, Eilonwy? The injured one?"*

"I ... I don't know," Eilonwy answered honestly. *"But I want to try for it, at least."*

"It won't be easy, getting him into the inn like that."

Eilonwy shook her head. *"We won't get him into the inn. We'll get Jaimes to come to him."*

Tathiel nodded, though his expression showed he was not entirely convinced that it would be as simple as that.

"And the other two? The young one and the other male? Do we take them to Larten with us?"

Eilonwy considered for a moment. *"We let them rest. Then we can send them back to Vyris or wherever they might find safety."*

Tathiel nodded again. "Then we're going."

"We're going," Eilonwy agreed.

Tathiel opened the flaps to the rear of the wagon once more, this time pinning them open with a length of rope suspended from the tarpaulin for just that purpose. "I'll give you two minutes to take from these fine and upstanding gentlemen anything you might find a use for, and then we need to get out of here before the scouts return and realize their cargo has rolled off of its own accord."

The two male elves didn't need to be told twice, and they clambered from the rear of the wagon with stammered curses and blinks.

Tathiel stood motionless, arms crossed as he watched the men pull weapons and purses from the dead with only the slightest of hesitations.

Eilonwy peered at the woman that remained. "And you?"

The elf shook her head. "I won't leave him."

Eilonwy's gaze flicked to the wounded elf as he inhaled a loud and shuddering breath. The female elf stroked his hair soothingly, whispering quietly into his ear.

The young elf with no tongue returned first, the pockets of his trousers stuffed with jingling coins and a pair of nearly new leather boots tucked under one arm. Under the other arm shone the hilts of two blades, their scabbards hardly scuffed and their belts dangling down to the boy's knees.

"She'll be taking one of those blades, if you don't mind," Eilonwy said to him, motioning towards the elf behind her.

The boy shrugged and let Eilonwy disentangle one of the weapons from the stash under his arm.

"Do you know how to use a blade?" she asked.

"Of course we know how to use a blade," the other male elf asked, lurching into the wagon once more. "What do you take us for, a bunch of clumsy human oafs?" His arms were more weighed down than the younger elf's, but he dropped a pair of shoes to the bottom of the wagon with a clatter. "Got those for you, Gilaine. I hope they fit. Took 'em off the smallest man out there."

The wagon shifted and jerked as Tathiel settled into the wagon's box and urged the horses into a manageable pace.

"Thank you, Asher," the female elf, Gilaine, said.

Asher shrugged, belting a sword around his waist while keeping a noticeably larger pair of boots pinned against his chest. The motion of the wagon did not disturb his balance in the slightest.

The younger elf made a gurgling sound, and a heavy coin purse fell to the wooden slats just beside Gilaine.

Eilonwy looked up at the young elf, but he only gave a proud, toothy grin before leaping from the wagon and disappearing around the side of it. Eilonwy heard Tathiel murmur and the wagon creaked as the boy took a seat next to Tathiel.

Gilaine stared at the purse, mouth open in a dumbfounded expression.

Asher snorted, finally sitting to replace his worn-out shoes with the stolen boots. "The boy might not be able to speak, but he does have a certain charm about him, doesn't he? And he knows what's what. Can't be leaving our kind to suffer in despondency and destitution, now can we?" He paused, looking from Gilaine and the unresponsive Mirith to

Eilonwy. "So there's no hope of removing these traps around our wrists?"

Eilonwy shook her head. "None that we've been able to find."

"And … our ears?" Asher asked hopefully, fingering the uneven cut where the tip of his ear had been shorn off. It was red and slightly inflamed, as if it were only just healing from an infection. "Any hope of getting those back, you think?"

Eilonwy thought of Jaimes, and of his work in Larten's inn. She shook her head again. "No. Nothing short of magical means, and even that would only be temporary. It wouldn't last."

Asher tugged on his fresh boots, the false cheer in his voice not entirely hiding the disappointment behind his words. "It was a silly thing to wish for, anyway. I still have my life. What are the tips of my ears to me?"

Mirith groaned in Gilaine's lap, and Eilonwy squatted, testing his temperature with the back of her hand. His skin was hot and clammy.

Eilonwy looked up at Asher, who was staring at Mirith with wide eyes set into a suddenly grey face. "The only thing I can do is help you find the men that cut your ears away."

Asher's face and eyes brightened momentarily, but the effect was forced. "You already have." Asher motioned towards his feet, now shod in the scavenged leather boots. "I'm wearing his shoes."

***

The return journey to Larten was slower than Eilonwy had anticipated. They stuck to forest trails, avoiding the heavier beaten roads and highways, and the wagon's wheels stuck in the soft soil every once in a while. They were lucky it had not rained in several days, or the trek would have been even more difficult. They ate together the first evening, the three able-bodied men sitting around a small fire while Gilaine and Eilonwy ate in the wagon with Mirith's prostrated figure between them.

Eilonwy had been of little help to the sick man, though she knew a little about herbal medicine from her study of Jaimes's books so many years ago. The problem was not in the lack of knowledge, but in the lack of ingredients. With every stop to unstick the wagon or rest the horses and themselves, Eilonwy searched the nearby woods for some of the plants she knew could help kill fever and fight off infection. The silent elf boy, who Asher had taken to calling Gabber, often accompanied her, but their efforts usually returned little more than handfuls of mushrooms and wild berries.

They were lucky enough to find a large patch of Serpent's Tongue, an herbaceous plant with red vines that forked every ten inches or so, and for which the plant was named. The leaves could be brewed into a mild tea that had some anti-inflammatory properties, and because it was the only thing that had been found with more potent medical properties than the few mint leaves Gabber had collected only a few hours before, Eilonwy stuffed her pockets with every leaf from the plant, silently praying to the Great Ones for the gift and asking forgiveness for likely killing the poor-vining foliage.

The mint and Serpent's Tongue tea smelled nice, but Eilonwy could see no noticeable change in Mirith's condition by the third day. If anything, he was growing steadily worse. In the evenings, when Eilonwy removed his bandages and cleaned them in boiling water taken from one of the many small tributaries of the Knife, she would examine Mirith's head wound. It was a cut to the side of his head, and the sight of it brought blurry and unpleasant memories back to Eilonwy. But it was longer and deeper than her own wound had been, and it oozed a thick red ichor that stank of infection. Mirith's ears, the tips of which had been savagely ripped away with a serrated blade down almost to where ear and skull met, were also red and swollen with deep infection.

By the time the Serpent's Tongue ran out, the putrid smell rising from his wound was strong enough to make them gag and could be smelled through the freshly cleaned wrappings and the mint leaves Eilonwy wrapped around the cut. The gore that seeped from Mirith's head was no longer a medium red in color, but was now a red so deep it was almost black.

Asher left them that third morning, wishing them farewell. When they offered him one of the three horses, a dappled gelding with blood dried on its saddle, he refused and left on foot. They were close to Larten, and it was entirely possible they would reach the sandy outskirts before nightfall. Asher was vehemently against getting any closer to a human settlement than absolutely necessary, and no one protested when he announced that it was time for him to part from their company.

Gabber seemed unsure if he should stay or go, and Eilonwy often caught him staring wistfully into the deep green of the wild forest, a gloomy expression on his face. But when Mirith took a turn for the worse, his breathing suddenly shallowing to almost nothing and his clammy skin growing deathly cold and dry, Gabber stayed faithfully by the wagon. He would disappear for several moments at a time, and Eilonwy was ready to snap at the quiet boy to either sit still or go away because she had no time to watch a wandering child, when he returned with a fistful of mint leaves and shoved them hurriedly into Eilonwy's hands.

Eilonwy grumbled a tired thanks and shoved the mint leaves into her mouth, chewing them furiously into a paste. The mint stung her tongue, making her eyes water, but she kept chewing.

Gilaine began to weep, collapsing against Gabber's shoulders in exhaustion and defeat. He held her awkwardly, staring at Eilonwy as she tugged the dying Mirith into her lap. Mirith's head lolled against her shoulder, the smell of the infection that was slowly killing him breaking through even the scent of the mint leaves in her mouth.

Eilonwy spat the wad of mint paste into a wooden cup and poured the last of their water over it, giving it a careful swirl. She tossed the empty water skin across the wagon, not even noticing where it landed, and tilted Mirith's head further back until his mouth hung open. She slowly poured the hastily made mint tea into his mouth, massaging his throat to coax the liquid down. Even then, much of it spilled from between his lips, and Eilonwy cursed.

When the cup was empty, she tossed it aside as well and beat a fist against the wooden boards that separated the wagon from the box seat where Tathiel sat. "Go faster, Tathiel! He won't make it much longer."

Tathiel spurred the horses, shouting curses at them.

TATHIEL

Tathiel bounced lightly in the saddle in time with the hoofbeats of the mare beneath him. He wanted to urge the beast to go faster, faster, but she was already nearing a full gallop, and saliva foamed at the horse's mouth as she breathed hard and fast. Her eyes were large and wide, and the whites showed clearly in the sunlight.

The gate to Larten loomed before him like a mirage, and Tathiel sighed with relief when he saw that it was open and unmanned. *"Nearly there, Eilonwy. I'll bring Jaimes back as soon as I can."*

Eilonwy did not respond, but she had not said anything to him since he had taken the horse and left the wagon nearly half an hour before.

He let his mount slow, pulling her to a slow trot as he entered the broad street that served as Larten's main road. He cursed, forgetting himself for a moment, and touched the first two fingers of one hand to the amulet that rested against his chest. The magic within the stone flared to life with a few choice words, and where someone may have seen a silver-haired elf a moment before, there was now a blond human with a forgettable face.

Tathiel led the horse to the trough just outside Mathius's inn and left her to drink. She snorted irritably when he brushed his hands over her neck. "Rest while you can, my darling. We'll be heading back in almost no time."

Mathius was behind the counter when he entered, and the captain-turned-innkeeper welcomed the fresh-faced stranger as Tathiel rushed past him.

"Not now, Mathius, sorry. We need Jaimes's help. He'll need a horse, if you can spare one."

Mathius spluttered, but Tathiel did not stay to make sure the man realized who had just rudely run past him and up to the guest quarters.

Tathiel pounded up the stairs and reached Jaimes's door in a handful of strides. He knocked harder than absolutely necessary, and he heard Jaimes curse inside. There was also the sound of glass clinking, and what may have been the heavy thud of a book hitting the floor.

"Dammit, Mathius, are you trying to scare me to death?"

Tathiel pushed the door open, fighting down a gag at the stench of whatever terrible concoction was boiling on the countertop. Jaimes's expression changed from an angry glare to one of surprise and confusion.

"Good, you already have boots on. Get some sort of medical kit together and let's go. Eilonwy needs your help."

Jaimes blinked. "E-Eilonwy?" He took a limping step closer. "Tathiel, is that you?"

"Of course it is." He waved impatiently. "Let's move, Jaimes."

"I-I …" Jaimes stammered, looking hastily around the room. "What do I need?" His face paled. "What's wrong with Eilonwy?"

"It's not her," Tathiel said, reaching for an old saddlebag resting on a nearby shelf and shaking it open. Dust and ash fell from the worn leather and onto the floor. "We've got an injured … friend." Tathiel cringed at his near use of the word elf in the inn. Even if they were alone at the moment, there was no telling how much of their conversation might be heard by other guests in the nearby rooms. "He's been getting worse, and now Eilonwy thinks he won't survive much longer. We've been riding straight for you for days."

Jaimes straightened, grabbing the bag from Tathiel. "Alright. What's wrong with this friend?"

Tathiel thought frantically. He wished Eilonwy had been the one to rush to Larten. She had the better mind for medicine. *If she would even answer me when I called to her, this would be easier.* But she likely had her attention focused on Mirith. "Fever, I know that. And infection. From a head wound."

"Alright." Jaimes grabbed several bottles from the bench top and dropped them into the bag. They clinked together, but didn't seem to break as they rolled against each other. "What has Eilonwy been using so far?"

"Mint, mostly. It was all we could find."

"And is your friend improving with treatment?" Jaimes turned and rummaged through a few more bottles, reading labels and muttering under his breath.

"I don't think so." Tathiel sighed. "We should get back. He was vomiting bile and blood when I left."

"Shit," Jaimes spat. "I'm glad you said something about the vomiting. Is it just blood and bile, no food?" He turned and reached for a waxed sheepskin sachet sitting on the same shelf the saddlebag had been resting on. He glanced at the label and tossed it in with everything else.

"He hasn't eaten in at least a few days."

"Is he responsive?"

"Is he what?"

"Responsive," Jaimes snapped, waving his arm about. "Is he awake? Does he answer when you speak to him?"

"No, he just groans occasionally."

Jaimes sighed, turning to face Tathiel. "Alright. Is there

anything you can think of that I should know? Any other symptoms?”

“No. That's everything I know.”

Jaimes nodded curtly and closed the bag with a jerk of the leather ties. “Now we can go. You might have to give me a hand on the stairs, Tathiel. I twisted my knee a bit getting everything together.” Jaimes stumbled towards him, his face betraying a faintly pained expression, and Tathiel noted that his steps were more labored than they normally were.

Tathiel eyed the lit burner on the worktop. “Will your things be alright here without you?”

“Hm?” Jaimes turned, spotting the source of Tathiel's unease and shrugging a shoulder. “It'll be fine. It just needs to boil for another half an hour,” Jaimes said. “Then it can simmer until I return. Best not to let it cool completely, I think.”

Tathiel stepped out of the doorway, letting Jaimes pass him on the landing. “Does Mathius know how to work that burner?”

“Great Ones, I doubt it.” Jaimes shut the door to his room behind them and locked the bolt with a small ornate key. He dropped the key into a pocket on the inside of his vest and patted it gently. “But it'll be fine,” he repeated.

Jaimes did not need help descending the stairs, though Tathiel remained close by, nonetheless. They left the inn nearly as quickly as Tathiel had entered, though Mathius was no longer behind the desk just inside the entrance.

“Our caravan is stopped along the Knife. I made the ride quickly enough, but night is coming, and my horse is tired.” Tathiel held the door open as Jaimes exited the inn. “But if we hurry, we can still— ” Tathiel cursed, spotting the empty post above the trough where he had left his horse. “She's gone!”

“Don't get your hair in a twist—I've just had her taken to the stables to be cleaned and fed,” Mathius said behind them.

Tathiel turned, ready to protest, but Mathius held the reins to two fresh horses in his hands. They snorted lightly, and one stamped a hoof impatiently against the hard packed earth in front of the inn.

"You ran right past before I could ask how things had gone, so I figured something was up. And then I found a horse nearly passed out from exertion right outside the door." Mathius passed the reins over, and Tathiel helped Jaimes into the saddle of one without taking his eyes from the former sea captain. "So I brought you both fresh mounts. They've been in the stable for a while, and they seem eager to get their legs moving again. Just bring them back in one piece, and I'll be happy to have helped."

"Thank you, Mathius," Tathiel said. "I didn't even think you'd recognized me."

Mathius snorted. "I'm sorry to say it, but you don't have the same skill that your sister does when it comes to those incognito looks you put together. They all look sorta the same," Mathius said. Tathiel noted the slight southern lilt that fell into a few of his words, and wondered if the old man was doing it intentionally, or if his few short years in Larten had already changed him. "And besides," Mathius continued, holding the reins of the stamping horse as Tathiel hoisted himself into the saddle. "You never change your eyes."

"Thank you, Mathius," Jaimes said. His words had a breathless quality to them, and he glanced about nervously as if he were only just realizing that he had left not only his room, but the inn as well. "I-I'll be back soon, I hope." He turned the horse with a little effort, pointing it towards the opened gate. "Let's go, Tathiel. Keep the gate open for us, Mathius."

They rode the horses hard again, Tathiel taking the lead. Mathius had been right about the mounts being eager. They took to a gallop with little need for encouragement, and only slowed when they grew too tired to maintain the pace they had set for themselves. They continued at a steady trot, and Tathiel glanced anxiously at the sky as the sun began to descend.

"What were you two doing?" Jaimes asked, guiding his horse closer to Tathiel's. "You left so quickly last time you were in Larten. I didn't get a chance to ask you what your plans have been while Alastor and Roland search for the Amulet of Fire."

"Nothing permanent," Tathiel answered. "A few errands for the others here and there."

"And this time?"

Tathiel sighed. "This time it was hunting down a group of slave traders that had been crossing into Vyris and taking elves from their homes. We rescued four, and it's one of the four that is sick."

"Slave traders." Jaimes shuddered in the saddle. "So close to Larten?"

"They were in Larten," Tathiel corrected, his tone more biting than he had intended. "They stopped at the inn. It's how Mathius knew about them."

"*Mathius* sent you after them?"

Tathiel turned in his saddle to face Jaimes. "Why does that surprise you? Mathius has always been honest with us about his feelings regarding Mothlenor's treatment of non-humans. He's been giving us information for years."

"I didn't know."

Tathiel narrowed his eyes at Jaimes, and the man shrank away a little. "We have all been doing our part, no matter how small it may be."

Jaimes broke the gaze that Tathiel held him with and bit his lower lip, eyes lowered. "You're all just moving on with your lives, as you said before," he murmured after a moment.

"I didn't say we were moving on. I said we were no longer children."

"Is there a difference?" Jaimes asked with a snort.

Tathiel frowned, pulling the reins on his horse slightly. His mount was getting spirited again, and in a few moments they would be able to finish out the journey to the wagon at a full gallop.

"There is a difference, yes."

Jaimes gave him a wry smile. "If you insist."

"Moving on means accepting what has come before. And we cannot accept the tragedies that have come to us and the people of Azimar because of the king. We will not move on until Mothlenor is stopped." He let the reins of his horse out, and it immediately increased speed. Jaimes followed Tathiel's example, and their pace increased. "Leaving childhood behind is inevitable, and with it comes the acceptance of responsibility and, hopefully, some maturity. That is what I meant before."

"Responsibility and maturity." Jaimes nodded, his face set into a scowl. "I'll remember that, Tathiel."

"I hope you do." Tathiel let the reins out even further, and urged his horse into a gallop with a kick to the ribs.

They rode in silence for the next several minutes, more from necessity than a desire for quiet. Tathiel sensed the distance between himself and Eilonwy shrinking rapidly, and he called out to her. *Eilonwy, we'll be there soon. Please tell me we're not too late.*

He could see the wagon in the distance in the fading sunlight. "Up ahead," he shouted to Jaimes. "Do you see it?"

Jaimes squinted, leaning slightly over the pommel of the saddle. "No, it's too dark."

"We're close."

A high-pitched keening wail echoed across the sandy stretch between them and the caravan.

Jaimes's face paled as he turned to Tathiel. "What was that?"

You were too late, Tathiel.

Jaimes stayed with them as they prepared Mirith's body for travel, though he was not needed. It was Gilaine's helpless and anguished cry they had heard as they neared the caravan, and her cries did not cease for a long time. So it was left to Tathiel and Eilonwy to clean Mirith's corpse, with occasional help from Gabber. The young elf was eager to help, but grew pale after prolonged exposure to the body. So his task was to comfort Gilaine as much as a mute elf could comfort a grieving soul.

When it was done, Tathiel took the two horses from the caravan's original pack of three and strapped them into the leads. He and Eilonwy wished Gabber luck and shared condolences with Gilaine before the two freed elves climbed into the wagon box and turned the horses towards the Knife and Vyris.

Jaimes passed the reins of one of the horses borrowed from Mathius to Tathiel. "Where will they go?"

"Home," Tathiel answered. "If they ford the Knife and enter Vyris before morning, they should be able to avoid further slavers."

Jaimes took Eilonwy's steadying hand as he stepped into the saddle of the second horse. "Why not bury their friend here? They would be faster on horseback."

Eilonwy shook her head at him. "If given the choice, would you want to be buried in a foreign land? Especially if your homeland was so close?"

Jaimes hardly hesitated to answer. "No, I don't suppose I would."

"Besides," Tathiel said, arranging himself in the saddle more comfortably, "there are rituals that Vyrisians follow when it comes to burying our dead that simply can't be done here."

"Like what?" Jaimes's eyebrow raised, his interest piqued.

Eilonwy climbed into the saddle behind Tathiel, wrapping her arms lightly around his waist. "Sorry, Jaimes. It's not something we freely share. Maybe you'll get to see it someday."

Eilonwy's voice sounded weary, and she leaned a little more heavily against his back.

Jaimes's shoulders slumped, but he only made a small sound of acknowledgment.

"Are you going to be alright, Eilonwy?" Tathiel asked his sister in a quiet tone.

"I just need some rest. Let's go back to Larten. Hopefully Mathius has a room for us."

They made the journey back to Larten in silence. Tathiel conjured half a dozen green witch lights for the horses and Jaimes to see by, and he led them over sandy and rocky terrain at a sedate pace. Eilonwy's weight grew heavier against him as she dozed, but not once did her grip around him slacken.

There was a figure standing at the gate to Larten. Tathiel saw the lantern before he saw the shadowed shape of the person holding it. When they were close enough that the witch lights might be seen by whoever stood at Larten's entrance, he doused them. Jaimes cursed lightly, but Tathiel took the reins of his horse and led both animals.

When he could finally make out Mathius's form in the shadows of the lantern the innkeeper held, Tathiel sighed and relaxed his body.

"Is that you, Jaimes?"

Jaimes's head lifted. "Oh, Mathius, thank the Great Ones."

"We've returned, and we brought Eilonwy with us," Tathiel said. His sister stirred at the mention of her name, but did not sit completely upright.

"Well, quickly now. The whole damned town is sleeping. Let's get you inside and to bed too, you lot."

"Oh, Mathius," Eilonwy murmured. Tathiel could feel her

lips moving against his shoulder. "What would we do without you?"

Tathiel and Eilonwy shared a room, and Eilonwy fell into bed without wishing Jaimes or Mathius goodnight.

Tathiel shrugged. "She's been up for days straight. She'll be more amenable in the morning."

He did not go to bed right away. Instead, he donned a disguise and went out to the stables. The horses they had borrowed from Mathius had already been unsaddled and returned to their pens, and Tathiel gave both an extra-large handful of feed into their bags, along with a soft thanks for their help. The mare he had first ridden to Larten slept in a pen at the opposite end of the stable, and Tathiel whispered a few kind words in her direction before leaving her to continue her well-earned rest.

He returned to the room he shared with Eilonwy. It was almost morning. The sky was still black, but the stars had shifted. The sun would be rising in a few hours.

"Tathiel?" Eilonwy asked from the bed. She sounded only a little more rested, and would surely fall asleep again momentarily.

"Yes?"

"Melonya will be coming to Larten tomorrow, correct?"

Tathiel thought for a moment, staring at the moon through the window of their room. Melonya was supposed to meet them on the fourth day after the full moon. "Two days, not tomorrow."

"Ah."

"Why?"

Eilonwy did not answer right away, and Tathiel wondered if perhaps she had fallen asleep again. But she spoke up again, slowly and unsure of her words. "I don't think I will be going with you to join Alastor."

Tathiel turned to face her, surprised. She sat up in bed, staring across the room at him. "Why not?"

"I want to stay here with Jaimes. I want to help him see that he is still the man we need him to be, despite everything he's been through."

Tathiel didn't want to argue. Not with Eilonwy, and not about Jaimes. Instead he sighed. He crossed the room and settled onto the bed beside his sister. He kicked his shoes off, letting them drop to the floor, and settled his arms behind his head. He felt his spine and the muscles of his back stretching. How long had it been since he slept in a bed?

"Two weeks, Eilonwy." He turned his head to face her. "After Melonya and I leave, I'll give you two weeks. Melonya will return to Larten to bring you to join Alastor and me. With or without Jaimes."

Eilonwy nodded. "Two weeks."

"If anyone can remind him that he's still the savior his Mark declared him to be, it would be you, Eilonwy."

Eilonwy settled back into the bed with a sigh. "I only hope I can."

Jaimes, you stupid, selfish, idiot. I hope you come to understand how lucky you are to have my sister's heart.

16
VASH

Vash watched silently as Jaimes shut the door and left her alone. She heard murmured words exchanged between him and the elf that had barged into their room, but the voices faded quickly as the two departed.

I didn't even get a chance to say goodbye. To tell him to be careful, or to remember his cloak.

Instead, she'd remained hidden in the fire produced by the many candles that littered the top of Jaimes's workbench.

Jaimes had been content to remain in his room with her, focusing on their work together, for so many days. What had changed to make him rush away so quickly?

Vash settled into a seated position, balancing on a light draft created by the shifting candle flames, and glanced at the small vat of liquid carefully arranged on the burner. It was still boiling happily away, despite the scowl she unintentionally fixed it with.

It was something that elf said. That Eilonwy needed Jaimes.

Vash's scowl deepened, and she reclined against a chaise of smoke and crossed her arms.

Eilonwy is an elven name. And the way Jaimes instantly jumped to help ...

Several distinct pops and a hissing sound drew her attention to the liquid again. It was beginning to boil over, and white froth foamed at the lip of the cauldron. And no wonder—the small flame that sat beneath it had condensed into a hot core of intense heat.

"Shit," Vash cursed, focusing on the tiny flame and willing it to cool. The concoction settled into a gentle boil again, and Vash hesitantly turned away from it again to stare at the door.

It's not like me to get so annoyed.

Or was annoyed not the right emotion she felt? Was it instead anger? Jealousy, even?

Jealous of what? How quickly Jaimes responded to that name? Anger that he could run off at the mere mention of some she-elf?

Vash glanced over her shoulder at the cauldron again. It was still behaving as it should be. She returned her attention to the door.

Why does it matter? He's a human.

"How long will you be gone, Jaimes?" she asked the empty room.

And who is she?

1 7

ANNA

Anna waded into the water slowly, descending the steps with care. She stopped when the warm water reached her torso, just beneath her breasts. She had kept her dress on, and the wet fabric clung to her and weighed her down, restricting her breathing slightly. Anna had grown accustomed to the slightly uncomfortable sensation with each attempt to contact the spirit resting in the baths, and now it was little more than a minor nuisance. Besides, she had a clean robe waiting for her in the antechamber.

Burners circled the bath at even intervals, each one laden with the precious oils and resin she had spent days scavenging for, and the heavy scent of roses and copal hung in the steamy air. It was enough to make her head swim, and she knew she would have to ask Ishta and Illa to air the bath out as soon as her work here was finished.

She had meditated.

She had prayed to the Great Ones, asking Imis for compassion and Elir for guidance.

She had sat in that perfumed room for hours, abstaining from food and drink, trying desperately to bring her arcane talents as close as possible to any latent Gift she may possess.

179

She had grown up in the Coven, after all. Her mother was Gifted, whoever she was. Only Gifted Coven women were given the right to procreate and produce offspring for the Coven.

If there was even a trace of the Gift in her veins, this would be the only time she would ever need to use it.

So please, Great Ones, let this work, Anna pleaded. *Great Elir, grant me the strength to see this task complete, and Great Imis, lend me your ability to reach into the world beyond and connect with the lost soul that inhabits this place.*

She repeated the mantra, invoking Elir's power and Imis's wisdom and clarity.

Then she waded into the deepest part of the bath, where the water reached to her neck, raised her arms until they floated on the surface of the pool, and closed her eyes.

"I call on my Coven sister, who was also Mother to us all." Anna's voice shook, and she took a steadying breath. "I call on you, Matriarch, whose soul still wanders this place, and ask that you make yourself known to me."

Anna's teeth chattered, despite the warmth of the water. She had expected a whisper of arcane energy, or a gentle breeze to blow across the bath, or perhaps a dazzling light to show her that she was no longer alone. But she felt nothing, and behind her closed lids, she saw nothing but black.

"Please," Anna sobbed. "I have so many questions, and you are the only one who can help me."

"I am here, Anna."

Anna opened her eyes in a snap, turning with a splash to the spot along the bath wall where the voice had originated.

Her Coven sister's body was a shadow, if shadows were made of light instead of darkness. She was incredibly thin. Her cheekbones were sharply accented in her face, and her eyes sat in huge hollows. Anna could see bruises circling her frail neck, and everywhere her eyes settled she saw bones showing prominently under ghostly flesh.

She leaned against the wall of the pool, close enough that Anna would only need to take a few steps before closing the distance enough to touch her.

But Anna did not want to touch her. She didn't want to feel the way those thin arms might wrap around her in an embrace. She did not want to feel the weight of someone who could be no more substantial than a doll. Not when the spirit before her had once been the Matriarch of the Coven. Not when she had been Mother to all the sisters, deserving of respect and affection. And, in Anna's case, a small amount of carefully concealed lust.

The spirit remained where she sat, her bright blue eyes fixed on Anna. They were the only thing about her that still seemed alive in any way. Everything else, her impossibly thin body, the way the water did not ripple around her as she shifted her weight, the semi-translucent quality to her that brought hairs to stand on the back of Anna's neck, it all spoke of death and illusion.

But her eyes were still very much alive.

Anna choked on the lump in her throat, then let out a strangled sob.

"Nevina."

18

ISHTA

Her opponent was large, but Ishta had beaten larger men. What concerned her more was how fast he was.

She ducked beneath another swooping grapple, her upper arm inches away from his sweating grip. Ishta struck him in the back with a powerful kick, hoping she'd struck something tender and delicate. The crowd surrounding them in a tight circle jeered as the man grunted in pain, but Ishta kept moving, keeping herself as far from those hands as she could.

Men so strong shouldn't be so quick as well, she thought, dodging a tired swing of the man's arm and delivering another kick, this time to his midsection. *But at least he's getting tired. A few more minutes, and I can exhaust him into submission.*

She maintained her distance, circling her opponent and dodging his increasingly slow and fumbling attacks. And then a strong arm grabbed her around the waist as a spectator pulled her close. He had a faint vinegary smell about him, and his profile as he knelt to inhale deeply at her neck seemed vaguely familiar.

"Get off!" she cried, and dealt him an elbow to the ribs.

Several men in the crowd laughed as the man that had

grabbed her released her and stumbled back, and the crowd pushed her back into the fight. Their shoving hands propelled her right into the embrace of the sweating behemoth she had avoided for so long.

"Caught ya now, little bird," the man slurred. His arms tightened around her, and Ishta felt the air squeezed from her lungs. "Haven't they told you yet? It's dangerous for a girl to be out after dark."

Over the pounding in her ears, Ishta could hear a large portion of the crowd cheer, even as a somewhat smaller section booed and cried foul.

Ishta kicked blindly, but her feet found nothing. She felt her spine popping, and her lungs began to burn.

"That pretty face is starting to turn blue, little birdie." He squeezed her harder, and Ishta's mouth opened in an agonized and soundless cry of pain. She would have screamed if she had the air for it. "I don't think little birds fly so well once they've had their wings snapped off," the man crushing her said through gritted teeth. "What do you say, should we give it a try?"

Ishta bent both legs and propelled them forwards, hoping against hope that she might make contact.

And she did. Something soft met the bottoms of both bare feet, and the man holding her drew in a sharp breath and dropped her.

Ishta landed gracelessly to the floor, tailbone first. The ground was made of hard-packed earth rather than cobblestone, but it still hurt. She lay back, breathing heavily and trying to shake the spots from her eyes. Her sides ached terribly.

There was a howl above her, and Ishta instinctively rolled to one side, propping herself up on both elbows where she stopped. Two huge fists pummeled the ground where she had been seconds before, and the man fell to his knees in the dirt, gagging and gasping for air.

Ishta took her chance. She leapt onto his back, locking an arm under his throat and squeezing tight. The man tried to stand, but Ishta wrapped her legs around his arms and pulled them back, locking her ankles together. His hands slipped from the earth and he crashed face first into the dirt. Ishta's nose smacked into the back of his huge bald head, and she instantly tasted blood. But she didn't let go.

The cheers this time were louder, and Ishta tightened her grip. "You've got the ugliest fucking face I've ever seen, but now yours is turning blue, you big fat pile of shit." Blood flecked the side of the man's face with the last word, and Ishta spat a thick wad of more blood into the ground beside them. "Give it up, before you pass out."

"N-no," the man choked. He tried again to stand, but Ishta tightened her legs, pinning his arms to his sides. She doubled down on her grip around his throat, tasting blood in her mouth as she ground her teeth in effort.

The man made a strained strangling noise, and she felt his throat working against her forearm. "Give it up! You're not getting out of this one!"

The man made an imperceptible nod, and Ishta groaned as she loosened her hold on the man. "Say it!"

"I … yield," the man gasped. The crowd erupted, but Ishta did not release him.

"Louder!"

"I yield!" His voice carried further, and more of the crowd responded to his words. Ishta instantly released him, slumping against his sweating back. He flexed his shoulder, attempting to shrug her off. "Get off of me, you filthy whore," he groaned. His voice was raw.

Ishta fought the urge to deliver one last kick as she stood and limped away. Something was definitely wrong with her ribs, and there was a good chance her nose was broken. Again. She never let it heal properly the last time she had taken a blow to the face.

Someone behind her was already announcing the next fight, but she didn't listen. The sounds of clicking coins was all she focused on, and that sound was all around her. She pressed through the crowd gathering for the following match, careful not to bump too hard into any of them. Her hand may have slipped unnoticed into a pocket or two, but she got little for the effort.

A short man stood close to the exit, waiting for her. His hair was a greasy grey, and he constantly stank of stale ale and stale sex. Ishta wasn't sure how he could afford much of either, but the stench never faded. "Little Bird," he said with a nod.

"Don't call me that."

"All the best fighters have a name, and you won't give us your real one. You take the one given to you, then." He spat, then sneered up at her. "Little Bird."

"Just give me my money and get out of my way," Ishta said with a wince.

"There wasn't much today," the man said, affecting a forlorn expression even while he clinked coins together in the pockets of his pants.

"Bullshit," Ishta snarled. "I heard them. They were crazy about the fight. You had to have made thirty off it at least."

"Oh, I made my share and then some," the broker said with a vacant nod. "You weren't so lucky."

"I won the fight," Ishta said, her patience nearly gone. "I get a portion of all the money you make from lost bets. That's how it works."

The broker shook his head. "Bets are made so quickly before a fight. And everyone was so sure you would make this fight a short and memorable one. But you took too long to get the yield."

Ishta growled, rounding on the small man. He was little more than half her height, and she had just taken down someone three times his size. He should have been intimidated.

But he wasn't. He never was. And from the corner of Ishta's eye, she spotted two men nearly the size of the massive creature she had just beaten straighten and move towards her.

Ishta gritted her teeth and forced a smile. Fresh blood leaked from her swollen nose, trailing around her lips to drip off her chin. "I got the yield as fast as I could."

Coins clinked in the broker's pocket, and he gave her a slimy grin. "Then perhaps next time you should get the yield a little faster."

Ishta sighed, realizing arguing with him would be pointless. "How much, then?"

"Sixteen."

She nearly cursed. Her last fight had earned her twenty, and it had been an easier one. And sixteen would get her nowhere near her goal. But it was better than walking away with nothing. "Fine," Ishta spat, stretching out a bloodied hand. "Sixteen."

The broker's slimy grin deepened into a smile, and he dropped some coins into her open palm.

He knew I would accept the sixteen. He had it waiting for me, clinking away in that pocket of his.

Ishta glanced at the pile of coins in her hand, counting quickly. There were fourteen round pieces of gold, the edges worn and the surfaces rubbed smooth, and four small copper bits, their edges cut into octagons and the brown metal tarnished green in a few spots.

"You said sixteen," Ishta said, heat rising to her cheeks. She wasn't sure if she was going to start crying or yelling, and neither would end well.

"Sixteen before my ten percent, Little Bird."

Ishta let out a choked laugh. "You and I both know you took your ten percent before the sixteen."

The broker shrugged. "You can take that, or you can leave it all and be escorted out and banned from returning. Your choice."

"You're using me," Ishta said. She straightened, her fingers curling around the coins. "I won't let you continue to do so."

The broker smiled again. "You want to try your luck at one of the other fighting dens? They'll use you in worse ways than I do, Little Bird."

He was right, and Ishta knew it. The masters of the other dens would have her taken to be raped and beaten before letting her fight.

Ishta ground her teeth, turned on her heel, and stormed out of the den.

"See you next time, Little Bird," the broker called after her.

Ishta spat blood and phlegm onto the dirt, cursing the broker under her breath.

The walk back to the castle was circuitous and tiring, but she arrived safely in the kitchens before an hour had passed. Some careful examination in the light cast by the oven helped her determine that the wounds to her sides were not serious, though she would have impressive bruising in the days and possibly weeks to come. Her nose was broken, but it wasn't the first time it had been and likely wouldn't be the last. She cleaned the blood from her face, tossing her tunic out to be cleaned later.

She was propped awkwardly on the kitchen table, one leg bent at the knee so she could inspect a potentially broken toe, when Illa walked in.

Her sister only stared at her for a moment, her face unreadable as she gazed over Ishta's half-naked body in the pale light. Ishta didn't move, unsure what to say or do.

Illa just gave a tired sigh and walked around the table, heading for the oven.

"I-I didn't realize anyone would be awake," Ishta said.

"Trissa had a nightmare," Illa said, tossing fresh coals into the fire under the oven. "I couldn't get back to sleep."

"This isn't what it looks like, Illa."

Illa snorted, her back towards Ishta. "I'm not an idiot. I'm sure it's exactly what it looks like." She disappeared into one of the larders, and Ishta heard banging and thumping as Illa rummaged around noisily. "You decided to take up fighting in one of the filthy dens in the city."

"I don't really have any other option." Ishta returned to examining her toe. It was swollen and hurt immensely to bend, but the bone was still straight. Broken, but not an ugly break.

"No other option?" Illa called from the larder. "And here I thought you were fighting just for the fun of it."

The sarcasm and pain in her sister's voice stung Ishta.

"There is only one reason someone goes down into those places," Illa continued. The banging grew louder, and Ishta winced as a pot clattered to the floor. "Money, Ishta. And lots of it. And there is only one thing anyone in Etritia needs a lot of money for. Only one thing they would risk getting beaten and broken for."

Ishta nodded. Illa wasn't an idiot. "You're right."

Illa appeared in the open doorway again. Flour and dust streaked her apron, and she held something under her arm. "Why didn't you tell me you were ready to leave? I thought we were going to stay here together—for Trissa. For Anna."

Ishta sighed, wrapping her arms around her chest. Even with the extra warmth from the coals added to the oven, there was still a chill in the air. "I don't want to leave. But I'm doing this for Anna."

"You're going to try to help her escape? So the two of you can run off and live happily together until the end of your lives?" Illa sniffed, and Ishta realized that her sister was crying. It was hard to see in the dim light, but Illa's chest rose and fell with uneven breaths and her shoulders shook slightly. "And what about me? What about Trissa? Will you leave us here to die in this place?"

"No." Ishta stood, wincing as she put weight on her broken toe and the muscles in her sides shifted over the bruised ribs. "No, that's not what Anna wanted."

Illa sniffed again, wiping her face with one hand. She stepped closer, falling into a seat at the table. Ishta looked her sister over more closely, examining her face. She looked tired. The kind of deep exhaustion that comes with the certain knowledge that there is nothing left to hope for. "What does Anna want, then?"

Ishta bent to retrieve her soiled shirt, pulling it on over her head with difficulty. Then she sat, very carefully, across from her sister. Illa did not once look up from her lap.

"Anna wants me to take Trissa."

Illa nodded. "Because Trissa is Gifted."

"And her father would abuse her Gift. She isn't safe here."

"No one is safe here."

Ishta didn't reply.

After a moment, Illa met Ishta's eyes. "How much is it to get Trissa out of the city?"

"Two hundred gold."

"A hundred each, then?"

Ishta nodded. "Now do you understand why I'm fighting? I have no other option."

Illa lifted a clay vase from her lap, setting it carefully onto the table. Ishta recognized the vessel at once. "Is that …?"

"Mother's concoction jar, yes." Illa patted the sturdy exterior half-heartedly. "I've been keeping it in the back of the larder for years now." Illa's eyebrow quirked, though her gaze was vacant. "And whenever I get a little bit of money, I put it away in here. I've been saving for us to leave, Ishta. But I don't have much."

Illa removed the lid from the jar and carefully tipped the contents out. Gold and copper pieces spilled out onto the table with a soft clatter. It was more than Ishta could count at a glance.

"How much is here?"

"At least sixty. But less than eighty. Not enough for me to come with you, but I hope it can be enough to help pay for passage for you and Trissa."

It was more than enough to cover what Ishta had not already earned. But … "Illa, I can't take this."

"You can," Illa insisted, sweeping the coins across the table towards her. "I know why Anna asked you to take Trissa, instead of me." Illa bit her lower lip for a moment, staring at the coins. "Just keep that little girl safe, you understand? And …"

"Yes?"

"Help her remember me when she gets older. And her mother."

Ishta dropped a hand over her sister's. "She will never forget you, Illa."

19

JAIMES

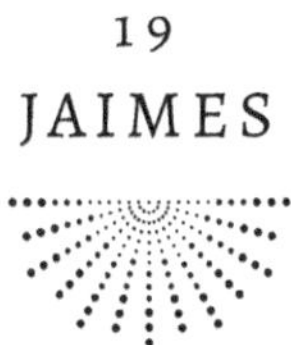

"Hello, Jaimes."

Jaimes awoke instantly, turning on his side to look out of the window set into the adjacent wall. The curtains were pulled back, and one shutter had been opened to let in a cool breeze. The sky was dark, and through the opened window, he could see thin clouds and countless stars.

"I wondered if I might hear from you. How have you been, Melonya?"

Deep contentment emanated from the dragon with her reply. *"How could I not stop to say a few words?"* There was a pause, and Jaimes had the brief and dizzying sensation of wind whistling over wings he did not have. It made his stomach flip excitedly, and he closed his eyes against the odd vertigo that gripped him. *"I have been well. Tathiel says you are behaving better than in the past. I'm glad to hear it."*

"Behaving? Like a dog? Did he really say that?"

Melonya's laugh was melodic and warm. *"He did not say that. But the sentiment was there, to an extent."*

Jaimes fumed silently for a moment, watching the clouds drift slowly across the small sliver of night sky that he could see from his spot in bed. *"When will you leave?"*

191

"Very shortly. We are meeting on the hill, if you want to say your goodbyes. I can't say when we might see each other again."

Jaimes hesitated. He knew which hill Melonya had meant, though she had been careful not to specify. It was the same hill they always met at, whenever the chance arose for her to come to Larten. The hill where his parents were buried. All three parents, including the mother he had never known and the woman that had cared for him as she had cared for her own son.

"You do not have to come."

"No, I want to," Jaimes replied quickly. *"It's just ... a hard trip."*

"Your knee?"

Jaimes sighed. *"Not just the knee. It hurts to see them. Their graves, I mean."*

Now it was Melonya that hesitated. *"I can't chance getting any closer to the town. I wouldn't ask you to come to the hill if there were a more convenient location, Jaimes."*

"I know." Jaimes sat upright, planting his bare feet on the floor. *"I'll be there as soon as I can. Don't leave before I get a chance to say goodbye."*

"Jaimes? Everything alright?" Vash's quiet voice called softly from a spot near the center of his worktable, where a cluster of candles formed a small ring.

"Everything is fine, Vash. I just need to step out for a bit." He grabbed a robe that lay crumpled at the end of the bed and tugged it on hurriedly.

"Is this about the dragon that just landed outside?"

Jaimes paused, one arm still fighting with the sleeve of the robe. "How did you know she's here?"

Vash's shadowed form rose from the cluster of candles, and her tiny arms stretched above her head. "I could feel it. They have a certain kind of power, dragons. It's easy to sense it when something as big as that suddenly drops from the sky and lands a stone's throw away."

Jaimes continued trying to shove his arm through the proper hole in his robe. "I don't think I'll ever understand how you elemental spirits work."

"Your sleeve is inside out," Vash said dryly.

Jaimes cursed, tugging the sleeve out and finally slipping his arm through.

"Does this mean that little she-elf will be leaving?" Vash asked.

"Eilonwy?" Jaimes tugged one boot on. "What makes you think she and Tathiel will be leaving?"

Vash was quiet for a few seconds, giving Jaimes the opportunity to search the dark floor for his other boot. When she answered, she sounded unsure. "They have the same kind of power the dragon does. I think. I don't really understand. But I thought they might be close. The elf siblings and the dragon, I mean."

"You're not wrong. Though it's strange that you can tell that much without even having the chance for a proper meeting." The floor was too dark, and Jaimes didn't want to kneel to search on his hands and knees. He'd never make it up the hill if he had to crawl around looking for a shoe. Instead he kicked the single boot he'd managed to find off. "And yes, they'll be leaving. And I don't know when they might come back. I ..." Jaimes faltered, thinking of Eilonwy, and the ring that had adorned her finger. "I want to say goodbye."

"Will you be long?" Vash asked around a stifled yawn. "Should I wait up for you?"

Jaimes shook his head, reaching for the door. "No, Vash. Get some rest. We'll start working on the next round of trials tomorrow."

He didn't wait for her reply before slipping out of the room. The hall outside was dark and chilly, and he wrapped his robe around him tighter as he maneuvered down to the first floor. He could hear faint snoring from one of the guest rooms he passed, but the inn was otherwise quiet. Jaimes thought of checking on Mathius's quarters, next to the kitchen, but decided against it. If Mathius wasn't already heading for the hill himself, he would be soon. He wouldn't miss a chance to wish the twins and Melonya good luck on their journey any more than Jaimes would.

He slipped through the front door of the inn, careful to silence the little bell that hung over the door so its ring would not wake anyone inside. His eyes were adjusting well to the darkness, and he forwent the use of one of the lanterns that hung on either side of the inn's door. The trek to the hill was a short one, but the cool night air cut through his robe and trousers and made his leg ache and his feet cold.

A large shadow eclipsed the myriad stars scattering the night sky, and voices drifted down from the hilltop. The shadow moved, a huge serpentine motion, and Melonya's voice washed gently over him. *"I'm glad you made it."*

One of the figures silhouetted against a single hovering witch light turned. "Jaimes, is that you?"

It was Eilonwy's voice, and some part of Jaimes ached slightly at the sound. "It's me, yes. I'm coming up."

Not gone, then. I still have time.

Jaimes began the climb up the sloping path to the crest of the hill. It was neither a difficult climb nor a long one under normal circumstances. *But then,* Jaimes thought bitterly as he limped along the path, *I will never have truly normal circumstances again.*

"Do you need a hand?" Eilonwy called. She stood at the end of the path, her face framed in the witch light, which bobbed slightly just above one shoulder.

"No." His reply was harsher than he had intended, and he shook his head, giving Eilonwy a carefree wave of one hand. "No, I'll be fine. Just a little slow."

In truth, his knee and the muscles stretched over his twisted shin were burning from effort. He knew it was impossible to hide how weak he was, but he still has some pride left in him.

Mathius was at the hilltop, and he and Tathiel were conversing in low voices when Jaimes reached them. Eilonwy waited nearby, brushing a hand absently over Melonya's shoulder and staring across the horizon.

Melonya was the first to greet him, stretching her neck to bump the crown of her head again Jaimes's forehead. *"It's good to see you."*

"And you, Melonya." Jaimes touched Melonya's neck. She was warm under the hard scales of her body. "You'll be leaving soon, I suppose?"

"We were waiting for you, Jaimes. Melonya would never let us take off without seeing your face." Tathiel turned towards Jaimes, his hand clasped around Mathius's upper arm.

Jaimes smiled. "I'm glad she's stubborn enough to make you stay for a few more minutes."

A rare smile crossed Tathiel's lips very quickly before fading away in the dark. "We're going to Vyris, it seems. Mathius had word from Alastor this afternoon. It should not be a long expedition." He embraced Jaimes, his arms strong and gentle around Jaimes's shoulders. "I hope we can see you again soon."

"I hope so too," Jaimes said, surprised by both Tathiel's affection and the news from Alastor. Tathiel released him, and Jaimes used the grip on Tathiel's shoulder to surreptitiously regain his wavering balance. "The Amulet of Fire is in Vyris?"

Tathiel nodded. "Your brother is headed there now, in the company of two elf women."

"Well, that bodes well for the women," Jaimes said sarcastically. "I'm sure he's entirely focused on the task at hand and not at all distracted by the prospect of winning a she-elf's fancy."

"Much less the fancy of two she-elves," Tathiel added. He gave Jaimes a gentle clap on the back. "We should be leaving now. We need to be deep within the woodlands before the sun begins to rise."

"Just a moment," Jaimes said, beckoning Eilonwy over. "I want to speak with your sister for a moment."

Tathiel left him, climbing the long stirrups and settling into the saddle nested between Melonya's shoulder blades.

Eilonwy stopped just out of arm's reach, and Jaimes held out a hand for her to take. She did, her expression unreadable in the night. "Jaimes? What's wrong?"

Jaimes pulled her closer, and she accepted his embrace without hesitation. "I just wanted to apologize. I shouldn't have acted as I did." He squeezed her gently, and her hand wrapped around his waist and held him. "I wish we had a little more time. To talk things over."

"Well, I'm glad you feel that way." Eilonwy released him, pushing away and meeting his eyes. "Because I'm not going with Tathiel."

"Wh-where are you going?" Jaimes stammered.

Eilonwy chuckled. "I'm not going anywhere. At least not right away." She gave him a gentle shake. "I'm staying right here."

"We've been arguing about it all day," Mathius said gloomily.

"You mean that you have been arguing about it," Tathiel corrected from Melonya's back. "She has her mind made up. And you can't change that."

Mathius grumbled something inaudible in reply.

Eilonwy's head tilted, and the bobbing witch light loomed close enough for Jaimes to see the confusion on her face. "Aren't you happy, Jaimes?"

His throat was suddenly dry, and his voice cracked as he answered. "Sure. Of course I'm happy. But why?" He cleared his throat, shaking his head. "I-I mean, what made you decide to stay?"

Eilonwy sighed. "Tomorrow. Let's talk things over tomorrow. Like you wanted."

Jaimes wanted to press the issue, but Melonya's voice stopped him. *"Two weeks, Eilonwy. Then I will return."* Her great wings spread, and Jaimes and Mathius both took several steps back. *"And when I do, I hope you might decide to join us, Jaimes."*

Jaimes did not reply, and Melonya did not wait for him. She launched herself into the air, leaping from a low crouch and buffeting the ground with wing beats. And she and Tathiel were gone, disappearing into the night without a trace.

<hr>

S hit.

Jaimes had managed to avoid any in-depth conversation with either Mathius or Eilonwy on the walk back to the inn. He claimed exhaustion, which they both accepted easily, and he was left alone with his thoughts as they walked. And his thoughts kept circling around the mysterious reason why Eilonwy would want to stay behind in Larten.

He took the stairs up to his room as quickly as he could, leaving Mathius and Eilonwy down in the kitchens to continue the argument they had apparently been having for the better part of the day. Jaimes didn't listen to a word of it.

Is it about the one who gave her that ring? Is that what she wants to talk about? "I'm sorry, Jaimes, but I want someone in my life that can go on daring adventures with me, and you just can't do that anymore"?

Jaimes bit his lip, pausing on a stair as the muscles in his calf complained.

But why stay for two weeks? Why not just tell me and be done with it? Then disappear into the clouds with her brother. He groaned, ascending the last few stairs and heading for his room. *And why did I have to tell her that I wanted to "talk things over"? What am I supposed to say to her?*

He opened the door to his room and quickly shut it behind him. The candles were still lit, and the window was still open. He staggered across the room and shut the window, drawing the curtains over the shutters. "Shit," he grumbled. "I'm in a mess now."

Jaimes turned towards the cluster of candles on the worktable. "Vash? Are you awake?"

"I am now," the spirit replied. Her figure drifted out of the candle smoke, large enough that he could have held her in both cupped palms. "What are you cursing about over there?"

"Eilonwy did not leave with her brother."

"Wonderful," Vash said. Her rich voice was heavy with sarcasm.

Jaimes lifted an eyebrow. "You sound upset."

Vash's arms crossed over her chest. "She distracts you. She's only been here for a little more than a day, and your work has already suffered for it. How long does she intend to stay?"

"Two weeks, I think."

Vash sighed heavily, and she sat on nothing, her knees bending as she found a comfortable position.

"It gets worse," Jaimes admitted. "She said she wants to *talk* tomorrow."

"What does that mean?"

Jaimes shrugged. "I don't know. I was hoping you might be able to tell me."

Vash laughed. "Why would I know what the she-elf is thinking?"

"Well," Jaimes began, hesitating. "I thought you might have an idea. Because you're a woman."

Vash didn't answer for a long moment, leaving Jaimes to

wait awkwardly. "You're an idiot, Jaimes. I don't tell you often enough."

"I thought it was reasonable enough," Jaimes said, collapsing onto the end of his bed.

"Just tell her you don't want to talk. You're too busy."

Jaimes shook his head. "I can't ignore her. We have too much history."

"History?"

Jaimes pulled his arms from the robe and let it drop from his shoulders. "We've been through a lot together. This injury to my leg …" He motioned towards his twisted leg, extending it slightly. "It happened while trying to protect her."

"So you feel obligated?" There was no derision to Vash's question, and Jaimes glanced over at the cluster of candles. Vash was standing once more, leaning towards him slightly. "I've never had the chance to have *history* with someone. Relationships aren't exactly an easy thing to have when you can stop existing at any moment."

"Pity," Jaimes said. "You make good company, Vash." He stretched out on the bed, lying with his head on the end closest to the fire spirit. "It's not just obligation. I care for Eilonwy. Very much. I'm just afraid of what she might say."

"And what might she say?"

"That I missed my chance to be with her."

"Do you think you have?"

Jaimes groaned, tucking his arms behind his head. "There was a ring on her finger. Meaning she has either married someone, or has promised to marry someone."

Vash was silent for a moment, then yawned loudly. "Her loss."

Jaimes sat up, turning to look at her. "I don't think you understand."

"I probably don't," Vash conceded. "But I know that if she can't see what I do when I look at you, then that's her fault."

Jaimes smiled. "Thank you, Vash."

Vash sat again, once more crossing her arms over her chest. "I also know that your work is going to suffer as long as she's around to occupy your thoughts like this. Either meet her and hear what she has to say, or stop acting like a child and forget her."

Her words struck Jaimes. *Like a child ... Is that what Tathiel has been trying to say all this time?*

He shut his eyes, feeling exhaustion settling in once more. "The world was already complicated enough without all of this."

2 0

NIEVE

The only sound was the neighing of horses and the crunching of hooves over dried leaves. Syrani rode in the lead position, her head swiveling around as she searched the woods for any signs of danger. Nieve took the rear position, but her attention was focused squarely on the arcanist in front of her. Alastor had done nothing but ride quietly along, occasionally conjuring small birds and sending them soaring into the sky. But his peaceful demeanor irritated her to no end. She wasn't sure if he was being intentionally off-putting or if it was his true nature, but Nieve disliked it very much.

And worse yet, there had been no sign of Halcia since they had left the village.

Syrani had not spoken of the golden dragon, but with every stop Nieve sensed that her friend's worry was deepening. Syrani was not sleeping or eating as she should, but she refused to be comforted with words from either the arcanist or Nieve.

So Nieve sat in her horse's saddle as they rode slowly along the faint forest trails, staring at Alastor's back. And as she stared, she tried to call out to the dragon and beg her to return.

"I don't know if you can hear me," she began for the dozenth time, *"but Syrani is hurting without you. Please. Return to her."*

"You're doing it wrong," Alastor said from his saddle. He had pulled his horse back, letting her ride closer.

Nieve sighed. "What are you talking about?"

"You're trying to call out to Halcia," Alastor said matter of factly, staring into his palms. His fingers were working diligently, making small signs and twisting strangely. "But you're doing it wrong."

"And how do you know what I'm trying to do?"

"Because I can hear you." He muttered a word, and a small bird took shape in the palm of one hand. It was very lifelike in appearance, but it did not move. "You're not channeling your thoughts properly, so they're just drifting about. Anyone paying any attention at all can hear what you're trying to say."

Nieve swallowed. "Including Syrani?"

Alastor looked up, glancing at Syrani's back, his eyes narrowed. "No, I don't think so. I should have specified." He turned over his shoulder to look at Nieve, one eyebrow raised. "Anyone within about ten feet of you can hear you."

Nieve gave the arcanist a sneer. "Then by all means, go ride ahead with Syrani, if it bothers you so much."

"It doesn't bother me," Alastor said, shrugging one shoulder lightly. "I was only going to offer to help you channel your thoughts better. So that maybe you can actually reach Halcia."

Nieve ground her jaw. "I don't need you to teach me anything. I can figure it out on my own."

"Very well. I have been trying to reach Halcia myself all day." He brought the immobile bird up to eye level, scrutinizing it carefully. "I thought you might have better luck, seeing as you know the dragon better than I do."

Nieve watched him work, oddly fascinated by the little creature he had woven together. "You overestimate our familiarity, arcanist." Alastor stroked the feathered plume of the bird, and Nieve's curiosity overcame her irritation with the human. "What are those birds, exactly? You keep conjuring them, but then you just let them fly off."

"They are messenger birds." Alastor curled his finger around the small bird and whispered into his cupped hands. When he opened them, the bird had changed slightly. It was larger, and its feathers had darkened from bright white with a pastel chest to black.

"Sending notes to your lover?" Nieve arched an eyebrow at him, recalling the nude figure she had found lying beside him after the Harvest Festival.

Alastor smiled. "The first was for Verelyn, yes." He stroked the bird's plume again, inspecting the small creature. "Then one to an ally in the Free Cities. And this one is for my uncle."

"Your uncle?"

The arcanist nodded. "He was supposed to be here with me. But he was called elsewhere. I just want to keep him updated on our progress."

"What are you two mumbling about back there?" Syrani's voice called.

She had halted her horse and turned it partway around, and she stared at them with dark and narrowed eyes.

Nieve jumped slightly, surprised that she had not noticed Syrani stopping along the path. But Alastor was evidently not caught unawares. He met Syrani's gaze with a friendly grin.

"Just talking about family, Syrani."

Syrani shifted uncomfortably. "Family?"

Alastor opened his palm, showing Syrani the immobile bird in his hand. "I was just telling Nieve about my uncle, and how he was meant to be traveling with us." He turned to share his grin with Nieve. "And Nieve was about to tell me about her family."

"Oh." Syrani tugged on one side of her horse's reins. "Well, stop dawdling. We have a long way to go yet."

Nieve watched her ride away. Alastor was whispering to the bird cupped in his hands again. When his lips parted from the gap in his fingers, a chirp sounded from the creature.

"Ah, there we go." Alastor held the bird in one hand, holding it out for Nieve to inspect. It was moving now, and Nieve let out a low chuffing laugh as the tiny thing tilted its head to look at her. It gave another chirp. "I think it likes you, Nieve. Would you like to say hello?"

Nieve stroked the feathers adorning its head, and the creature's eyes closed briefly. "Hello, little bird."

Alastor pulled the bird close again, holding it within an inch of his nose and whispering softly. Nieve tuned the words out, giving the arcanist privacy. A quiet moment passed before Alastor released the bird into the sky with a gentle toss into the air.

Nieve watched the bird fly off, winding through the trees until it disappeared from sight.

"Did you see the way she reacted when I mentioned family?" Alastor asked. His gaze was also on the direction the bird had gone, though he had surely lost sight of it before Nieve had.

"What?"

"She's uncomfortable with even the mention of family, it seems."

Nieve frowned. "So?"

Alastor took his horse's reins in hand and clicked his tongue. Nieve followed him, staring over the arcanist's shoulders at Syrani.

"I would be willing to bet that it's not just Halcia's

absence that bothers her. But whatever, or whomever, she might have left behind in Vyris is also eating away at her."

MOTHLENOR

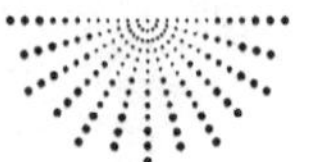

Mothlenor bent over the *Daemonica*, though he was not truly reading the ancient tome. He'd devoured its contents the same night he had pulled it from his brother's treasure room, and had taken care to read it more thoroughly when time allowed. Each subsequent read had given him less and less to learn, until he had stopped paying attention to the words written on the pages.

But holding it open before him, feeling the power within the sacred text, that still brought him joy.

He brushed a hand lightly over the open book, relishing the way the dark energy bound between the covers of the leather-wrapped volume seemed to almost caress him in return.

A ring on the smallest finger of his left hand warmed suddenly, and when he glanced at it, the clear stone set into the center flashed a deep indigo. Even as quickly as he noticed it, the sensation faded.

A proximity alarm, disarmed as soon as it went off. The indigo flash indicated Anna, so he did not prepare for an intruder climbing the stairs of his tower. Instead, he flicked a wrist and released a small amount of arcane energy, willing the door to open.

Mothlenor watched Anna ascend the last several steps to his study. At first he could only see the top of her head, unadorned with any crown. She never wore her crown, not even to the increasingly infrequent council meetings. Next came her face, set into a disinterested stare with one brow slightly raised. Her shoulders were bare, the deeply scooped neckline of her dress exposing flesh down an inch or two below her collarbones. And with each step, more of her came into view. There was no seductive charm in the way she walked, but he was entranced regardless.

"Anna," he breathed.

"My lord," she returned as she entered the study and shut the door behind her.

"A beautiful sight as always, my queen."

Anna's mouth quirked, but she said nothing. He wasn't sure if the movement had been the beginnings of a smile or a scowl.

The scent of her wafted towards him, and he let it drift over him. Hers was an intoxicating scent, and it was again today. But it was different. There was no hint of the jasmine that usually accompanied her, though the strong smell of arcane energy still surrounded her. Instead, the floral notes that enveloped him as she approached him were something half remembered and that he could not quite put a name to.

He stood when she stopped before his desk, then circled around the wide slab of scarred wood to bring himself closer to her. "Are you feeling better?"

"Better?" Anna asked, her eyebrow raising higher.

"You've spent the last several days in your rooms." He put a hand on her waist, pulling her towards him. She did not resist, but there was no eagerness either. "I assumed you were ill."

Anna's skin was warm through the fabric of her dress,

which was in a deep green color, made of thinly woven wool. *She could have anything she wanted, and she chooses cheaply made wool.* He pressed his mouth to her collarbone, inhaling the familiar scent he could barely recall.

Anna instantly stiffened. "I was ill, yes. I didn't realize you were aware."

"Of course I was aware," he murmured as he kissed first her shoulder, then her collarbone again. "You are an important part of my work, Anna." His hand was on the small of her back, and he pressed her closer to him. "You were missed."

"My lord," Anna said, her voice strained. "Perhaps this should wait. I am still not fully recovered, and your work—"

"The work can wait an hour more, Anna." He kissed her neck, grazing his teeth lightly against her skin. "As for your illness …" He kissed the hollow under her jaw, using his free hand to dig into her dark hair. It was slightly damp. "I'm content to risk illness."

That smell. What is it?

Anna pushed against him, bracing both palms against his chest. "I don't want to do this, Mothlenor. Not today."

Mothlenor stared at her. She had never outright refused him, and she had never used his name before. There was a hardness in her eyes that he recognized unmistakably as hatred. When was the last time a woman had stared at him with so much hate in her eyes?

And then it came to him.

Nevina.

And the intoxicating smell that clung to Anna suddenly had a name.

Roses.

"You would refuse me, Anna?"

The look in her eyes did not change. "I simply think it would be best to focus on your work today, as we are undoubtedly behind schedule."

He hesitated, thinking, and they stared at each other for a long moment. *Why roses, Anna? Do you know what the scent of them means to me?*

Mothlenor released Anna. "You are correct. Your absence has put us far behind in our research. Distractions would be ill-advised." He returned to the opposite side of the desk to sit once more in his chair. "Perhaps we should take a few moments to purge the castle of any other distractions to our work?" He tilted his head slightly, watching Anna for a reaction. "A few of the remaining servants? Trissa?"

Anna's eyes went wide. "What do you mean?"

Mothlenor shut the book that still lay open on his desk. "There are far too many diversions surrounding us, Anna. Why not remove them all?"

"But …"

"And if the princess is not a Gifted child, then she is of no use to us. She is only another thing to draw our focus away from where it is meant to be. She should be disposed of."

"Disposed of?" Anna leaned against the table, her weight on her forearms. "She's your daughter! You couldn't want to kill her."

Mothlenor raised an eyebrow.

That was not my meaning, but if it's how she takes it …

"I have done much worse to people I loved much more."

Anna bowed her head low. "Please forgive me. I will do anything, if only you'll allow Trissa to remain here with me."

Mothlenor went around to stand before her. He tucked a hand under her chin and pulled her head up. "I am willing to forget that this unfortunate event has taken place. On two conditions."

He half turned, keeping his eyes on hers, and grabbed the first book from his desk that his long fingers touched. He pressed it into her hands, ignoring the momentary regret he felt when he realized it had been his copy of *Daemonica* that he had chanced upon. "First. You keep working to help me break my brother's curse or kill Ajax. No distractions. No excuses. Begin with this."

Anna's face twisted as her hands closed around the book, and he wondered if she could feel the same arcane energy he felt when he held it.

"And second. When I call for you to join me in my bed, you will come willingly. And you will be an …" He searched for the right word. "Enthusiastic lover." He frowned. "Despite your preferences." He drew himself up, letting his expression settle into stony indifference. "Or you will never see Trissa again."

22

JAIMES

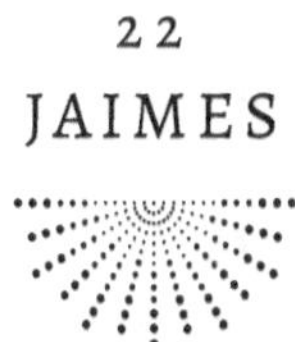

J aimes took a deep breath before opening the door to his room. He had managed to avoid Eilonwy for a few days now, but she was becoming more and more insistent. He was sure she would soon stop accepting the excuse that he was too busy with his work to have their "talk" whenever she stopped by. He refused to even open the door for her, which Vash chastised him endlessly for.

It couldn't be helped, he decided. The logical part of his mind told him that putting off any bad news Eilonwy might give him would not make it easier to bear when the time eventually came to face her. Despite knowing that, he was still terrified.

But now he was running low on a few ingredients from his mother's garden, which meant venturing downstairs and seeking out Mathius's assistance. And if Eilonwy was waiting for him, there would be no avoiding her.

How long will it take for her to say that she does not love me? That someone else has taken her heart, and that whatever we may have felt for each other in the past is dead?

Jaimes looked down at the slip of parchment in his hand and reread the short list for perhaps the dozenth time. The list was complete, as it had been every time he had checked it before. Every ingredient he had been using for his restoration potion was listed. In alphabetical order, even.

"This is ridiculous," he muttered to himself. "Just get on with it, dammit!"

And he opened the door to the hall outside.

There was no one waiting for him outside his door. And when he neared the stairs, the landing was empty. He could hear chatter from the dining room downstairs, as well as laughter and the general sound of merriment as Mathius's guests dined.

And there was no sign of Eilonwy.

Jaimes took the stairs as quietly as he could, though he knew he would never be able to fool Eilonwy's elven hearing.

He heard dishes clattering together in the kitchen, and Mathius appeared in the doorway beneath the stairs he stood on. The former sailor held an impressive number of beer mugs in each hand, their tops white with froth.

"Mathius," Jaimes hissed in a whisper, leaning over the railing to catch the other man's attention.

Mathius turned, looking up at him. "Well, there you are!" He beamed, wrinkles forming in the corners of his eyes as he did. "I was worried you'd gone back to hiding like a turtle in its shell."

Jaimes descended the rest of the stairs, turning the corner on the landing and stopping before the innkeeper. "Mathius, I just have a quick request, and then I really have to get back to work."

"I'm afraid I can't, Jaimes." Mathius turned and headed for the dining room. "It'll have to wait until tomorrow."

"T-tomorrow is fine, I don't care." Jaimes held the parchment up, taking a hobbling step. "Just let me—"

Mathius halted with a sigh, turning to give Jaimes an exasperated look. "Yes?"

"Just let me give you this list," Jaimes finished lamely. He held the list out for Mathius to take, but Mathius just indicated his full hands with a pointed look at each collection of ale mugs he held. "W-Well …" Jaimes stammered, searching for a convenient pocket he could tuck the list in.

The list was snatched from his hand by long pale fingers. "I'll take that."

Eilonwy stepped around Jaimes, reading over the list. Her hair was a light shade of brown, but just as long and straight as it naturally was. Three pairs of thin braids pulled much of it away from her face, knotting somewhere on the back of her head that Jaimes could not see. She had darkened her skin slightly, too. Just enough to give it a faintly tanned appearance. And, through her long lashes, he could see her eyes. They were bright green, as they always were. Her half of the Amulet of Water was tied in a complicated braided leather thong that sat snugly against the hollow of her throat.

And a long, ugly scar ran from her left eyebrow over her temple, and back into the hairline behind her rounded ear. It stood out against the tanned color of her skin like a jagged white tear.

"You remember my niece, of course," Mathius said with a faint hint of a smile. "Eilen."

"Eilen?" Jaimes asked, staring between Mathius and Eilonwy. He gave Mathius an incredulous glare, noting the apron Eilonwy wore and the tray of mugs she held aloft with one hand. "You're letting her work here?"

Mathius let out a snort of laughter. "I didn't like the idea at first. But I'll be damned if I said she wasn't a natural."

"Am I to understand that you need these ingredients to continue your work?" Eilonwy asked sharply, ignoring Mathius.

"Y-yes," Jaimes said. He looked at Mathius, but Mathius only gave him a knowing wink and turned to head into the dining room.

"And you can't continue working if someone doesn't collect these for you?" Eilonwy gave him a narrowed look.

"I would collect them myself," Jaimes said, clearing his throat. "Only, my leg makes it hard to—"

"I'll collect them for you," Eilonwy said brightly, giving him a wide smile.

"Y-you will?"

"Of course, Jaimes," she said coyly, slipping the list into a pocket of her skirts. "And when I bring them to you, we'll sit down and have that little discussion you keep trying to avoid."

"I don't think that's really necessary—"

"Well, I do." The smile faded, replaced by a hurt expression. "I can't believe you, Jaimes. Going to all this trouble to forgo a bit of unpleasant conversation."

Jaimes shook his head, fumbling for words. "I-I … Well, that's not at all what—"

Eilonwy stepped forward, stretching the arm that held the tray of drinks out and bringing herself as close as possible to Jaimes. She leaned forward, staring into his eyes. "You'll get your ingredients. I'll get to speak my mind." And then she gave him a quick kiss on the cheek and spun away on her heel.

Jaimes held his breath as she paused in the doorway to the dining room. Cheers erupted from the guests at her appearance, and Eilonwy smiled and made a small curtsey before disappearing from his view.

Jaimes let his breath out in a long exhale.

"Shit."

"I think you're letting this grow out of proportion, Jaimes." Vash hovered over her cluster of candles, her legs stretched out like she might have been lounging on a chaise. Her arms were extended behind her head, and she stared at him through drifting tendrils of smoky hair. "Regardless of what she might say, Eilonwy is still your friend. You ought to stop acting like she's coming to rip your heart out and eat it in front of you."

"I know, I know." Jaimes ran his hands nervously through his hair, then immediately smoothed the mess back down. "I just can't seem to control it." He rubbed at his stomach, which had taken on a sour and unpleasant sensation ever since he had returned to his room. "Elir curse it, I think I might be sick."

"You're panicking," Vash said flatly. "Take some deep breaths."

"Panicking!" Jaimes laughed. "Panicking? This is panicking?" He groaned as his stomach flipped unexpectedly. "I think I'm dying. My heart is racing. I-I can't get a good breath." He fell to the bed, suddenly faintly dizzy.

"Don't forget the sweating."

Jaimes examined the front of his tunic, where a dark stain had appeared right above his chest, between his pectorals. "Dammit!"

"Deep breaths, Jaimes," Vash supplied helpfully. "Everything will be fine."

"Easy for you to say. You're just a bit of fancy smoke. Do you even understand what love and friendship are?"

Vash was silent for a long moment.

"Vash …" Jaimes took a deep and shaking breath. "I'm sorry. That was horrible of me. I didn't mean it."

"I'm sorry that I can't be of more help to you."

Her voice was firm, but there was a strange quality to it that pained him to hear.

There was a knock at the door, and Jaimes bolted upright. Across from him, Vash's figure simply vanished. It was a trick he very much wished he also possessed.

"Jaimes, are you in there?"

It was Eilonwy's voice, of course.

"I'm here," Jaimes mumbled. He took another deep breath, cursing the sweat stains on his tunic and smoothing his hair one last time. "Come in."

Eilonwy opened the door, taking a cursory look around the room. "Did I hear a woman's voice?"

Jaimes took another deep breath, clasping his hands together and tucking them between his knees. "It's just me in here."

It wasn't technically a lie, because Vash's disappearance made it true. But it still felt wrong to omit the truth of Vash's existence.

Eilonwy opened the door wider, bringing in one of his mother's flower baskets laden with brightly colored flowers and gently grouped leaves. "I brought everything from your list. Plus a few things that seemed to fit with the rest." Eilonwy motioned towards the worktop, where candle wax had pooled in globs all over the surface. "Shall I set them here?"

Jaimes jumped to his feet, then swayed slightly as another dizzy spell took him. His leg flared in pain, and he winced slightly. But he managed to wave at Eilonwy. "Sure, sure. But just leave the basket, I can take care of it."

"Jaimes, you're sweating." Eilonwy set the basket carefully on the tabletop, away from Vash's candles, and had a hand on Jaimes's forehead before he could protest. "It's not a fever, though you are warm …"

"It's nothing, Eilonwy." Jaimes brushed her hand from his face. "It's just a little stuffy in here sometimes."

"It's all the candles you're using." Eilonwy seemed to be counting the growing collection of stubs and half-used wax tapers. "Mathius said you'd been going through a lot of them lately. Why do you need so many?"

Jaimes sidestepped around her, gently guiding her away

from his worktable without actually laying a hand on her. "They're for my work. I work a lot of late nights."

Eilonwy let herself be led away from the table, and she took a seat on the edge of Jaimes's bed. Jaimes remained standing, settling himself against the opposite wall, one hip pressing against the short edge of the table.

Eilonwy raised her eyebrows. "Well?"

"W-well what?"

She smiled, her nose wrinkling slightly. "You said you wished we had more time to talk together. Was there something in particular you wanted to say?"

Jaimes felt sweat forming in several new places. "N-no, nothing in particular. I just enjoy your company."

Her eyebrows raised again. "You have a funny way of showing it."

Jaimes ignored the quip. He knew it was true.

"And what about you? You said you wanted to speak your mind. I suppose you have something in particular to say?"

Better to be done with it quickly. And then I can start to put it behind me.

Eilonwy sighed. "I do, but I don't think you'll like it."

"Ah." Jaimes nodded, his suspicions confirmed. "I think I know what you're going to say, Eilonwy."

Eilonwy sighed again, this one apparently of relief. "Thank the Great Ones. That makes it easier." Her head tilted, and she gave him an imploring look. "Will you come, then?"

Come? To the wedding?

The very idea made him sick.

"I-if you would like me to be there, then I would be happy to come," Jaimes said.

Eilonwy nodded. "Good. I'm sure your brother will be happy to have you there with him."

"Alastor?" Jaimes asked. He frowned, remembering the last time he'd seen his brother.

Alastor had said he was getting married, hadn't he? But it was a joke. Wasn't it?

Eilonwy stood, reaching around Jaimes for the basket she had brought in. She began pulling plants out, sorting them into small piles on his table. "Of course. Who else?"

Jaimes clenched his jaw. "Who else, indeed."

Alastor had become quite the favorite among every woman he met, but Jaimes had never guessed that his charms would work on even Eilonwy.

Eilonwy's back was to him. She was lifting glass jars and inspecting labels. Many of the empty ones she filled with plants she had brought up from the garden. Some jars were still half full, and some plants she had brought him did not have a jar to go into. He briefly wondered what she might have thought fitting to collect with the rest of the specimens he had requested that he had not already considered, but the thought was pushed aside by the anger simmering away at him.

Anger at himself, for being foolish enough to think Eilonwy would wait for him to heal his leg.

Anger at Alastor, for pursuing the woman he knew Jaimes loved.

And even anger at Eilonwy, for her callous disregard for the feelings she had to know he felt for her.

"Melonya will be returning to Larten next week, if all goes well." Eilonwy plucked bright red petals from a cluster of flowers and dropped them into an empty jar. "From there, the two of us can travel to Vyris and meet up with our siblings, and hopefully—"

"Vyris?" Jaimes straightened, suddenly unsure.

Eilonwy turned towards him, a few red petals in one hand and a half-plucked flower in the other. She raised her eyebrows at him again, giving him a faint smirk. "The Amulet of Fire *is* in Vyris, after all."

"The Amulet of Fire is in Vyris?" Jaimes repeated. Had he

not understood Eilonwy at all?

Eilonwy tossed the flower onto the tabletop, giving him a concerned look. "I thought you knew all this? Were you not paying attention at all when Mathius and I were discussing it on the way back to the inn? After Tathiel left?"

Jaimes shook his head.

Eilonwy sighed. She crossed her arms, rubbing a petal between her thumb and forefinger. "Alastor sent a message to Mathius. He found the Rider, though there's some sort of complication between the Rider and her dragon. And she knows where the amulet likely is."

"In Vyris?"

Eilonwy nodded. Jaimes noticed the pads of her fingers were beginning to stain a faint red color. And on the fourth finger of her left hand, the hand holding the petals, was a small ring.

"And this has what to do with me, exactly?"

Eilonwy let out a frustrated sound and rolled her eyes. When she spoke, she did it slowly, enunciating each word carefully, as if she were speaking to a child. "I want you to come to Vyris with me. And help us find the amulet."

"What?" Jaimes recoiled, backing further into the wall he leaned against. "No! I can't."

"But you just said you would!" Eilonwy glared at him, tossing the petals angrily onto the table to land beside the flower they were pulled from. "What has gotten into you?"

Jaimes held his arms up defensively, palms facing her. "I thought I was agreeing to something else. I didn't realize that's what you were talking about."

"What in the world could be more important than finding the amulets, Jaimes?" Eilonwy grabbed his arm, gripping it tightly. "Please come with me. We need you."

We, Jaimes noted. *Not I.*

"You don't need me." Jaimes shook his head. "I'm not the same person I was on the *Kingfisher.* I can't be the man you need me to be." He looked down at her hand, noticing the small ring adorning her finger again. "I'm sorry, Eilonwy. I meant to be that for you, but clearly I'm not."

Eilonwy shifted her grip, pressing her thumb into the space above his wrist. He felt a jolt of arcane energy pass through the pad of her thumb and into his flesh.

The Mark on the inside of his arm responded instantly to her magic, and a bright rune glowed on his flesh.

"Do you remember what I said this Mark means?"

Jaimes nodded, staring at the glowing symbol.

"Say it, Jaimes."

Jaimes shook his head. "No."

Eilonwy exhaled sharply, annoyed. "It means 'Savior'. And do you remember when I gave it to you?"

A memory surfaced. His parents' graves, illuminated by a witch light. Eilonwy's hand on his arm, much like it was now.

Jaimes blinked, surprised to see that his vision was closing with tears. "How could I forget?"

"So then you remember that I gave you this Mark *after* the *Kingfisher*? Not before."

Jaimes pulled his arm from her grip. "Eilonwy, please."

She was uncomfortably close. He detected a faint woodsy scent about her, mixed with the sharp tang of arcane energy, and he saw flecks of silver in her bright green eyes as they stared up at him. He felt the heat of her body radiating out to him, and it made his stomach cramp.

"If you were deserving of that Mark then, after everything you and I went through together, then you are still deserving of it now. You *are* the man I need you to be, Jaimes." She stepped away from him, and her eyes left his. "I wish you could see it as easily as I do."

She left him in dumbfounded silence.

Jaimes spent several minutes staring at the inside of his wrist, where a red spot in the shape of Eilonwy's thumb stained his skin.

23

ANNA

Night had passed hours before, but there would be no sleeping for Anna. Trissa had been difficult to get to bed, and she had seemed stressed and unwilling to leave Anna's side when Illa had tried to coax the young girl to her own room. So Anna had lain in bed with her daughter until she had finally fallen into a deep sleep.

It was easy enough to be convinced to do so. Her life had been threatened only the day before, and Mothlenor's words still haunted Anna's every waking moment.

And when Trissa was at last asleep, Anna rose from her daughter's bed and slipped out into the front room.

She had hidden the horrible book Mothlenor had given to her in a small box atop the mantle. From the first instant her fingers had touched the book's cover, Anna knew it was no ordinary book. She felt the malcontent and *evilness* of the book, and the thought of Trissa stumbling across it made her skin crawl. So she put it out of the girl's reach, and concealed it within an old trinket box that she often kept above the fireplace, and hoped her daughter would not sense its presence.

Anna removed the book, fighting the eerie sensations that

swarmed her as her hands clasped around it. She sat by the fire, hoping the warmth might help her keep the *Daemonica's* awful presence at bay long enough to make some decent progress through its pages. She had tried reading it the night before, but had given up after only a few paragraphs of the ancient text. The longer she held the book, or kept her eyes focused on the words it contained, the more unsettled and ill she felt.

And if she did not make an effort to assist Mothlenor, what would he do to their child?

So Anna read from the vile tome. And she continued reading, despite the mounting unease and malevolence she felt stirring within her. She thought she could hear sounds. Inhuman growls, deep and far away. Whispers just beyond the edge of her hearing. But if she drew her attention away from the *Daemonica* to find the source of the noises, they disappeared.

Hallucination or construct, she couldn't tell. But she was sure the book she held was the cause.

She read on, finishing each page as quickly as she could and turning to the next. She did not want to have to stop and linger on any given line any longer than necessary. Anna was determined to finish it and return it to Mothlenor as soon as possible, and forget that he had ever tasked her with reading something so *wrong*.

But she did stop. And reread the last passage a second time through. And then a third.

And then Anna shut the book, though she was little more than halfway through, and dropped the book to the floor at her feet. Instantly, the sounds surrounding her, which had grown closer and louder without her realizing it, vanished. The wearying sensations of insects crawling over her flesh and some thick and viscous liquid oozing over her body disappeared.

Physically, she was exhausted. Her muscles ached from

sitting in the same position for perhaps hours, perhaps only half of one. She couldn't be sure.

Mentally, she was awake and alert. And afraid.

The passage she had read had covered the art of Calling. Mothlenor was no amateur when it came to that particular skill, and Anna knew he had half a dozen wraiths at his command. He sent them into Azimar and Vyris irregularly, searching for clues to the whereabouts of the amulets or the small group of misfits that led the opposing hunt for the same. He had even used them to destroy his brother's body, to conceal the true circumstances of Areanath's death.

Surely he must know it already.

But Mothlenor had never suggested such a simple solution to his predicament.

And he already has all he needs to do it.

Anna bit her lip, curling her legs under her and staring at the discarded *Daemonica*.

What if he has missed it?

Would she tell him that there was a possibility he could get everything he needed to find the former Commander Ajax and destroy him? That he could search for and find the amulets with only a single wraith?

Would she betray Nevina, and doom all Azimar and all Vyris to the same way of life that Etritia now had?

Anna shook her head. "No. If he knows this possibility exists, then he's abandoned it for a reason. And if he missed it …"

If he missed it, I won't let him learn of it.

There was a soft knocking at the door to her rooms, and Anna tensed.

"Anna? It's me. Are you awake?"

Anna let out a shaky breath and stood to unlatch the door.

Ishta waited out in the hall, and she slipped in quickly before Anna had even opened the door completely. "I've finished making preparations. I can get Trissa out, but we have to do it tonight."

There were bruises on much of Ishta's face. Many were faded and healing, but many more were dark and fresh. There was an ugly cut across her nose, which appeared to have been broken several times in the recent past.

"Ishta, what happened?" Anna tried to recall if Ishta had looked so beaten the last time she had seen her, only to realize that it had been several days since they had last met. "What have you been doing, you're covered in—"

"Anna, there isn't time to explain." Ishta pushed past her, heading for Trissa's room. "We have to leave tonight. I'll get Trissa ready while you pack some of her things."

Anna followed behind her hesitantly. This was precisely what she wanted. She wanted Trissa to be safe and away from her father. But now that the time was here for her to say goodbye to her daughter …

"Alright, let's be quick about it."

Ishta was already opening the door to Trissa's room. Instead of a sleeping young girl lying in bed, they found Trissa awake and sitting in the center of her room.

"Nanny Cookie woke me," Trissa said, turning to face them as they entered. She held one of Ishta's handmade toys close to her chest, and she had swapped the nightgown Illa had dressed her in for some heavier clothing. Her feet were still bare. Trissa always had trouble putting on shoes. "Is this when I leave?"

Anna nodded. "Yes. This is when you leave."

Trissa made a sound like a hiccup, and Anna wondered if she has been crying. "Can you help me with my shoes?"

Ishta exchanged a glance with Anna. "I'll get some of her belongings packed away." She retreated a respectful distance, leaving Anna with her daughter.

Anna dropped to her knees. There was a pair of thick woolen stockings on the ground beside Trissa, as well as her favorite boots. Anna pulled one of the stockings over Trissa's small foot. She wondered how much longer the stockings would fit her daughter. Would they wear out before she outgrew them?

"These are good stockings to wear. They'll keep you nice and warm where you're going."

"And where am I going?"

Anna swallowed, forcing down the lump in her throat. "Somewhere safe. Somewhere where no one can hurt you." She slipped the second stocking on, and gave Trissa a gentle pat with both hands. There was still so much baby fat to her small legs. Anna wondered what her daughter might look like when she was older. She could see parts of the woman Trissa would become. Her face would thin out, and her cheekbones would be slightly prominent in a rounded face. She would be on the shorter side, perhaps. Like her mother. And would she be a skilled witch? Would there be anyone left in Azimar to teach her how to bend and manipulate arcane energy?

Anna slipped Trissa's feet into the boots one at a time, then began lacing the first one. "Do you remember how to do this?" She moved her fingers slowly, letting Trissa watch each movement.

"I can remember." Trissa reached for the laces on the second boot, mimicking Anna's movements. The result was slightly loose and lopsided, but it would hold.

Anna tightened it and gave Trissa a smile. "Very good."

"Anna." Ishta had returned, one of Anna's old clinic bags stuffed full and tucked into the crook of one elbow. "We have to go."

Trissa put one hand in Anna's and the other in Ishta's, and Ishta led them out of the bedroom.

"Ishta, wait." Anna pulled the other woman close and kissed her quickly on the lips.

Ishta's eyes widened, but when she wrapped an arm

around Anna and pulled her close, her grip was strong and warm. She returned Anna's kiss, pressing gently and lovingly, and when they parted their foreheads rested against one another's.

"I don't know if we might ever have that chance again. I didn't want it to pass by."

"We'll have the chance again, I promise." Ishta kissed Anna's cheek. "And maybe then, at last, there will be no tears."

Anna sniffed, though it was meant to be a laugh, and wiped her face with the back of her free hand. *I won't hold you to that promise, Ishta. Just forget me.*

But to Ishta she nodded and said, "I hope so."

Ishta kissed her once more. "I love you, Anna. And I will never love another."

"Ishta ..."

"And I know you feel the same," Ishta said firmly, pressing her palm to Anna's face. "Even if you're too afraid of what might happen to me to admit it aloud."

Anna nodded, unable to answer.

Trissa stood beside them, a hand in each of theirs, staring up at them with a childish expression of awe.

Ishta sighed, turning away from Anna. "Let's go."

The bruised and battered maid checked the hallway outside before escorting them out.

"I've secured passage out of Etritia. Where should I take her after we pass the old farmlands?"

Ishta's voice was a low whisper, and when Anna replied she did so at the same volume. "You have to find Layle. She can help you protect Trissa."

"Layle?" Ishta asked. "Is that the girl who escaped the dungeons?" They reached the end of the hall, and Ishta pulled them down a darkened corridor. Anna recognized the path as the one leading towards the kitchens. From there, the garden path would take them out to the main square, where Ishta could guide Trissa through the dark city to freedom.

"Yes, but I don't know where she is."

"She's with my cousin. I can find Arella, and Layle will be there, too." Trissa's voice was confident in the dark, but her words made Anna's stomach twist.

Layle named her Gifted grandchild after one of the other girls Nevina lost in the dungeons. The youngest one. Little Arella.

Anna tried to shrug off the unease that weighed her down. "There you have it. Trissa can guide you to them."

They made another turn, and Anna knew they were nearing the kitchens.

"Almost there. Once we leave the castle, navigating the city will be a slow process. But I know I can get her out of here, Anna."

"You aren't going anywhere," a deep voice called from the far end of the hall, just in front of the kitchens.

Anna felt a familiar chill as a wave of arcane energy rolled towards them. Lights lit in their sconces along the walls, one after another, illuminating the darkness ahead of them. When the energy hit them, Trissa yelped and buried herself in the skirt of Anna's dress. The sconces behind them did not ignite, but remained dark, leaving their retreat cast in deep shadow.

At the end of the hall stood Mothlenor. His arms were bent at the elbows, so that both hands were tucked into the billowing sleeves of his robe. He stood alone, blocking their only means of escape. They could turn and run, but Anna knew he would be on them before they could take more than a few steps. She knew his power better than most. There was no leaving the castle now.

Ishta had surely reached the same conclusion that she had, but she stepped forward, bending slightly at the knees and bringing both fists up into a fighting stance.

No words were exchanged, but no words needed exchanging.

Mothlenor gave Ishta a contemptible grimace and extended one hand, palm out.

Anna sensed the resulting energy attack more than she saw it, and Ishta did not react in time to avoid it. She was thrown back by an invisible force, hitting the stone floor and sliding into the darkness behind them with a heavy thud.

"Ishta!" Anna turned, nearly stumbling over Trissa in her hurry to reach Ishta. But a large hand clamped around her upper arm, and she was yanked further into the brightly lit corridor.

"How dare you try to subvert me!" Mothlenor snarled in her ear. She turned to face him, trying vainly to free her arm from his hold. "Did I not tell you that I know everything that goes on in my castle? In Etritia?"

"Let go, Mothlenor," Anna cried, prying at the fingers tightening around her upper arm with her free hand. Trissa still clung to her dress skirt, and the small child was pressed between them as they struggled.

"I am your king! And you will address me as such!"

The hand around her arm disappeared, and Anna managed a half step back before Mothlenor's long fingers pressed into the flesh around her throat. Her airway was not cut off completely, but her breathing came harder, and she felt arcane energy flooding into her body through his touch.

"Please, let go," Anna begged. Her skin burned where his fingers touched her, and Anna was not sure if it was from the icy frost of his usual arcane energy, or if the fire that lit his eyes had extended into the grip he held on her.

Somewhere below her, where she could no longer see, Trissa was crying loudly.

"I never should have removed your cuffs, Anna. You denied me a Gifted child for years, only to give me a squealing and Ungifted brat." The fingers pressing into her throat tightened.

"S-stop … please," Anna struggled to say.

"Then, when I finally have something in my grasp that you care for more than your own miserable life, you conspire with your *lover* to take it from me." Mothlenor's teeth were bared in a hideous grin, and his grey eyes were wide with madness.

"Please …" Mothlenor's grip tightened again, and Anna's words were choked off. Her head was pounding, and she could find no purchase to pry away at his hold on her.

"Stop it!"

Anna felt movement around her hips, where Trissa was undoubtedly trying just as vainly to push Mothlenor away.

"Don't kill her!"

Mothlenor growled and, without looking down, struck at Trissa.

Anna heard Trissa fall to the ground, and the girl let out a surprised huff as the wind was knocked from her.

Mothlenor pressed Anna into a wall, and she would have lost her footing if he had not already lifted her feet from the ground. She held fast to Mothlenor's forearm, trying desperately to relieve some of the pressure from her neck. She tried to beg again, but it came out as a gasping wheeze.

"If you kill her, you will never find what you are seeking, Mothlenor," a young voice said from out of Anna's line of sight.

Mothlenor's grip loosened slightly, and he turned in surprise.

Trissa sat on the stone floor, her hair and clothes in disarray. But she stared up at Mothlenor with eyes that were too old to match the rest of her face. "Let her go, or you will never see an Amulet of Power for as long as you live. And your life will be short and full of misery."

The voice that came from Trissa was not entirely hers. It

was much too old. The voice of Trissa if she were an adult, perhaps.

Mothlenor released Anna immediately, then stooped to offer a hand to Trissa. "It seems I was mistaken, my lady. You are not the Ungifted child I thought you were."

Anna slumped to her knees on the floor, coughing. "N-no, Trissa …"

Trissa found her feet and gave Mothlenor a frightened look. Her eyes were their normal shade, and her voice had returned to its usual childish timbre. "Please don't hurt her."

"I will not hurt her, my darling," Mothlenor said to Trissa, his voice soft and eerily warm.

Ishta staggered out of the dark. There was a fresh scrape on her cheekbone, or perhaps it was one that Anna had not noticed before now. "Get away from her, Mothlenor."

Mothlenor's head snapped up and turned to look at the approaching woman. Anna knew what his intentions were before he moved, and she brought a hand up to stop him.

But Mothlenor was too fast. He was always too fast.

The same hand that had closed around Anna's throat now held Ishta's. Anna let a jet of fire escape from the palm of her hand, aimed for Mothlenor's head, but he waved it out of existence like it was nothing more than an annoying insect. He lifted Ishta from the floor with ease, but he did not look her in the eyes as he had Anna. Instead, he was watching Trissa.

"Can you tell me, Trissa, what might happen if I kill this woman now? What might befall my plans if she does not survive the next few moments?"

Trissa wailed, but did not answer. She looked from Ishta's darkening face to Anna.

"She has no control over it yet, she can't See whenever she wants," Anna cried. "Let Ishta go!"

Ishta let out a gasping breath, her eyes wide and her face red.

"It's such an intimate way to destroy someone, don't you think?" Mothlenor said, fixing his gaze on Anna. "To feel them struggling to breathe. And to feel that struggle begin to weaken."

Trissa let out another wail, tears streaming down her face.

"Trissa, if you can tell me right now that I will be better off leaving this woman alive, I will release her."

Ishta's face was an alarming shade of red, and her body was beginning to slacken.

Trissa could only cry, staring at Ishta.

Anna rose to her feet, using the wall Mothlenor had pressed her against as support. "If you don't release her, I will never tell you how you can get the amulets before Ajax does."

Mothlenor's arm dropped, letting Ishta's feet rest against the floor. Ishta drew in a ragged breath.

"I am listening, Anna."

Anna hesitated. She had promised herself that she would not let him find out what she had read in the *Daemonica*, and now she was willing to trade that same information to save Ishta's life.

"Anna, don't," Ishta said. Her voice was hoarse and strained.

"I will give you one minute to explain, Anna." Mothlenor's arm lifted slightly, and Ishta let out a strangled gurgle. "If you fail to tell me what you have learned, I will kill this woman right before your eyes. Then I will take her soul and make a new wraith. And when the time comes that you have lost your usefulness to me, she will be the one to devour your flesh and bones." Mothlenor's face was unreadable. "You know that I will not hesitate, Anna."

Anna thought of the Coven, stolen from their fortress and beaten and raped. She remembered the ultimatum Mothlenor had given them all before shutting those that had refused him away in the dungeons to die. She did know indeed that he would not hesitate.

"If you have a soul that is powerful enough, you can form it into whatever shape you desire," Anna said quickly. "It doesn't have to be a normal, human-shaped wraith. If the soul is powerful enough, you could funnel your own arcane energy into it, and shape it into something bigger and stronger than a normal wraith could be."

Mothlenor's eyebrows raised, and his arm lowered.

"If the soul is strong enough, you wouldn't need a dragon's egg. You could make a dragon wraith, and imbue it with some of your own power."

Mothlenor's arm dropped further. "If the soul is strong enough."

"You have such a soul in your possession." Anna silently begged forgiveness as Mothlenor's eyes lit up.

"Nevina."

Mothlenor dropped Ishta to the floor. She stumbled, but did not lose her footing. Mothlenor turned to her, and Ishta shrank back at his glare. "If I ever see you again, I will kill you." He stepped to the side, motioning towards the kitchens. "Leave. Leave the castle, leave Etritia, I don't care. But do not set foot in this place again."

Ishta looked from Mothlenor to Anna. "Anna …"

"She can do nothing for you now," Mothlenor said. "Leave."

Ishta walked past him slowly, keeping her sights on him. When she reached Trissa, she put a hand on the girl's head. Trissa's tears had started to dry, but she clung to Ishta's waist.

Ishta soothed her as best she could. One of her arms hung limply at her side, so she could only hold Trissa close with one hand. "It's alright, Trissa. It's alright."

"Please, you can't go," Trissa wailed.

"I'll be fine," Ishta said.

Trissa pulled Ishta down into a hug, and Ishta dropped to

her knees to embrace the young girl. Trissa buried her face into Ishta's neck, sobbing and whispering quietly to her.

"That's enough," Mothlenor said in a warning tone.

Ishta stood, releasing Trissa. "Take care of your mother for me, will you?"

Trissa nodded, and stepped obediently into Mothlenor's beckoning arm. His cloaked arm covered her like a large bird covering its young.

And Anna watched as Ishta staggered off for the kitchen and disappeared into the darkness.

24

ISHTA

Ishta stumbled through the dark passageway, passing the kitchen and exiting through the door that opened onto the stretch of dry earth where a rose garden used to be. She leaned against the door, letting her head fall forward as she drew in several breaths.

Mothlenor's first strike, whatever magical method he had used, had caused her to land painfully on one side of her body. Her hip ached, and she was sure she'd find a bruise there. Her entire arm was numb from the impact, but everything moved fine when tested. A temporary discomfort that would surely pass.

More alarming was the swelling to her neck. It almost felt as if Mothlenor's hand was still closed around her throat, and it would likely get worse before it got better.

Ishta touched a hand to her throat and winced at the sharp pain it introduced. She could feel raised welts forming, and her skin was uncomfortably warm.

But she was alive. She had briefly lost consciousness, and the fear that had gripped her as she felt her body relax just before her mind slipped into darkness had not left her.

But she was alive. Alone, and still struggling to breathe, but alive.

Ishta suppressed a cough as she looked around the empty space before her.

The rose garden was long gone, but there was still a bench centered in front of an empty fountain shaped in the likeness of the goddess Imis. Water no longer flowed from the pitcher in her grasp, and the basin at her feet was full of leaves and debris.

Ishta took a slow breath, fighting back tears and ignoring the tenderness in her throat.

She set off for the market square, long ago emptied of all stalls and merchants. Even the lanterns hanging from long poles at even intervals were unlit. It made crossing the open space easier, because Ishta could slip from shadow to shadow unseen—though there were not many people out at this hour. Even the drunks were sleeping in piss-filled alleys.

Ishta found the hidden entrance to the barn even in the dark, and slipped in silently.

"Dars," she called in a loud whisper. "Come out, I need to talk to you." She waited a moment, eyes adjusting to the deeper black of the inside of the abandoned building. "No games this time, old friend. It's too urgent."

There was a shuffling sound off to her left, and Ishta turned toward it.

"No time for games?" Dars's gruff voice asked. "What's so important that there's no time for games?"

"I'm leaving. Now." Ishta turned and rummaged along the wall by the broken timber that served as their makeshift door. Her bag was still right where she had left it, as she knew it would be. "I want you to come with me."

"Where are you going?" Dars asked, approaching her slowly. He stank of stale piss, and his breath was sour.

"I'm going to go meet Gallant. I'm leaving Etritia, remember?" She turned back towards him, pulling on the cloak from the top of the bag. "I was supposed to take someone with me, but my plans have changed. I can take you instead, if you want to come." She pulled the cloak over herself, wincing at the pain in her side, and tugged the hood down low over her face.

"Leave Etritia?" Dars shook his head violently. "No. No, I don't want to."

"Dars," Ishta sighed, reaching for him. "You can't take care of yourself. You need me with you."

He slapped her hands away. "No! I have to stay here."

"You don't have to stay," Ishta said in a gentle tone. "You can come with me."

"No." Dars took several steps away from her. He disappeared into the shadows, only the vague outline of his form visible. "I promised I would stay here. And do my part."

Ishta shouldered her bag, watching Dars retreat deeper into shadow. "I guess this is goodbye, then. I can't come back. If I do, Mothlenor will have me killed."

There was no reply, and Ishta waited a moment, staring into empty blackness. She felt an odd pain in her chest, a kind of loneliness that she was not accustomed to.

I will really be going this alone, won't I?

She thought of the words Trissa had whispered in her ear as they embraced for the final time.

"Go east. You will find the one you're searching for."

At least she wouldn't be alone forever, if Trissa was right. She would find Layle. And then …

And then what?

"Goodbye, Dars. I hope we can meet again sometime."

Ishta was at the southern gate in only a few minutes. Gallant was guarding it, as he had said he would be. She recognized him easily enough, and when she stepped into the light of the lantern hanging from the gatehouse, he turned to her and spat a wad of phlegm on the ground at her feet.

"I see you've made it back. Where is your companion? There were to be two of you, correct?"

Ishta pitched her voice low, affecting the most masculine voice she could. "My plans have changed. I will be traveling alone."

Gallant smiled, half of his face cast in shadow. "Do you have the two hundred gold marks?"

Ishta ground her teeth. "You mean one hundred. It was two hundred for two people."

"My prices have gone up." Gallant's smile deepened.

Ishta had the two hundred, but she had been hoping to use the spare coin for traveling. But even a few coins could buy her a hot meal or two. "One hundred and fifty."

Gallant shook his head. "Did you forget that I don't negotiate?"

Ishta growled. "I have to leave tonight. What will it take to convince you to let me go?"

Gallant's head tilted and he stepped closer. "It will take two hundred gold marks."

Ishta hesitated, chewing the inside of her cheek as she contemplated. She could make it without any coin to travel with. It would be rough, but she'd managed rough for several years now. "Fine," she snapped. "I don't seem to have much choice."

Gallant waved her towards the guardhouse. "We'll go through here. Have a drink with me, drop the coins, and I'll unlock the exterior door and let you go free."

Ishta pulled the hood of her cloak down lower over her face. "Alright, but let's do this quickly. I don't have much time."

Gallant opened the door to the guardhouse, and Ishta was surprised by the inky blackness that greeted her. As her foot crossed the threshold, the hairs on the back of her neck rose, and the stink of wine filled her nose.

Ishta instinctively ducked just as an arm shot out from

the darkness to grab her. The weight of her bag shifted, and she was pulled back as Gallant's heavy hand tightened around the strap crossing her back and tugged.

Ishta fell into the door frame, a jagged piece of broken stone digging into her side. She groaned, then tried to duck a second time as a silver flash descended towards her face. The knife missed her, but her movement propelled her into Gallant's waiting arms.

The heavy knight wrapped both arms around her in a hold that lifted her from the ground, and from the shadows of the guardhouse emerged a King's Guard every woman in Etritia had come to fear.

Dirk passed the knife he held from one hand to the other, his dark eyes flat and cold in the lantern light. "Did you think you would not be recognized, Little Bird?"

Ishta's stomach twisted, and she wriggled in Gallant's grasp. His grip on her did not loosen.

"How do you think anyone that comes to us begging for passage out of Etritia gets the coin they need?" Dirk asked, approaching her slowly. He passed the blade to his opposite hand again, the movement quick and liquid. "They all go to the fighting dens. Not many come back with the coin, though. And those that do …" Dirk smirked, his eyes keeping their flat expression. "They do not make it out of the city alive."

"We have orders to kill anyone that attempts the crossing, Little Bird," Gallant said, his breath hot on her neck. He had a heavy, sour stink to him, and it made her nauseous. "But for a woman to come to us … it would be a waste to just kill you and be done with it."

Gallant shifted his grip to a one-armed hold, and his other arm steadied him as he stepped towards the guardhouse. Ishta rammed a knee into his side, then gasped as she felt the hard rings of chain mail. Gallant gave a low chuckle, though the impact of her knee made him stumble slightly.

"Get her inside," Dirk said as he held the door open. "Before anyone sees."

Gallant took another couple of steps, Ishta squirming in his grasp as he went. Then he stumbled and fell to his knees, dropping Ishta.

Dirk cursed and leapt forward, letting the door clang shut.

Ishta rolled to avoid him, only realizing after she did so that Dirk was not reacting to her at all.

Ishta got to her feet before Gallant and dealt him a hard stomping kick to his head. Gallant crumpled to the ground again, and Ishta took the opportunity to check her surroundings.

Dirk was in a grappling contest with none other than Dars. The former first knight took a glancing blow to the jaw without so much as a grunt before twisting Dirk's wrist until the King's Guard dropped his weapon. The knife fell to the cobblestones with a clatter, and Dars kicked the hilt out of Dirk's line of sight with the heel of one bare foot.

Ishta watched the skittering blade roll out of the firelight, then dove after it before it could be lost entirely. The hilt was still warm, and Ishta fought the squirming sensation in her gut as she hefted it experimentally before charging for the two men still locking arms.

Dirk twisted, throwing Dars off balance. Dars fell with a surprised shout, and his hold on Dirk was broken. Dirk immediately turned, and Ishta saw the angry grimace and his dark, flat eyes as his attention focused on her.

Ishta froze, the blade held tightly in one hand, as Dirk stomped towards her. She held the blade out in front of her, the tip extended. "Stay away from me."

Dirk snarled and stomped closer. Ishta could smell the wine on his breath as he reached out for her. His hands fell to grab her shoulders, and none of Ishta's fighting instincts took over to stop him. She could have avoided him. She could have attacked him before he touched her. But she did nothing.

Dirk also froze, his eyes widening.

He released her shoulders and stepped back, both hands pressing to a spot on his abdomen. Something wet and warm and slightly sticky rolled over Ishta's hand, and she looked down to see that the blade she held was covered in blood to the hilt. She hadn't felt it stab him.

Dirk stumbled further back, tumbling over an uneven cobblestone and falling onto his back. Blood seeped between his fingers.

There was a groan behind her, and Ishta turned in a panic to see Gallant squirming on the ground. Dars stepped over the large man, one bare foot on either side of his torso, and knelt to grab his head.

Ishta turned away quickly, but her eyes fell on Dirk as he bled across the stones.

She shut her eyes as the sharp sound of a snap echoed softly behind her. She kept them closed until she felt Dars's reassuring hand on the small of her back.

"You did well, for a house cat."

"I didn't mean to kill him," Ishta whispered. The coppery scent of blood filled the air.

"You did what had to be done." Dars took the knife from her hand.

She thought he might keep it, but he only wiped the blade on the black surcoat Dirk wore. With a few quick tugs and the sound of tearing cloth, he ripped the white embroidered symbol from the surcoat, then held the knife out for her to take.

Ishta wiped her hand on her cloak before accepting the weapon. "I don't want this, Dars."

Dars shook his head. "You make the kill, you keep the spoils." He shrugged. "Besides, you're goin' ta need it out there, I imagine."

Ishta slipped the dagger into a loop on her belt. She would make a better spot for it later. Perhaps a concealed sheath inside her boot. But the belt was fine for now.

Dars held the scrap of cloth out for her. "This too."

"No, you keep it. You collect them."

Dars shook his head again, more forcefully this time. "You make the kill, you keep the spoils."

Ishta took the fabric and tucked it into a pocket of her trousers, feeling faintly sick. "What are you going to do?"

"Get rid of these two, first."

Ishta watched him examine Gallant's body, ripping the sigil from the second King's Guard's surcoat and pocketing it for himself. "Will you come with me?"

Dars gave her an exasperated look.

"Alright, I understand," she said, both hands raised. She pulled her bag higher up on her shoulder. The strap had torn during the struggle, but not much. She could mend it. "Thank you, Dars. For coming to see me off. I would have died without you."

Dars shrugged, then yanked a silver object from around Gallant's neck and tossed it to her.

Ishta caught it without thinking, and was surprised to realize that it was a key.

She examined it. It was large and heavy and covered in small spots of rust. "Think it opens the guardhouse doors?"

"Only one way ta find out."

Dars stood in the doorway to the guardhouse as Ishta entered the small and dark room. There were narrow stone steps that led up to a closed door set into the ceiling, and Ishta watched the door warily as she made her way across the room. On the wall to her left, across from the stairs, was a large wheel of iron and wood, with a pulley system that extended down into the floor and up into the ceiling through small gaps in the stonework. Ishta gave it a cursory glance, her eyes adjusting to the dimness, and wondered is that was how the heavy main gate was lifted. An iron-studded door waited across the room, and Ishta pressed her ear against the wood and listened for a moment.

No sounds could be heard from the far side of the door.

Ishta held her breath and slipped the heavy key into the hole beneath the handle. The door would unlatch from this side without the key, but if she ever found a way back into Etritia, she might be able to use the key to return to the city.

The key slid effortlessly into place, and when she turned the key's bow, now warmed from her holding it, the latch released. Ishta held her breath and pulled the door open.

Beyond the door was a set of stairs that wound down the outside of Etritia's walls. Further ahead was nothing but grass and night sky, and in the distance she could see structures that she recognized as old farmhouses and stables. To her left, across from the sealed main gate, was a second set of stairs. Ishta guessed there was a second door much like the one she had just opened.

She shut the door again and hurried back to Dars.

"I'm leaving," she said breathlessly. "And I'm taking this key with me. Maybe I can get a second one made somewhere, and we can try to get more people out of here soon."

Dars nodded. "I won't stop you tryin', house cat."

Ishta pulled out the small wallet that had been meant for Gallant. "Do me a favor, Dars." She poured a small number of coins into the palm of her hand and dropped them down her boot, then held the wallet out for Dars to take. "Get this to my sister, Illa. You remember her, right?"

Dars's head tilted. "Illa? The little kitchen wench?"

Ishta made a face. "Don't call her that where she can hear you, Dars." She closed his fingers around the wallet. "Give this to her, and tell her to wait for me before she leaves. Tell her that escape was a lie. That the King's Guards kill anyone that tries to buy passage out of Etritia. And tell her ..." Ishta paused, thinking of what Dars might best remember. "Tell her I'm sorry."

Dars nodded. "Alright."

"Do you remember all of that?"

"I remember," Dars snapped.

Ishta sighed, unsure if he would recall it all long enough to deliver her message and the money. "Thank you, Dars."

Dars shuffled his feet. "Wait, house cat."

Ishta hesitated, hoping he might change his mind and come with her after all. "Yes?"

Dars pointed back to Dirk's prone body, and Ishta grimaced. "You mind if I take his boots?"

Ishta nodded, forcing a smile. "Consider them yours."

LAYLE

Layle stumbled from the bedroom she shared with Arella, groggy and still exhausted despite the mid-afternoon nap. Arella was sitting quietly in their small living space, staring at the heavy black kettle that hung from a hook inside the fireplace.

"I didn't intend for you to sit and stare at it when I asked you to watch the kettle for me," Layle said, giving Arella's hair a tousle.

"Oh, I wasn't staring at it," Arella said, turning to give Layle a reassuring look. "I was talking to Trissa."

Layle nodded, though the admission made her uneasy. Now that Arella had made Layle understand exactly who she was conversing with, though the means were outside the child's understanding, Arella spoke freely of her conversations with the princess. Layle checked the contents of the kettle, leaning her head into the fireplace. The fire was little more than glowing embers now, and the stew she had spent the early part of the afternoon putting together was fragrant and thick. "You remember what I told you, right? Never tell her where we are, or who exactly you are, or—"

"Or anything about us," Arella finished. "I remember. She doesn't ask me those things."

Layle nodded again, pulling the kettle from the fireplace and carrying it over to the table to cool. "What did you talk about today, then?"

Arella stood, following her grandmother to the far side of the room, where a cupboard hung from the wall. She dutifully held out her hands as Layle stacked a pair of bowls and a small stack of freshly laundered linens and placed them in the child's palms. "She told me that Nanny Nevina was sending someone to find us."

Layle froze at the sound of her mother's name. "Who is she sending?"

Arella shrugged, dropping the dishes and linens onto the table next to the kettle. "A man. She didn't know who. She also said that Queen Anna was sending someone else to find us, too. Trissa's Auntie Ishta."

Layle scooped a healthy portion of the stew into one of the bowls and handed it to Arella. "Here, go ahead and eat. It's hot, so be careful."

"I haven't got a spoon," Arella protested.

Layle was already retreating to the bedroom again. "You know where they are. I'll be back shortly."

By the time she returned to the living area, Arella was licking sauce from the inside of her bowl, the spoon lying forgotten to one side. Arella parted from the bowl long enough to give a disapproving comment. "Your stew got cold. There's fat on the top of it now. I bet you won't like it."

Layle dropped the chest she had already filled by the door and brought the still mostly empty one over to where Arella sat. "I'll feed the rest to the pigs. They don't care what it tastes like." Her arms ached from carrying what was arguably not very much.

I'm getting so old, now. I can feel it.

"What are those for?" Arella asked, eyeing the chests. She

gave Layle a confused and pained expression. "Are we leaving?"

The hurt in Arella's eyes reminded her of her son, Arella's father. His eyes had a similar look to them every time he realized it was time to move again. Though the color was not the same.

"We have to leave, Arella. We don't want to be found."

"Not even by someone Nanny Nevina sent?"

Layle gave a low chuckle. "No, not even by someone she sent."

"What about Trissa's Auntie Ishta? The queen sent her."

"We especially don't want to be found by anyone the queen sent."

"Why?"

Layle could feel Arella's eyes on her as she hurried about the room collecting items and depositing them into the chest. How had she accumulated so much? Was it just from their time spent here? Had she grown comfortable with her life in this place? "If the wrong people find us, we could be in danger. *You* could be in danger, Arella."

The little girl turned in her seat and watched Layle scramble to gather their belongings. "But Auntie Ishta *isn't* the wrong kind of people. She needs our help."

Layle gave the room a cursory glance. Most of her herbal supplies had been in the bedroom and were now neatly packed away. Even the book she had been writing, *The Practical Witch's Guide to Practical Medicine*, was carefully tucked away among some clothing.

Her son would be proud of her for that one, she knew.

"Grandmother?" Arella asked.

Layle turned. Arella did not often address her as such, and reserved the moniker for when Layle's attention was focused far from where it was needed most. Layle stopped in the center of the room, clasping her hands behind her back. "Yes, Arella?"

Arella straightened, pausing to consider her words carefully. Layle's lips twitched in a faint smile. This was a practiced habit they had fallen into ever since Arella's first mention of Trissa and the Coven. As long as Arella could maintain her composure, Layle would address whatever the young girl could articulate. Their conversations about sensitive topics had become much easier to have, if they were now a little slower to commence.

"Do you not want to help the queen?" Arella asked finally.

Layle shook her head. "No, I don't."

An ugly expression crossed her granddaughter's face, but was gone quickly. Then Arella continued. "Why? Is it something she did?"

Layle had to take a moment to find her answer. She gave Arella a signal to wait, and paced the room, one hand on her chin. They did not have time for this, but she and Arella had made a promise to have these sorts of conversations as the need arose, and she didn't want to lose Arella's faith in her.

"Yes, and no." Layle sighed, coming to a rest in front of her granddaughter again. "Anna was in the Coven. I've told you that. In fact, we grew up together. We played together as children, though that changed some when I proved myself to be Gifted and she did not." Layle paused. Arella's attention was focused on her. "When Anna agreed to help the king in exchange for her freedom, she abandoned us all."

"She was afraid of dying, wasn't she?" Arella asked. Her voice had a hard tone, and Layle suspected the girl might lose her temper soon.

Layle raised a hand to quiet Arella. "I bet she was. Which I can understand and forgive. But that's not all. We have both left the Coven behind us. And now the Coven's magic has found a way to start bringing us together again." Layle made for the mantle of the fireplace, where one last item sat, waiting to be packed with the rest of their more important belongings. "I can't speak for Anna, but I know that I am very afraid of what lies ahead. And I am not sure I am prepared to return to that life I used to have."

Layle cradled the white dragon's egg in her hands, mildly surprised by the weight it had. It was not often handed, and she normally forgot it was even on the mantle at all. But now Layle held it very tenderly and very carefully, as she had once held Arella when she was only a little larger than the egg was.

"You're afraid?" Arella sounded uncertain, and Layle took a moment to consider if she had ever confessed feeling fear to her granddaughter.

Layle nodded. "I am."

"So, you want to run away?" Arella's tone shifted, sounding older and more mature than it had any right to sound. It sounded very much like Layle's own mother's voice.

Like Nevina's voice.

Layle nodded again, unable to meet Arella's eyes. She focused instead on the white egg in her hands. "I do. It's what I have always done."

Arella slid from her seat, her bare feet slapping quietly against the stone floor of their little cottage. "If the Coven's magic is pulling us all together again, is there any point to running away?"

Layle let out a watery chortle. "Probably not."

In the back of Layle's mind, she heard her mother's voice.

"There is no sense in running from fate. Fate will always find you."

She could not decide if it was a memory or her imagination.

Arella gently pulled the dragon's egg from Layle's grasp and held it close to her chest. Layle wanted to give a soft warning, but it would be unneeded. Arella knew what she held, and she was gentle with it. "We could leave. We could run away, and leave our life here behind. And we would still be found." Arella tilted her head, staring down at the egg cradled in her arms. "Or we could stay. And wait for fate to find us. And maybe have a home waiting for us when our destinies are done."

Layle did not comment on Arella's talk of fate and destiny. These were not ideas that the young girl had learned from her. No, Arella had learned those things from someone else. Trissa, perhaps?

Nevina?

Was that possible?

Layle sighed, wiping her eyes. She had begun crying at some point. She wasn't sure when. "I did just plant all those silk leaf seedlings, didn't I?" She forced her shoulders to relax. "It would be a shame to leave them behind."

Arella smiled and passed the egg back to Layle, who placed it back into its place on the mantle.

It was very warm to the touch.

SYRANI

They camped at the foot of a dilapidated bridge. It was made of hardwood and treated with tar to keep the water that splashed from the Knife from rotting the timbers away. Human made, without a doubt. It should have been replaced long ago. If her people had made it, Syrani knew, it would last centuries more before reaching the same state of decay that it had now.

They could have crossed the bridge before nightfall, but Syrani insisted that they remain within Azimar for one more night. Her excuse had been that the woods of Vyris could be dangerous to navigate at night. It was true, but that was not her reason for wanting to remain in Azimar for as long as possible.

She did not want to admit, even to herself, that her true reason for remaining on this side of the Knife was a selfish one. Syrani did not want to voice aloud her fear that, were she to cross the bridge they camped beside and venture into Vyris, she might never see Halcia again. She would be alone. Alone in her thoughts, though she had grown accustomed to that while living within the arcane bubble that shielded

Nieve's village from outsiders. And alone in a deeper, harder to define way.

It scared her to think of that loneliness. And she hated herself both for the fear and for the dependence she was realizing she had on Halcia.

She also suspected that Nieve and the arcanist knew exactly why she had requested they stay in Azimar for another night.

But she did not know what else to do.

The arcanist passed her a wine skin, slightly warmed by both the fire and his body heat. He had worn it on a strap around his torso all afternoon, though Syrani had never caught him drinking from it while they rode.

"I thought you might enjoy a little taste of home before we crossed the water," he said, crouching to rest beside her. "Nieve has gone to check the traps you set. I expect she'll be back shortly."

Syrani took the bladder hesitantly. She wanted to ask which home he meant, Vyris or the village? But she thought better of it, and simply pulled the cork from the stopper and drank.

She had almost expected Vyrisian wine, but what touched her tongue was instead the earthy taste of the tea Nieve's father enjoyed so dearly. It was still slightly warm, and she wondered if the arcanist had kept it close for that precise purpose.

She tea soothed her some, and she stoppered the skin again and held it out for the arcanist to take. "Thank you."

He shook his head, refusing the tea. "No need to thank me. The Elder thought you might want some, and asked me to see that you got it. He prepared the mixture. I just added some water to the skin when the time was right."

"That was ..." Syrani searched for the right word. "Thoughtful. On both of your parts. I appreciate it, arcanist."

The arcanist smiled. It was not unpleasant, though Syrani

wondered if it was the same smile he has used on Verelyn or if this was a friendlier one. "Please, call me Alastor."

It unnerved her how similar this man beside her resembled the human she had come to accept as her brother. Even his eyes were the same shade of blue. His hair was longer, and he had an effeminate habit of brushing it away from his eyes. But it was the same as well.

Syrani nodded. "Alright, Alastor."

Alastor shifted in the dirt, settling completely down. "I'm surprised there are no Etritian outposts on this bridge. Every other crossing over the Knife has at least one small posting of King's Guards."

Syrani uncorked the wine skin again. "It is too far into the woodlands. The boundary between Vyris and Azimar is weaker here. It would not be safe for them."

Alastor nodded. "That makes sense."

There was a quiet moment, during which Syrani offered Alastor the tea again. Alastor once more refused the skin.

"Do you have family in Vyris, Syrani?"

Syrani was surprised by the question, and she took a long sip of the lukewarm tea while she weighed her answer. "My mother was still in Vyris when I left."

Alastor lifted an eyebrow. "What about your father? Brothers and sisters?"

Syrani fingered the stitching of the wine skin. "My father died before I came to Azimar. I had a brother, of a sort. He was human. He also died."

Alastor's dark eyes lit up, but he only said, "I'm sorry to hear about that."

Syrani's curiosity was stronger than her desire to abandon the topic. "What about you?"

"An uncle and a brother," Alastor answered quickly, his eyes narrowing. "But let's go back to your family for a moment. Your brother was human?"

"Yes," Syrani answered hesitantly.

The light in the arcanist's eyes grew brighter. "What was his name?"

Syrani let out a long sigh, setting the skin of tea aside. "It was Hasani."

The arcanist nodded. "My father."

"Yes," Syrani admitted. "You knew that already. How?"

The arcanist shrugged. "My father was last seen fleeing into Vyris. He had a golden dragon's egg with him. You have a golden dragon." He drew his own skin from inside his vest. This one was smaller, and when he pulled the cork from it, the pungent scent of rich wine reached Syrani's nose. "There are few enough dragon eggs and dragons and men fleeing into Vyris to put it all together."

Syrani stared at Alastor as he drank lightly of his wine. "You seem to be handling the knowledge well."

Alastor shrugged again, his lips smacking together as he savored the wine. "I have gone my whole life not knowing him. My mother and uncle never gave up hope that he was alive, but I didn't bother to maintain such delusions myself."

Another silence stretched between them. Finally, Syrani gave Alastor a light pat on his knee. It was awkward, she knew. But she was not accustomed to even the smallest displays of affection, and the motion was as uncomfortable to her as she hoped it would be comforting to Alastor. "He was a good man. And I was glad to call him my brother."

Alastor nodded, his face angled away from hers.

"He is buried in Vyris. He was given a proper burial, and has his own burial tree. Next to my father's. If we have the chance …" Syrani hesitated, wondering if she could actually follow through with the words she was about to utter. "If we have the chance, I will take you to see him."

"Thank you, Syrani."

Nieve emerged from the woods, much to Syrani's relief. She carried three hares in the grip of one hand, and she dropped them unceremoniously in the warm light of the arcane fire Alastor had conjured. She reached them and stretched out a hand for Syrani's wine skin without a word.

Syrani offered it up without hesitation, but Alastor made a low warning noise and held his own out for Nieve to take. Nieve's eyebrow quirked and she took Alastor's skin instead, drinking deeply from it.

Syrani scoffed. "Neither of you have any sense of taste."

Nieve ignored the comment, though Alastor chuckled.

"We have a good catch for dinner, though the traps were not out for long. It seems the wildlife in this region are not accustomed to being hunted."

"And were we followed?" Syrani asked. She thought not of men with swords and ill intentions, but of the young Eysa and her eagerness to follow in Syrani's footsteps.

"We were not. No one should know we are here."

"Actually," Alastor said, getting to his feet. "I have some companions who are on their way to aid us. They should arrive before nightfall."

Nieve rounded on him instantly, and Syrani did not interpose herself. "You are bringing others of your kind here? Who?"

Alastor protested, but Syrani couldn't catch the words he used to defend himself. An odd sensation tickled the back of her neck, and she looked across the bridge to the far side of the Knife. The waters coursed beneath the bridge, the sound steady but not overly loud. There was nothing on the far side but trees and tall grasses.

Nothing that she could see, at any rate.

But she could feel something approaching them. Something familiar.

"Halcia?" Syrani cried, jumping to her feet. The skin of tea tumbled from her fingers, but Nieve caught it before it fell to the dirt and handed it back to her.

"What about Halcia?" Nieve asked. "Is she back?"

"No," Syrani answered after a moment of hesitation. "It is

not her. But …" The sensation grew stronger, creeping over Syrani's skin and into her mind. "But it is someone very much like her."

There was the sound of rushing wind, and a shadow swept over their heads, almost close enough for her to reach up and touch.

"It's Melonya." Alastor stood at Syrani's side, watching as the great blue dragon came to a thunderous rest at the opposite end of the bridge. "I'm sorry, I should have said sooner."

Syrani's shoulder's tensed as Melonya's presence continued to grow stronger in her mind. "It's alright. It was just …"

"Startling?"

"Yes," Syrani breathed.

A single figure descended from the strange saddle that was affixed to the dragon's back and made its way towards them, crossing the bridge briskly.

"Hello!" Alastor called, waving an arm over his head.

"It's an elf," Nieve said in surprise.

"I told you they wouldn't really be *my kind*."

"Tathiel and Eilonwy, and their dragon Melonya, correct?" Syrani asked.

"Yes, though I don't see Eilonwy," Alastor remarked.

Tathiel, a male elf with long silver hair and a trim figure, stopped with perhaps another two dozen steps between them. "Well met, friends of Alastor." He crossed his arms over his chest and bowed in greeting, the tips of his long fingers pressing gently against the opposite shoulder. "I am Tathiel. And this," he motioned towards the dragon behind him. "This is Melonya."

Melonya had not moved, other than to settle down on her haunches. *Well met, friends. I am sorry if my appearance surprised you.*

Syrani's breath caught in her throat. Melonya spoke with a different lilt to her words than Halcia's, and the sensations and emotions pouring from the older creature were more powerful and stronger than any Syrani had experienced from her golden companion. But the way Melonya's voice sounded …

"You sound just like Halcia. Like you could be sisters," Syrani said to the blue-winged beast across the water.

"We are sisters," Melonya answered simply. *"And I feel the pain her absence brings you."*

Syrani didn't respond. There was no reason to.

"Where is Eilonwy?" Alastor asked. "I thought you were both coming?"

Tathiel crossed the remaining distance at a leisurely pace, though the calm in his steps did not entirely hide the irritation in his demeanor. "She has decided to remain in Larten for a time. With your brother."

Alastor snorted. "Regret letting her stay already?"

"I could not have stopped her. You know that." Tathiel extended a hand to Syrani in greeting, and she shook it. "I am pleased to meet another Rider, Syrani."

"As am I." She indicated Nieve, and Tathiel shook hands with her as well. "This is Nieve, my friend. She will be accompanying us on our journey."

"Into Vyris, yes?"

"Yes," Syrani confirmed. "To the mountains in the southwest. Do you know them?"

"Only by map, I'm afraid. My sister and I come from a Homewood further north. There are no mountains where we are from."

"We can't leave without Halcia," Nieve protested, much to Syrani's surprise.

"Nieve, please," Syrani said, giving Nieve a light touch on the arm. "We can't stay and wait for her to return."

"I agree with both of you," Alastor said. "We need Halcia, and it would be foolish to continue waiting around and calling for her."

Syrani felt her neck warm. How had he guessed that she spent much of their time riding through the woods of Azimar calling for the great gold dragon?

Tathiel gave Alastor a hesitant look. "What are you proposing?"

"I am proposing that you and Syrani take Melonya and search for her. Convince her to rejoin us."

Tathiel's look deepened into uncertainty. "Melonya is meant to return to Larten for my sister in less than a fortnight."

Alastor clapped the elf on the upper arm. "Then I suggest you find her quickly."

Tathiel sighed, then turned to Syrani. "Alastor is right. We will need Halcia if we are to retrieve the Amulet of Fire."

"I know," Syrani murmured.

"We can wait until morning, if you wish. Or we can leave now. I leave the choice to you."

Syrani looked across the bridge. It was a short journey, really. Only a few hundred feet over fairly calm waters. The bridge was old, but sound. It had taken Tathiel only a moment or two to cross. Melonya waited for her there, her serpentine head turned so that she could focus one large eye on her.

But Vyris was also on the opposite side of the Knife. A whole different world awaited her over there. A world she had not wanted to venture into without Halcia by her side.

If I do not cross now without her, I will never cross with her.

"We can leave now."

Syrani stepped away from the others, not even wishing Nieve and Alastor a goodbye. She landed one foot hesitantly on the decaying boards of the bridge.

A single step towards Vyris. One she had not wanted to make even a moment before.

Then another step.

And another.

And soon Tathiel was at her heel, following her.

And Melonya's voice, so much like Halcia's that it unnerved her, called across the Knife to her.

"We will find her, Syrani. And you can make this crossing again with her wings beneath you. I promise you."

2 7

JAIMES

Jaimes's stomach rumbled, but he ignored it, focusing on the warm cauldron in his right hand and the glass jar in his left. "This is it, Vash. Our next test sample."

"Careful," Vash warned, her figure floating close to his shoulder, now roughly the size of his forearm. "Don't spill any."

"I know what I'm doing, Vash." He noted the annoyance in his voice, but did not apologize for it. She would understand.

"Do you think this one will go well?"

"I can't imagine why it shouldn't. This is probably the closest I can get with my current lab."

"You mean your bedroom," Vash said with a snort.

"I make do where I can." The cauldron emptied nicely into the jar, leaving little room left. And not a single drop was spilled. "If I can market this to Mathius's old Mercantile Guild contacts, I can use the funds to build a better lab."

His stomach rumbled again, louder and more painfully this time. When was the last time he had eaten?

"How shall we proceed?" Vash asked.

"We'll start as we usually do." Jaimes motioned towards a

small cage on the opposite end of his worktable, where a fat rat squealed from the inside of a metal and wood cage. His tail and one rear leg were bent and clearly broken, but the injuries did not stop the rat from rattling at the confines he found himself in.

"Where do you get these rats?" Her words were steady, but Jaimes noticed the way her minuscule face grimaced at the cage.

"This one was rescued from the inn's cat, who must have found it down in the larder." Jaimes lightly capped the jar, leaving enough of a gap for the steam and excess pressure to vent off. "If I can fix him, I'll let him go. I doubt he'll come back without thinking twice."

"Alright. Are we ready to begin?"

Jaimes shook his head. "A quick lunch first, I think." He plucked a red and orange flower, a type of chrysanthemum, from its place in a large jar, and held it close to the flame Vash was contained within. "This is for you. To celebrate."

A smoky hand reached out to take the flower from him, and Vash smiled down at it. "A bit presumptuous, don't you think? Still, I've grown tired of eating nothing but melted wax and whale oil. A flower would be a lovely delicacy." The flower withered and wilted, and even browned slightly as it was pulled into the burning flames. But it did not disintegrate into blackened ash.

Jaimes winked at her. "I knew you would like it." He turned and hobbled towards the door, already considering what he might ask Mathius to bring him. And the weather was nice. Would it be too indulgent to eat outdoors? "I'll be back soon, Vash."

"Wait!"

Jaimes turned, surprised she had called him back and more than a little annoyed at the further delay to quieting his rumbling stomach.

"You're going to eat out there?" Vash sounded more

impressed than concerned. "Aren't you worried that you'll run into your little she-elf?"

Jaimes considered for a moment, then shrugged. "There's no point in hiding from her any longer. We've both shared our thoughts on the matter." *And I'm just glad she didn't approach that* other *subject.* "Besides, I'm too famished to care if she wants to start another argument about it." Which surprised him; he normally went without eating anything substantial for several days while in the thick of his experiments.

He gave Vash a quick smile, which she returned, though it was hard for him to see from across the room. "I'll see you in a bit. And then we'll see if that flower was premature or not."

There was music coming from downstairs, and Jaimes glanced over the banister that enclosed the open floor the second-story rooms were arranged around as he made his way to the stair. He could see a pair of fiddlers, and he recognized the tune they played almost immediately. He found himself whistling along, and the song added a spring to his step he was not used to having. It was a faster tempo than he was accustomed to hearing, but the shanty was a popular one he'd heard many, many times from sailors traveling in from Hythe or Emery.

A drunken chorus rang out from the patrons in the dining room, and Jaimes joined for the last few lines in a low mutter as he descended the stairs.

Though my sailor's creed will bring me strife
Upon the salty sea,
My heart still beats for my fishy wife.
My siren calls to me.

He had never understood how a song with such sad words could have such a cheery melody. Unless he misunderstood the lyrics? The song told the story of a sailor who fell in love with either a siren or a mermaid, it was hard to be certain, and then had to leave her when his ship set sail again.

When he finally found her, the mermaid, or siren, or whatever she was supposed to be, immediately drowned him. Though how the unfortunate sailor was supposed to then be telling his story was never explained, and the final verse was often accompanied by drunk sailors boisterously clanging mugs of ale and grabbing for a handy barmaid, if there was one, and giving her a sloppy and slobbery kiss on the cheek.

Even if it doesn't make sense, it's still damned enjoyable.

Jaimes rounded the corner of the stairs, spotting Mathius standing in the doorway that led to the dining room. There was a broad smile on his face, and he was clapping his hands with the beat being stomped out by the singers to keep the fiddlers in time.

"Having a little celebration, Mathius?" Jaimes had to raise his voice to be heard over the next chorus being drunkenly sung by patrons he could not quite see yet.

"Oh, Jaimes!" Mathius started, waving him over. "Come and see. I told you they loved her. Just look at her go!"

Curious, Jaimes stepped closer, letting Mathius drop an arm around his shoulder and give him a hearty shake.

The tables of the dining room had been pushed against the walls to make an impromptu dance floor. Three dancers were twining and spinning around each other in time with the music provided by the two fiddlers Jaimes spotted from above. Cheering the dancers on were about a dozen men, sailors from the looks of them, with drinks clutched in tanned and calloused hands and ale splashing over their clothing and onto the floor.

The two men dancing were red in the face and breathing heavily, the dance and drink exerting them to the point of fatigue. But they were smiling broadly and laughing. Between them, her skirts flying as she spun and twirled with her alternating partners, was Eilonwy. Her face was not red, and there was no sweat on her brow. If she was breathing heavily, Jaimes did not notice. Her hair, darkened by the glamour spell she'd woven about herself, danced and tossed about as she moved. Her feet, bare to Jaimes's surprise, were lightning quick, and her laugh was hearty and lovely. The Amulet of Water, bound to a leather strap around her neck, bounced against the hollow of her throat as she linked arms with one of her two partners and skipped in a small circle.

The earth opened up to swallow Jaimes whole.

Or so it felt, as he watched Eilonwy dance.

A heavy weight settled in the pit of his stomach. Beside him, Mathius resumed his clapping and even joined his voice with those of the patrons for the last line of the verse in which the sailor's ship encounters a storm and is threatened with capsizing.

Jaimes turned away quickly, heading for the stairs.

They seemed longer and steeper than they had been just a moment before. And all he could hear was the rhythmic thumping of boots on the floor of the dining room, like the beating of his own racing heart.

Vash was startled by his sudden appearance. The chrysan-themum he had given her was missing several of its small petals, as if she had been plucking them off one by one. "I thought you were going to have a bite to eat—did you forget something?"

Jaimes shut the door behind him, his breaths coming in shallow pants. "Yes. I did," he said numbly. He could still hear the beat of the shanty below him, a steady drumbeat that echoed in his skull.

He made for the worktable, reaching for the small jar of elixir he had painstakingly distilled and concentrated for the last several days, the final product of more than three years of testing and experimenting.

"Are you alright?" Vash asked.

He uncorked the jar and downed a mouthful of the liquid inside. It was still warm, and had a minty and flowery taste that was simultaneously pleasant and awful.

"What are you doing?" The flower fell from Vash's tiny hands, burning away into nothing more than smoke and a small pile of ash.

Jaimes almost gagged on the liquid, but he managed to swallow it. "Proceeding with the testing phase." He recapped the jar and set it on the table once more. Half of the liquid was now gone.

"On yourself?" Vash's form increased in size, bringing her overall height to about the length of Jaimes's torso. She swept closer to him, the heat from the huge cluster of candles supporting her figure making the air in front of Jaimes shimmer. "Are you insane? What if there are side effects?" Her hands reached for him, but dissolved as they drew closer to his face. There was a pained look in her eyes. Her face shifted and contorted like an unsteady flame. "I can't help you, Jaimes."

Jaimes took a deep breath. He could almost feel the warm liquid sitting in his stomach. *How long before it takes effect?*

"I'll be fine," he reassured her. He sat on the edge of the bed, trying to control his breathing.

"Dammit!" Vash cursed, whirling in a half turned and drifting as far in the opposite direction as her candle flames would allow her to go. "What were you thinking?" She spun around again to face him. "This was that she-elf's doing, wasn't it? Did she start another row with you? What did she say this time?"

Jaimes shook his head. "She said nothing. She didn't even see me. I just— Oh …" Jaimes pressed a hand to his abdomen.

"What? What is it?" Vash returned to him instantly, scrutinizing him.

"Just some tingling in my stomach. Nothing serious."

"Tingling. Not burning?"

"Just tingling." Jaimes hesitated. "But it's spreading. Fast." Now his chest and upper arms were alight with the eerie prickle, as were his hips and down into his rear and thighs.

He couldn't tell if it was his skin that crawled with the sensation, or the muscles of his body that were experiencing it. "It's not painful. Just … odd."

Vash shook her head. "I don't like this. I can't believe you could do something so stupid."

The tingling sensation in Jaimes's body reached his knees and elbows, and he gasped. His twisted knee gave an agonizing stab of pain, then the feeling faded. It happened again as the tingling spread to the improperly healed bones of his leg. The tingling increased to an intense burning as it worked its way over the old injury, and Jaimes would have fallen if he were not already sitting.

"What's going on?" Vash asked in a panicked voice.

"I … I think it's working." He groaned, falling back against the sheets of his bed. He tried to control his breathing, but the pain made it difficult to do more than pant between gritted teeth.

"Jaimes!" Vash cried out. "Are you okay?"

"I'll be fine," Jaimes managed through pained grunts. The burning in his injured leg was fading, leaving behind a strange numbing effect. He sat up carefully, his head feeling light and dizzy. He lifted his injured leg experimentally. "It doesn't hurt."

Vash sighed. "Well, at least there's nothing permanent."

"No, you don't understand." Jaimes stood, putting equal weight on both legs. His stance was a little off, due to the odd twist that was still in his knee and calf, but he was standing evenly on both feet. "My leg doesn't hurt at all. No pain, no aching. I don't feel anything." Jaimes bounced lightly on the balls of both feet, a feat that would have left him in agony twenty minutes before. There was no pain. Jaimes laughed.

"It … worked?" Vash asked tentatively.

Jaimes nodded, walking to the door and back, his steps quick and only a little uneven.

"It worked!" Vash clapped her hands together, a spark igniting where they met. "I can't believe it worked!"

Jaimes stopped, turning to face her. "Of course it worked. The two of us are brilliant together, Vash."

"You should stay up here for a while longer, just to make sure we can record any side effects," Vash said quickly. "I'll make a note of the temperature the elixir is at, in case it degrades as it cools or gets too hot."

Jaimes headed for the door again. "Make a note of the temperature, sure, but I'm heading back downstairs."

"What? Why?"

"There's something I want to do before the elixir wears off."

Vash laughed. "That's not funny, Jaimes."

Jaimes rounded on her, his neck and cheeks warming in anger. "I'm not trying to be, Vash. I have something I want to do, and I have no way of knowing how long this elixir will last. It will take days to make more, and by then it will be too late."

Vash shrank away, startled, then her head tilted. "Jaimes, your face is very red."

Jaimes wiped his brow, where beads of sweat had started to tickle at his skin. "Well, it's damned hot in here. All these candles I've lit for you … they make the room unbearable."

"You've never complained before."

The sweating was getting worse, and he was panting now. "I've been a gentleman about it, yes. But it really is quite warm in here."

"Great Ones above," Vash cursed. "You're dripping in sweat."

Jaimes panted again, trying to get a cool breath of air into his chest. His lungs didn't seem to expand as he sucked at the air. His chest felt heavy; his muscles burned and ached. "I … I can't breathe …"

"Jaimes?" Vash came as close as she could, but she was still several inches away from him. "I-I can't do anything! You have to get some help."

Jaimes stumbled to the door, the heat of the room making his head swim. He struggled for each breath, his chest constricting. The hall outside wasn't any cooler, and he had to use the railing to pull himself towards the stairs. His legs didn't seem to respond to the commands his brain sent them.

What is happening?

He was able to navigate the first three or four stairs, each one painfully slow, before his legs gave out beneath him and sent him sprawling down to the landing with a heavy crash. The back of his head smashed against a wooden step, and he came to a stop staring up at the ceiling.

Am I dying?

"Jaimes?"

There was a soothing hand on his shoulder, and Mathius's face swam into view above him.

"What's wrong, boy?"

Jaimes tried to explain, but only a strange and breathy wheeze passed between his lips.

"Eilen! Get over here!"

There were hurried footsteps as several pairs of stomping boots made the wood under Jaimes shake.

"Jaimes!" Eilonwy's voice drifted towards him, and more hands clung to him. "Help me get him up!"

The world swam, and Jaimes's head lolled uselessly onto his chest. Someone laughed. "Can't hold his ale, can he?"

Eilonwy was whispering, to him or to Mathius Jaimes couldn't tell, but they were moving back up the stairs.

"Oi! What's wrong with his skin? He got some sort of plague?"

"No, no, 'course not," Mathius answered cheerily. "Just some bad bruising. Clearly the poor boy's been roughed up. But Eilen will get him seen to, lads. No worries!"

"Maybe Eilen will take me to bed and rough me up after

she's done with the boy?" More laughter followed that sentiment, and Eilonwy paused on the stair long enough to give a friendly retort. Jaimes only caught a few words. His whole body was heavy, and he could no longer feel any of his extremities.

I'm sorry, Eilonwy.

Somehow Eilonwy was carrying him all on her own. Mathius's voice drifted up from the floor below. She was speaking to him, but he couldn't make out the words.

I just wanted to dance with you.

When he awoke, Jaimes was on his bed. His shirt had been removed, and there were damp cloths draped across his chest and forehead. His whole body ached, and when he tried to move his arms and legs, pain lanced through them.

"Don't move." Eilonwy was sitting on the bed beside him, and at her words Jaimes stilled.

"What happened?"

"I could ask you the same." Her face was expressionless as she pulled the cloth from his chest and folded it with nimble fingers.

"How long was I asleep?"

"An hour. And you weren't just asleep."

"Wh-what do you mean?"

Eilonwy tossed the cloth onto the floor, and it landed with a softly wet slap. She glared at him. "You died, Jaimes." Her eyes were rimmed in red, and even as she spoke more tears threatened to fall. "Your heart stopped beating. I almost lost you."

"I'm sorry." It was all he could think to say. "I was just trying to—"

"I know what you were trying to do." Eilonwy stood. Her

hand reached for his face faster than he would have thought possible. He couldn't have flinched from her if he'd wanted. But she did not strike him. Instead, she yanked the cloth from his forehead and tossed it to sit with its companion. "The same thing you've been trying to do ever since you started holing yourself up in this room."

He sat up slowly, grimacing at the pain. Dark lines radiated across his chest, their crisscrossing heavily concentrated above his heart. "What are these markings?"

"That's the toxin still working its way out of your system."

Jaimes stared at the markings. "The elixir did this?"

Eilonwy scoffed. "Elixir? There are enough painkillers and poisons in that 'elixir' to kill ten men. And you drank it undiluted. And on an empty stomach, no less."

"How did you know?"

Eilonwy moved to the table, where a plate with half a loaf of bread waited. "I had to induce vomiting. It didn't help much, but it bought me a few moments more to save you." She brought the bread over to him, holding it out for him to take. "Eat."

"Why?"

Her eyes hardened. "It'll help absorb more of what's still left in your stomach."

He took the bread from her. It was warm. Mathius must have made it while he was asleep. Or dead. "Will I be alright?"

Eilonwy crossed her arms over her chest, staring down at her feet. "The worst is long over. You'll be fine soon."

"I'm sorry."

"I said eat."

Jaimes ate. It was slow, and though the bread was soft and fresh in his hands, it was hard to swallow. His throat didn't seem to work properly, and he still couldn't feel his hands and feet well.

"I thought you were going to die. Right there in front of

me." Eilonwy spoke slowly, avoiding his gaze. "I thought you were going to leave me behind."

Jaimes swallowed another mouthful of the bread. He was hungry, and he'd already eaten nearly all of it, despite the soreness in his throat. "But you saved me. How?"

Eilonwy sighed. "I had to use magic, how else?"

Jaime coughed on a chunk of bread that stuck in his throat. "I would have died otherwise?"

"Yes." Eilonwy finally looked up, her eyes very serious. "You would have."

Jaimes nodded, though he felt faintly ill. "Then I'm glad you did what you had to."

Eilonwy bowed her head once more and did not answer, though she wiped at her face with the palm of one hand.

Jaimes brushed a few stray crumbs from the sheets, the heaviness to his limbs fading. "I know I scared you. And I'm sorry. I wish I had a good reason for what I did, but I was just being selfish."

"And incredibly foolish."

"Incredibly." Jaimes nodded. "I won't let it happen again, I promise."

Eilonwy's fingers tapped against her upper arm. "You said you wanted to dance with me."

Jaimes nodded. "Yes." He should have known she would be able to hear those thoughts running through his mind. There was no arguing it now.

"Do … do you still want to?"

Jaimes sighed, giving Eilonwy a smile. "More than anything."

"Can you stand?"

Jaimes stood. It was not an elegant movement, but he was able to keep both feet on the ground. "My leg hurts."

"More than usual?"

"No," Jaimes said with a sigh. "The same as usual."

Eilonwy held out a hand for him. "Come here, then."

He did. She put one of his arms around her waist, then lifted the opposite hand until his elbow held a loose L shape. Her palm pressed lightly against the palm of his raised hand, and her other hand settled gently against his bare chest, between sternum and shoulder. "The traditional Vyrisian dances I grew up knowing are a lot more … intimate than anything I've learned in Azimar." She cleared her throat softly, avoiding his gaze. There was a slight redness in her face that was endearing. "I hope you don't mind that I've picked one of those."

"Not at all." Jaimes's face warmed. "But I don't know if I can—"

"You can, don't worry." Eilonwy's smile was more reassuring than her words, and Jaimes relaxed the sore and aching muscles of his body. "I'll take the lead, and perhaps next time we get a chance like this, you'll be a little more confident in your abilities."

Next time …

"Alright."

And so they danced. It was not the heart-racing dance of the sailors that he had seen Eilonwy perform. This was slower. And far more intimate, as Eilonwy had said. She taught him the moves without words, using only gentle presses of her hands against his palm and chest. There was a softness to Eilonwy's movements that left Jaimes feeling slow and stupid and clumsy with his leg, but Eilonwy never let him stumble or misstep. There was enough surety in her steps for both of them, and he learned the motions under her quiet tutelage in only a few minutes. And beneath it all, he could sense more than hear, the gentle hum of music that coursed through Eilonwy's thoughts as they danced together.

And then it was over. The dance had led them across the small room, and they stopped when their hips bumped against the sill of the shuttered window. Eilonwy's hands fell from his, but he was not quite so ready to part. His hand remained around her waist.

"Normally," Eilonwy started, her cheeks regaining their embarrassed glow, "we would turn and continue back the way we came. But I think that's enough of a lesson today."

"I'm sorry, Eilonwy," Jaimes blurted.

She gave him a raised eyebrow. Her bright green eyes stared up at him curiously, the tiny flecks of silver in the irises sparkling in the candlelight.

"I've been very selfish over the years, and I didn't realize how much it was hurting you. I could have saved us both a lot of grief if I had been less of a coward. And if I had spoken my mind from the start."

"Ah." Her forehead creased with the scarcest of frowns. "And what will you say now?"

What, indeed?

"I would say …" He paused, taking her hand in his and giving the knuckles a kiss. "I would say that I am sorry I could not be the man you wanted in your life. And that I hope whoever it is that you've bound yourself to realizes how lucky he is. And that he does not make the same mistakes I have."

Eilonwy's head tilted, and she stepped out of his arms. "What?"

"Your husband, or betrothed, or … or whatever he is," Jaimes stammered. "I wish I were in his place, is what I'm trying to say."

Eilonwy let out a startled laugh. "I'm not married."

"But … the ring on your finger …" Jaimes laughed himself, gesturing towards her left hand. "You can't say it's just coincidence."

"It's not coincidence, it's part of the glamour I'm using." Eilonwy rolled her eyes and pressed her fingertips to a spot above her eyebrow.

Jaimes shook his head, not sure he could believe there was still hope. "That's a cruel joke, Eilonwy."

"It's not a joke." Eilonwy's voice grew defensive. "It was at Tathiel's insistence. If I am in a human town or city, I have to have the ring on. Do you know how unsettling it can be to walk around so many licentious and utterly disgusting men while being something that even remotely resembles a female?"

Jaimes frowned. "I guess I don't."

Eilonwy continued, crossing her arms and pointing at him accusingly. "You tell a drunkard no, and he insists you meant yes. You tell a drunkard no, you're promised to someone else, and flash a tiny piece of metal wrapped around your finger like … like …" She struggled for her next words. "Like some sort of tether, and he suddenly has basic language comprehension skills. Especially if there happens to be a tall and menacing-looking man standing close at hand. Tathiel has had to play the part of my husband on so many occasions that I've lost count. It's infuriating!"

Her anger was startling, but also heartwarming in a way that he couldn't fully understand. "I guess it doesn't matter that you could smite them where they stand, or kill them a dozen times over in the time it takes for them to have a drunken piss."

Eilonwy laughed, short and bitterly. "It does not."

"The ring … it's fake, then?"

She nodded, her eyes sparkling again, and her lips curved into a smile. "It's a fake."

"Thank the Great Ones." Jaimes made an exaggerated motion of piety, one hand falling across the dark lines staining his chest as his head fell back and he gazed towards the ceiling. It brought another laugh from Eilonwy. "Then, if it is not too bold and stupid of me, I've had something I've been meaning to give you for a very, very long time." He maneuvered around her, shuffling through a few items on a nearby shelf.

"This is a sudden change of heart," Eilonwy remarked.

"As you said, I died. I was almost gone from this world forever." Jaimes found the carefully wrapped item he was looking for and blew dust and ash from it before turning around. He held it out for Eilonwy to take, fighting back the nerves that told him this was a foolish idea. "But you saved me, and I won't let that go to waste."

And if there was ever a good time to be a stupid, lovestruck idiot, I suppose it is right after nearly dying.

Eilonwy sat on the bed, her eyes alternating between him and the gift she held. "How long have you had this?"

"Since before we left the *Kingfisher*." A thought struck Jaimes, and he reached for the package again. "I-it might be tarnished. Maybe I should check to see if it needs cleaning, and give it to you some other time."

Eilonwy pulled the package away from him. "If I give it back to you now, I doubt I'll ever see it again. I can handle a bit of tarnishing."

Jaimes sat beside her, staring nervously at the floor while she undid the old wrappings.

"Jaimes … it's beautiful." Her lips pressed against his cheek, and Jaimes's face instantly warmed. "Thank you."

He looked up at her. She was already fastening the silver comb into her hair behind her ear. The long scar that stretched across her scalp was now more prominent with her hair pulled away from it. "Are you sure you like it?"

She quirked a smile at him. "I love it." Her hands fell, and she turned her head so he could inspect her handiwork. "What do you think?"

The silver comb was pinned in her hair, its gently hammered leaves and small emerald stones both untarnished and brilliant. "It looks lovely. I think it'll look even better with your natural hair color."

Eilonwy made a small, thoughtful sound, and touched the Amulet of Water that rested against the hollow of her neck. Instantly, her features shifted. The dark brown hair lightened into silver. Her ears, previously the small and rounded ears of a human, elongated and developed the prominent tips of a Vyrisian elf. Subtler changes were harder to pinpoint. Her face changed shape, becoming longer and more angular. The same was true of her limbs. And her chest shrank noticeably, the muscles in her shoulder and arms now more toned and defined. It took very little time, but the effect was mildly surprising to see. Jaimes hadn't realized how sophisticated and complex her glamour spell had been.

"What about now?"

Jaimes smiled. "Just as I thought. It's perfect."

"What do we do now?"

"Now?" He hadn't thought that far ahead. Jaimes shrugged. "I guess now we just … continue on? I bet Mathius is waiting to hear from you."

Eilonwy shook her head. "Jaimes, you idiot. That's not the answer I was hoping for."

"Oh." Jaimes paused, thinking. "Then what answer are you looking for? I'm not really sure what to say."

Eilonwy kissed him again, her lips pressing firmly against his own. Her arms wrapped around his neck, and out of instinct his own tightened around her waist, pulling her closer to him.

She separated from him, and her mouth breathed warmly against his neck and ear. "How about you say nothing, and I'll take the lead again?"

Jaimes nodded, understanding her intentions and feeling foolish for not realizing it sooner.

They were undressed in no time. Jaimes tried to hide the scars that made his leg ugly and unattractive, but Eilonwy did not let him.

As hideous as he felt, she was just the opposite. There

were faint tan lines on her upper arms and on her torso. Her thighs were larger than her skirts suggested, and there was an old scar along the outside of one of them. He thought to ask her about it, but it didn't seem the appropriate time. All of her was soft skin and hard muscle and prominent angles and wonderful curves, and all of her was perfect.

He lay against sheets and covers he did not often use, and she was on top of him, taking the lead as she'd said she would. And all he could think, in the moments when his mind could form words and not just focus on the perfect woman with him, was that this was the kind of magic beds had been made for. And why had it taken so long for him to discover this with her?

They kissed, more times than he could count and more passionately than he had ever imagined a kiss could be. And somehow, miraculously, she did not stop moving. They were all quiet, hot breaths and warm bodies, and he could not be certain he knew where one breath ended and the next one began.

And when the muscles of her body stiffened, and a low, sighing moan escaped her mouth, it was the most perfect sound in the world. When it happened again, a few moments later, he could not have stopped his own body from responding in much the same way.

And then it was over, and he was both exhilarated that it had happened and upset that it was over so soon.

Eilonwy lay beside him, one arm over his abdomen.

He kissed the knuckles of her hand again, then let her arm rest against him once more. "I love you, Eilonwy."

"Will you still love me in the morning?"

"I will always love you."

Across the room, Vash hid herself away in the core of a single candle flame. Her eyes were shut tight, her ears covered by hands formed from fire and smoke. Yet she was still far too present in that room for comfort. She wished she could disappear entirely. Perhaps chase a smoke trail out of the window or up the chimney. But the window was shuttered closed, and the fireplace was empty and too far away for her to reach on her own.

And if she left this room, Vash knew there was little chance of her being able to return.

And she did not want to be gone from this place forever.

So she hid in the candle flame, and tried to block out the sweet nothings that were whispered into ears made of flesh and blood. She tried to ignore the sound of laughter and of bedding being turned down as the couple behind her prepared for sleep.

She tried to disregard the faint pops and puffs of steam as the tears that fell from her eyes evaporated before they had even fully formed.

She was a Spirit of Fire, and fire did not cry.

2 8

EILONWY

She watched him sleep. Jaimes was a quiet sleeper. He did
not snore, and he did not toss and turn like many others
did. He slept soundly and peacefully.

Eilonwy traced the dark markings on his chest. They
were lighter, but they would take time to fade completely.
She was fascinated by the small, dark hairs that grew on his
chest. Elves did not grow much hair, just as they did not
often sweat or pant or exert themselves to the point of
extreme fatigue. But Jaimes did many of those things, and it
never ceased to amaze her.

He was even sweating now.

Eilonwy frowned, taking a moment to check for a fever.
There was none. Which meant … what exactly? Exertion?
From …

Eilonwy's face warmed; it was possible, despite her
efforts to reduce exactly such exertion. He had died, in the
technical sense. It was fitting to ease any burden she could
for him.

It would have been more fitting not to have engaged in
such activities for a while longer, but if she had not acted as
she did, would such a chance ever have occurred again?

Watching him sleep, his chest rising and falling with even breaths, Eilonwy regretted nothing.

It was warm in his room, that was all.

And no wonder, Eilonwy thought as she scanned the room. *So many candles, and the window is shut tight. He must sweat and steam in here constantly.*

She arose from the bed, careful not to disturb Jaimes as he slept. His shirt, which she had removed and discarded onto the floor in her haste to revive him, fit nicely. It was easier to discern from the rest of the mess of fabrics scattered around. And it smelled like Jaimes, which Eilonwy found comforting and relaxing.

Eilonwy opened the window, pulling open the shutters and letting the cool breeze in. It smelled of salt, with hints of the sea and beer and smoke and the sweet scent of baking bread from further down Larten's main thoroughfare. The sky was dark and filled with stars, and she stared up at the sparkling lights of the heavens. There was no moon tonight.

A new moon. Melonya will be coming in a few more days.

A candle guttered behind her, the sputtering sound drawing her attention. Eilonwy watched the flame flicker once before it went out. The others around it shifted in the breeze from the window and stilled.

So many candles. Why does he need them all?

Eilonwy crossed the room, counting the candles clustered together to form a misshapen lump of melting wax and tiny flames. There were over a dozen, and no two were exactly the same size. She sighed, staring at the mess the burning candles had made. Wax crusted the surface of the table in a large pool, and there was more than one burn mark where an errant hand or elbow had evidently sent a fire searing into the wood.

Eilonwy sighed, then blew the candles out. She could have used magic, but there was something more intimate in the mundane act. They went out in groups of two or three, until they were all gone and the room was dark.

It was also cooler, which Eilonwy hoped would make Jaimes more comfortable as he slept.

But she did not want to leave him. Not yet.

So she grabbed Jaimes's leather-bound notebook and settled into bed beside him to read by starlight.

Halcia lay in a small cave set into the side of a hill. The hill was only slightly larger than the cave itself, which was small and cramped. She would be too large for it soon, but it had been her home for years now.

And it will be my only home, now. Until I outgrow it and am forced to find another place.

A light mist hung in the air, dampening the earth at the entrance. The leaves of the trees outside grew heavy with moisture, until water dripped from them in fat drops. A few handed on Halcia's head, which stuck out into the forest.

She could have moved, could have curled into a tighter ball and pulled her head in from the wet. But she did not have the heart to care about the water condensing and dripping down her scales.

Halcia had listened to the fading pleas of Syrani as she begged her to return. It had been hard to ignore them, and even harder to eventually block them out so that she could not hear them.

The human Syrani had taken to the elven village had also called for her, his voice coming to her in less desperate notes, but still earnest. Halcia was sure Nieve was also reaching out for her, though she never heard her.

If another hour or two had passed, Halcia was sure she would have given in to their pleas. She would have left her small den and sought them out. She would not apologize for leaving, not until Syrani admitted that she had been in the wrong, but Halcia would have gone back.

But the voices faded and eventually disappeared.

They have gone on without me.

It was precisely what Halcia had wanted, but now she found that she did not want it at all.

I am truly alone.

Halcia was almost always alone. Syrani's presence in the elven village meant that they could not communicate, and in the months that passed between each of Syrani's excursions, Halcia grew comfortable in the silence of her absence.

But knowing that there would now only ever be silence . . .

What will I do? Go further south? Find some small, uninhabited place to live?

She drew a deep breath and let it out in a great sigh. Moisture plumed out as the water collecting in the hollows around her nostrils was forced out.

Go to Vyris? There is plenty of woodland there. I could be happy in the woods.

And she might find Syrani again. Out of luck, not out of seeking. And she might welcome her back. Perhaps.

A foolish wish. Nothing more.

Halcia slept to pass the time. The mist departed, and the sun shone against the scales of her head and much of her neck. Birds sang in the trees around her, delighting in the warmth of the sun and the gentle breeze that stirred the leaves. Halcia felt their minds touch hers briefly before their attention moved on. She did not let them bother her.

Halcia only slept, and her mind tracked the passing of

time by the change in the songs of the birds and in the change of the heat on her body as the sun moved across the sky. Sometimes her sleep was deep enough that even the sun and the birds did not register.

In those moments, she dreamt.

She dreamt of flying, with Syrani on her back. The wind was crisp and cool and invigorating on her scales and under her wings. And everywhere she looked there were trees. They were not the heavy conifers of the Azimar woods she knew. These were even larger, and many were of varieties she did not recognize. Their branches stretched and inter-twined and formed huge canopies of broad leaves. The greenery was so thick that she could not see the floor of the forest except in the few spots where no trees grew.

This is Vyris, she thought. *This is the world Syrani left behind.*

Halcia dipped her left wing, pulling into a tight circle. She scanned the horizon, looking for landmarks or anything that could help her determine where she was. There was a moun-tain range in the distance, the unfamiliar peaks covered in snow. And to the opposite side, the trees changed. They grew shorter and more familiar, and then thinned until there was nothing remarkable about them at all. The glittering waters of a river could be seen just beyond.

That is the Knife. Halcia stared at the water, fascinated by the way the sunlight played along the surface. *Vyris is much larger than I thought.*

"*Halcia!*" Syrani called. Her laughter was carried on the wind, bright and cheerful. Syrani had never laughed like that before.

Halcia could feel Syrani's hands on her back, just between her shoulders. They felt real.

This is a dream, but it is one that I do not want to leave.

Halcia turned again, this time dipping her right wing and aiming her flight toward the distant mountain range. She beat her wings, gliding on a current of air that would take her close to the snowcapped summit.

The distance closed impossibly fast. Halcia had only to form the idea that she wanted to explore them, and the mountains were suddenly before her. She spread her wings wide, letting the air catch in the thick webbing and slow her down. Syrani's weight shifted, and only then did she realize that there was a strange sort of saddle fastened to her back and around her chest. It was comfortable enough that she had not noticed its presence until Syrani had moved and caused the odd contraption to press into her back.

There were not many places to land comfortably. The only promising spot Halcia could find was a large summit with a slightly depressed top covered in white. The gusts her wings created caused the snow to eddy and swirl, and when Halcia finally landed all four legs on the ground a great plume of the fine stuff went airborne.

It did not settle back down.

Halcia drew a breath, and inhaled the light snow with the crisp air. It burned her throat and lungs, and Halcia let out a hack and gagged.

This is not snow. Halcia bared her teeth, staring at the white powder around her. *It's ash!*

"Halcia!" Syrani called again.

Halcia turned, surprised that Syrani had left the saddle without her noticing. Syrani stood at the far end of the mountaintop, her back to Halcia and her arms spread wide. Thick black smoke obscured the horizon, ascending high enough to cover the sun.

"Syrani?"

Syrani fell forward, over the cliff edge and into the haze beyond.

"No!"

Halcia leapt forward, taking two giant steps before vaulting off the edge herself.

There was only fire and smoke below the cliff.

Halcia tried to orient herself, letting her wings slow her descent. She could see no sign of Syrani and no sign of the beautiful woods she had flown over. Everything was obscured by black smoke and a red haze of flame. The smell of burning wood and seared earth flooded her nose, and the blackened clouds stung her eyes.

This is the madness Syrani is running towards.

The air was thick and dark, and there was still no sign of Syrani.

This is just a dream. I can wake up.

The redness beneath her grew brighter. She could hear the crackling of wood as it burned. She felt the heat of the flames beneath her.

Wake up!

She did not wake. She continued to fall into the depths of the fiery inferno that had consumed everything in sight. Flames began to lick at her scales. First along her back, then across her neck. The pain was excruciating, and yet she still did not wake up.

"Halcia! Where are you?"

It was Syrani's voice, calling for her. She was still out there, somewhere in the flames and smoke.

Please wake up, Halcia begged herself. *This cannot be the end.*

Halcia awoke.

The sun was bright overhead, and the heat from it burned against the scales of her neck. Birds sang in the trees closest to her, unaware of the horrible images that had frightened her.

Noon again already? Have I slept for an entire day?

Halcia stretched, pulling her head into the coolness of the cave and curling into a tighter ball.

It was only a dream. She yawned, wondering if more sleep would bring more dreams. *It was the sun's warmth I felt. There was no fire. No smoke.*

But it had felt real. And those calls for her had sounded real enough.

But it was only a dream. Syrani is in Vyris by now.

Syrani would be wrapped up in the insanity the human brought with him, and Halcia wanted no part of it. She knew why the arcanist was searching for her, and she had no interest in scouring the world in search of lost trinkets.

Halcia could feel the imbalance in the world, but she did not care to make any effort to correct it.

What point would there be in it? I am a relic of a forgotten age. There is no future for me in Azimar or Vyris, and I will not risk myself for a world where I have no future.

Halcia tightened herself into an even smaller ball, covering her head with her tail. She would begin to cramp soon, but the heat of the day would fade before she had to stretch herself out again.

I could not keep even my closest companion by my side. Syrani left me. Others would leave me as well.

Outside, the world fell silent. The chirping of the birds ceased, and the only sound was the wind through the trees.

"Halcia, I know you're here somewhere. Please, answer me!"

Halcia lifted her head in surprise. The soft concussive sound of large wings beating the air echoed through the woods.

"She is close, Syrani. I can feel her presence," a second voice said.

This voice was also female, but it was not human or elven. The words brought with them intense sensations that struck Halcia and were redoubled within her. Feelings of deep longing and affection and an intimate familiarity that was both comforting and disconcerting resonated within Halcia.

She scrambled for the exit to her cave, squeezing her body through and out into the open. *"Syrani?"*

"Halcia!"

The sound of wingbeats came again, and a shadow fell over the woods. Halcia could not see the creature that flew overhead, but there was only one other land dragon in existence.

"Melonya?"

The new voice came again, her words bringing a fresh wave of emotions that Halcia did not fully understand. There was worry and concern, as well as a fair amount of pride and excitement. *"We have come to ask you to join us once more, Halcia. Your companion could not be parted from you."*

"Please, Halcia, don't leave," Syrani begged. *"I couldn't bear it if I lost you again."*

The shadow fell overhead once more, larger now that Melonya was descending.

Halcia thought of the dream she'd had. Was that Syrani she had heard, calling for her as she slept? Or had it been a part of the dream, as she had thought? And Halcia recalled the way Syrani had let herself fall from the ash-covered cliff, falling to the fires below.

"Nor could I bear it if I lost you," Halcia admitted.

The shadow circled for a third time, slow and very low. Halcia watched the dark shape approach, the sun behind Melonya's large body making it impossible to see her clearly. Halcia waited, her eyes squinted against the sunlight, as Melonya came to an easy landing and stopped several large strides away. She was much smaller than Halcia, barely half her size. Her body was a beautiful tapestry of blues and purples and hints of silver, lithe and unadorned with spikes, unlike Halcia's own, which was bulkier and crested in spines along her back and on her head and tail.

Melonya stretched, the front half of her body straightening in the same way a cat's might after a long nap. Her long neck and thin V-shaped head bowed, and Halcia realized the other dragon was bending in formal greeting.

Halcia returned the gesture, feeling slightly foolish, and

straightened. Syrani was already climbing down from Melonya's back, and she was being helped by a tall silver-haired elf. The saddle on Melonya's back was the same that Halcia had been wearing in her dream, she was sure of it.

"I'm glad to finally meet you, little sister," Melonya said. At once, Halcia understood the pride and excitement that Melonya had exuded. It was pride in her, in Halcia, and Melonya's excitement at meeting her.

She didn't understand the basis for either sentiment. *"Sister?"*

Melonya laughed, deep and pleasant. *"Do you think it chance that two eggs have been found, when there should be none? We must have come from the same clutch, only to be separated somehow."*

"But ... we don't look alike." Even as she said it, Halcia realized that it did not matter. She wasn't sure how she knew, but she knew it all the same.

"We are sisters, Halcia. If not by parentage, then by fate."

Syrani rushed towards her, and Halcia instinctively dipped her head to welcome her companion's embrace. "Halcia, I'm so glad I found you." Syrani wrapped her arms around Halcia's neck in a tight hug. "I don't want to lose you again."

"Syrani ... I still want no part of this quest."

"Is there nothing I can do to change your mind?" Syrani asked. Her words were muffled as she pressed her face in Halcia's shoulder.

"I do not want to risk my life for a world I do not belong in, Syrani. I am not meant for Azimar, or for Vyris. The people of this world would destroy me if they knew I existed."

Melonya settled on her haunches, the male elf resting his hand on her side. *"Not only are you wrong, Halcia, you are also selfish."*

"You may call it selfishness," Halcia snapped at the other dragon, *"but I call it preservation."*

"You are still wrong, sister." Melonya was unperturbed by Halcia's outburst, or so it appeared. *"There is only one man that proves any real danger to you. And Mothlenor would not kill you."* Melonya's lips curled back from her teeth, which were longer and sharper than Halcia's own. *"He would enslave you. You would wish for death, I imagine."*

Halcia hesitated. Syrani was staring at her, arms still clasped around her neck as if fearing Halcia might fly off if she let her go. It was not out of the question. *"All the more reason not to involve myself in this insanity."*

"You are involved, whether you desire it or not," the male elf said. "Your birth has involved you. Your fate is entwined with our own, and there is nothing to be done for it but act the part you were born to play."

Syrani released Halcia long enough to gesture towards the elf. "Halcia, this is Tathiel, one of Melonya's companions."

"I know who he is." She addressed Tathiel, turning a hard eye on him. *"Where is your sister, elf? Where is Eilonwy? I heard she was the passionate and companionable one of you two."*

Tathiel's jaw twitched. "She is trying to convince one of our friends of the same thing we are trying to convince you. That we are all needed if we are to stop Mothlenor. That we must all do our part."

"Our part?" Halcia laughed at the absurdity. *"And what will my part be after the amulet is retrieved? Will it then be to swear my life away to you, Melonya? The older, wiser sibling?"* She snapped her jaws, startling Syrani. *"Or will I be free to leave this land, and live as I wish?"*

Melonya's answer was sorrowful. *"You are always free to do as you wish, Halcia. We are only asking for your help. You can still choose to ignore us."*

That answer surprised Halcia. She considered it for a moment. How hard could it be, really? To find an amulet and retrieve it? What harm would there be in that?

"Please, Halcia. Come to Vyris, at least. We will have to

return to my old Homewood. You can meet my mother. See my father's burial tree. Learn my history. And your own."

"I ... I'm not sure I want to."

"The task ahead cannot be done without you," Tathiel said. There was a sense of annoyance and urgency to his voice, and he did not stray far from Melonya's side, as if he were expecting to be leaving at any moment.

"Hush, Tathiel. The choice is hers to make. Not yours." Melonya settled further down, folding her great blue wings against her back and kneeling comfortably on all fours. *"Though I suspect that Halcia and Syrani are not being entirely open with each other."*

"Open?" Syrani asked, turning to face the other dragon and her companion. "What do you mean?"

Tathiel sighed, crossing his arms irritably. "Melonya has a habit of thinking herself some great emotional healer." He gave Halcia and Syrani both a critical glance. "I think she may be right this time."

Melonya let out a short chortle, but it died quickly. She eyed Halcia and Syrani carefully, her voice very serious. *"You may have a strong connection, but it is not as strong as it ought to be. You are companions,"* Melonya insisted. With the words came a flurry of emotions that were gone again before Halcia could identify even a few. *"Your lives, your souls, should be one. There should be no secrets or hidden feelings between you. You should know each other as intimately as you know yourself. More so, if possible."*

"It was easy for Eilonwy and I," Tathiel said. There was more kindness to his voice now. "We were already twins, growing together and knowing the other as well as siblings could. To add a third, Melonya, was little effort."

"But you, Halcia, have been left alone for too long. And Syrani, you have shut yourself behind a ward and cut yourself away from the closest friend you could ever have. It has weakened the love you should have for each other."

"What do we do, then?" Syrani asked. "Is there a way to restore what we've lost?"

"Yes." Melonya bowed her head again. *"Halcia, come to Vyris with us. Even if you choose to leave us to the hunt for the Amulet of Fire alone, you may still be able to strengthen the bond between you and your companion. Give yourselves time together, and it may not be too late."*

Halcia thought for a long moment. She did not want to lose Syrani, and the dream memory of Syrani falling from the cliff and into the inferno below replayed itself over and over in her mind.

"I will go to Vyris."

3 0

FERRAND

Ferrand could not see the redoubt through the blizzard, but he knew it was close. He inched along, his feet crunching heavily through inches of snow layered with crusts of ice. The trail was marked with black pennants, and he could only just see the next one a dozen or so steps away. The flag was torn, ripped by sheer winds and perhaps wildlife, but it was still attached to the iron reinforced stake that had been driven deep into the ground.

When he reached it, Ferrand paused, blowing hot air over his fingertips and searching for the next marker through the grey and white storm. It had not even been half a mile since the last rest stop, but his body was already nearly frozen through again. He hated traveling so far north, but the fur-clad figure, gender indeterminate even by voice through the heavy garments, had insisted that this was the place Ferrand wanted.

If he was wrong ... if I was lied to ... I'll kill him.

Even his thoughts came slow and sluggish in the deep chill.

Ferrand didn't see another marker. Instead, firelight glowed faintly in the distance, and Ferrand hoped it was the redoubt he wanted, and not just another rest stop. He blew on his fingertips again, the heat of his breath not even making it through the huge fur gloves he wore, and stumbled off towards the light.

It was the redoubt, a small refuge tucked into a swell of solid stone and permafrost and surrounded by a twisting line of spiked barricades. A wolf's pelt hung to dry over a fire pit dug into a protected corner, where the wind could not get to it so easily. The smell of the beast's carcass was still fresh on the frozen air. There were people here, even if he could not see them.

A wooden door was set into the face of the stone, evidently the entrance to the redoubt. Ferrand shuffled towards it, blowing on his hands once more. But a curved blade dropped around his neck, and Ferrand froze.

"You've come far from your cozy little castle this time, Ferrand," a cool female voice said.

Ferrand turned, sizing up the woman that had slipped behind him. She was several inches shorter than him, and her head was badly shorn, with small patches of light hair still present next to fresh cuts along her scalp. She was covered in furs from various species, though her arms were bare. Or arm, rather. The left one ended just below the elbow in a nasty and twisted stump.

"Dix," Ferrand said, trying to match his tone with hers and failing. The cold that steeped into his bones made his teeth chatter.

And to think I once called this place home.

"I see you're just as lovely as ever. I love what you've done with your hair."

Dix sneered at him, dropping the curved blade away from his throat. "I got a bad case of the fleas from a skinny little fox. I made him into a hat, but the hat had the last laugh of it."

"That's what happens when you don't clean the fur properly. You ought to know that." Ferrand grimaced at the cuts on her head, wondering why he was surprised that Dix had done the job herself. One of the cuts was oozing a pale pink liquid, catching the light of the campfire in a grotesque display.

"And you ought to know that I prefer my furs while they're still hot and fresh." Dix smiled at him. She was missing more teeth than he recalled.

"As much as I enjoy your company, Dix, I'm here on business."

"I know why you're here, Ferrand. I was waiting for you in the pass. I was supposed to be your guide." Dix smiled again, then spat unexpectedly just to the right of Ferrand's shoulder. Her phlegm left a wet spot in the deep snow.

"The pass?" Ferrand asked. The pass had been a narrow cleft in the mountains, covered in snow and creating a wind tunnel that would have killed him if he had tried to pass during the blizzard that now covered the north. He had been lucky, and had gone through the pass two days before with little trouble. "You should have been guiding me all this time?"

Dix rolled her neck and shoulders. The muscles in her missing arm flexed and stretched, causing the twisted nub where the arm ended to contort briefly. "You're a big man, Ferrand. You can handle a little snow and wind. This was your birthplace, after all."

Ferrand sighed, the wind taking the warmth from his breath before it had even plumed before him. "Where do we go from here?"

Dix pointed to the entrance of the redoubt with her blade. "Through the door, of course."

"Bitch." Ferrand turned his back on Dix and headed for the door again. It was a simple one, set poorly into the stone. Wind whistled through holes in the planks and around the edges. Dix followed him as he entered, and Ferrand was not at all comforted by her presence.

"Down the hall and to the left," Dix whispered in his ear. Her breath was hot and sour. "He's waiting for you."

Ferrand didn't need to ask who 'he' was. It was the same as it always was. Though why they had made him come this far into the badlands of the north was beyond him.

Probably just to irritate me.

But he strode down the tunnel entrance, the small amount of warmth afforded by the protective stone around him and the door behind him already working to thaw his fingers.

There was a light ahead at the end of the tunnel. He could smell food, and his stomach rumbled. The scent of some sort of meat hung in the air. Wolf, or maybe bear. It was hard for him to distinguish the various game of the north by smell alone anymore. There was also the indistinct sound of a meal being eaten. Dishes clinked, a cup clattered, and someone let out a loud belch.

Ferrand followed Dix's directions, which led him closer to the light and the food. When Ferrand entered the chamber, there was only one man seated inside. He was huge, with a bare chest covered in dark hair and a face covered in scars. His arms were nearly as large as Ferrand's torso.

"It's about damned time you got here, Ferrand Whoreson. I don't like to be kept waiting."

The muscle in Ferrand's burned jaw twitched at the name. "I disowned my father. His deeds are not mine to bear in name, Jorvun."

Jorvun took a slow sip from his mug and set it down again. "Your mother was a Nameless, Ferrand. Your name could only come from the deeds of your father. Until you earn a new one for yourself."

"I have no father," Ferrand insisted, straightening and glaring down the length of the table at Jorvun.

"Perhaps," Jorvun acquiesced. "But there are many here who still remember Fenris the Whore, who would lie with any man or woman that could give him scraps from their table. And we all remember the child that stuck to him more firmly than his own shadow. To us, you will always be Whoreson." Jorvun stabbed at a cut slab of unidentifiable meat from a trencher in front of him and dropped it to his plate. "Still, your father was one of my favorite little pets, and I would not deny my aid to his son." Jorvun motioned to the seat closest to Ferrand. "Sit."

Ferrand sat. "Do you have news for me? I doubt you would ask me so far north, or ask to meet with me in person, if there wasn't some good news to share."

Jorvun sliced a bite-sized piece of meat off the bone and chewed thoughtfully at it for a moment. Dix joined him, sitting at his side and using her blade, shaped like a crescent moon, to trim a long strip of burnt meat from the larger slab. She wound it around the blade with a flick of her wrist, then leaned back to chew languidly at the meat.

Ferrand stared at the trencher, trying to identify the beast it came from. It was too small to be a bear, and too fatty to be a wolf. His stomach rumbled again.

"Eat with us, Ferrand, and we can discuss my news on full bellies," Jorvun said.

"And what is the meal my host has provided?"

"Ah yes." He motioned towards the trencher. "You remember Renfrid, don't you?"

Ferrand fought down a gag. "Renfrid?"

"My latest pet. Perhaps you never got to meet him." Jorvun cut another bite-sized piece from the steak on his plate. The motion was sharp and emotionless. "He tried to stab me in my sleep."

Dix laughed, then finished the long strip of roasted Renfrid with a series of grotesque sounds. She looked and sounded like a starved dog gobbling down a bit of scrap meat.

"I appreciate the hospitality, but I must decline." Ferrand wanted nothing more than to leave the redoubt, but he couldn't just turn around and walk away. Not without knowing why Jorvun had asked him to come so far.

"Are you sure?" Jorvun asked. "I can assure you, it's quite fresh. This is the last of his left leg, and it was only cut away this morning. Tomorrow, we shall begin with the right leg. Unless Renfrid passes in the night, in which case we will have to spend the morning salvaging whatever meat we can get from him before it begins to spoil."

"Once you get past the cutting and get to the cooking, human is no different than any other animal." Dix wiped her mouth with the stump of her left arm. "And it's far better when you clean the beast yourself, I've always thought."

"I'll take your word for it, Dix," Ferrand snapped.

Jorvun laughed. He leaned back in his chair, arms resting over his belly. "You can't blame him for not being quite like us, Dix. He's a southerner now, remember? No more cold and hunger. He gets to live in a fancy castle, with all the women and drink he can handle. It's made him soft."

Dix spat, glaring at Ferrand as she did.

"Do you have news for me, Jorvun?" Ferrand asked again.

Jorvun eyed him. It felt like being sized up by a very large bear. Jorvun was calm now, but that could change at a moment's notice.

"I've found one of the items you've been asking for."

Ferrand sucked in a breath. *After all this time ...*

"Which one?"

Jorvun fished an item from his pocket and set it on the table. "See for yourself." He flicked it with one huge forefinger, sending it rolling down the table to meet Ferrand.

Ferrand caught it. "Another dragon's eye." It was much smaller than the one he had gifted Mothlenor so long ago, and that Ajax had stolen. That one had fit nicely into the palm of his hand. This one was only slightly larger than the gold coins the Azimarians used for currency. "It's small."

"Taken from a breeder, several hundred years ago."

Ferrand turned it over between his fingers, inspecting the small artifact. There was a deep chip in the surface. "It's damaged." He looked down the table at Jorvun again. "Is this a joke to you?"

Jorvun frowned. "I have been assured that it will still work. As for the size, I imagine your king can find a way to amplify the images the eye shows him."

Jorvun was probably correct about the second part, but Ferrand didn't trust him to sell him a damaged dragon's eye with only the promise that it still worked. "I won't accept this, Jorvun. You can do better."

"Perhaps I can," Jorvun said. His voice was low and dangerous. "But it has taken us years to find this one. How long do you think it will take to find a better one? And how long do you think your king will tolerate you returning empty-handed?"

Ferrand thought for a moment, turning the eye over in his hands. He inspected the chip again. If this was the best that could be done, then this was the best that could be done. And this eye could be used to find Ajax. And once Ajax was killed, the original dragon's eye could be returned to its rightful owner. "The damage is not so bad as I thought it was." Ferrand closed his fingers around the eye. "Are you certain it will still work?"

Jorvun nodded.

"Good." Ferrand stood. "I'll have the agreed-upon price brought up as soon as I return to Etritia and can have its authenticity verified."

"I don't think so," Jorvun said, also rising to his feet. "I get paid now."

Ferrand sneered. "Do you think I am foolish to bring that much gold to these mountains?"

"Your gold means nothing, Ferrand. We don't need it here."

"Then what do you want? Women? Drink? All of both that you can handle?" Ferrand sneered, his burned face twisting painfully. "I don't have any of that with me either, as you can see."

Jorvun smiled, and the expression was far more unpleasant on such a large man than it had been on Dix. "I want to see if Fenris the Whore's son can live up to his father's name."

Ferrand swallowed. "What?"

Dix laughed, a short and terrible sound.

Jorvun did not laugh, but instead leaned forward. The table groaned under his weight as his forearms pressed down onto the wood. "I have no pets at the moment, Ferrand Whoreson. And the nights are long and cold this far north. Stay three nights with me in my hall, paltry as it may be, and the eye is yours to take when you leave."

The burned half of Ferrand's face twitched furiously. "No."

Jorvun laughed, straightening once more. He picked up the partially eaten Renfrid steak and tore a chunk away with his teeth. "Come now, Ferrand," he said as he chewed. "How do you think your king will react when I send word to him that you refused my generous offer? Suffer humiliation with me here, or risk death in Etritia."

Ferrand pocketed the dragon's eye. "You will pay for this, Jorvun."

Jorvun smiled again. "Not before you have paid for the dragon's eye, Ferrand the Whore."

JAIMES

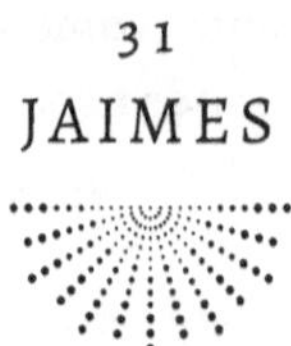

Pain in his leg awoke Jaimes. It was the same dull ache it always was, and he lay for a moment under the covers, trying to recall the vivid dreams he'd had.

He and Vash had found a strong and natural pain remedy. He had tested it on himself, though he had a hard time remembering why. Then, he and Eilonwy …

"Are you awake over there?"

Jaimes sat up slowly, his jumbled memories falling into place again. Eilonwy sat at his table, a book in her hands. His face warmed. "You're still here."

Eilonwy smiled at him. She had adopted her disguise once more, and her clothes were different than he remembered them being before. "I'm here again, yes."

Jaimes flexed the fingers of his left hand. They were tingling, and compression lines crossed his forearm. He must have been sleeping deeply. "How long was I asleep?"

"A little more than a day."

"That long?" Jaimes untangled the bedding from around his legs and stood. His voice was hoarse, and he was hungry. There was something off about the room, but his bladder was protesting too loudly for him to understand what it was.

"You needed the rest. You died, remember? Things like that tend you wear you out, I imagine." Eilonwy gave him an odd smile.

He hobbled for the door, and Eilonwy rose to stop him. "Where are you going?"

Jaimes shrugged, giving her an embarrassed smile. "You just said that I was asleep for more than a day. I'm off to do what most people do when they first wake up."

Eilonwy nodded her head knowingly, then relaxed back into her chair.

Jaimes maintained what little composure being half naked and barefoot could afford him until the door shut behind him, then he hobbled as quickly as he could for the privy at the end of the hall. It was unoccupied, thank the Great Ones.

When Jaimes returned, Eilonwy was just as he had left her. She set her book aside and stood to face him. "Here, I've brought you something." She held out a small glass jar for him, one of his own if he wasn't mistaken. Inside it was a thick white cream.

"What is it?" He pulled the cork stopper out and sniffed the contents. They had a pungent medicinal smell to them. A very familiar medicinal smell.

"I've taken the last of your solution and blended it into a cream base. After the … reaction you had drinking the liquid, I thought a topical application might be more suitable." Eilonwy folded her hands together in front of her and rocked on her heels. There was a proud glint in her eyes.

"I didn't think about that." Jaimes dabbed at the cream, rubbing a small amount between his fingers. There was a brief cooling sensation, then nothing.

"Of course you didn't. You're a man. Men don't typically think about creams and the like." She winked at him. "Sometimes the vanity of a woman can come in handy." She motioned for him to sit down. "Try it out. I want to see how well it works."

Jaimes obediently sat, and she took the jar from him and slathered his twisted leg in the thick cream from thigh to just above his ankle. There was an interesting cooling sensation on his skin, but it faded after only a few seconds.

"Well?"

Jaimes flexed the muscles of his leg. "There's no pain." He smiled, but it faded quickly. "But my leg still looks like it always has."

Eilonwy stoppered the jar again and held it out for him. "You wanted something completely natural. No magic whatsoever. That can only get you so far."

Jaimes knew she was right.

"You should be proud of yourself, Jaimes. Most witches would have found ways to get these same results by blending magic with herbal medicine. Those remedies create a dependence on arcane users." She pointed at the jar. "That can be mixed up and used by anyone with even the most basic of apothecary knowledge. You've done something wonderful for Azimar."

Jaimes turned the jar over in his hands. *Something wonderful for Azimar. The best compliment I've heard in some time.*

"How long do you think it will last?"

Eilonwy's head tilted as she considered the question. "Each application? Several hours, I would imagine. And with a jar that size, I think you have maybe two weeks' worth of cream there."

Jaimes shook his head. "No, the hollyvine extract would go bad before then. It only lasts for a few days."

Eilonwy nodded. "Which is precisely why I added cannabis extract to your tonic before blending it into the cream."

Jaimes laughed. "Cannabis extract? That wouldn't work."

Eilonwy crossed her arms. "It wouldn't work to do what you were aiming for, no. But for general pain management, it works very well."

She was right. Again.

Jaimes narrowed his eyes at her. "How did you know about the hollyvine?"

"I read your notes." Eilonwy turned and held up the book she had been reading from for him to see. It was his notebook. "You've made an astonishing amount of progress in the last few weeks."

"That notebook is encoded," Jaimes said with a smirk.

"With a simple symbol substitution." Eilonwy rolled her eyes. "It took me less than five minutes to figure it out."

It was more complicated than a symbol substitution, but her point had been made. "You're brilliant, Eilonwy."

"I know." Her expression was smug, but the hint of red to her cheeks told him that she was pleased and a little embarrassed by the comment. "Actually, there is one symbol I still haven't figured out." She opened the book to one of the last pages and held it up for him to see. "This one here. The small one that looks like a hatch marked V. What does that one mean?"

Jaimes smiled. It was Vash's symbol. He used it whenever she was overseeing a step in their experiments. *Eilonwy has no idea that Vash even exists—*

"Vash!" Jaimes stared at the unlit candles on the tabletop, then at the cold fireplace. "You put the fires out?"

Eilonwy's eyes were large. "You were sweating. I didn't see the point in having so many candles lit."

"Shit." Jaimes ran a hand through his hair. "Light one again. Hurry."

"Alright." Eilonwy reached for the flint striker on the table.

"No!" Jaimes put a hand out to stop her. "You have to use magic to light it."

"Jaimes, what has gotten into you?" Eilonwy was staring at him with a confused and hurt expression.

"Please, just do it."

Eilonwy lit a candle with a smooth wave of two fingers.

Jaimes leaned towards the candle, careful not to let his breath blow it out again. "Vash?"

There was no answer.

"Another one."

"Jaimes—"

"Another one!"

Eilonwy lit another candle.

"Vash? Are you there?"

Her reply was weak and tired when it came. "I'm here, Jaimes."

Eilonwy's hand went to her mouth. "A fire spirit. I didn't know she was there." Eilonwy addressed the second candle flame, where a minuscule figure could be seen. "I'm so sorry."

Jaimes quickly relit the remaining candles with the flint striker while Eilonwy continued her apologies. His hands were shaking. He didn't want to admit how afraid he had been that Vash was never going to answer. Once all the candles had been lit, Jaimes pulled a flower from the closest jar and held it out to the flames. "Here, Vash. I hope this will help you feel better."

The flower burned away immediately. "Thank you, Jaimes." Vash's voice already sounded stronger. "How long was I gone?"

Eilonwy bit her lip before answering. "A day. Give or take a few hours."

"It always feels longer," Vash said.

"Vash, I'm sorry," Jaimes said. "I'll find a way to make sure it never happens again."

Eilonwy put a hand on his shoulder. "I already know a way."

Jaimes sighed. "You do?"

Eilonwy nodded. "In my Homewood, we sometimes conjured fire spirits and kept them during festival nights. They're easier and safer to keep alight than actual fires, and they seem to love being out in the world for a whole day. We put them in spellbound jars and feed them flowers and bugs, and they give us light to sing and dance by."

Jaimes grimaced. "That sounds a little barbaric."

"It's not." Vash shook her head, which now was roughly the size of Jaimes's thumb. "I've been to a few of those festivals. We dance and sing with the elves, and we get to sit and stare up at the stars and enjoy ourselves for an entire night. For some of us, those nights are the most memorable ones we will ever experience."

"Please," Eilonwy said to Vash. "I would be honored to make a spell jar for you. You would be free to go wherever you please, so long as someone carried you."

Vash hesitated, then gave a curt nod. "Alright."

Eilonwy worked quickly. The jar she took from the collection on Jaimes's table, dumping the herbal contents and blowing broken bits of leaves and dirt out of it. Jaimes watched her, offering more flowers and weeds to Vash, who ate each one quickly and with thanks.

Eilonwy muttered a spell over the empty jar, and the glass flashed a dull blue. Then she snapped a lit candle stub that was nearly entirely melted from its holder. The holder was covered in hardened wax, and some clung stubbornly to the tiny candle. Eilonwy repeated the incantation over the candle, though there was no colorful display this second time. Then, with long and nimble fingers, she dropped the lit candle into the bottom of the jar. It bounced before settling against the smooth bottom, but did not go out.

"There." Eilonwy held the jar up. "That should do it. The candle won't melt away, and the glass will not discolor or break if dropped."

Jaimes blinked. "That was quick work."

Eilonwy shrugged. "My mother was a good teacher when it came to these sorts of things." She held the jar close to the fiery form of Vash. "Are you ready?"

In answer, Vash shrank down to about the length of Jaimes's smallest finger and drifted inside the jar. "It's a little snug," she said softly.

Jaimes smiled. "I'll find a bigger jar for you soon." He took the jar from Eilonwy, holding it up so he could easily look inside. "Where would you like to go first, Vash?"

"Outside, I think. To start with." Her voice was muffled and distorted by the glass surrounding her. "And then, when the time comes, I want to go with you, Jaimes."

"Go where?" Jaimes squinted at the tiny figure inside.

"Don't be stupid, Jaimes." Vash crossed her arms over her chest. The motion was so small he almost couldn't see it. "You're going to Vyris with your she-elf. You've already made up your mind, I can tell."

Jaimes felt his cheeks warm. How had Vash come to know him so much better than he knew himself? He had decided to go to Vyris with Eilonwy as soon as he realized that their night together had not been a dream. As soon as he had recalled the scar on her hip, and the way the comb he had finally given her looked in her hair. Jaimes looked up at Eilonwy. She was still wearing the comb, and there was a hopeful light in her eyes.

"Will you really come with me?" Eilonwy asked.

"I'll go anywhere with you, Eilonwy."

Ishta pulled her cloak more tightly around her as she stumbled over the uneven ground. The thin fabric was all that kept the sharp chill of the night air from biting too deeply into her skin, but she still shivered with every gust of wind.

Who knew it could get so cold on the plains?

Her feet and knees ached, and her face and hands were wind chapped and raw. She had followed Trissa's whispered instructions, keeping her nose always pointed east as she walked. It had taken hours to leave the view of Etritia behind and the better part of a day before she had left the surrounding farmlands behind as well. The once lush land was overgrown and home to wild game, and the homes and roads she had once explored as a child were in ruins. And now, in the middle of a cold and cloudy night, she had traveled far beyond any lands she knew.

And she was afraid. More than the fear of the unknown surroundings, or of the dark or the countless things that might be sharing the night with her, Ishta feared that she would never see Anna again. As she walked she thought of

Anna's voice and face. She thought also of Illa, and Trissa, and of Dars. But her mind was constantly drawn towards Anna, and she clutched the heavy key that settled into the pocket of her cloak until her hands were numb with cold.

Ishta had yet to come across another town, and she had never learned her maps well enough to know if any lay along the path she took. The air smelled damp, and thunder rumbled in the distance. Ishta searched for anything that might protect her from the coming rain. All around her was shadowed in darkness, but she could see nothing larger than a shrub to shelter beneath.

"Trissa could have mentioned how long this journey would take," Ishta muttered bitterly.

But it was not fair to be mad at the princess.

"I'm just cold and tired," Ishta said with a sigh. "And very hungry. I didn't mean it, Trissa."

Could the girl hear her if Ishta spoke out to her?

Better than being alone in the dark.

Ishta thought of the princess, remembering the way her voice had sounded when she had spoken to Mothlenor as a Gifted Coven child. It had been both eerie and fascinating to witness, and Ishta was not sure she would ever want to see such a strange thing again.

"If you know of any place that could keep the rain off, I would appreciate it."

Thunder roared nearby, making Ishta jump and curse. Lightning followed quickly behind it, momentarily blinding her.

In the darkness that followed, an afterimage burned into her eyes by the flash of light quickened Ishta's sore and blistering feet.

By the time she reached the little cottage the lightning had shown her, rain was falling. Fat drops soaked her in only a few minutes, and it ran down her face and back in rivulets. The water was colder than the wind, and Ishta's teeth chattered painfully. The thunder was closer, each one more deafening than the last, and she hurried to the door of the small house and beat on it with a heavy fist. Almost immediately, a light brightened behind the shuttered windows.

"I told you before, I don't take kindly to threats," a woman shouted from within the house. "Leave me in peace, or I'll make sure you regret ever calling the King's Guard here."

"Hello?" Ishta jumped as another crack of thunder shook the world around her. "Hello? Can you please help me?"

There was muttering and some mild cursing from within the house, and the door opened slightly. A single eye, surrounded by wrinkles and with an eyebrow that was more grey than black, peered out at her. "Who are you?" the woman barked. "What do you want?"

"Just to get out of the rain, if you don't mind," Ishta said. "I'm not King's Guard, and I haven't brought any with me."

"Who said anything about King's Guard?"

"You did. Just now."

The woman narrowed her eye. "I guess I did." The door opened wider, revealing a hunched woman a foot or more shorter than Ishta and well into her later years. "Come on then, before you drown out there."

"Th-thank you," Ishta stammered. As the door shut, she peeled her wet cloak from her shoulders. The woman took it and shook water droplets onto the floor.

"Ah, you're a young lady. Should have said so. I wouldn't have made you stand out there quite so long."

Ishta smiled politely, casting a cursory glance around the home. Herbs and drying flowers hung from every rafter, giving the whole room a sweet and earthy aroma. The woman herself was barefoot and wearing a thinning skirt and a sleeveless wool shirt. She jingled as she walked, the sound arising from the countless bangles around her wrists and ankles.

The woman made a fuss of hanging Ishta's cloak above

the fire, which was little more than glowing embers. "Now, tell an old woman why you were out wandering in the rain, hm?"

Ishta shrugged. "I got lost in the dark. It was only luck that I found your house."

The woman laughed. "Luck, huh?" She motioned for Ishta's to strip, and Ishta did so with little hesitation. She was too wet and too cold to argue over modesty.

Her clothing fell with heavy slaps onto the stone floor of the cottage, and Ishta's bare feet left wet footprints as she struggled to remove her waterlogged boots. "What would you call it, then?" Ishta asked as the woman wrung water from her shirt.

"Might be luck. Might be coincidence. Might be fate."

Ishta snorted, rubbing warmth into her upper arms.

"You don't believe in fate, little girl?" The woman turned a pair of beady eyes on her. "It believes in you." She nodded towards a wooden bench that sat along one wall. "Drag that closer to the fire. Should be a blanket underneath you can use to warm yourself up."

Ishta did as she was told, crossing her legs awkwardly on the bench and wrapping the blanket over her shoulders and thighs. The woman was arranging the rest of her clothing in the fireplace, which now burned warmer and larger. "What do you mean, fate believes in me?"

"Well, it believes in all of us, doesn't it?"

Ishta's chills were subsiding even as the wind and rain outside grew louder. "You make it sound as though it were alive."

"Not alive, no." The woman sat with a groan on a small chair in front of the fire. "But fate has a way of knowing."

Ishta shook her head. *Of all the places to get stuck, it has to be in a crazy woman's house.*

The woman held out her palm. "Give me your hand, little girl."

Ishta reluctantly removed her hand from the warmth of the blanket she had cocooned around herself and put it into the woman's.

The woman flipped her hand over, palm up, and peered at it sidelong. "Interesting," she said after a moment. "It seems fate has an interest in you."

Ishta pulled her hand away. "What makes you say so?"

"It's all there. In your palm. Where fate has laid out her plans for you."

Ishta stared at her hand. "What does it say?"

The woman laughed. "What would be the fun in telling, darling?"

Ishta must have made a face, because the woman laughed again.

"Would you like some tea? Something hot to melt away the ice in your bones?" The woman pointed beside Ishta, where a small cup sat just within her reach. It was filled nearly to the brim with steaming and faintly yellow liquid. "It's dandelion."

Ishta carefully took the cup in hand, cradling it to her chest. She had seen occasional tricks from Anna, but nothing so silent and imperceptible. *Suddenly, worrying about the King's Guards makes sense.* "You're a witch."

"And you are seeking a witch."

Ishta shook her head. "But you're not the one I'm looking for."

"Ah." The witch nodded. "No wonder you've yet to ask for my help."

"You've already helped. You let me into your home and out of the weather." Ishta sipped the tea. It was pleasantly sweetened, and Ishta's heart warmed when she recognized the taste of honey.

"And you are interesting company. I would be happy to host you through the night."

Ishta did not want to think what the witch meant by

"interesting", though she was sure it had something to do with what the old woman had seen in her palm—if there had been anything there to read at all. Ishta dipped her head respectfully. "Thank you. I only wish I knew where to go when morning comes."

The woman smiled wider than ever, and Ishta could see small gaps where a few of her teeth were missing. "As I told you. Fate believes in you, and she has led you to one who can guide you in the right direction."

Ishta straightened. "You know where Layle is?"

The woman raised a hand to hush Ishta. "I don't know anyone by that name. But there are not so many of us with arcane skills left in the world, and we have a habit of trying to know where others like us are. Never know when you may need a friendly face and an understanding heart." The witch leaned back in her chair, looking very small and frail in her worn and oversized clothing. "If you head east, you will eventually find another witch. Whether she is the one you are searching for, I can't say. But she can at least point you in another direction, if you need it."

Ishta finished her tea, staring at the fireplace. *East. Like Trissa said.*

"Done with your tea?"

Ishta looked up, surprised that the woman had stood without her noticing. She held a hand outstretched, reaching for the tiny cup Ishta was using.

Ishta spared a quick glance at the bottom of the cup, where tea silt and a few dandelion greens clung. She passed the cup over. "Are you going to read it?"

The witch snorted. "I'm going to refill it for you."

"Will you really tell me nothing of what you read of fate's plans for me?"

The witch considered for a moment, then answered with deliberate care. "The path you are meant to travel is a long and narrow one. Danger lurks to either side, and the end to your journey may not be at all what you desire. But you must never stray from the course fate has chosen for you."

33

MOTHLENOR

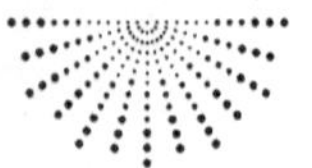

Mothlenor stared at the passage of the *Daemonica* that Anna had shown him. He had almost dragged her back to her quarters, Trissa wailing behind them, and had taken the ancient book back. But he had first made her find the passage dealing with the formation of a dragon wraith and let him read it for himself.

There had been no specific mention of dragons, but there had been a small note about the creation of wraith beasts from stronger souls, which would be more powerful, more resilient, and more dangerous to control. But the soul in question had been in his possession for years. Surely it would be a simpler feat than the *Daemonica* made it sound.

And I missed it. I have read this tome countless times, and it never entered my wildest ideas ...

He'd shut both Anna and Trissa in their quarters, locking the door behind him. No key would open it, no magic would break the seal. No magic weaker than his own, at least. They would not be permitted to leave until he had determined what to do with them. Nothing went in or out of the room, not even food, without him being present to watch the transaction.

The castle was so quiet now. Without Anna and Trissa wandering the halls, and without half as many servants as they had employed only a few years ago, he almost never saw another soul while walking through the castle. Even Ferrand was still gone.

When his brother had been alive, it had always been bustling with people.

No matter. All will be right again soon enough.

Mothlenor shut the book and took a deep breath.

From under his robe, he pulled a small vial bound on a leather strap. He could have kept it on a fancy chain, but it somehow felt more fitting to leave it on such a base thing as an old worn strip of leather. The contents of the vial were milky and moved like something that was neither liquid nor smoke, but a mixture of both. He gave the vial a small swirl, holding it up to the sunlight that streamed through the open window of his tower study.

The soul within danced and swirled for a moment before settling into a lazy eddy once more.

"Nevina." Her name came out like a longing sigh, and he had to shake his head to clear the image of her face that it had conjured. "I promised you that I would not turn you into one of my wraith pets. I said I would save your soul for something special." His fingers closed around the vial again, obscuring the shimmering contents within. "The time has come for me to fulfill my promise to you."

He unstoppered the vial, then quickly pressed his thumb over the opening. Nevina's soul would surely still be very strong, and it would still search for an escape until he bound its power to his.

With his free hand, he brushed a thin layer of dust from the table in front of him. The table was old, the stone surface worn and cracked. It had been damaged slightly in the move from the woods outside the castle to his tower, and Ferrand had seen to it that the men responsible had been severely punished. But it was still whole, and it was still powerful. The energy that was bound into the old altar was very much alive and active, and it would once again prove useful for the art of Calling.

The altar housed a small collection of arcane trappings, but there was only one piece that interested him: the ruby-topped needle in the leather pouch that his fingers were hurriedly unwinding. When he had last used that same needle, it had been to summon Nevina to his chambers on the night she had died. It seemed fitting to use it once more to reanimate her spirit.

He carefully brought the long needle to the thumb that pressed against the mouth of the vial. He could feel Nevina's soul squirming against the pad of his thumb, apparently sensing freedom and desperately trying to slip away.

Mothlenor slipped the thin needle between the meat of his thumb and the rim of the vial and stabbed himself in the fattest part of the pad. There was no sensation of pain, and it wasn't until he saw the tip of the needle dipped in red that he was sure he had actually drawn blood.

He tipped the vial several times, washing the white soul within in his blood. It began to darken. He placed his free hand on the altar's surface, drawing the dark energy that clung to it into him. He was practiced enough in the art of blood magic that he could Call Nevina's soul on his own, without the aid of the altar's power, but precautions were always wise. And the altar had never failed him before.

"Nevina," he said, imbuing his voice with power. "You are mine to Call. You are mine to control."

The soul squirmed against the sides of the glass vial. It was now a dark pink, almost red in color. He continued tipping the vial, massaging his thumb against the rim until more blood seeped out of the small puncture.

"Nevina," Mothlenor repeated. "Your soul is mine to command!" He poured more power into the summoning.

The air around him warmed, and he felt sweat accumulating on his brow.

The soul was blood red now, but still it squirmed and fought against the binding spell. He stabbed at his thumb again, then a third and fourth time. Each one hurt more and more, as he focused more on making himself bleed than on making the process painless.

He could deal with a bit of pain for this. Pain was nothing.

"Nevina!" He slammed his palm against the altar, pulling more energy from the reserve it held into him. The hair on his arms stood, and the space around him crackled with energy. His breathing was labored, and the air around him was hot and heavy. "You are mine to Call, and I Call upon you now!" He conjured an image of a great and terrible beast, with wings of fire and a body of smoke. "I give you the power of flight and of destruction. Find the ones that seek to undermine me. Destroy them."

The vial in his hand was warm, and whatever was now inside was no longer beautiful and pure. It was a red so dark it was almost black, and it bubbled like thick sludge. And still it fought to escape the tiny glass prison it was in.

"For this task I Call on you. And for this task, you are mine to command!"

The vial shattered, startling a gasp out of Mothlenor's mouth. Glass stuck into the palm of his hand and littered the floor. His whole hand was bleeding, and he stared at it in numb shock and pain, vaguely aware that the black thing that was inside shot straight for the open window and disappeared into the open sky.

"Nevina …" Mothlenor murmured.

I have failed …

Mothlenor hurried towards the window, hoping there might still be time to capture the escaped soul and try the binding again.

There was a loud shout and a shrill scream from the street below, and a large shadow passed overhead. Before Mothlenor had the time to look up, the shadow was already gone.

"Nevina?"

Above him, a great and terrible roar shook the stones of his tower.

34

TIRYN

S and shifted under Tiryn's feet, but he maintained his balance as he marched through the desert. Nunor was not as graceful, and the gold earth sucked at his heavy shoes with every step. He tired much faster than Tiryn. He also sweated and stank a lot more than Tiryn.

"We should have bought horses," Nunor grunted for the hundredth time.

"Horses would not fare any better than us here," Tiryn said through parched and cracked lips.

Nunor growled, each step sending sand flying skywards as he wrenched his foot free. "You got any water?"

Tiryn did, and he passed the half-full skin over his shoulder to the dwarf. When Nunor returned it, it was noticeably lighter. They would run out soon enough, and what then?

"Keep talking, Tiryn," Nunor said. "I think it helps keep my head going right."

"Where was I?"

"The gate in Thessala."

"Ah, yes." Tiryn took a long look around them, searching for anything that might shelter them for the night. Evening

319

was still a long way off, but they were traveling slowly, and any excuse to pause for a reprieve in the shade was a welcome one. "My father opened it. It wasn't often used, and we weren't sure where it would take the survivors. But we ushered them through anyway. The women and children first, except for those women who could fight. It didn't take long."

"And then?" Nunor asked. "I'm guessing you didn't get the best of the King's Guards that were there, did you?"

"We did well enough, considering the circumstances." A memory flashed through Tiryn's mind, and he shook it clear. "There could have been a lot more casualties, if not for my father."

"Aishe," Nunor said with a snort. It almost sounded like a curse coming from the dwarf. "The same elf that killed my ancestor. And now I carry a cursed name."

"I thought you said you did not bear my father any ill will?" Tiryn said. His voice cracked. His throat was dry, but he dared not sip from the last of their water.

"I don't. If it had not been your father, it would have been someone else's. Nimel Halfhelm was a fool. He was born a fool, and he died a fool." Nunor stumbled wearily, catching himself before he fell to his knees. Tiryn offered Nunor a hand, and the dwarf took it and let himself be pulled to his feet again. "What happened then?"

"The Waypoint was opened and we got the women and children out. And then the King's Guards broke into the inner square, right where the Waypoint was." Another memory surfaced, and Tiryn could not shake it free. Bloody cobblestone and a pale, feminine arm and the sound of men yelling paused Tiryn's feet. "I lost friends in those next few moments. People I had known all my life."

"But …" Nunor started, stopping beside Tiryn and staring up at his face. His eyes were squinted so tightly that they may as well have been closed. "But you got most of them to safety, right?"

Tiryn nodded. "My father and I held them off long enough for everyone to get through the Waypoint. And then we were going to go through." Tiryn let out a dry chuckle. "I think we both realized it at the same time."

"What?"

"That if we both went through, there would be no one to close the gate. The King's Guards could just follow us through."

Nunor nodded. "So your father went."

"I didn't give him much choice in the matter. I hit him square in the chest with an arcane blast and knocked him through."

Nunor laughed wearily. "That doesn't surprise me in the slightest." He wiped sweat from his brow, using his long and unruly beard as a handkerchief. "And then?"

"The arcane blast damaged the Waypoint, but not enough to close it." Tiryn shook his head again, trying to sift through the resurfacing memories to find the ones that mattered. "I hit it again. And there were a couple of King's Guards trying to rush through it. I think one of them got caught in my arcane blast, because I saw his body later." Tiryn swallowed again. His throat was so dry, and there was no shade in sight. "I fainted. Arcane sickness."

Nunor made a sound of acknowledgment. It sounded hoarse and scratchy.

"And then ..." Tiryn hesitated. He couldn't share what happened next, not even to Nunor. He couldn't share the time he spent mourning, and the hours he spent burying his friends.

"And then Roland showed up?" Nunor supplied helpfully.

"That's right," Tiryn said. His voice was thick, and it wasn't entirely from the strain of speaking with such a dry throat.

"I've heard the rest of the story before." Nunor's breathing was heavy. "The second Waypoint that led to the Coven. What you found there."

Tiryn nodded, though he suspected that Roland, like himself, had not been able to share every detail of what had transpired within the halls of the Coven's home.

Nunor stumbled again, this time falling to his knees in the sand with a curse.

"Let's take a rest, Nunor. Just get our breath back for a moment."

"I'm fine," Nunor growled. "Just give me a hand up."

Tiryn did so, pulling Nunor to his feet once more. He stayed close to the dwarf, in case Nunor should fall again. "Your turn for talking. I don't have anything left in me to say." He lifted the water skin to his mouth, but pressed his lips tight together so that the water left inside only splashed across his mouth. He held the skin out for Nunor to take, and the dwarf drank greedily from it. "Will you finally tell me what Darlyth said to you that has us nearly killing ourselves in this desert?"

Nunor grumbled something under his breath.

"What was that?"

"I said you didn't have to come with me, you pointy-eared pain in my ass."

Tiryn smiled. "Of course I did. I would never let a dwarf think he was braver than an elf."

Nunor only rolled his eyes.

"What did Darlyth say?"

"He's dying."

Tiryn frowned. "I'm sorry. I know you care for him."

Nunor groaned and passed the water back to Tiryn. It was nearly empty. "I knew his passing would come eventually. The stubborn bastard is nearing a hundred now. That's a long life for a dwarf." Nunor shifted his ax on his hip and suddenly picked up speed, passing Tiryn with huffing breaths. "And Darmon would be a great king in his father's place, under different circumstances."

"But?" Tiryn asked, sensing the hesitation in the dwarf's words.

Nunor gave an exasperated sound. "You heard him yourself, Tiryn. He is too hungry for war, too eager for bloodshed." Nunor braced a hand against a sand dune as he clambered over the shifting earth. "I worry for Doldural's future, and what Darmon may bring to my people."

Tiryn ascended the dune in a couple of long strides. "So we find the Amulet of Earth before Darmon takes the throne. We're here in this cursed land for that reason. But a few days of rest and respite and, for Great Ones' sake, *planning* would not have made much difference one way or the other."

Nunor shook his head, letting out another guttural growl. "Darmon will not be swayed from war against Etritia just because the amulet has been returned. He will march the dwarfs against men for the violation of the treaties, and for the suffering Mothlenor has caused our people."

Tiryn stumbled in the sand, sending the dune crumbling as both he and Nunor slipped and rolled down the opposite side. His descent stopped at the foot of the disintegrating sand hill. Tiryn groaned, letting his head fall back into the sand. Nunor spluttered and grumbled inches from him.

"Then why am I here? I'm exhausted. I will never be able to get the sand from my clothes. And I'm sweating." Tiryn tried to sit up, but his body was too fatigued to respond properly. He groaned again, wiping sand and sweat from his face. "Elves do not sweat."

"Oh, quit your damned whining about a little perspiring." Nunor sat up and shook sand from his beard. "We're here now so I can find the amulet and bring it back to Darlyth and be named his heir."

Tiryn let out a dry chuckle. "You? King of the dwarfs?"

"Better me than Darmon."

Tiryn shook his head. It was getting hard to think clearly. "I thought your family name kept you from even joining any of the higher Orders, much less becoming *king*."

Nunor nodded. "Those with cursed names, like Halfhelm, are treated like the lowest families and Orders are treated. Which is to say, not too poorly. But not as well as our talents might otherwise grant us. But Darlyth will change my family name if I bring the Amulet of Earth to him."

"And then he would make you king?"

"I don't want to be king," Nunor said with another growl. "But if the options are war or taking the crown, then I'll take the damned crown." Nunor stood with a great deal of effort. "Get up, you pointy-eared shit." He held a hand out for Tiryn to take. Nunor's stature only gave him enough leverage to help Tiryn sit up, but his sturdy shoulder was enough for Tiryn to use for balance as he got to his feet. "You're getting weak, old man."

"I'm fine." But Tiryn's body was heavily fatigued. He could feel the weight of their long walk through the sands in his limbs, and he still had no idea if Nunor had any idea where they were going.

"You're not fine, Tiryn." Nunor once more shifted his ax on its belt and continued on. "But we're almost there."

"Almost where?" Tiryn searched the distance, but could see nothing but a haze of heat.

Nunor pointed at a dark stain on the horizon. "Your sharp eyes can't make that out, Tiryn?"

Tiryn shook his head, squinting at the shape Nunor had indicated. "There's nothing there. It's only a mirage."

"A mirage?" Nunor laughed, turning to face him. "That's no mirage. That's our salvation."

Tiryn took a step toward the black patch far off in the desert heat. His knees buckled, but not enough for him to fall. "What?"

"That's a tent. A big one. And it's no more than a mile

away." Nunor retreated to where Tiryn wobbled on his feet, bracing Tiryn's weight with his own stocky body. "Get your legs back under you." He wrapped one of Tiryn's limp arms around his shoulder and put his own arm around Tiryn's waist. "Salvation awaits."

35

NIEVE

The horses were tired, as was Nieve. She had been wondering for several hours if she had been right to insist on accompanying Syrani and the lewd and annoying arcanist on such a ridiculous errand. She cared for Syrani, of course. It was hard not to grow fond of someone that shared your home for so long, even if they tried to distance themselves. But Syrani had been gone for some time now, and Nieve was stuck wandering aimlessly through the Vyrisian woods with the arcanist.

Alastor let his horse meander under the trees and drummed his fingers against the pommel of his saddle. He sang, loudly and poorly.

"There once was a girl at the Cardyn fair,
With ruby lips and flaxen hair.
A smile and a kiss began our affair,
And then she knelt down low."

Nieve groaned. This was his fourth or fifth such song. Each one detailed some encounter with a woman and the explicit sexual aftermath of their chance meeting. Whether the songs were of real events or imagined ones Nieve neither knew nor cared.

"Please, for the love all the Great Ones gave us, stop singing." Nieve rubbed at her temples, holding the reins to her own horse loosely in her hand. "If I have to listen to another one of your stupid verses about getting sexual favors from attractive women, I might just have to kill you."

The arcanist laughed. "Come on, Nieve. I can't sing about it, I can't talk about it, I can't joke about it. I suppose you want to tell me not to even think about it."

Nieve closed her eyes briefly. "If by *it* you mean sex, then yes. That would be helpful." She rolled her head and shoulders, annoyed by the tension she felt in those muscles. "Most people can go a few hours or, dare I suggest it, a few days without thinking about *it*."

"I am not normal," Alastor said with a snort. "Haven't been for a few years now."

"Give it a try, would you?" Nieve said with forced politeness. "My sanity and, by extension, your life depend on it."

"Oh, fine." Alastor's face had a sour expression, but she was sure it was fake. "I'll keep my thoughts to myself."

"Thank you," she said with an exasperated sigh.

They continued in silence. The reins of Syrani's horse were fastened to the saddle of Nieve's horse, and the three animals walked slowly along a worn game trail with only a few gentle course corrections from their riders. Nieve had no way of knowing where the trail would lead, if it would lead them anywhere at all, but wandering through Vyris was a little better than waiting at the Azimarian side of the river that separated the two lands from one another. So she simply followed Alastor, who was following the trail, and said nothing at all.

"Nieve?" Alastor cast a quick glance over his shoulder at her.

"Yes, arcanist?"

"I … apologize, if I upset you." Alastor cleared his throat and straightened in his saddle. "It's just that I feel very comfortable around you. Like I don't have to pretend to be some uptight ass. I can be my very odd self."

Nieve laughed. "You feel comfortable around me? How many times have I threatened to kill you?"

Alastor turned again, giving her a sly smile. "And how many times have you made even the slightest thing to act on those threats?" He put his back to her again. "Admit it, you think I'm wonderful."

"I most certainly do not," Nieve protested. "In fact, I think you're vile and repugnant, and if I have to mortally wound you to prove it, then maybe I will."

"You're lying. I'm starting to grow on you."

"Like a disgusting lesion I have to cut away, perhaps."

Alastor stopped his horse, shifting his weight in the saddle so he could face her fully. "So I *am* growing on you." He gave her another smile, and his dark eyes flashed glee-fully. "Was it the songs?"

Nieve grimaced and shook her head. "Why are you like this? Can't you be civilized?"

Alastor shook his head, his smile unchanging. "Afraid not." He resumed their slow walk, clicking his tongue to get his horse moving again. "Have I told you the story of the first 'attractive woman' I encountered?"

"Great Ones spare me," Nieve muttered.

Alastor's head tilted as if he were thinking. "It was five, six years ago. My brother and I were searching for an uncle of ours, who had been a sailor on a merchant ship." Alastor waved his hand. "The who and how of it all are not impor-tant, but at one point …" Alastor paused, turning his head slightly to catch Nieve's reaction. "I ended up in a lake with a water nymph."

Nieve raised an eyebrow, but said nothing.

"As it turned out, that water nymph had killed our uncle and his entire crew. Seduced them until they willingly swam out into the depths of the lake. And then she drowned them."

"That's horrible." Nieve frowned, staring at Alastor's back. "I can't imagine what a death like that must be like."

"I don't have to try imagining it," Alastor said. His tone was even and relaxed as he spoke. "I lived it, very nearly to the end." This time, when Alastor turned to look at her, there was no smile on his face. Instead there was an oddly pained expression. "It was ecstasy. Every moment was pure bliss. And when I was pulled from the lake, spitting water and gasping for air, I tried to go back to her."

Nieve said nothing. She wasn't sure what could be said.

"I was in that strange time when one is neither a boy nor a man. And that moment, when the nymph put her arms around me and began to drag me down, ruined me. I have never been quite the same since." He laughed suddenly, a high and strained laughed that chilled Nieve. "Whether I'm trying to find that same bliss in other women, or trying to drown myself in sex, I can't really say. But I am not normal, and I am not civilized."

"Arca— Alastor," Nieve began. She swallowed, then started again. "Alastor, I'm sorry. I didn't mean—"

"Now that you know, do you think I'm a monster?" He asked the question lightly, keeping his gaze on the trail ahead of him. "I saw your face when you found Verelyn and I together the other morning."

Nieve hesitated, then asked, "Have you ever hurt a woman?"

Alastor shook his head. "No." He turned to look at her. "At least, never physically. And I try not to do anything to hurt them emotionally, either."

"Explain."

Alastor stopped his horse again, and Nieve did the same. There was an uncomfortable and pained look in his eyes, but his face remained neutral. "I don't … hunt for women. I only sleep with those who are interested. I take precautions against giving her children." He raised a hand, gesturing strongly. "And I'm never her first, I always make sure of that. And I never make promises to return."

Nieve considered for a moment, watching Alastor. Gone was the aloof arcanist that sang of lewd encounters. The man that waited patiently for her answer was ashamed and afraid of what she might say.

"You are not a monster." Nieve rocked her hips, urging her horse forward again. "You had a traumatic event in your life that changed how you interact with many people. You recognize it, and try not to let it harm those around you." She rolled her eyes at him as her horse drew level with his. "Frankly, I think you overestimate your deviation from the average human male." She passed him, taking the lead on the trail. "What I don't understand is why you felt the need to tell me."

"Because I want you to be able to trust me." Alastor laughed, and it sounded much more like his normal laugh. "Which I realize is probably the exact opposite of what you're likely feeling now."

"Honesty leads to trust." Nieve shrugged. "You may have just done the best thing to earn my trust. Time will tell."

"You think so?"

Nieve turned and gave him the prettiest smile she could muster. "Either that, or I'll grow tired enough of your disgusting songs that I finally kill you."

Alastor returned the smile. "Have you heard the one about the busty lass with the tight round—"

"Yes," Nieve said, interrupting him before he could finish the line. "That was the second one you sang. Please don't repeat it. That one was particularly distasteful."

Alastor chuckled, then was quiet for several seconds. "Nieve?"

"Yes?"

"Thank you."

Nieve tried and failed to stifle the smile that crossed her lips. "Don't thank me yet. I may still decide to kill you."

Whatever Alastor meant to say in return was lost as a large shadow crossed overhead. The green-hued air around them grew momentarily dark, and the deafening sound of rushing wind followed close behind. The horses whinnied and stopped, and Alastor and Nieve both searched the sky above.

"Only one dragon. They must not have found Halcia." Nieve struggled to hold both horses in check. "Syrani will be upset."

"No," Alastor said slowly. He squinted up at the sky, his head tilted. "No, I think that *was* Halcia."

"Then where is Melonya?"

There was a loud rustling in the trees overhead, and Nieve instinctively tossed the reins of her horse to Alastor and drew her bow. She came to her feet, planting both on the seat of the saddle and balancing on the shirking animal as she nocked an arrow and aimed for the commotion in the canopy overhead.

"Wait!" Alastor held a hand up, and Nieve hesitantly loosened her draw on the bowstring.

A figure slid down the trunk of a nearby tree and landed on the needle-covered forest floor with hardly a sound. Tathiel straightened, brushed his hands together and dusted a few errant pine needles from his tunic, then tilted his head to look up into the higher branches of the tree expectantly.

"Tathiel," Alastor said with a relaxed sigh. "As elegant and graceful as ever."

Tathiel held out a hand as another figure slid down the same trunk and came to a less than perfect stop at the bottom. Tathiel's hand was a steadying presence as Syrani found her balance and tousled needles from her hair.

"That was … less than pleasant," Syrani said. Her face was slightly flushed, Nieve noticed.

"How did you find us?" Alastor asked.

"And, if that was Halcia, then where is Melonya?" Nieve added. She replaced the arrow she had removed from the quiver on her saddle and dropped back into a seated position, catching the reins as Alastor tossed them to her.

"Halcia smelled the horses." Syrani answered Alastor's question first, crossing the short distance and pulling her horse's lead from a ring on the cantle of Nieve's saddle. "We found you before we even had the time to begin a proper search."

"Explains why you didn't give us a shout before dropping in," Alastor noted with a pointed nod towards the tree Tathiel and Syrani had descended from.

"Remind me not to go flying with Tathiel again," Syrani muttered under her breath to Nieve. "He's a bit of a madman when it comes to returning to the ground."

Nieve snorted, and was surprised to see that Syrani had a small smile as she mounted her horse.

"Melonya left for Larten. She's supposed to be meeting Eilonwy there tonight." Tathiel stepped closer as well, but remained on his own feet because there was no horse for him to ride.

"And Jaimes?" Alastor asked. "Will my brother be joining us?"

Tathiel shook his head. "I don't know. I hope so."

Syrani clicked her tongue and kicked her heels into her horse's sides, guiding the animal off the trail. "Halcia and I will guide us to my Homewood. I hope we can find some rest there before we head for the amulet."

"Halcia will help us, then?" Nieve asked, turning her horse to follow Syrani. "That's great news."

Syrani stiffened slightly, and it was Tathiel who answered. "Halcia is not sure where she stands on this quest of ours. She agreed to come into Vyris with us, but has yet to decide if she will go further."

Nieve stopped her horse once more. "Oh." She stared at Syrani's retreating back, stiff and straight.

She always holds herself like that when she's upset.

Nieve and Tathiel exchanged a glance as Tathiel crossed her horse's path and took up a leisurely pace off Syrani's flank. "I'm sure Halcia will make the best choice she can," Nieve said. "We'll find a way to the amulet, with or without her."

Alastor gestured silently for her to follow Syrani ahead of him, but Nieve shook her head. Alastor shrugged, then urged his mount forward. Nieve brought up the rear, keeping some distance between herself and Alastor. She tried to recall the tips the arcanist had given her when she had tried to reach out to Halcia. Alastor had said her thoughts were not channeled properly, whatever that meant.

Nieve closed her eyes, picturing the great golden dragon she wanted to reach out to. She could see Halcia's huge amber eyes, narrowed in anger as she argued with Syrani. Nieve focused on those eyes, set into a serpentine face scaled in varied hues of gold and yellow. And it was those eyes that she spoke to.

"Thank you for returning to Syrani. I can only hope you choose to stay with us. Please, forgive me for never treating you as a friend. I ... I want to fix that, if you'll let me."

Nieve opened her eyes once more. Her horse had stopped, no longer guided by its rider. And Alastor had also stopped, his own horse turned across the path so he could watch her. She gave him an annoyed sigh, flicking the reins and putting her horse into motion again. "I suppose I did it wrong again?"

Alastor smirked at her, shaking his head. "No, actually. I was going to say you did a much better job this time. I felt something passing from you, but I heard nothing."

Nieve lifted her chin as her horse maneuvered around his. "I told you I could figure it out myself," she said proudly.

This time, Halcia responded. There were no words to the message. What came to Nieve from the golden dragon was a blend of intense and conflicting emotions. For a few short seconds, Nieve felt the distress and anxiety and happiness that filled Halcia as she flew ahead of them. And then the emotions were gone.

Nieve nodded slightly, shifting her grip on the reins. "I understand," she muttered under her breath. "I'm sorry, Halcia."

MELONYA

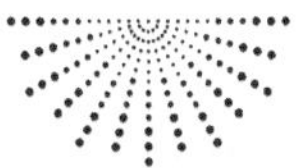

Melonya smelled Larten before she saw it. The air smelled of salt and the sea, even among the clouds. It was a refreshing scent that was becoming the smell that came to mind whenever she thought of home. The woods of northern Vyris smelled of cedar and pine, and that was where she had grown up. But the salty sting of sea air in her lungs and nostrils was what now felt more comforting. And beneath the smell of the ocean came the acrid tang of ale and human sweat and animals. That was how she knew Larten was close, though she could not yet find it through the cloud cover.

"Eilonwy?" She called for her companion, sensing their connection like a figure in the dark. She knew it was there, she just wasn't entirely sure where.

Eilonwy found her. *"Melonya! You're almost here?"*

Melonya altered course slightly, aiming for the direction Eilonwy's presence originated from. She folded one wing slightly, her silent glide on the air current turning into a curved descent. *"I will be soon. Larten is just coming into view."* Beneath her, dozens of miniature lights loomed out of the dark. They were little more than pinpricks, and a couple of them appeared to be moving.

"We'll meet you on the hill," Eilonwy said, and then their connection was dulled. Not broken, only set aside for the moment.

Melonya directed her attention to another presence in the dark. *"She said 'we.'"*

"Come again?" Jaimes asked.

"Eilonwy said that 'we' would be heading for the hill."

Jaimes was distracted; his thoughts were jumbled and hard to understand. *"Yes, we're leaving the inn now."*

We. He said it, too.

Melonya flexed the muscles of her shoulders, bringing her wings up and slowing her descent. *"Does that mean you're coming to see Eilonwy off, or that you're coming with us?"*

Jaimes paused. His mind settled, focusing on her. *"I'm coming with you. I don't want to leave Eilonwy."*

"Good." Melonya saw a light in the distance leave the walls of Larten behind. The figures holding the torch could not be made out, but Melonya was sure it was Eilonwy and Jaimes. *"I'm pleased to hear it."*

"You don't sound pleased."

Had he sensed it, then? The concern and fear she had felt? Of course he had. Jaimes had an uncanny ability to read her emotions better than anyone else.

"I am ... worried. About you." Melonya was honest. If she were anything but, Jaimes would see through it easily. *"But my worry should not keep you from joining us."*

"It won't." There was a hard and bitter edge to his words, and guilt colored Melonya's thoughts. Jaimes must have noticed, and his next words were softer. *"Your concern is touching. But I will be fine, with two lovely ladies like you and Eilonwy by my side."* His focus shifted briefly, and when his attention was once more on her, he quickly added, *"We'll be at the hill shortly. See you in a moment."*

Melonya aimed for a low-hanging cloud and flew into it, using it to hide her form from any who might be watching the night sky from below. The moon was a thin sliver high in the sky. There was not quite enough light to make her entirely visible. But a large shadow was frightening enough, and she did not need Larten to stink of fear as well as ale and animals.

She circled south, coming in low from the sea, and came to a gentle landing on the top of the hill that marked Larten's graveyard. It was set apart from the rest of the city, and the trees and fencing that surrounded it made for excellent cover. And no one dared go to the graveyard at night. No one except Eilonwy, Jaimes, and Mathius.

Mathius crested the top of the hill first, a torch in his upraised hand. Eilonwy and Jaimes were only a few steps behind him. Jaimes leaned surreptitiously on Eilonwy for support, and a witch light bobbed over his opposite shoulder to guide him.

Mathius dropped the torch into a sconce staked into the ground just beyond the closest ring of burial cairns. "Melonya, you beautiful creature. I am happy to see you, and sad that you will take my best employee and my longest tenant with you when you go."

"*Mathius, my favorite former sea captain,*" Melonya began. She spoke so that all close by could hear her—she had never been able to get Mathius to understand how to communicate directly to her. "*I still can't forgive you for making Eilonwy work in that den of drunkards you call an inn.*"

"He couldn't have stopped me if he wanted to, Melonya. You know that." Eilonwy had dropped whatever human disguise she had been wearing, and Melonya was mildly surprised to see a silver ornament adorning her hair. It pulled her light hair away from the left side of her face, making her scar prominent and easy to spot.

Melonya felt a trickle of pride at the sight of her

companion wearing her old wounds with confidence. *Like a warrior,* she thought.

Jaimes and Eilonwy exchanged a glance, apparently both having sensed her emotions and the reason for them. If Eilonwy blushed, Melonya could not see it in the darkness.

"I was not fond of the idea, myself. Teach a new pint slinger during one of the busiest weeks of the season? But she learned so quickly, and those *drunkards* loved her!"

"Pint slinger?"

"Pint slinger, draft tosser, beer maid, whatever you want to call her." Mathius yawned loudly, rubbing his face with his palms. "She was an excellent one."

"Are we keeping you from your bed, Mathius?" Jaimes asked. His arm was around Eilonwy's waist, and Melonya was sure it wasn't entirely for her support.

"I'm getting tired in my old age, Jaimes."

"And fat," Melonya added with a pointed nod at the slight belly the innkeeper was beginning to grow.

"It will happen to all of you eventually. Except perhaps Eilonwy." Mathius shook his head, looking between Melonya and the couple standing behind him. "Damned elves and your eternal beauty."

"Go on, Mathius. Get back to the inn. We'll see you soon." Eilonwy gave Mathius an easy smile. "And be sure to tell that old fool with the eyepatch that he still owes me for losing in Mills."

Mathius laughed. "He'll claim handicap, on account of the patch."

Eilonwy put a hand on her hip, her weight shifting defensively. "You and I both know that patch is just for show. Did he think we wouldn't realize when he came back from the privy with it covering the wrong eye?"

Mathius laughed harder. "Don't worry, I'll warn him you're still out for gold."

"Keep an eye on my study, will you?" Jaimes asked. "Everything is packed away, but—"

"Yeah, I'll peek my head in every once in a while to make sure it's all still standing." Mathius waved Jaimes's concern away and approached Melonya. "Give an old fat man a hug, would you?"

Melonya obliged as best she could, surprised Mathius wanted to embrace her. She draped her long neck over his shoulder and let him wrap his arms around her. He smelled of bread and ale and roasted lamb. It made a faint hunger stir in her belly.

"Take care of them, will ya? All of them, I mean," Mathius whispered. "Bring them all home to me. I'm counting on you."

Melonya couldn't answer, not without Eilonwy and Jaimes hearing her as well. But she flexed her neck, drawing Mathius a few inches closer, then released him. Mathius dropped his arms and gave her a sly wink. Melonya returned the wink, though it felt unnatural to do so.

"Come on, you two," Mathius said, gesturing for Jaimes and Eilonwy to approach. "Jaimes, you can get that arm off her, I'm not taking Eilonwy back with me."

Jaimes immediately dropped his arm from Eilonwy's waist as Mathius embraced them both in a tight hug. He kissed each of them on the temple and tousled Jaimes's long hair. "Take care, you two. I know you'll be fine, so long as you stick together. Tell your brothers I said hello."

Jaimes nodded, and Eilonwy muttered a soft acknowledgment.

Mathius separated from them and pulled the torch from its sconce. "I'll be off, then. Don't forget your way back, now."

They watched him descend the hill until he was out of sight.

"Well, come on. This saddle pinches when it's empty, you know."

Melonya settled down on her haunches, and Eilonwy used the bend of Melonya's back leg to boost herself into the rear seat of the double saddle.

"Give us a minute, Melonya. This is Jaimes's first time riding in this contraption of Tathiel's." Eilonwy reached out a hand, and Jaimes used Melonya's front elbow and the supporting grip from Eilonwy to clamber into the front seat. He did it with a good deal of speed and apparently little pain from his leg.

"Jaimes, did you finish your research?"

"No. But Eilonwy helped me make a suitable alternative. The effects will not last, unfortunately, but for now I'm fairly pain free." Jaimes was shifting his weight experimentally in the seat, and Melonya curled her neck to see him clutching a bag tightly to his chest.

"What's in the bag?"

"More of the cream." Jaimes rearranged the bag's weight. "Among other things."

Melonya eyed the bag. There was something strange in the bag's contents. *"One of those things wouldn't happen to be a fire spirit, would it?"*

"It would. Her name is Vash, and she's joining us on this adventure of ours."

"The more we have, the merrier we'll be," Eilonwy said, settling back and giving Jaimes a tap on the shoulder. "Hold on right there, the little metal bar."

Jaimes grabbed the bar with both hands, his knuckles instantly going white. "I know you and Tathiel do this all the time, but this is safe for humans, right?" He gave Melonya an imploring and pleading look.

"Safe for humans, fire spirits, and anyone or anything else that climbs onto my back."

Eilonwy gave Jaimes another tap on the shoulder. "I've got you from back here, and Melonya will never let you fall. Unless you want to."

Jaimes's face paled. "Why would I want—"

Melonya turned and took two large and lumbering steps into the wind before leaping into the air.

Jaimes cursed and pulled back on the bar, stretching Melonya's shoulders back.

"Eilonwy ..." Melonya said to her companion, struggling to bring her wings wide enough to hold her weight as she ascended.

"Jaimes, don't pull! Just hold!" Eilonwy shouted into the wind.

Jaimes must have heard her because his pull on the bar loosened. Melonya continued their climb up, her wings unhindered.

What would Jaimes be doing with a fire spirit? Not that she truly cared. He had surely been lonely; she could not blame him for befriending an elemental.

And what about his leg? Could he keep up with the rest of them, if it came to it? Could he fight, if he had to? How would Eilonwy react if he were to be injured? Or worse, killed?

"I'll be fine," Jaimes said to her.

She had hurt him. She could hear it in his voice.

"I'm sorry. But Mothlenor will not make gathering the remaining amulets an easy task. I'm sure he has something planned for the last two, even if we beat him to the Amulet of Fire."

"But you don't seem concerned about any of the others, Melonya. Just me."

Melonya hesitated, then opened her thoughts deeper to him. Buried beneath the immediate concerns for Jaimes's safety were fears of losing one of her companions, or of seeing one of her friends die. *"That's not true at all."*

Jaimes sifted through the fears she kept hidden away. Imagined visions of Tathiel staring up at her with vacant, dead eyes. Eilonwy with a second wound to her head that would not stop bleeding. And Jaimes himself, dying from a sword wound he was not fast enough to avoid.

"I worry about all of you."

"I'm sorry," Jaimes said in a soft tone. *"But I will no longer stay behind."*

37

SYRANI

Syrani hesitated at the edge of the tree line. If the woods behind her were filled with tall elms and firs, then the woods before her held trees that were impossibly vast. Their trunks were smooth and pale and large enough around that her entire party could not form a ring around a single tree. The bark was unblemished and unknotted, and the lowest branch could not be reached with even the most practiced leap. The roots of the trees twisted along the ground. In some places, roots from neighboring trees wound around one another and became one before disappearing beneath the earth again. And all around them the air smelled of magic.

"Syrani?"

Syrani turned over her shoulder and her horse stamped a foot irritably beneath her. They were all staring at her. The arcanist's face was dull and uninterested, while Tathiel's face was entirely blank. Only Nieve showed any concern or worry.

"Syrani, do you want to go around? Find another Homewood to rest in?" Nieve asked.

"No." Syrani turned to face the imposing trees again.

"There isn't another Homewood for several days, and this is the one that is closest to the amulet."

"If you need another moment—" Tathiel began, but Syrani nudged her horse forward before he could finish the thought.

They passed beneath the shadows of the nearest trees, taking their horses two abreast. Tathiel walked on foot beside Syrani, his eyes on the wide trail ahead of them.

No one said a word. Even the birds seemed quiet, though Syrani heard an occasional trill and saw a flash of brightly colored wings. One such bird hopped along the trail beside them for several feet, its head tilting and turning as it examined them with interest.

A Sunset Starling, Syrani mused, noting the orange chest and dark purple feathers along the back and wings. *I haven't seen one in years.*

The starling gave a short trill punctuated with a chirp, then flew off and disappeared into the trees.

"We are being watched," Tathiel said in a low voice. "I spotted movement a hundred feet or so off the trail."

Syrani nodded. "I'm surprised you saw them. The starling was their scout." Syrani rolled her shoulders and relaxed in the saddle. "They will present themselves soon enough. Just proceed as if you hadn't noticed them."

Tathiel made no indication that he had heard her, and his head remained fixed in a forward position.

The elves watching them stepped onto the trail only a moment later. There were ten of them, each with an ornate bow ready and aimed at the four of them. Syrani halted, giving Nieve a warning look before she could pull her own weapon. But Nieve remained still, her chin lifted and shoulders squared. Syrani gave Alastor a similar look, and the arcanist pushed the right sleeve of his tunic up to the elbow and raised his arms in surrender. Tathiel crossed his arms over his chest, his feet hip width apart, keeping his hands away from the blades on his belt and the bow on his back.

"Well met, kinsmen," Syrani said in Vyrisian. She examined the elves around them, recognizing several of their faces. Nearly half were female, and they all wore light leather armor and carried Vyrisian blades on their hips. "I see we have grown skeptical of even our own kind since I was last home."

"You travel with a human," the one directly ahead of them said. He was a tall elf, with dark hair and a dark scowl. "I'm sure you can forgive us for our concern, kinswoman."

"I have a Mark, if you would care to inspect it," Alastor said. His Vyrisian was good. Nieve had complained about his pronunciation at great length. But Syrani disagreed.

He speaks it better than his father ever did.

At the mention of a Mark, an elf stepped forward and took Alastor's right arm in hand. Syrani saw the exchange out of the corner of her eye, but kept her focus almost entirely on the elf that had spoken.

"Is that you, Alduin?" Syrani asked, and an elf to her right stiffened. "You have grown very well these last few years. I remember you as a little child, and now you've begun to mature nicely. I bet your father is very proud of you."

"Syrani ..." the elf in front of her said quietly.

"And you, Paneth?" This time, a female elf to her left instinctively lowered her bow. "Has your brother beaten my marksman record yet?"

Paneth laughed. "Not yet. But who could, cousin?"

"Syrani." The elf's tone was a warning now.

"You recognize me. Yet you block my path and point weapons at my companions and me."

"You travel with a human. And these elves are not from our Homewood."

Syrani gestured to Alastor. "You recognize him, too, do you not?"

The elf hesitated, his bow arm quavering slightly. "I see the resemblance, yes."

"Then you know this *human* is the son of my sworn brother." Syrani gestured wildly at Alastor, her frustration mounting. "He is Marked. And not by me. He is as dangerous to you as Hasani was."

The elf sighed, but did not drop his bow. Some of his followers had, though, and Syrani took that as a sign that they would eventually be granted passage.

"This," Syrani motioned next towards Nieve, who had stepped closer and now waited with her horse an arm's distance from Syrani's right knee. "This is Nieve. Her family took me in when no other family would. She is the first and closest friend I have had since leaving this Homewood." She extended a hand towards Tathiel, who bowed as she introduced him. "This is Tathiel. His Homewood is to the north. You may know him better as one of the twin Riders of the dragon Melonya, who found the lost Amulet of Water."

"Then that was your dragon we saw?" another elf asked. This one Syrani did not recognize, and his features suggested he was Azimarian, not Vyrisian.

"No," Tathiel said. There was an odd look to his face, and it took Syrani a moment to realize that he was enjoying this encounter. "Melonya is with my sister."

"Then who—?"

"I am the dragon's Rider, Cariel," Syrani said. "And I am asking for passage."

Cariel finally lowered his bow. "Why did you come back, Syrani? Your mother wept for weeks after you left. And now you walk back in here like you've been gone a few days and not a few years." Cariel stepped off to the side of the trail, and the elves with him followed his example. "Think of what you're doing to her before you get her hopes up, Syrani."

Syrani led the way through the outskirts of her Homewood, guiding her horse slowly over the winding path. Cariel followed behind, but his entourage disappeared into the trees as silently as they had appeared. Syrani was sure they were off to tell others of the Homewood about the riders that were heading their way, and about the news of a second dragon.

It was strange, being home again. Everywhere Syrani looked, everything looked exactly as she had anticipated, and yet nothing like she had thought it would. She had only been away for a few years, but she had expected the place to be different somehow. It was nearly the same as it had been when she left it, though there were a few faces she did not recognize as they neared the center of the Homewood. The strangers were Azimarian elves, for the most part, though a few Vyrisians were dotted through the scattered numbers. Word had evidently reached the ears of many who called the Homewood theirs that a group of travelers had arrived. Syrani caught many of the elves staring as she led the party closer to her Hometree. When the elves spotted Alastor, many scowled and muttered in low tones to one another. Others watched as he passed with confusion evident on their faces. Still others recognized Syrani right away, and she waved at a few old friends, too anxious to exchange any words of greeting.

When a young dark-skinned elf emerged from a Hometree and rushed at Tathiel, assorted shouts went up to stop the child. But Tathiel laughed and held his arms out to embrace the youngling.

"Gabber!" Tathiel exclaimed. "It's good to see you, too." Tathiel gave the young elf a tight embrace. "Where is Gilaine? Did she come here with you?"

"I'm here, Tathiel." A she-elf emerged from the same Hometree the young one had come from. She was tall and severe looking, and she wore a black leather band around her upper arm. Syrani made an involuntary shudder when she noticed that the women's ears had been carelessly cut off.

Her embrace with Tathiel was more dignified. They grasped arms just below the elbow for a brief moment, then separated. "We were welcomed here, and my husband was given a place to be buried. This will be our home for as long as we are permitted to stay."

"Syrani?" The third and final elf to emerge from the Hometree was another female. She was older than the first, with darker hair and softer, kinder features. And Syrani knew her very well.

Syrani dropped from her horse's saddle and offered the reins to Tathiel. "I see you're still giving shelter to those who come in need of it." Syrani could not meet her mother's eyes, but could not find a suitable place to rest her gaze either.

"Syrani …" Her mother embraced her. "I thought I would never see you again."

"I didn't intend for you to."

She nodded. "I know." She gestured towards the Hometree—Syrani's Hometree. "Let's discuss this over tea. I hope your friends will join us." Her mother released her, and Syrani's mixed emotions of longing and discomfort faded as her mother stepped away. Her mother reached instead for Alastor. "You must be a son of Hasani." The smile she gave the arcanist was warm and welcoming. "It's as clear as the starlit sky on a summer night. Did Syrani tell you that your father lived with us for over a decade?"

"She did. She also said that was why she didn't knock me over the head and leave me for dead when she had the chance." Alastor smirked, giving Syrani's mother's hand a gentle shake paired with a dignified bow of the head.

Her mother tsked. "That does not sound like the Syrani I raised."

"Mother," Syrani said. "Please. Just let the past go unmentioned."

Her mother ignored her. "But I also didn't raise a daughter that would steal her brother's belongings and run away from home, either. That must have come from her father's side, Imis bless him."

The mention of both her father and Hasani broke her already stressed restraint, and she snapped angrily. "Mother, enough. We haven't even wiped the dust of the road from our clothes, and you've already brought up things I would rather leave forgotten." Syrani brushed a few stray strands of hair from her face. She wanted to bathe. She wanted to sleep and to try to mend what had become broken between her and Halcia. She sighed, wishing that there were far fewer spectators around to witness. "May we take a few moments to rest, and explain why we have come to your Homewood?"

Her mother raised an eyebrow. "*My* Homewood. Not *our*."

Syrani was silent. Beside her, Nieve dismounted, giving Syrani a cautious and concerned glance.

Syrani's mother nodded curtly. "Very well. Rest, of course." She waved toward a pair of Vyrisian males. "Have their horses stabled with my other guests', and see that their belongings are brought to my Hometree. I will accept responsibility for these visitors."

"Responsibility?" Nieve asked. "Are we a concern?"

"Anyone who does not call this Homewood theirs is a concern to us these days." Syrani's mother motioned towards the Hometree, which still waited with its trunk twisted open for admittance. "Please, make yourselves feel welcome."

Tathiel and the two elves he seemed familiar with took the lead, and Tathiel bowed respectfully to her mother as he passed. Alastor offered her mother his arm, which she took with a soft comment on his knowledge of the Vyrisian language.

"Syrani?" Nieve waited for her to follow, but Syrani could not urge her feet to move.

"Go on without me. I want to stretch my legs a little."

"Would you like company?"

"No." Syrani shook her head. "No, I want to be alone for a while."

Nieve pursed her lips together, but did not argue.

"I'll be back shortly, I promise. I just need …" *What do I need?*

"Go on. We'll be waiting for you." Nieve gave Syrani's shoulder a gentle touch, then followed Alastor and the others into the Hometree.

Syrani took a deep, slow breath, squared her shoulders, and began walking.

No one stopped her as she passed through the heart of the Homewood. She walked briskly, and the one or two old friends that waited for a chance to approach remained where they were. They knew where she was going.

Syrani made it to the outskirts of the Homewood uninterrupted and found what she wanted within a few moments. She sat in the dirt, crossing her legs and resting her hands on her knees.

"You've grown, Father," she said to the tree before her. It was much larger than it had been when she had left her Homewood, but it still had many, many years before it could be a Hometree.

How long does it take for the tree to completely consume the body it was placed in? Is my father still there, or is the tree all that is left of him?

Syrani was silent for a moment, staring at the smooth white bark of the tree. A trail of ants was climbing up the tree, and Syrani watched their march with disinterest. "So many things have happened since I left. The egg hatched. The one you meant to destroy. Halcia is supposed to be my companion, but …"

Syrani sighed, closing her eyes and bowing her head. "I've done everything wrong, haven't I?"

The tree did not answer.

"If you were here, you would tell me that my mistakes are a part of my growth. That nothing is permanently damaged. Mistakes can always be mended, if only partially." She opened her eyes again. "I just hope you're right."

She sat in the quiet peace of the growing Hometree for some time. Syrani sensed a peaceful warmth emanating from the trees around her, each of them a burial tree much like the one that she addressed. Whether she imagined the welcoming atmosphere or not, she didn't much care. It was still better than returning to the Hometree and facing her mother.

She heard Alastor approaching before he spoke. The noise was no doubt intentional, and she waited until he was sitting beside her to acknowledge his presence.

"Arcanist."

"Syrani," Alastor replied in a voice that was just as dry and unemotional as hers. "Your mother said you would be here. She made a comment about revisiting the past on your own terms or something."

Syrani scoffed.

"This is your father's burial tree?" Alastor asked.

Syrani nodded. "It is."

"And … this is your way of immersing yourself into your old life? Starting with the dead, and working towards the living?"

Syrani scowled at him. "You have no idea what you're talking about."

Alastor shrugged. "Then enlighten me. Why come to this place first? Why not start with your mother? She seems to have missed you a great deal. Or even begin with some of the friends you left behind?"

"I'll get around to them eventually. But this is where I

need to be right now." Syrani adjusted her position, pulling her knees to her chest and wrapping her arms around them. "My father would understand how difficult it was to return."

"Why did you leave at all?"

Syrani shook her head. "I don't know."

It was a lie. She knew exactly why. And being here, in front of her father's burial tree, only reminded her of her reason.

Alastor said nothing, and she kept their comfortable silence for a long moment. Then she pointed to a nearby burial tree. It was much smaller than her father's, but she was surprised to see that it was flourishing. "That is your father's burial tree."

Alastor straightened. "I'm shocked it's doing so well."

Syrani raised an eyebrow. "So am I. It's not unheard of for a human to be given a burial tree, but they usually do not survive the first year."

Alastor moved closer to the second tree, brushing a hand against the bark. "What does it mean, that his tree is still growing?"

Syrani shrugged. "That he had a strong soul, I suppose."

Alastor nodded absently. "My mother would have agreed with that."

Syrani hesitated, watching as Alastor stared reverently at his father's burial tree. "Vyrisians believe that as long as the tree is alive, the soul that is bound to it can hear you when you speak to it."

"Is that right?" Alastor sat back on his heels, cupping his chin in one palm and inspecting the tree.

Syrani stood. "Would you like some time alone here?"

Alastor turned to give her a quizzical look.

She raised an eyebrow again. "You and your father have a lot to talk about."

Alastor thought for a moment, his brows pinching together, then nodded. "I think I would. Thank you, Syrani."

Syrani bowed her head slightly and turned to depart. But she did not leave without a gentle touch against Hasani's tree, followed by a similar brushing of her fingertips against her father's.

"Syrani."

"I am here, Halcia," Syrani answered. She could hear Alastor speaking in a low voice behind her, and she tuned his words out so as to not overhear. *"Are you in the Homewood yet?"*

Syrani heard a chorus of laughter and loud chatter, and she knew the answer to her question before Halcia confirmed it.

"I am surrounded by elves, and they will not stop touching me," Halcia grumbled.

"Try not to show too many teeth. These people are friendly, and it would be best to keep it that way."

Halcia's displeasure was nearly palpable. *"Then please tell them to stop petting me like I'm some sort of docile dog."*

Syrani sighed, quickening her pace. She found Halcia in the center of the Homewood, where the trees were less dense. There was enough room for her maneuver around, but not enough for her to walk for than a step or two in any direction. Halcia was surrounded by a tight ring of onlookers, but none were closer than an arm's length away. None except Nieve, who stood between the Vyrisians and Halcia with her arms stretched wide.

"Please, that's enough touching!" Nieve cried.

"The beast nearly bit that boy's arm off!" an older elf cried. He gestured towards the young dark-skinned elf Tathiel had called Gabber. Gabber, for his part, seemed unbothered by any potential harm that may have come to him. He stared at Halcia with wide eyes and a slackened mouth.

"She doesn't spend much time around others," Nieve explained. "You frightened her, that's all."

"They did not *frighten me,"* Halcia protested.

If Nieve heard her, she made no indication.

"Is it dangerous to have a dragon here in the city?" another elf asked. "Is it feral?"

"If Halcia was feral," Syrani said loudly, drawing the attention of many of the gathered crowd, "do you think she would have let any of you lay a hand on her?"

"Are you responsible for this animal?" the first elf asked. He glared back and forth between Halcia and Syrani with an anger that surprised Syrani. He was Azimarian. His less prominent ears and slightly rounded facial features made his expression look nearly human.

"I am, but I would refrain from referring to her as an animal again."

As if on cue, Halcia let out a low rumble of displeasure.

The elf glowered deeper. "You should train her better, young lady. She snapped at that boy."

"Halcia?"

Halcia couldn't hide her shame. *"It wasn't at him, precisely. He has something on his wrist that let off some sort of strange energy. It startled me. I snapped at it, not at him."*

Syrani frowned. "If Halcia meant to hurt the boy, she would have. It was a warning, nothing more. Now please, disperse. She has traveled a great distance, and she needs rest."

The crowd dissipated reluctantly and with much muttering. The outspoken Azimarian made a point of proclaiming loudly that feral beasts should not be permitted within the city, no matter how fascinating they might be.

Syrani motioned towards the boy. "You, come here."

The boy approached. As he drew nearer, Syrani could see where his ears had been cut away. It made her stomach turn.

"Tathiel called you Gabber, right?"

The boy nodded.

"Are you alright? She didn't hurt you, did she?"

"Of course I didn't," Halcia said indignantly.

"Hush, Halcia," Syrani said, giving the dragon a sideways glance. Nieve stood close by, eying the departing elves.

Syrani turned back to Gabber. "Are you alright?"

Gabber nodded again.

Syrani held out a hand. "May I see your arm?"

The boy held out an arm. His tunic was heavily worn, and there were old stains that were undoubtedly blood. Under the cuff of the tunic was a metal bangle. Syrani tapped it with a finger, and was unsurprised when it reacted to her touch with a flare of arcane energy.

Gabber stared at the bracelet uncomfortably. Syrani held out her other hand, and Gabber obediently placed his other arm in her palm. A matching bangle circled the other wrist as well.

"What are these?"

The boy hesitated, then tapped his mouth with the tips of his fingers and shook his head.

"I … don't understand," Syrani said. "You don't know what they are?"

"He doesn't speak, Lady Syrani." The female elf that Tathiel embraced earlier approached. She held her arms out, showing a matching set of bracelets on her own wrists. "They are arcane cuffs. They prevent us from using magic. We were captured by slave traders."

"And the slave traders? They were the ones that cut off your ears?" Syrani asked. She fought the urge to touch the tips of her own ears.

The elf nodded. "They also took Gabber's tongue. We have been developing a way for him to communicate with us, but not many of the elves here take the time to bother with it."

"I'm sorry to hear it," Syrani said slowly. "Where are the slavers now?"

"Dead," the elf said flatly. "Tathiel and Eilonwy killed

them and helped us escape." She interlaced her fingers, and Syrani had the distinct impression that she was fighting the urge to ball her hands into fists. "My only regret is that they died quickly."

"And the cuffs?" Nieve asked. She stood beside Gabber, staring at the metal cuffs with an ill look.

"Nothing can be done about them."

Syrani took a deep breath. "You have suffered a lot."

The elf shrugged. "I was always far more deadly with a blade than I ever was with magic. I will survive." She sighed, motioning towards Syrani's old Hometree. "Your mother has prepared a small meal. And your old room has been set up for you to sleep in."

"I'm not hungry," Syrani said quickly. In fact, she was very hungry. But the thought of sitting for a meal with her mother was too daunting to consider.

What was it that Alastor said? I was immersing myself into my old life by starting with the dead? I am not yet ready to face the living.

The elf bowed. "Your mother was hoping to spend some time with you this evening, but I can tell her that you need rest before anything else."

Syrani grimaced. "She's probably waiting right inside the barrier to welcome me home."

The elf said nothing, but a small smile crept over her face.

"I'll come along shortly," Syrani said. "But I have no intention of dining tonight."

The elf bowed again, then motioned for Gabber. "Come on, then. Tathiel will be waiting for you. You promised to teach him how to curse in your new language."

Syrani waited until they were out of earshot, then turned to Nieve. "Do me a favor, would you?"

Nieve nodded. "Of course."

"Distract my mother so I can get to bed without her pestering me."

There was a knock at the door to her bedroom, and Syrani hurriedly wiped a few tears from her face. "Who is it?"

"It's me," Nieve answered softly from the far side of the door. "May I come in?"

"Sure," Syrani muttered.

Nieve slipped inside, only opening the door hip width before quietly shutting it again. She was barefoot and wearing a sleeveless top that barely reached her mid-thigh. "Your mother is still downstairs, waiting for you to come inside."

Syrani groaned.

"Dinner was hardly over before she made me strip and bathe, and she took all my clothes to wash. All of them! Even what I had in my bag." Nieve crossed the room on soft footsteps. "She just left me this ridiculous … thing to wear."

"It's normal bed attire in Vyris," Syrani murmured. "I'm wearing the same thing."

"Well, I'm not Vyrisian. Give me pants or give me nothing. Not this ridiculous nonsense."

"You are part Vyrisian, aren't you?" Syrani watched in confusion as Nieve climbed into bed and curled under the bedding. "What are you doing?"

"My room is on the other end of the house. I'm sleeping with you tonight. Do you know what Alastor would say if he saw me in this?"

Her hair was still damp, and Syrani could smell soap on her skin. "Do you know what he would say if he found us in bed together?"

"Something crude, no doubt." She pulled the bedding to her chin. "Is this real down?"

Syrani shrugged. "I think so."

"Well I guess it's safe to assume you didn't leave Vyris because of a lack of amenities."

Syrani fell back into her pillows. "Goodnight, Nieve," she grumbled.

Nieve was quiet for only a moment before speaking again. "Do you want to talk?"

"About what?" Syrani asked.

"What has you crying alone in the dark, perhaps?"

"I am *not* crying."

Nieve turned to her side and propped her head up on one hand. "But you were. I may not know you as well as some of those elves we saw out in the Homewood today, but I know when you're upset." Nieve shrugged a shoulder. "Do you want to talk?"

Syrani groaned. "No, I do not want to talk. I want to be left alone to sleep."

"The road here has been a long one, hasn't it?" Nieve yawned but did not lie down again. "But if I were returning to my Homewood after fleeing with a dragon's egg I stole from my dead brother, I think I would have a lot to keep me awake at night."

"Nieve, you don't know anything about this. Leave it alone."

"And if my friend noticed that I was hurting, and she offered to listen to the thoughts that were torturing me, I might share them. If only to make sure I got a good night's rest."

Syrani rolled over to her side, putting her back to Nieve. "You and I are not much alike, Nieve."

"Alastor says you went to see your father's burial tree."

"Alastor needs to learn how to keep his tongue in check."

Nieve chuckled at that. "I don't disagree."

Syrani chewed on the inside of her cheek for a moment, then blurted out, "I don't know why I thought it was a good idea to come back here."

"Because it's the closest Homewood to the amulet. And because going around it would add a lot of time to our journey," Nieve reminded her.

"It's not only that."

"Then what is it?"

"I thought …" Syrani sighed. "Never mind."

"You thought?" Nieve pressed, leaning closer.

Syrani could feel hot tears threatening to fall. "I thought I was ready to be forgiven. But I'm not."

"Forgiven?" Nieve asked. "For what? Stealing Halcia's egg?"

Syrani shook her head. "I didn't steal the egg. Hasani gave it to me. He told me that he and my father were going to try to destroy it."

"Before they died?"

"Yes," Syrani breathed. She sniffed, and Nieve put an arm over her waist. "Hasani gave it to me because he knew I could get back to the Homewood before the demons that were chasing us caught up. He wanted me to finish what they had planned to do."

"You mean he wanted you to destroy the egg?"

Syrani nodded.

"But you didn't, clearly."

Syrani looked at Nieve over her shoulder. "I tried to destroy the egg countless times. Nothing I did worked. I smashed it with hammers, stabbed and cut at it, and threw enough energy to bring the entire Homewood down at it. Nothing left a single mark."

Nieve's brow furrowed. "Then why did you leave? You tried to do as they wanted, but it couldn't be done. That's not your fault."

"I knew," Syrani said slowly, "that if the egg remained in my Homewood, Mothlenor would keep coming to look for it. I had already lost my brother and father. Who else would I lose if he found our Homewood?"

"So you left to protect your Homewood."

Syrani's shoulders shook as she wept into the covers.

"Syrani, calm down." Nieve held her tighter. "You did what you had to. There's no shame in that."

"I left my Homewood to take the egg back to Mothlenor." Syrani choked. "I was going to give it back to him, on the condition that he leave Vyris alone." She took a ragged breath. "The only thing that stopped me was Halcia hatching from the egg."

Nieve was silent, and Syrani took several steadying breaths. "When I saw that helpless little creature, I knew I couldn't let him have her. But I was willing to trade the thing that Hasani lost his memory and lost his life to get. I was going to let my father's and brother's deaths go to waste. *That* is what I need forgiveness for, Nieve."

Nieve squeezed her gently. "No matter what your intentions might have been, you never made it to Etritia. Have you ever considered that Halcia would never have hatched if you had not left Vyris?"

Syrani nodded. "I have, but I can't be sure it makes a difference. And what of our relationship?"

"What about it?"

"Halcia and I are not as close as we should be. I've seen Melonya and Tathiel together, and their bond is much stronger than ours."

Nieve rested her chin on Syrani's arm. "You've already said it's because you two spent so long on opposite sides of an arcane shield. You never had the time to connect properly. But that can still be fixed."

Syrani wiped more tears from her face. "What if it can't?"

Nieve relaxed into the bed again, but her arm remained draped over Syrani's waist. She yawned. "Why couldn't it?"

"What if Halcia knows, deep down, that I tried to kill her?"

38

ISHTA

Ishta sat at the table closest to the rear exit and positioned herself so that she could see the main entrance to the tavern. The place was small, poorly lit, and very loud, all of which suited her just fine. She didn't remove her hood until she was sure no one would pay any attention to a single woman drinking quietly alone. She would have stood out in most other places, but here the tables were full of boisterous men spilling ale and loosely dressed women laughing loudly and often, and she didn't think anyone would notice her.

And then a barmaid dropped a heavy mug on the table in front of her, causing Ishta to jump, and her thoughts of going unnoticed were quickly shattered.

"Sorry, darling. Didn't mean to startle," the woman said with an easy grin. "Ale fine enough?"

"That's fine, yes. And something to eat, if you don't mind."

"Any preference?"

Ishta shrugged. "Whatever I can get down the fastest. I don't plan on lingering."

The woman nodded. "No problem. But the matron would skin my ass if I didn't tell you we've still got a few rooms left, if you change your mind." She smiled again, nodding towards a plump and severe-looking woman standing behind the counter and filling mugs.

Ishta nodded her thanks. "I understand, but no thank you."

The woman winked cheerily, wiping ale from her hands with a fold of her skirt. "Just a moment, then."

Ishta drank greedily from the mug. It was difficult enough in Etritia to come by ale that wasn't more water than alcohol, but this was rich and heavy and perfect.

"Trying to go for a swim in it, darling?" the woman asked with a chuckle.

Ishta swallowed a large gulp of the amber liquid and wiped foam from the corner of her mouth as the barmaid dropped an assortment of plates in front of her. "Sorry?"

"You're drinking that down awfully quick," the woman remarked, nodding towards the mug. "You need another?"

"In a moment, perhaps," Ishta replied, eying the dishes. There was bread spread with a generous pad of butter, a wedge of soft cheese, and a cluster of fat grapes that made Ishta's mouth water. "The road is long and dusty."

The barmaid laughed. "Ale is good for parched throats. I'll be back with another mug for you."

Ishta could hardly wait until the woman's back was turned before pulling a handful of grapes from their vine and shoving them into her mouth. They burst with the slightest pressure, and a sweetness Ishta had not tasted in years flooded her mouth. She spat the seeds indelicately into the palm of her hand and discarded them, reaching next for the bread. It was soft and sweetly scented, and Ishta savored the feel of fresh bread in her hands for a moment. Bread was more common in Etritia than grapes and ale, but to have such a fresh loaf all for herself was uncommon. And butter was unheard of for anyone but Mothlenor and Anna.

Ishta chewed slowly, savoring the meal. She added cheese to the bread, smashing it into a sort of sandwich. It may have looked unappealing, but it tasted divine. The grapes she pulled off one by one and eat each with deliberate care.

This will surely be an expensive meal, Ishta thought as she emptied her mug. But it was too perfect to fret over the price for more than a moment.

"Here you are." The woman dropped a second mug in front of Ishta. "Anything else you need from me?"

Ishta swapped her empty mug for the full one and pulled it close. "Just some information, if you don't mind."

"Oh?" The barmaid raised an eyebrow. "I'm not in the business of spreading rumors, but I could find you someone who might be."

"No, no." Ishta held out a hand to stop the woman before she could call for anyone else. "Not that kind of information." Ishta held her mug to her mouth but didn't yet drink. "I'm looking for someone. To help me with a problem."

The barmaid's eyebrow lifted higher. "What kind of problem?"

"It's a kind of family problem," Ishta said, giving the woman what she hoped was a convincingly fearful look. "The kind that could get an unwed girl into a lot of trouble if her family found out."

The barmaid straightened. "Ah."

Ishta clutched at the woman's arm. "Is there anyone here that could help? I've been searching and searching, but I haven't heard a word of any herbalist or witch woman or—"

The woman hissed in a sharp intake of breath at Ishta's words. "We haven't got anyone like that here, you understand?"

"I understand, but—"

Across the room, a pair of men roared in laughter and slammed their mugs together. The woman jumped at the sound, her face paling. "You see those two over there? They're King's Guards. If they heard talk like that, you wouldn't be the only one they carried out in chains."

One of the men at the table shifted in his chair, reaching for a passing woman and pulling her across his lap. Ishta spotted the white embroidered patch stitched to his leather vest.

"They're not wearing armor," Ishta remarked.

"I think it's time you went on your way." The woman turned to go, taking Ishta's empty mug with her. "Great Ones care for you, darling."

"You don't know where I could find someone—"

"We have no one like that here," she insisted.

Ishta sighed. "How much do I owe you?"

"Forget the money. Just get out," the woman said in a hushed tone. "And don't speak of things like that again."

The woman left, bustling around the few tables that separated them from the counter, then leaned in close to the matron's ear and spoke several words. The matron's eyes settled first on Ishta, then on the two King's Guards at the nearby table.

Ishta took several quick swallows of the second mug of ale and rose to her feet. She dropped a single gold coin on the table and slipped through the back exit as quick as she could. It led to a small covered pen with a few fat hogs and a dozen chickens.

Ishta stepped through the muck and over the low fence that separated the pen from the alley that ran behind the pub. It was dark, but she could see torches at the mouth of the alley.

"Great job, Ishta," she muttered to herself. "Haven't heard a damned word on where to go yet, and you ruin your first decent meal by opening your stupid mouth."

"You there!" a woman's voice called.

Ishta froze, touching the knife on her belt.

"I'm talking to you," the woman called.

Ishta turned slowly. The tavern's matron stood in the alley with her arms crossed over her chest. She was taller and broader than she had seemed inside, but Ishta sense no malice from her.

"I heard you had a question that needed answering."

"Do you have an answer?" Ishta asked slowly.

It would be silly to hope …

"Go east," the matron said. "There's a house on the outskirts of a small village a few days from here. You might find what you need there."

"Thank you," Ishta said.

"Anyone foolish enough to ask questions like that in a public space doesn't need to be in the kind of condition you're in. I'm doing everyone in Azimar a favor, I think." The matron held something up for Ishta to see. "Take this."

Something small and shiny flipped through the air, and Ishta caught it easily. She held it up to inspect, surprised to see that it was a gold coin.

"You'll need it more than me. I've heard her prices can be steep."

ALASTOR

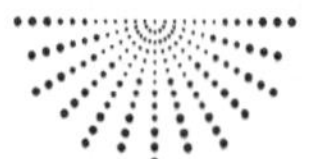

His pants were still gone when Alastor awoke. Gabber had woken him with a series of annoying taps to his forehead, right between his eyebrows.

"What?" Alastor mumbled, staring blearily at the young elf.

Gabber made a motion that looked like he was putting food to his open mouth, then gave Alastor a quizzical look.

"Morning already?"

Gabber nodded, then repeated the motion.

Alastor sat up and placed his bare feet on the floor. He hated going barefoot. It felt unnatural. "I suppose I could eat. Has our host finished with my clothing?"

Gabber made a chortling sound, the only noise Alastor had heard from him. It was quite a good one, and conveyed nearly as much sarcasm as actual words might have.

Alastor sighed. "She could have at least warned me before stealing all of my clothing. I'm not usually one to go around with everything swinging with every step."

Gabber grimaced and shook his head.

"Go on." Alastor waved him away. "I'll be out in a moment."

When Alastor finally roused enough courage to leave his guest quarters and follow the scent of richly cooked food, he immediately met Tathiel in the hall outside. Tathiel wore the same thigh-length shirt as he did, though he seemed far more relaxed as he fell into step beside Alastor.

"You seem … comfortable," Alastor remarked, giving the elf a nod.

"You forget that I am Vyrisian. This is normal attire for me. Though I don't typically wear it so late in the day."

"Can you tell me why all of my clothing has disappeared?" Alastor asked. He pulled lightly at the fabric as it rode up his thighs, threatening to expose parts of him that he would rather Tathiel not see.

"Vyrisians value cleanliness."

Alastor waited, but when it became clear that Tathiel would provide no further explanation, he pressed further. "And? When can I expect to be properly dressed again?"

Tathiel gave him a mischievous smile. "You'll have your pants back soon enough."

Syrani's mother, Lethas, was already in the dining room when they entered, as was Gabber, though Gilaine was thankfully not present. And sitting very close to each other on a long dining cushion were two more friendly faces.

"Jaimes! I'm glad you decided to join us." Alastor approached his brother and carefully arranged himself in the spot at Jaimes's side. There were no proper chairs to sit on, only a motley assortment of ornate blankets and cushions arranged on very low stools. They surrounded a round table that rested only a few inches from the floor and spun in a slow circle. Alastor spotted what looked like a huge mound of fresh rolls smeared with some sort of fruit glaze and waited for it to near his grasp. Tathiel promptly sat beside his sister, giving her a brief kiss on her forehead. "When did you two get in?"

"Only a couple of hours ago," Jaimes said, taking the

topmost roll for himself. "Just long enough to bathe and get a short rest."

Alastor gave his brother a quick look over. His hair had been trimmed, but not cut, and the haggard look he'd had to his eyes when Alastor had last seen him was gone. And he also wore the damned Vyrisian shirt. "I see you've also been ransacked by the clothing thief?" Alastor said, casting a playful wink over to Lethas, who quirked a smile in return.

"I like it," Jaimes said, surprising Alastor. "It's very comfortable. But you'll forgive me for not standing up to greet you."

"It's a little more customary for couples to wear them to bed together, but given the circumstances …" Eilonwy let the statement falter, selecting a slice of an odd-looking fruit Alastor did not recognize and offering it to Jaimes. "Though I suppose you and I didn't exactly go against tradition, either."

Jaimes went faintly red in his cheeks and neck as he took the chunk of fruit from Eilonwy and ate it. "I suppose we didn't," he said around a mouthful of food.

Alastor smiled, reaching for a roll as it at last spun close enough for him to reach. *Good for you, Jaimes. It's about time you put your head on properly.*

"You must be Eilonwy and Jaimes," Syrani's voice said from behind him.

Their attention immediately went to her, and she nodded at each of the newcomers. Nieve stood beside her, and she scrutinized Jaimes. "You're the arcanist's brother?" Nieve asked. When Jaimes nodded, mouth too full to speak, Nieve shrugged. "The resemblance is hard to see. You don't look nearly as impetuous and foolish as your brother."

Alastor sighed. "It's a long story, but we're not actually related. But I'm sure Jaimes takes your comment as a compliment."

Jaimes swallowed and choked out a laugh. "Oh, I do, believe me."

"This is Nieve, my friend," Syrani said, gesturing towards the Azimarian elf. "You can forgive her for her crudeness or not, she doesn't seem to care either way." Syrani bowed, bending her arms so that she could touch the fingers of each hand lightly against the opposite shoulder. "I am Syrani, companion to Halcia, who you surely saw outside."

Eilonwy returned the gesture, coming to her knees to do so. After an embarrassed glance between both elf women, Jaimes gave Syrani a wave of the hand still holding a small piece of sugared roll and muttered a hello.

"And how is it that the two of you are wearing clothes?" Alastor asked, interrupting the greeting ritual.

"It's because Syrani slipped in without me noticing," Lethas commented. "And I'm assuming Nieve has borrowed something from my daughter, because Gilaine is only just returning your belongings to where they should be."

Nieve shrugged. "Those little dresses are ridiculous. Just look at Alastor."

"They are traditional Vyrisian attire," Syrani said forcefully. "If you had grown up wearing them, they wouldn't look quite so … *ridiculous*, as you put it."

"Please, Syrani, have a seat and eat something," her mother insisted, motioning at a vacant spot beside her.

"There isn't time. We should continue on our journey."

Alastor snorted, grabbing at what looked like a pastry ball. "You haven't even told us where it is we're going."

"Into the mountains," Syrani answered.

"I gathered as much," Alastor said, pulling the puff pastry open to inspect the inside. It was filled with minced fruit and some sort of thick sauce that smelled wonderful. "You seemed to know exactly where to go as soon as you heard that poem of Areanath's. But you haven't told us where the amulet is or how you know you've got the location right."

"Syrani," her mother began. "Take a few moments to explain, then you can be on your way."

"You explain, mother. You've been aching to tell stories of the past." Syrani crossed her arms, glaring at the table instead of at her mother.

"It is not my story to tell. I wasn't there. But you and your father—"

"I don't want to talk about my father!"

Syrani's outburst stilled everything in the room but the table, which continued its slow circle. Alastor found himself wondering whether it was powered through mechanical or arcane mechanisms, then shook his head and cursed himself for his idle thoughts.

Syrani and her mother both sighed, then Syrani sat beside Alastor, letting Nieve take the final spot beside their host.

Lethas did an excellent job of hiding the pained expression that crossed her face, but Alastor noticed it before it disappeared. "Syrani and her father saw the Amulet of Fire when it first appeared on the mountain. As I said, I was not present, but my husband told me about the experience afterwards." She paused, pouring a glass of amber liquid from a jug that had come her way. "They were out hunting. It was one of the many things they always did together, ever since Syrani could hold a bow." She smiled briefly, and Syrani grimaced.

Alastor pulled the closest plate and offered it to Syrani. She said nothing, but took some of whatever was presented. Alastor didn't even bother to check what it was.

"They were on their way back with an elk or a deer or some sort of—"

"It was a boar," Syrani corrected, not looking up at her mother. "We caught a boar."

"A boar, then," Lethas said. "They were on their way back to the Homewood with this boar, when they felt an immense surge of arcane energy. When they looked up, they saw a streak of light soar across the sky. It lit up the clouds like a small sun, my husband told me. It was daytime, but they could easily track the way it moved overhead. And then it landed in the mountains, at the top of a peak we've always called the Starlit Summit."

"The Starlit Summit?" Nieve said. "It sounds lovely."

"The view from the top is wonderful," Syrani's mother said. "You can see the whole valley below. You can see the entirety of our Homewood. And at night, the stars sometimes line up like they're touching the peak."

"Have you been to the Starlit Summit before, Syrani?" Alastor asked.

"No."

Lethas shook her head. "When the star landed at that mountain, it hit with such a tremendous force that it destroyed the peak. It's nearly flat now. And the Homewood agreed not to allow anyone to climb the summit again."

Alastor looked from Syrani to her mother. "But we can go, correct?"

Syrani's mother laughed. "I doubt anyone would try to stop a group with two dragons in their number."

"May we go now?" Syrani asked in annoyance. "Your questions have been answered. The streak we saw that day was clearly the Amulet of Fire, the 'mislaid star' your poem spoke of."

Alastor nodded. "I don't think we need to linger much longer."

Syrani jumped to her feet. "Then there's no time like now."

Alastor laughed. "Most of us could use a few minutes to get dressed properly, if you don't mind."

Syrani glanced about the table, apparently realizing she and Nieve were the only ones prepared to depart. "Then I'll help you. Let's go."

Alastor blinked. "I'm sorry? Help me with what?"

Lethas stood, motioning for Gabber to do the same. The young elf had been sitting so quietly that Alastor had all but forgotten he was there. "My daughter is looking for a way to continue to avoid me. Humor her, Alastor. Please."

Alastor managed to stand without embarrassing himself too much, and Syrani followed him at an uncomfortably close distance as he made his way back to the room their host had loaned him for the night.

"I should have known she would have housed you here," Syrani said, surveying the room.

Alastor grabbed the first pair of pants he found in the neatly folded pile that lay on the bed and quickly stepped into them. "Why is that?"

"Your father stayed in this room."

Alastor paused with the waist of his pants still around his thighs. "Did he?"

Should it feel strange, knowing I've shared a room with a parent I never knew? Because it doesn't.

Syrani touched the end of the bed, her fingers hardly making a dent in the soft covers. "I spent many nights in here with him." She turned toward him, and Alastor twisted his hips away with a low curse as he tied his bottoms around his waist. "Talking. No more. We stayed up talking on a regular basis."

"About what?" Alastor grabbed his boots and a pair of wool stockings and sat on the edge of the bed. He was sure this particular pair, a mottled green set that happened to be his favorite, had been thinning at the heel. But they looked nearly new now, with no sign of age. The color even looked more vibrant, and the ties that held them tight around his ankles were less frayed. "I can't imagine you being one to lie under the stars and chat about your hopes and dreams."

"That's exactly what we did."

Alastor chuckled, but when he looked up at Syrani, her face was faintly red.

"He was a brother to me. I felt loved and safe in his presence." Syrani let out a shaky breath. "And I miss him."

Please don't start crying. I never know what to do when someone cries.

Alastor set his booted feet on the floor and rested his elbows on his knees. "My mother missed him a great deal, too. She told me stories about him when I was growing up. It was never quite enough to make me feel like I knew him, though. Maybe you and I could talk about him sometime, if you wanted. Try to remember him better." He gestured over his shoulder. "Hand me that tunic, would you?"

Alastor tugged the wretched Vyrisian shirt over his head and found Syrani waiting with his own in her hand. He nodded his thanks and stood.

"Hasani had a small scar," Syrani began, touching a spot on Alastor's chest between his right shoulder and his collarbone. "Do you know how he got it?"

Alastor shook his head. "No, my mother never mentioned it."

"He never remembered either."

Alastor slipped his arms through the sleeves of the tunic. It felt softer than he remembered. *Just what did those women do?*

"What did my father remember?"

Syrani frowned. "Almost nothing. His name was about all he ever regained, and even that took a few months."

"But you knew he had a family?"

"He wore a wedding band," Syrani said. "He couldn't remember anything about his wife, or where she might be. I think he believed she had been killed by the same demons that almost killed him."

Alastor shook his head, straightening the top around his hips. "She died from an illness when I was first reaching adulthood." He grabbed his sword belt and his cloak. "Let's go, the others are probably waiting for us."

Tathiel was waiting for them, but Eilonwy and Jaimes were nowhere to be seen.

"Where are they?" Alastor asked, not even bothering to clarify who he meant.

Tathiel motioned further down the hall with a jerk of his chin. "Down there. By the sound of things, they have no intention of being ready soon."

Alastor rolled his eyes. He heard nothing, but Tathiel had better ears than he did.

"And you're just going to stand here and wait?"

Tathiel shrugged.

Alastor stormed down the hall, pausing just beside the open door. Now he could clearly hear what Tathiel had alluded to.

Normally, he would be inclined to give his brother a pat on the back and a carefully chosen joke, but Syrani's anxiousness had infected him. Alastor reached a hand inside the doorway, aiming blindly, and sent a quick jolt of arcane energy towards the sounds.

There was a yelp from Jaimes, and a curse from Eilonwy.

"Now isn't the time for that, Jaimes. Get your asses outside. We have an amulet to track down, remember?"

There was scrambling from within the room and a string of profanities from both halves of the couple, but Alastor ignored it and returned to Tathiel.

"I think they'll be ready to go shortly."

Nieve met them outside the Hometree with Gilaine and Gabber. "Lethas was kind enough to pack up the rest of our meal for us to enjoy on the road." She held up a strange-looking basket with a concave bottom. "She insisted that the fruit dumplings be eaten warm."

Syrani sighed. "Pack it on my horse. We'll eat her damned dumplings however we can manage."

Alastor followed Syrani around the Hometree and into the heart of the Homewood. Halcia was still where she had been the night before, though now she was joined by Melonya in the crowded space. The two dragons lay side by side, their long bodies pressed against each other. And they were both purring in steady rhythm.

"Halcia, we are preparing to depart. Have you had enough rest?" Syrani asked, approaching the golden dragon and giving her shoulder a gentle rub.

"I'm not going."

"What?"

"I agreed to come to Vyris, but I never said I would go after the Amulet of Fire with you." Halcia's purring stopped, and after a brief moment Melonya's did as well. *"I will be here when you return, I can promise you that. But I will not go into the mountains with you."*

"I have tried to persuade her into changing her mind," Melonya said. *"But she is adamant that she will remain here."*

Syrani's brows knitted together and she scowled. "Fine. We will see you again when we return with the amulet in hand, Halcia. I hope you can be prepared to leave the Homewood as soon as we arrive." Syrani checked the straps around Melonya's belly that held the double saddle taught. "I have no intention of staying another night here."

"Syrani ..." Halcia said softly.

Syrani silenced her with a raised hand. "No. You're right, Halcia. You said you would come this far. I should be grateful for that."

Alastor felt a firm hand on his shoulder, and Tathiel spoke quietly in his ear. "Go with her, Alastor. She's been distressed ever since we entered this Homewood. Be a friend to her, like your father was."

Alastor grimaced, watching Syrani climb nimbly into the saddle on Melonya's back and strap herself in. "I don't know what she wants to hear from me. Besides, Melonya is your —"

"Melonya will be fine without Eilonwy or myself for a time." Tathiel's hand on Alastor's shoulder squeezed briefly. "Just be a friend for her, Alastor. That's what she needs."

"Are you coming, arcanist?" Syrani asked, staring at him. "Or perhaps I should call for Nieve to join me?"

Alastor shook his head. "I'm coming." He fastened his sword belt around his hips as he crossed in front of Halcia towards Melonya.

Halcia let out a hot breath of air through her nostrils, blowing up dirt and leaves around Alastor's feet. Alastor paused, giving Halcia a sideways look.

"Take care of her."

Alastor made no sign that he had heard the threat in Halcia's words, but he gave her the smallest of nods before accepting Syrani's hand up into Melonya's saddle.

As he fastened the leather belts that would keep him in his seat, Alastor marveled at how fast the morning had moved. He'd not even been able to finish his pastry ball.

Trissa had finally fallen asleep, her small fist curled against Anna's chest. The roar they had heard terrified them both, and Trissa had refused to sleep in her own bed. Anna was content to hold her close, knowing what had made that horrible noise. She stroked Trissa's hair, trying to stay awake and alert.

The door to the hall opened with a bang, causing Anna and Trissa both to jump.

"Trissa?" Mothlenor's voice called from the front room.

"Mother?"

"Hush," Anna whispered. "You remember what I said to do."

Trissa nodded and slipped from Anna's bed just as the door to Trissa's room opened with a force that shook the walls. Trissa dropped to her front and crawled under the bed as quickly as her small limbs would let her.

"Where are you, Trissa?"

Anna got to her feet, standing between the door and the bed.

When Mothlenor opened the last door, it was with a gentle push. Somehow that gentleness was more menacing than the crashing that had come before. "Where is she, Anna?"

"What do you want with her?" Anna asked. "You have your dragon wraith. We heard it hours ago."

Mothlenor scowled. "The wraith alone is not enough to stop those criminals. I need Trissa's Gift to track them down."

"And if she doesn't want to help you?"

"She has no choice in the matter," Mothlenor answered coolly.

Anna lifted her chin, staring him in his hawkish eyes. "She's your daughter, Mothlenor. You can't treat her—"

Mothlenor slapped her hard across the face. She had expected something of the sort, but it still knocked her to the ground. Anna caught Trissa's frightened gaze looking out from beneath the raised frame of the bed and quickly turned away before Mothlenor could notice.

He leaned over her, one hand pinching her chin between his thumb and forefinger. His hand was bandaged, and the rough cloth scraped against her skin as he tilted her face up to meet his eyes again. "I am your king, Anna," he said in a slow and even voice. "You really must remember to address me as such."

Anna jerked her chin from his grasp. "You can't treat your daughter like a slave."

Mothlenor's head tilted and one thick eyebrow rose. "I would never dream of it." He straightened, offering a hand to Anna. "But she will help me. Or her mother will be killed."

Anna ignored the offered hand and sat against the bed. "You wouldn't kill me. Not after everything I've done for you."

She knew it was a foolish thing to believe, and Mothlenor's cruel smile only further solidified the thought. "You know I would, Anna."

There was scuffling from under the bed, and Trissa appeared on the far side. "Please, don't hurt her."

Anna kept her gaze locked on Mothlenor but addressed Trissa. "You don't have to help him."

"Ignore her, Trissa. Come with me." Mothlenor also addressed Trissa without breaking eye contact from Anna. "Help your father make Azimar the country it was destined to be."

"Will you leave my mother alone?" Trissa asked in a soft voice.

Anna stood, pushing Mothlenor away from her. He didn't budge in the slightest, and when she tried to hurry around to Trissa's side, he grabbed her around the waist and held her to him. "Your mother will not be harmed, so long as you continue to assist me."

Trissa's face was puffy, her eyes swollen. Her face contorted as she tried to hold back more tears.

Anna shook her head. "Don't do it, Trissa. Remember the promise you made me."

Trissa sobbed, balling her hands and rubbing her eyes. "I'll help. Just leave her alone."

Mothlenor released Anna, and she rushed to Trissa's side, falling to her knees beside her daughter.

"Where can I find the men that are following my brother's quest?"

Trissa closed her eyes, and Anna pulled her close. "You don't have to tell him anything."

"I am waiting," Mothlenor said in a calm voice.

"I'm trying," Trissa said, squeezing her eyes more tightly.

A strange sensation brushed against Anna's skin like a draft of cool air that left a tingle on her arms and neck. Trissa instantly relaxed, her shoulders drooping slightly.

Anna turned to Mothlenor, but he made no indication that he had noticed anything strange.

"You don't have to say anything," Anna whispered to Trissa. "Or lie, if you feel you have to answer."

"Answer me, Trissa. Or your mother will—"

"She has never tried actively using her Gift, Mothlenor," Anna shouted over her shoulder. "It will take time for her to learn to control it." Anna stood, placing Trissa behind her. "You may never get the answers you want in time."

"They are scattered throughout the known world," Trissa said in a voice that was not entirely her own. Anna turned in surprise to see Trissa staring across the room at Mothlenor, her eyes bright and alert. "To the south, in the desert, are two who seek the Amulet of Earth. In Vyris are several who seek the Amulet of Fire. And one man will be waiting in a tavern for his destiny to find him, though he has not reached this meeting place yet."

Mothlenor straightened, lifting his chin. "In which of those parties is the man known as Ajax?"

"Ajax, now known as Roland, is the one that will be waiting for his fate to arrive."

Mothlenor mused for a moment, then addressed Trissa again. "Which of these three groups is the closest to finding another amulet?"

Trissa tilted her head. "Those in Vyris are on their way to collect the Amulet of Fire as we speak." Her eyebrow raised, and she suddenly looked several years older despite the childish chubbiness to her cheeks. "You will not reach them in time to stop them."

Mothlenor scowled. "We'll see about that." He held a hand out. "Come, Trissa. It seems we have much work to do."

Trissa blinked, and the aged look to her eyes faded. She stepped towards Mothlenor, then stopped again, hesitating. "What about Mother?"

"Trissa stays with me." Anna put a protective arm around her daughter, once more pushing Trissa behind her. "I'm her mother. I know how to take care of her."

"Trissa will come with me," Mothlenor said in his danger-ously soft voice.

"I'll go," Trissa said. "As long as you leave my mother alone."

"It will be as you ask, my daughter." Mothlenor extended his hand a few more inches, and Trissa stepped around Anna to take it.

"No, don't!" Anna reached for Trissa, but it was too late. In the time it took for Anna to blink, Trissa and Mothlenor were both gone. Whether he had vanished them away to his tower or had simply used his ability to bend time to make a hasty retreat with her daughter in hand, Anna couldn't guess. But there was a sharp tang of spent arcane energy in the air, and Trissa was gone.

Anna ran for the door, hoping against hope that it would be unlocked.

It wasn't.

She tried the handle, pulling and pushing on the door with all her might. But it would not budge.

"Trissa!" she screamed through the wooden door.

There was no sound in the hall beyond.

"Trissa!"

She pounded on the heavy wood, beating it with first an open hand and then with fists.

"Please, bring her back!"

There was no answer from the castle beyond.

41

JAIMES

They built a small camp at the foothills of the mountains. The flattened top of the Starlit Summit was easily seen until they reached the edge of the valley, then it all but disappeared. Melonya assured them that she was leading them correctly, and Jaimes did not mind the slow and steady pace they rode at, even if Eilonwy spent much of the journey at the head of the caravan, listening to her dragon companion as she guided them through the woods.

Nieve, however, was less pleased with the speed they traveled. She grumbled at every indecisive split in the path. She grumbled as they reached the mountain and saw the full scale of the journey ahead. And she grumbled loudest of all when Eilonwy announced that they should stop for a rest, because there was no way up on foot and it would take time for Melonya to find a suitable place to leave her riders and return down the mountain to ferry the rest of them up.

"Are you sure there isn't another way up?" Nieve asked, scowling up at the mountains.

These were not the gently rolling tree-covered hills that could be found in Azimar. These were sheer cliffs of stone.

382

Jaimes felt his palms sweating just looking at them and anticipating the thought of having to scale the terrain.

"Not unless you're keen on climbing up," Eilonwy said with a shrug. "Which wouldn't be an issue, if not for …" Eilonwy stopped, her cheeks flushing slightly as she gave Jaimes an embarrassed look.

"If not for me," Jaimes finished. "It's alright to admit it. Even without a twisted leg, I don't think I could make that climb."

Nieve bit into a yellow and green fruit Jaimes did not recognize and chewed thoughtfully. She grimaced, then spat the entire mouthful onto the ground.

"You're supposed to remove the skin," Tathiel said, scoring another of the same fruit and peeling away the brightly colored skin to expose pale white meat beneath. He passed it to Nieve. "Try it now. Mind the pit."

"Why are there so many foods that I don't recognize in Vyris? The climate isn't too different from much of Azimar," James noted.

"Because Vyrisians use magic to grow crops that would not normally do well in this area," Eilonwy explained, still staring up at the faraway peaks. "We used to trade with Etritia, but when Areanath became king he halted many of our trade agreements. It was in an effort to placate his brother's concerns of reliance on other species. That was many decades ago. I doubt even your parents ever had the chance to try some of what can be found here."

"Those of us in Azimar do much of the same. Though I suppose we only deal with more native crops." Nieve bit into the fruit, wiping juice from her chin and giving Tathiel an appreciative look as she chewed. "My mother used to cook a dish that used something very similar to this."

"I think I've found an easy climb up," Eilonwy said, blindly gesturing for Nieve to join her.

Nieve stood at her side, cupping a hand under her

partially eaten fruit to catch the juice that dripped from it. "Show me."

"If we start there," Eilonwy said, pointing to a spot on her left, "we can double back up this way …"

Jaimes let her words drift away. There was no way he could keep up, not once the climb became a vertical one. He reached into the bag at his feet, pulling out the spelled jar Eilonwy had made for Vash. She was still inside, and appeared to be sleeping, curled around the top of the candle stub and looking like little more than a puddle of inky fog. "Vash, are you alright?"

Her tiny body stirred. "I'm fine, Jaimes. Just getting a bit of rest."

Jaimes's brows furrowed. "Are you tired?"

Vash stretched and once more curled up around the wick of the candle. "That she-elf that made a fuss about cleaning your belongings doted on me quite a lot. It's been a long time since I've eaten as well as I did earlier. And now I just need a long nap."

Jaimes chuckled. Apparently he and Nieve weren't the only ones enjoying their host's meals. "Let me know when you're awake again, and I can catch you up on what we've found out."

Vash made a tired and dismissive sound, and Jaimes tucked her jar back into his bag. Vash and her small glass home were the only contents of the small shoulder sack, and Jaimes wrapped the bag around itself to make sure there was enough darkness for Vash to sleep by. And to give the glass a bit of padding, though Eilonwy had promised that her spell would keep it from breaking even under most extreme circumstances.

"May I join you?" Tathiel stood beside him, giving Jaimes and the bag both a curious look.

"Sure," Jaimes replied, tucking his bag between his knees. "I was just checking on something."

"The fire spirit," Tathiel said with a nod. "Eilonwy told me about her."

Jaimes cast a glance over his shoulder, noticing that he and Tathiel were the only two present. "Where did Eilonwy go? And that grumpy friend of Syrani's?"

Tathiel sat, his legs crossed and back straight. "They're scouting out a path up the mountain."

Jaimes sighed. "I won't be able to make the climb, Tathiel."

Tathiel nodded. "I know. And Eilonwy knows. But Nieve seemed eager to move forward. I don't think she's comfortable with the idea of being apart from Syrani." Tathiel brushed dirt from his clothing in slow, careful movements. "If they find a promising path, they'll return and we can decide if we want to split up and start making the climb."

"It would make it easier on Melonya if she only had to make one more trip down the mountain instead of two."

"It would."

There was a quiet moment, and Jaimes got the distinct impression that Tathiel was trying to approach a topic he did not want to discuss.

Jaimes sighed, wondering if he should have known that a moment like this would come. "What's on your mind, Tathiel?"

Tathiel frowned, staring at the dirt that still clung to his clothing. "Have you ever been told why twins are so special in Vyris?"

"Because they're rare."

Tathiel shrugged. "They are rare, but that's not the entirety of it."

"Go on," Jaimes said, curious where Tathiel would lead the conversation.

"Vyrisians believe that twins share their souls. Each couple, when they conceive a child, produces a single new soul that will grow to experience life. And if the birth results in twins, those two children share that new soul."

"Alright," Jaimes said. "You can make two bodies, two minds, two hearts, but—"

"But only one soul," Tathiel said, nodding.

"So you and Eilonwy share a soul?" Jaimes asked.

Tathiel shrugged. "If our beliefs are correct. But there have been a few things that make me wonder if it might be true after all."

"Melonya hatched for both of you," Jaimes supplied. "I asked her before which of you was her real companion, and she could only say that you both were."

"Melonya is the easiest example. But the Amulet of Water was found in two pieces, as well. As if it knew that the soul that would carry it was split between two people."

"Interesting." Jaimes grimaced. "A little strange if you think too hard on it, but interesting all the same."

"Vyrisians also believe that when a couple is formed, their souls combine and eventually become one."

"Ah." Jaimes straightened. "I think I know what you're trying to say."

"Do you?" Tathiel laughed lightheartedly. "Because I'm not sure that I do, so any advice would be helpful."

Jaimes snorted, and then both of them fell into an uneasy silence.

"Are you … worried about Eilwony and me?" Jaimes asked.

"No." Tathiel's reply was quick and confident. "I worry about what will happen to my sister after you are gone, but …" Tathiel gave Jaimes a reassuring smile. "But I trust my sister's judgment, and I like you very much, Jaimes."

"Thank you. I feel a lot better."

Tathiel frowned. "Why?"

"In Azimar, when a brother comes to have a nice chat with his sister's lover it usually involves threats of bodily harm." Jaimes shrugged. "Or so I've been led to believe, anyway."

Tathiel laughed again. "I don't think I need to do that for Eilonwy. She's more than capable of inflicting bodily harm all on her own if she needs to." Tathiel twisted, giving Jaimes his full attention. "But I do have one request."

Jaimes felt a sudden uneasiness. "Alright."

"If something happens to me, I want you to take the Amulet of Water and carry it."

"What?" Jaimes recoiled slightly, casting a glance down to the shapeless lump that was covered by Tathiel's tunic. "W-why me? Why not give it to Eilonwy?"

Tathiel sighed. "If I die, the part of my soul that is in me will die as well. It will not go to Eilonwy."

"So?"

"So, I worry that my sister cannot carry the full burden of the Amulet of Water with only half a soul." Tathiel gave him a pleading look. "But if you took it, the one who will eventually grow to share a soul with Eilonwy as I do now, she will be alright without me."

"Tathiel, you don't even know if this whole soul business is actually true. And you want to base the future of the amulet on that?"

"Does it matter?"

"It matters to me!" Jaimes said. He tried to stand, but his leg flared painfully and he fell back into a sitting position. Tathiel caught him, making his descent easier and less painful than it could have been. "Tathiel, what if you're wrong?"

"If I am wrong about the ways our two souls are connected, then so be it. But I am not wrong about you, Jaimes." Tathiel pointed to Jaimes's right forearm. "We both know what your Mark says. And I know that I trust you." Tathiel gave him another look, this one more desperate than pleading. "Will you accept my request?"

"Yeah, I'll accept it." Jaimes sighed, shaking his head.

There was the sound of stones clattering together, and

both Tathiel and Jaimes turned to see Eilonwy making her way back down the path she had pointed out to Nieve. They stood, Tathiel giving Jaimes an arm to lean on, and waited for her to reach the ground again. It only took her a moment, and Jaimes was astonished by the speed with which she moved.

How can I ever keep up with her?

"The path is a good one," Eilonwy said as she approached, brushing her hands together. "Nieve is still up there."

"How quickly do you think we could reach the top if we followed it?" Tathiel asked.

Eilonwy's nose scrunched as she thought. "An hour? By then, Melonya should be ready to bring Jaimes and I up. We can tether the horses and the six of us could be searching for the amulet together in no time."

"You'll wait for Melonya with me?" Jaimes asked, surprised.

"Of course," Eilonwy said, flashing him a quick smile. It made his breath catch. "I don't want you to think I've abandoned you." She gave Tathiel a pat on the shoulder, urging him on. "Go. Nieve said she wouldn't wait for you, and she's a fast climber."

Tathiel was moving in an instant. Jaimes watched him for a moment, once again surprised by how quickly elves could move.

"Give me a hand with the horses, will you?" Eilonwy asked, giving him a chaste kiss on the cheek. "Then maybe we can have a nice picnic while we wait for Melonya to retrieve us."

Jaimes touched the spot where her lips had touched his skin. He found himself wishing very much that Tathiel's talk of souls combining and being shared was all true. He couldn't imagine sharing his with anyone else but Eilonwy.

ROLAND

Roland drank slowly, watching the other patrons around him. Though it was late at night, the place was still packed with sullen and sour men and a small number of women that doubled as the bar's swill-swingers and as evening entertainment for the men that were willing to pay.

Roland had seen one woman, a middle-aged one with an attractive face, disappear out of a side door with a man so drunk she had to help him stay on his feet. She had returned not ten minutes later, grimacing and trying to fix her now tangled mess of light brown hair. The man had not returned.

It was not a bad town, he had gathered from watching the men who sat and stared into their mugs. It was only a tired town. There were no King's Guards to keep the people here afraid. The work did that well enough for them.

And Nevina was sure Layle would be found in this area.

Roland watched another group of men enter the pub, stamping the dark dust of the mines from their boots and shaking dirt from their hair. Two of them still carried their picks, slung into a loop on belts that crossed over their chests. A table was prepared for them before they had even finished brushing themselves clean, and they sat and coughed into their full mugs and conversed in quiet tones.

They always coughed, Roland noticed. Cough, drink, cough again. Like they could remove the dust from their skin and clothes, but never from their lungs. Which was probably true.

Roland realized he was staring and turned away, focusing on the remains of his own drink.

"Can I get you another one?"

Roland looked up. It was the middle-aged woman with the hair that she had not quite been able to fix properly. "No, thank you. But I will take a room, if you've got it."

The woman wrinkled her nose. "We've got one, but it's not a good one. Just a cramped space in the attic. Pretty sure there are mice up there."

Roland smiled. "I'm sure it's better than no bed at all."

The woman shrugged. "Will your friend be staying as well?"

Roland raised an eyebrow. "My friend?"

She jerked her head to the far end of the pub. "Small fellow in the corner. With the hood." She narrowed her eyes. "He asked about our strange resident outside town, too. I thought you might know each other."

Roland looked where she had indicated. There was indeed a small man sitting in the opposite corner with his back to the wall. His hood was pulled low over his face, and all Roland could see of him were the pale hands that gripped his mug. It was still full, and Roland was sure he had not been there a few moments before.

"Did he just arrive?"

The woman nodded. "Just walked in behind the last shift coming up from the mines."

The man lifted his mug to his lips and seemed to drink very deeply. When the mug hit the table again, the foam that had crested the top was gone. "When he finishes that drink, would you mind sending him another? Tell him it's from me?"

"No problem." The woman's eyes narrowed further. "Sure you don't want me to tell him you're here?"

Roland shook his head, giving her a nonchalant wave. "No, let the boy have a drink before I put him to work."

The woman relaxed. "You're a good one, aren't ya?"

"Try to be," Roland answered, keeping an eye on the man across the room. *Someone else looking for Layle, huh?*

"Is our lady on the hill in some sort of trouble?" the woman asked.

"Pardon?"

The woman tilted her head, looking Roland over. "I could see you being a King's Guard, maybe. With those strong shoulders and arms you've got." She gave him a seductive wink, then nodded back to the other man. "But your boy over there sounds like he's hardly got hair on his chest. Can't be King's Guard, I bet a night in the hay on it."

"We're not King's Guard," Roland said quickly, taking another sip of his drink.

"So our lady shouldn't be expecting no harm from ya?"

Roland shook his head. "No. We only require her … services."

"Ah." The woman nodded. "Maybe I'll save you a trip up the hill, then." She put a hand on her hip, then held up three fingers. "She's got three rules." The second two fingers vanished, leaving one behind. "One, you pay in advance. She's open to bartering, and will trade for just about anything." The woman gave Roland a severe look. "But you pay first."

"Alright," Roland said, amused.

"Second." The woman held up a second finger. "No asking for love potions or anything of that nature. She'll just slap ya silly and send you on your way. I've heard she'll make you something to help the man downstairs get up at night, but—"

the woman chuckled suddenly "—if anyone here has got that sort of thing from her, I haven't noticed."

"Oh, I don't need that sort of thing," Roland reassured the woman.

"I didn't think ya did, you manly beast, you." She winked again, then lifted the third and final finger. "Third rule." She grew serious. "Nothing that can harm another, man or animal. No poisons, venoms, or anything of the sort. Not only will she slap ya silly, but she'll alert our mining boys. And those fellows will do more than slap ya."

"Do people ask her for things like that?"

The woman nodded solemnly. "No one around these parts, but the strangers that come through sometimes do."

Roland nodded.

"Fourth rule."

"I thought you said she had three?"

The woman gave him a stern look. "She has three, but we have a fourth."

Roland frowned. "Alright."

The woman leaned close. She smelled of stale beer and fresh sex. "You tell no one that you don't trust as well as your own mother about her." She straightened again. "Our lady on the hill might be a grumpy bitch, but she's our grumpy bitch. And the child is a darling. The last thing we need is for them to be whisked away by some Etritian knights in their spit-shined armor."

"The child?" Roland asked. Across the room, the stranger in the hood was finishing off his mug of ale.

"Her daughter. Or, she says it's her granddaughter. But she's too young to be a grandmother already." The woman turned, noticing Roland's attention had left her. "I'll get that drink for your friend now. I'll be back, so don't wander too far."

Roland watched the woman hustle to the bar, fill a couple of small mugs with some dark liquid and leave it on the counter for the gentlemen there to take. Then she grabbed a larger mug and filled it with ale from a keg against the back wall. This one she carried to the stranger, who looked up as she approached. They exchanged a few words, and when the woman pointed over at Roland, Roland waved at the pair of them. Then he stood, slapped several coins onto the table, and left through the same side door he had seen the woman use earlier.

He did not have to wait long.

The man slipped quietly into the shadow of the alley, crouching low and staying close to the wall. Roland waited until the young man had passed his hiding spot, then he dropped from the weathered eave to land behind the man in the cloak. Roland slipped an arm around the man's neck, but was surprised when his hold was broken before he had even locked it in place. There was a sharp pain to his ribs as he took an elbow to the side, then another elbow flashed up towards Roland's face. He blocked it before it could strike him square in the nose, and he drove a fist into the man's back.

The man drew in a sharp breath and staggered forward. Roland made to follow, but a kick aimed at his leg knocked him to one knee. If it had hit a few inches higher, it could have damaged his knee. As it was, he would have a wonderful bruise for several days.

The man turned, bringing his other leg up into a kick that would hit Roland's jaw. But Roland caught it on his upraised arm with a pained grunt, then latched his opposite hand over the slim leg. Instead of pulling his attacker down, he lunged forward, lifting himself off the ground and driving both of them to the opposite end of the narrow alley.

Roland landed on top of the stranger, who let out a high-pitched yelp of pain before wrapping both legs around Roland and throwing him off. Roland felt inside his vest and pulled out a dagger. As they landed, with Roland now on the ground and the stranger on top of him, Roland slipped the dagger under his attacker's arm and up to his neck.

Roland felt a touch of cool metal against his own skin.

The stranger was panting, and Roland was ashamed to realize he was also breathing heavily.

"What do you want with Layle?" Roland asked, mindful of the blade at his throat.

"Commander Ajax?" The voice that came from under the hood was not a man's at all, and when the stranger pulled her hood away, Roland recognized the face beneath.

"You're one of Cookie's daughters …" he said, remembering where he had last seen that face. "Illa?"

The woman shook her head. "Ishta. Illa is still in Etritia." She dropped her blade into the dirt. "What are you doing here?"

"I could ask the same of you." Roland did not remove his blade.

"The queen has asked me to find the Coven girl that escaped the dungeons all those years ago."

"Why?" Roland spat. "So she can kill her, like her husband killed the rest of them?"

Ishta raised her hands, straightening until Roland's blade was no longer against her neck. "So that Anna's daughter might be saved from Etritia." Ishta shook her head. "Anna has been trying to save us, and when she found out from Nevina that there was still a member of the Coven—"

"Nevina is dead," Roland said.

Ishta nodded. "She is, and I don't really understand everything, but I trust Anna. And Anna said that Nevina told her to find Layle." Ishta sighed, shaking her head. "Something about Nevina's soul being trapped in this world."

Roland nodded. "Nevina told me to find Layle as well."

"How can Nevina speak with you? You're not from the Coven."

"It's a long story." Roland put his blade back into his vest.

"How do you know the queen well enough to call her by her first name?"

Ishta lifted an eyebrow. "It's a long story." She stood, offering him a hand. "Know a place we can talk?"

Roland sat up and took her offered hand, letting her help him to his feet. "How does a small space in the attic sound? We may have to share with some mice."

"So, you're saying Nevina gave you this healing ability so you could help get the dragon's egg out of the castle. And that's why you look the same as you did when I was a child?"

Ishta stood with her back to him, her shirt lifted so he could inspect her. There was a dark bruise forming where she had taken his punch, but she seemed unfazed by his gentle prodding at the surrounding skin.

"My friend seems to think she accidentally cursed me. Though curses are supposed to fade when the caster or the cursed die. This one hasn't, for some reason." Roland straightened, giving Ishta a tap on the shoulder to let her know he was finished with his examination.

"I wouldn't have believed it if I hadn't seen it myself. That graze on your head …" Ishta turned, tugging her shirt down and staring at the side of his face with narrowed eyes. "It's completely gone."

"You'll get used to seeing it happen," Roland said with a sigh.

"Is there anything it can't fix?"

Roland shrugged. "I've been stabbed, eviscerated, broken some bones … It's all healed. The worse ones take a little longer. When Ferrand cut my belly open it took weeks to heal completely. But that may have been from the blood loss." Roland lifted his own shirt, showing a thick white line that stretched across his midsection. "Now I just have this lovely reminder of him."

"Must be nice," Ishta remarked, bending slightly to take a closer look at the scar. "To know you can't get hurt."

Roland shook his head. "It definitely hurts. I just haven't died yet." Roland let his tunic fall again. "I've been told it's made me reckless over the years." He stepped away from Ishta, leaning against a support beam and crossing his arms. "What about you? You seem to know how to handle yourself."

Ishta shrugged, grimacing slightly and touching the bruises to her back. "There are only a few ways to make money in Etritia now, and they both involve selling your body for someone else's entertainment."

Roland nodded slowly. It didn't surprise him that Etritia had fallen so far, but it hurt to hear it. "You chose to fight?"

"Better to beat a man bloody in the den than to let him beat me bloody in the bedroom." Ishta bit her lip, staring at the straw-covered floor of the crawl space they had rented from the pub. "And I wanted to know how to protect Anna. And Trissa and Illa."

"You seem to care about the queen a great deal," Roland said, noting the agitation in Ishta's movements.

"Because I love her," Ishta said, glaring up at Roland. "Does that bother you? That Anna and I care for each other?"

"No." Roland shook his head. "It doesn't bother me. There's power in love, Ishta."

Ishta relaxed, then let out a low chuckle. "If Dars knew I'd gotten the better of you …"

"Dars is alive?" Roland asked, straightening. "Is he alright?"

Ishta bit her lip again. "He's alive. But his mind is going. He can't take care of himself anymore. I tried to get him to come with me, but he refused."

Roland sighed, rubbing his face. "He always was a stubborn old bastard."

"What about Layle? Do we ask her to try to save the
queen and Trissa, or do we ask her to join you in finding the
rest of the amulets?"

"Is one any different from the other?" Roland asked.

Ishta shrugged again.

"We tell her what we know. Maybe she or her granddaughter will know what path to take."

"Maybe Nevina will speak to you again and share some
more of her insight."

"Maybe." Roland gestured towards the bed, which was
little more than a sad and sagging woven cot covered in
molding straw and a thin and ragged wool blanket. "Take the
bed. I'll sleep on the floor."

Ishta nodded and pulled the blanket back, then groaned.

A family of mice had made a nest in the bedding, and
several infantile rodents squeaked and squirmed in the
sudden brightness of the single oil lamp Roland had
procured from the pub woman.

Ishta carefully draped the blanket back over the tiny
vermin. "Think there's enough floor space for both of us?"

43
SYRANI

Melonya landed at the top of the Starlit Summit with a thundering crash of white powder. They had seen the fine dust that covered the top of the mountains from far away, and Syrani had thought it to be ash from the amulet's fiery descent so many years ago. After all, it had looked so much like a falling star, and the amulet they sought was the Amulet of Fire.

So when she and Alastor unstrapped themselves from Melonya's back and tumbled to the ground, Syrani was surprised to realize that it was snow. It flew up in fluttering drifts and settled in her hair and on her eyelashes, and she realized it had been foolish to think it could have been anything else. Ash would have washed away long ago.

"Great Ones take it, it's f-fucking cold," Alastor said between chattering teeth. "Can you not feel that?"

Syrani tilted her head. "No. Elven children learn to adapt to extreme temperatures before we reach our twenties. The cold has never been much of a hindrance."

Alastor's breath fogged with each breath, as did her own. He blew onto his fingertips. "A trick like that would be nice to have right about now."

"If you don't think you can remain here—"

"I'll be fine," Alastor said, waving her off and turning to trudge further into the slightly concave summit they found themselves in. "Watch your step. There's a bit of rubble under all this snow."

"The others are still waiting for me," Melonya said, crouching low and folding her wings. *"Tathiel and Nieve will arrive shortly. They decided to climb their way to the top."*

"They're climbing?" Alastor said in surprise, turning to give Melonya an incredulous stare. His cheeks and the tip of his nose were bright red, and he held his hands close to his mouth, breathing intermittently on them.

"Nieve is a very good climber, though her expertise has been limited to the trees around our village."

"And Tathiel can be very competitive," Melonya added with a roll of her great blue eyes. *"I'm sure he's found a way to make a game of their ascent."*

"Great." Alastor pulled the hood of his cloak over his head. "I hope they brought a blanket or two."

"I will return with Eilonwy and Jaimes as soon as I can. The more of us that can search this place, the faster we can retrieve the amulet and return to the base of the Homewood." Melonya crouched deeper then leapt off the summit and into open air.

Syrani watched her with interest. The way she dove off the cliff was oddly feline, and when she opened her wings to begin her descent, Syrani was momentarily transfixed by the gossamer way the thin leathery webbing of her wings caught the wind.

"Syrani!" Alastor called. "Stop dawdling and start digging!"

Syrani brushed a layer of fine snow that Melonya's departure had sent into the air off her shoulders. "I have a more intelligent solution, if you don't mind."

Alastor was bent over, shoveling snow aside to clear a path no wider than his hips. He had only managed to clear a foot or so, and only down several inches. He gave her a look from beneath one arm. "Yeah?"

Syrani planted her feet and extended her arms. Concentrating on a patch of snow not far from where Melonya had left them, Syrani took a deep breath and sent arcane energy through the palms of her hands.

A strong gust of wind swirled where her attention was focused, and snow circled up into a loose vortex. Syrani concentrated further, and the swirling snow tightened. The winds increased in strength, until nearly all the snow was spinning in a cyclone no larger than a sapling. Syrani sent the vortex over the edge of the cliff, the snow it held with it, and let it fall apart.

Alastor nodded, wiping his nose on the sleeve of his tunic. "Not bad." He assessed the now cleared spot, a rough circle about five feet in diameter. "I bet I can do better."

Syrani stepped aside, waving Alastor forward.

Alastor made a show of stretching, then stood in much the same way Syrani had, with feet planted firmly and his arms outstretched. With a sideways glance at Syrani to ensure she was watching, he sent a long and steady stream of wind across the ground. Rather than focus on one small spot to clear it entirely, he instead swept over a larger area and sent a great deal of snow falling over the edge of the summit. When he stopped, a long and wide tunnel had been carved through the drifts of white powder, exposing the few inches of harder packed snow beneath. Alastor dusted his hands together, a satisfied grin on his face.

Syrani nodded in approval. "Good enough."

"And it takes less energy. We'll tire more slowly." Alastor took a few steps to his left and planted his feet again, preparing to repeat the process.

A hand reached up over the edge and gripped the top, and Nieve's irritated and snow-covered face appeared. "I would appreciate a warning next time, arcanist."

Tathiel appeared beside Nieve, and used both hands to quickly haul himself over the lip of the cliff and onto the snowy mountaintop. He brushed snow from his shoulders and head and offered a hand to Nieve. "I believe I've won."

Nieve glared at him as she pulled herself over the edge and rose to her feet. "What are you talking about? I reached the top first."

"The bet was for whoever could stand on the top first, not just who reached it." Tathiel gave Nieve a faintly smug smile. "You reached the top before I did, but I stood on it first."

Nieve grimaced. "Semantics."

"Nevertheless …" Tathiel said, his smile widening.

Nieve rolled her eyes. "Fine. You won."

"If you two are quite done acting like children," Syrani said loudly, drawing the attention of all three of the others, "we should get to work clearing the snow away."

"I would recommend being a bit more careful than Alastor. If the amulet is buried in the snow, we don't want to send it flying off the mountain." Tathiel made his way towards the center of the summit, where the snow was deepest.

Alastor blew on his fingertips again. "It would be our luck that the amulet was in that mess I just blew away."

"It wasn't." Nieve passed him, stopping to stand close to Syrani. "We would have noticed when it all came down on our heads."

"We'll start in the center," Syrani said, ignoring Nieve and Alastor. "Go slowly, as Tathiel suggested. If you see something, shout."

They met in the center of the concave summit, their backs to one another. Syrani raised her hands again, and to either side of her Nieve and Tathiel did the same.

"You feel it, don't you? The amulet?" Tathiel asked, leaning close to her.

"I feel it." She had felt it the moment Melonya had landed

atop the cliff. There was a strong energy here, but she could not pinpoint where it originated. The power the amulet emanated was strange and unfamiliar, but Syrani could feel it calling to her all the same. "It's here."

The work was quick with all four of them blowing powdery snow from the center of the summit towards the edge. But they had not even cleared half of the area when Tathiel and Syrani both called a stop.

"Did you find it?" Alastor asked.

Tathiel shook his head, sending white flurries cascading from his hair.

"We've cleared enough. We must have missed it," Syrani said.

Nieve sighed and walked back over the packed snow and ice to the middle of the summit. "But we've cleared nearly everything away." She knelt and dug through the last inch of frost. "There's nothing here but ..." Nieve hesitated, then dug faster, widening the hole she had created. "Give me a hand."

They all joined her. Syrani knelt on the ground, ignoring the sharp pain caused by pointed rocks digging into her legs, and clawed at what little remained to cover the stone of the mountain. The amulet continued to call to her, the feel of its pull stronger and more urgent than it had been even a moment before.

They cleared away a patch large enough for the four of them to huddle around. Syrani stared at what they had uncovered, quietly seething.

"How thick do you think the ice is?" Nieve asked.

Tathiel sighed, crouching closer to inspect it. "Thick enough to make this an unpleasant task."

Syrani stared at the faint red glow of the Amulet of Fire buried beneath a heavy layer of crystal-clear ice. *It's so close ...*

"Melonya can help, can't she?" Syrani turned to Tathiel. "She can breathe fire, right?"

Tathiel shook his head. "No. She can't."

Syrani let out a dry laugh, falling back to sit on her heels. "So that's why."

Alastor reached a hand out for her, momentarily blocking her view of the amulet. "What is it?"

"You said Halcia would be needed to complete this quest." Syrani met Alastor's gaze. "And now I know why." She pointed to the amulet and to the ice that held it well out of their reach. "Melonya may not be able to breathe fire, but Halcia can."

HALCIA

Halcia remained where Syrani had left her, waiting. She stared in the direction of the Starlit Summit, though she could not see it through the trees. The amulet was up there. She felt its energy reaching out for her. It felt like an old companion that she had all but forgotten was now calling her name.

It would be so easy to answer, but those visions I saw …

So Halcia did not answer the amulet's call. She waited for Syrani's return, hoping that her friend would forgive her for refusing to join them.

Was it foolish to be concerned that what she had seen might come true? The mountain and the valley had been engulfed in flames. How could such an inferno have started, if not by Halcia herself?

No, better to remain as far away as she dared. Syrani and the others could collect the amulet without her help.

"Thinking of Syrani, little hatchling?"

Halcia made a startled noise, surprised that she had not heard Syrani's mother approach.

"Yes. I don't enjoy being apart from her."

Lethas nodded. "I am all too familiar with that struggle."

Halcia turned once more towards the mountain, settling to rest with her snout on her forearms. *"Did she leave because of me?"*

"Yes."

Halcia let out a long breath. It steamed the air in front of her nose. *"Do you resent me for it?"*

"No."

Syrani's mother stood beside Halcia's shoulder, placing a hand on her scaled back. "Your place is with Syrani. Why are you still down here in the valley?"

Halcia shifted, settling deeper into a comfortable lounging position. The amulet's call was growing stronger, but she had no intention of leaving that spot. *"I … saw things. In a dream. I don't know if it was meant to be a warning of what might come to be."*

"Dreams can sometimes bring portents of the future." Lethas knelt in the earth beside Halcia's head, stroking her neck. "But sometimes a dream is just a dream."

"How am I to know the difference?" Halcia asked.

Lethas shrugged. "You can't."

Halcia lifted her head, wishing she could see the Starlit Summit through the trees. *"Do you think I should go?"*

"I think Syrani needs one of us. And she would rather have you at her side than me."

Halcia turned to see the sadness in Lethas's smile and the hurt in her eyes. *"I'm sorry. I know she—"*

A loud screeching cry cut off the rest of Halcia's words.

Halcia felt a tremor run over her spine and Syrani's mother let out a startled gasp. The noise was unlike any she had ever heard before, and its sound was painful to hear. There was agony and anger in the noise. Halcia sensed it as easily as she could hear the startled cries of the elves of the Homewood. She stood, searching for the source of the terrifying howl. If it was some sort of animal, it had to be close.

And if it is close …

"Demons," Lethas whispered. "Not again, not here again."

"Are you sure?" Halcia asked. *Demons in Vyris …*

"I will never forget that sound."

Gilaine approached at a run from the direction of Syrani's Hometree. "What's going on? There's talk of demons coming to our Homewood."

"Find Gabber," Lethas ordered sharply. "Tell everyone you can to get inside their Hometree." She stood, her gaze sweeping the nearest line of trees. "It is not safe out here."

"What about you?" Gilaine asked.

She was only a little faster with her question than Halcia was. *"What can I do?"*

"I need to find my daughter," Lethas said. "I need to protect Syrani."

"It's too dangerous," Gilaine protested.

"Halcia will take me." She waved the other elf off. "Go— get to safety."

Gilaine ran, casting one final look back over her shoulder at the pair of them.

Lethas braced a foot awkwardly against Halcia's elbow, trying to lift herself up onto Halcia's back. "We still have time to reach my daughter."

Halcia hesitated. In her mind's eye, she saw fire and smoke and Syrani falling to her death. *I cannot bring anyone else into that.*

"No," Halcia said firmly. She stood, straightening the leg Lethas was using for leverage. A human would have fallen to the ground, but Lethas only stumbled back a few steps.

She gave Halcia a fearful look. "No? You still won't go?"

"I will go," Halcia said, crouching down again and rolling and stretching her arms where wing joint met shoulder. *"But I will not take you with me. You are needed here."*

"I am needed where my child is," Syrani's mother protested.

"She is not a child any longer. But there are children here that

need you." Halcia dipped her head in the direction Gilaine had run off towards, and Syrani's mother turned just in time to see Gilaine fleeing back through the network of Hometrees with Gabber's hand in her own. *"Stay here. Protect your people. I will find Syrani and the others."*

Another shriek filled the air, louder and closer than it had been before. Halcia's eye watered in pain at the sound. She could feel it as well as hear it.

Syrani's mother covered her ears with her hands, then looked to the sky as a large cloud swiftly passed overhead. "What was that? Another dragon?"

Halcia shook away the tremors that ran along her spine and watched the shadow disappear from sight. *"That was your demon. And he is heading straight for the Amulet of Fire."*

MOTHLENOR

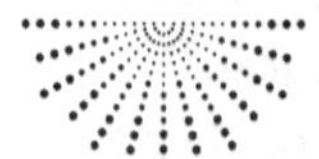

Mothlenor's eyes were closed, but still he could see. It was not the comfortably drab walls and careful clutter of his study that he saw, but instead he watched trees and rolling hills pass beneath him. He could feel wind on his skin and heat in his chest, and he could also feel the hard floor beneath his feet and the coolness of his tower. The duality was unsettling, despite having connected in much the same way with his older wraiths. He had closed his eyes after enduring only a second of the doubled vision his connection gave him, but there was nothing to be done about the extra sensations of touch.

He found he could not hear the rushing sound of the air around him, and he found he did not miss it.

The only sound he heard was Trissa's soft crying in the far corner of the room. She had not stopped weeping since he had pulled her from Anna's bedroom and magicked her into his tower.

His demon's vision was all in shades of grey, and it lacked the normal depth he was accustomed to. He would have questioned if that was how all dragons saw, but his demon had been fashioned from a human soul, not a monster's. The only reason he could find for the disparity was an apparent lack of power in the bond he had forged with Nevina's soul. Despite their combined strengths, which had been enough to shape her spirit into a beast of wing and shadow, it had not been enough to overcome something so trifling as complete color blindness and a lack of depth perception.

The demon altered course, trees appearing and disappearing from his field of view in rapid succession, and Mothlenor suppressed a groan of discomfort as his stomach somersaulted.

"Find the summit. We should be close now."

The demon's gaze scanned over the horizon, focusing briefly on each mountaintop in the far distance until it found one with a strangely flattened top.

"There. Trissa said they would be there."

The demon made for the summit with little effort on his part. A shadow blotted the sky, and the demon focused on the dark shape. The shapeless form was enlarged, and Mothlenor let out a sharp hissing breath.

"The dragon. The dragon that should have been mine."

The image enlarged further still, and the dragon turned, one large wing dipping as it arced gracefully to face the demon. Its back was momentarily exposed, and Mothlenor urged the demon to concentrate on the riders. He could not see the details of their faces, but the long ears of a Vyrisian elf were unmistakable on one of them.

"And elf and a human. The dragon Rider and Hasani's son."

Mothlenor stared at the human, trying to find some resemblance between the young man and his brother's advisor. But the demon's vision was too blurred and unfocused for him to see anything more than a rough estimate of his frame.

He drew in a breath, his heart beating hard in his chest.

"Kill them."

JAIMES

"**D**emon!"

Jaimes wasn't sure who said it first, Melonya or Eilonwy. Melonya's reaction to the screeching cry was sudden, and Jaimes clung to the bar that ran between his chest and Melonya's spined neck as she turned to face the coming danger.

"What's going on?" Tathiel asked all three of them.

The fury in Melonya's voice was nearly palpable. *"A demon approaches. In the guise of a dragon."*

Jaimes could see the black shape on the horizon. It was still a good distance away, but the gap between them was closing quickly. He suppressed a shudder at the sight of the dark thing.

"Can we get to the mountain in time?" Jaimes asked Melonya.

"It is possible, but—"

"No," Eilonwy interjected. *"You'll lead it right to the others. Can we distract it? Keep it busy while Tathiel and Syrani search for the amulet?"*

Jaimes almost choked, but a determined satisfaction rolled over him instead. Melonya's emotions were almost too strong for Jaimes to disregard entirely.

"I would be happy to do so."

"You don't expect to actually destroy that thing, do you?"
Jaimes asked, watching the demon draw closer with each
beat of its wings. It was strangely formless, like a dark storm
cloud with large eyes and an expansive wingspan.

"Eilonwy, don't be foolish!" Tathiel urged his sister. Jaimes
could no longer see him, but he was sure the four that stood
atop the Starlit Summit had stopped all work to melt the ice
above the Amulet of Fire. *"Lure it closer, and we can work
together to destroy it."*

The demon screeched again, louder and more horrible
than it had sounded before. Jaimes wanted to cover his ears,
but he didn't dare to release his grip on Melonya's saddle. It
wouldn't have helped anyway. The sound the demon made
burned through his mind, and Jaimes groaned in pain as it
echoed through every part of his conscious being. He
couldn't understand or describe the pain. He only knew no
living creature could make a noise like that.

There was a gentle hand on his shoulder. "Jaimes." Eilonwy's voice was in his ear. Her actual voice, not the one she
used to speak with Melonya. He felt her breath on his cheek.
"Jaimes, if you want Melonya to leave you somewhere while
we go to meet this thing—"

"No." Jaimes shook his head. "No, I'll stay right here."

She squeezed his shoulder, and there was a sultry quality
to her voice that surprised him. "Good." Eilonwy kissed him
on his temple, a warm and lingering kiss that steeled his
heart. "If we get close enough …" The hilt of a sword, Eilonwy's sword, appeared by his elbow. "Cut it."

Jaimes took the sword, then turned as Eilonwy retreated.
She was standing in the saddle, only her feet strapped lightly
into the stirrups and her elven balance keeping her from
sliding from Melonya's back. "What are you going to do?"

Tathiel was shouting for their attention as the demon
neared, both aloud and through their connection. Alastor's

voice joined in, but Jaimes ignored them both. He could smell and taste the acrid tang of arcane energy on the air. Eilonwy's focus was on the demon before them, and her arms spread out from her sides, elbows bent and palms glowing ominously. "I'm going to see what makes it hurt."

Melonya and the demon clashed in a soundless mess of wings and smoke. It was all Jaimes could do in those first few seconds to keep his hands on both the sword and the metal bar that he supposed was meant for this exact kind of situation. He ducked his head low as a dark mass that may have been a tail or a wing passed overhead. At the last moment he raised the point of the sword, not even bothering to swing. The metal passed through the cloud and met no resistance. The demon made no sound of pain.

Melonya rolled, and Jaimes cursed and tried to keep from vomiting, his eyes shut tight against the sudden appearance of trees where before there had been clouds. He heard a snap of huge jaws, and hoped it was Melonya biting at the demon and not the demon biting at him.

"The sword did nothing!" Jaimes yelled, hoping Eilonwy would hear. His stomach rolled as Melonya righted herself. "I hope you're having better luck."

Eilonwy growled loudly, and Jaimes opened his eyes in time to see a large blue-green orb strike the dark cloud and fade away into nothing. The demon remained unscathed.

The shadowy mass reared, and Melonya rose to match it.

The demon lunged, the front legs aiming for Melonya's neck. Melonya swerved to avoid the claws, only to be hit in the side by the demon's long tail.

Melonya's pain was agonizing. Jaimes felt the icy cold of the demon's spiked tail as if it had been driven into his own body. Melonya screamed and gave a guttural roar, and Jaimes and Eilonwy both screamed with her. Somehow, Melonya rolled away. Jaimes managed to keep hold of Eilonwy's sword and maintain a fairly upright position. The demon had retreated, but was already turning back for a fresh attack.

"Melonya!" Eilonwy's attention was only for her companion, and her barrage of arcane energy stopped. *"Are you alright?"*

"I'll be fine."

Jaimes noted the strain in her voice and the way her movements slowed. She could not avoid a second strike like that one.

"Melonya, we need to retreat." Jaimes settled into the saddle again, his eyes fixed on the demon. *"Swords are useless against it, and Eilonwy's attacks don't seem to harm it. We need to find something that will hurt it."*

Even as he finished the thought, a bright orb of red and orange soared through the air and struck the demon in the back, between the wings. The demon screeched, the sound almost human and yet still the earsplitting cry that had announced its arrival. It crumpled, falling several feet before righting itself and circling away.

"Fire will hurt it, you idiots!"

Syrani was addressing them, her voice strong and authoritative. *"Now draw it closer so we can hit it properly."*

Melonya raced for the summit as quickly as she could, which was noticeably slower than she could have a few moments before. Jaimes could see all four of their allies standing at the edge of the ridge. Behind them, the ice that held the Amulet of Fire was still thick, but there was a nice depression forming in the center. The four of them seemed to be clustered together around something, and as Melonya drew near Jaimes realized it was another huge fireball that they were building together. Their combined efforts were producing something far larger than any single one of them could make on their own.

"How did you think of that?" Jaimes asked.

"Syrani, of course," Alastor answered. His voice was terse. *"One to hold the shape and toss it, the others to get it formed."*

"Just like when we were children, Eilonwy," Tathiel added. *"Except it's a big ball of superheated flame instead of a rock."*

"Shut up and concentrate," Syrani admonished. *"On my order, we launch."*

Jaimes chanced a glance behind him to see that the demon had returned. It was headed right for Melonya, mouth open and glowing red eyes, making the image it cast terrifying. Melonya's wings beat steadily but not quickly enough to keep the demon from gaining on them.

"Melonya …" Jaimes warned. She was between the demon and the fiery orb Syrani and the others were constructing.

His stomach sank as Melonya ignored him. She continued flying furiously for the summit, the demon closing on her and the huge arcane flame growing larger.

"Melonya!" Jaimes said again. *"Get out of their way!"*

"That's it, I'm done," Nieve said. Jaimes could hear her, actually hear her shouted words over the sound of the wind and Melonya's wing beats.

"Hold on, Jaimes," Melonya answered at last. Jaimes could see the muscles in her shoulder tense, and he grabbed the saddle bar with his free hand. The knuckles were white.

"Now!" Syrani shouted.

Melonya exploded upward in a completely vertical incline. Her tensed muscles drove her wings down in one huge lunge, bringing them clear of Syrani's attack on the demon. Jaimes's head fell back at the sudden change in direction and momentum, and before he shut his eyes tight against the nausea that threatened to make him vomit he saw the red-orange glow of an arcane fireball hit the demon neatly in its shadowy face.

"Shit," Jaimes groaned, clutching everything and anything around him to quiet the very panicked voice in his mind that told him that he was about to fall from Melonya's back and plummet to his death.

"Great Ones damn you, Jaimes, get me out of this bag right now or I'll singe every hair from your body!" a tinny and high-pitched voice shrieked from his bag, which he had all but forgotten about and which he now held pressed to his midsection with his elbows.

"Vash?" As Melonya leveled out again and the nausea quickly faded, Jaimes released the saddle bar with a shaking hand and fished Vash's jar from his bag.

Vash was pressing vainly against the cork that sealed the jar, trying to force it open. She glared at him as light brought her tiny form into view. "What's going on?"

"There's a demon. Shaped like a dragon." Jaimes could faintly hear Syrani giving the order to throw arcane fire at the demon at will, as their last attack had apparently done little more than slow it down briefly. Eilonwy stood in her half of the saddle, using Jaimes's shoulder to steady herself as Melonya dove down closer to the summit. Jaimes didn't get the chance to grab the bar. "The only thing that seems to hurt it is fire, but we aren't doing enough to destroy it." He pulled the stopper from the jar, and Vash immediately rose from the small candle flame until her waist was even with the lip of the jar. "Can you help us?"

Vash hesitated. "Show me the demon."

Jaimes cursed as Melonya changed direction again; he had been too distracted to catch any warning in time to act. He lifted Vash's jar as high overhead as he dared and twisted to give Vash the best possible view of the demon that he could. To his surprise, the demon was still chasing after Melonya, and her sudden course changes were attempts to shake it from her.

Vash lifted herself further from the jar, her tiny arms straining to hold herself high above the candle flame that constrained her.

The demon snapped its jaws shut, missing the very tip of Melonya's tail by little more than a foot. For its efforts it received a small stream of fire between its glowing eyes from Eilonwy's outstretched hands. The demon flinched, but did not slow down.

Vash nodded, and Jaimes retracted his arm, closing his eyes briefly as Melonya performed some stunt that he didn't quite have the stomach to fully appreciate.

"I need fire," Vash yelled. "A lot of fire."

Jaimes repeated her request to the others. Syrani was the only one to reply, and it was curt and angry. *"We have nothing left to give!"* Her voice faded for a moment, and Jaimes watched a small ball of fire soar towards the demon. It fizzled out before it reached the shadowed form. *"None of us can make more than a little spark of flame, now."*

"I can."

The voice that came over the wind was a welcome one, and a collective sigh washed through Jaimes and his companions through their connected minds. A large ball of fire, somehow more intense than the ones conjured before it had been, slammed into the underside of the demon and sent it careering off course with a scream. The sound was definitely one of pain, intense and lasting, but Jaimes could not decide if the creature that made it was male or female. Or somehow both.

Halcia emerged from the trees at the base of the mountain, speeding towards them in a steep ascent. Her approach had been silent and unseen, and Jaimes was immensely grateful that she had arrived when she did.

"Halcia," Syrani began, but Halcia cut her off.

"Is that a fire spirit you have?" Halcia drew level with Jaimes, staring at the jar with one large golden eye.

"I need a strong stream of fire," Vash said, lifting herself from the jar again and addressing Halcia directly. "As much as you can give me."

Halcia dipped her head and fell back. The demon was already approaching again, though it was noticeably slower than it had been a moment ago.

"Jaimes."

Jaimes turned to Vash. Her face was too small to see properly, but he sensed the stress in her words.

"Throw me into the fire."

"What?"

Vash slapped a tiny hand against the lip of the jar, and flame briefly licked the edge. "You have to throw me into the fire."

Jaimes shook his head. "Why? What would that do?"

"I'm a fire spirit, Jaimes," Vash said in an annoyed tone. "What do you think it would do?"

It would make her huge. Large enough to—

"You can't be serious." Jaimes glanced back at the demon. It was now heading for Halcia, but Melonya was moving to intercept. Halcia remained fairly still, her golden wings keeping her aloft in more or less one spot. And her chest was glowing.

"It will work," Vash insisted.

"What if it doesn't?" Jaimes was not looking at Vash now. He was staring at Halcia's exposed chest, where the scales of her body were brightening into a shimmering gold.

"It will work. Trust me."

Jaimes nodded. "Alright. Let's do it, then."

"Whenever you're ready," Halcia announced. Her chest was too bright to look at, and her voice was strained and thin.

"Fire first," Vash replied when Jaimes relayed the message.

Melonya was nearly in range, but the demon was closer to Halcia than they were. He wasn't sure he could make such a throw.

He stood in the saddle, one hand still holding Eilonwy's sword, the other holding Vash's jar, and sighted over Melonya's shoulder and down her long neck. Feeling like a fool and with his stomach twisting every which way, he kissed Vash's jar for good luck, then pulled back his arm back to throw. *"Now, Halcia!"*

There was an eruption of red-orange flame just as Vash's jar left his fingertips. And after the jar made its first rotation in the air, Jaimes realized he should have asked Eilonwy to make the throw.

The jar reached its apex as Halcia's flame struck the demon. Vash's jar seemed to hover for a brief second before beginning its descent.

It wasn't going to make it into the fire.

"Shit."

A small blue-green orb shot over his shoulder and struck the jar, knocking it up a few more feet and propelling it into the streak of intense fire that spewed from Halcia's mouth.

The effect was instantaneous.

A huge woman-shaped column of fire slammed into the demon's chest with a terrific cry of fury. Vash, in her dragon-sized form, had wild hair of black smoke and a muscular body of white-hot flame. She straddled the demon's back, the heels of her bare feet digging into its underbelly. The demon screamed, and Jaimes was sure it screamed with the voice of both a man and a woman. The woman's shout was one of pain, while the man's was one of anger.

Vash curled a thick forearm around the demon's throat and cut both voices off.

They fell towards the ground together, the demon's wings limp and unmoving, Vash's face twisted in a feral grimace.

Halcia's fire sputtered once, then died.

Both Vash and the demon disappeared before reaching the trees. Jaimes blinked, staring at the empty space where the two creatures of smoke and fire had been. They had been locked together in a fighting embrace. Vash clearly had the upper hand. And then they simply vanished.

A collective cheer went up from the Starlit Summit, but Jaimes did not join in.

"Vash …"

Eilonwy's hand was on his shoulder again, and Jaimes slumped back into the seat of the saddle.

"Take us down, Melonya," Eilonwy said. "We'll find her."

Jaimes didn't recall the trip back to the ground. Eilonwy had a rough guess of where the jar might have landed after she had used the last of her arcane energy to bump it into Halcia's fire, and she assured Jaimes that the spell she had put on it would have protected the jar even after such a long fall.

But Jaimes said nothing. His mind's eye replayed the sight of Vash's huge form wrestling with a demon and then disappearing with a blink.

When Melonya landed, Jaimes tried to untie his legs and feet from the stirrups, only realizing then that he still held Eilonwy's sword. He returned it and ripped away the ties keeping him in the saddle. He felt a sharp stab of pain when he stumbled to the ground, but he limped away. He followed an aimless course, searching the ground and stepping over roots and stone and searching for the jar.

"To your left, Jaimes. There's something there."

Jaimes turned as Melonya suggested, pushing through low branches and tall weeds. There was a glint of something in the verdant and undisturbed undergrowth, and Jaimes reached out to feel the smooth and unmistakable feel of glass in his hand.

The jar was intact, just as Eilonwy promised it would be. But the flame of the candle had gone out, and there was no sign of Vash anywhere.

Jaimes shook the candle from the jar and turned back to search for Eilonwy. She was already behind him, staring at the candle in his hand with a faintly pained look.

"Light it again. Please." Jaimes held the candle out for her, and after a long moment, Eilonwy produced a tiny flame between two fingers and lit the wick.

"Vash?" Jaimes called.

There was no reply.

He waited several seconds, then called her name again. Still, she did not answer.

He blew the candle out, then held it out for Eilonwy. "Again. Please."

It took her longer to light the candle a second time, but it was done.

"Vash? Please answer me."

Silence.

He blew the candle out once more and held it out again. "Please, Eilonwy."

Eilonwy shook her head, taking the candle from him. "I can't Jaimes. I don't have anything left."

Her face was pale and tears were forming in the corners of her eyes.

Jaimes held his arms open and Eilonwy stepped into his embrace. They held each other quietly for a moment. He could feel the candle Eilonwy held pressing lightly into his back, just as she surely felt the jar he held against her own back.

Eilonwy smelled of smoke and burned arcane energy and of the woods, and he ran a hand through her silver hair and tried to fight back tears.

"I've lost her," he muttered in a thick voice.

"I'm sorry."

"She saved us, and now she's gone."

47
VASH

Vash welcomed the dragon fire with open arms, letting it consume her. She was a spirit of fire, and there was no fire quite like what a dragon could produce. The energy and heat of it became her own.

She leapt from the jar and towards the demon, letting the golden dragon's breath propel her forward. Fire spirit and demon collided in a tangle of flame and smoke, but Vash was quick to get the upper hand. She wrapped her arms around the demon's neck, amazed by the power in her grasp, and locked her feet beneath the beast's belly. She had feet! When was the last time that had happened? When was the last time she'd had the energy necessary to free herself from the tethers that so often restrained her?

For a second her only thoughts were of her newly formed limbs.

And then the demon squirmed and screamed, sounding more and more human with each cry, and Vash's attention was once more focused on the black thing in her grip.

She felt herself begin to fall. Wind tousled the smoke of her hair and made the demon's form shift slightly. But Vash's hold was firm, and it did not escape her.

When the energy of the dragon fire began to wane, she pulled the demon even closer, blending demon and fire spirit.

"When I go," Vash whispered to the demon, "I'm taking you with me."

There was a hissing in the air as her tears burst into steam.

Spirits of Fire cannot cry, she reminded herself.

And then the fire went out, and there was nothing but darkness and cold.

4 8

NUNOR

Nunor awoke with an ache in his head so deep and painful that he could feel it in the base of his skull. The first noise he made, before even opening his eyes, was a groan. The second, which would have been the first if the first had not been involuntary, was a string of curses in both Azimarian and dwarfish. For good measure, he finished it off with a Vyrisian word that he wasn't entirely sure was a curse but sounded like it ought to be. A heavy cloth was pressed against his eyes and over his forehead.

"You're awake, then?" Tiryn asked. Nunor could feel the elf's strong hands on his shoulders, pressing him back when he tried to sit up. "Steady now."

"I can't fucking see anything." Nunor tried to brush the cloth away from his face, but his arms didn't seem eager to cooperate. "Get this damned thing off me, Tiryn."

The cloth disappeared, and it was only then that Nunor realized it had been cool and moist. Nunor blinked several times, but still he could see very little.

"Tiryn." Nunor swallowed, groping for his friend's arm in the blackness. "I think I've gone blind."

"You're not blind," Tiryn reassured him. "It's night. There are no lights."

"But the moon, the stars, I don't see them."

"We're in a tent."

Nunor was silent for a moment, straining to make out the shapes around him. Slowly, the objects closest to him took form. There was a chair, and some other small piece of furniture. And the clearest thing he could see was Tiryn's face, which stared at him with an amused grin.

Nunor sat up slowly. "If you tell anyone about this, I'll have your ears made into a pair of beard charms."

Tiryn's barely visible smile widened. "I wouldn't dare."

Nunor lay down again. Even the smallest movement made his head throb horribly. "What happened? Where are we?"

"What do you remember?" Tiryn asked.

"The fucking desert."

Tiryn nodded.

"And we were talking about Darlyth. And then …" Nunor tried to remember, but thinking too hard made his head hurt. "A tent?"

"This tent, yes."

"So, we made it?" Nunor laughed. "I bet I dragged your ass all the way, didn't I?"

"Not quite, Master dwarf," a feminine voice said from behind him. A woman entered the tent through a flap only a few feet away, and with her came a cold breeze from outside. The woman was wrapped in thick clothing, and in the dark it was difficult to make out her face. "Your friend here managed to drag you to within a good stone's throw from our tent before he passed out beside you. Luckily my husband was outside checking the traps, or we would not have found you in time."

Her voice was pleasantly accented with a half-familiar lilt

that Nunor could not put a name to. She wasn't Azimarian, and he was sure she wasn't Vyrisian either.

She knelt and set a small oil lamp on the ground between them and fumbled with the clasp that held it shut with her left hand.

"Please, allow me," Tiryn said. He opened the clasp and lit the thick braid that served as the wick. Nunor noticed that he used the flint striker the woman passed to him rather than a bit of arcane energy, but made no comment on it.

Nunor shut his eyes against the sudden brightness, but his eyes adjusted to the red glow quickly and he opened them again. Nunor sat up again very quickly, instantly regretting it when his head swam, and took a second look at the woman.

Her skin was dark brown, so dark as to be nearly black, and her eyes were large and the startling color of amber. Her hair, which was cropped to just beneath her chin, was fashioned into countless thin braids and decorated with rings of precious stones and silver metal. Her face was young, not yet beyond the prime years of a human life, and was thin from long battles with fatigue and hunger. And Nunor knew at last where the lilt in her voice came from.

"You're one of the Elori," Nunor said in wonder.

"I am. I am called Suvusa." Suvusa sat, crossing her ankles and leaning against a heavy trunk that took up much of the space under the tent. Her feet were bare, and the soles of her feet were thick and calloused. "My husband is Hiriscu. He should be in shortly with food and fresh water."

Nunor shook his head and frantically smoothed his beard with both hands. "I have never met an Elori, my lady."

"There are not many of us left to meet, I am afraid," Suvusa said with a sigh. "But I am happy to know that our dwarfen friends remember us."

"The Elori and the dwarfs were allies long before the treaties across Vyris and Azimar were signed," Nunor explained to Tiryn.

"I know who the Elori are."

"Your friend awoke some time before you did, Master dwarf. He has told my husband of your adventure in the desert." Suvusa tidied the thick cloak and blankets that wrapped around her, covering her dark legs against the cold of the desert night. "You could both have died. I hope you understand that."

"Then I am even more grateful for your presence, my lady," Nunor said gravely. "I only hope it could have been under more flattering circumstances. This is hardly the grand hall of Doldural that an Elori deserves to be treated to, and I am as unfit a guest as any dwarf could be for an Elori to host."

Suvusa laughed sharply. "This is my home, and when my husband dragged you in, you were covered in your own vomit. What better way to make a fast friendship?"

Nunor cursed, and Suvusa laughed again, hard and long. It was a pleasant, manly laugh, cut short when a thin wail rose from the cloak clutched tightly to her chest.

"No crying now, Rushavi," Suvasa said, tossing aside the blankets to expose a dark breast and a small infant. "We are in the presence of an old friend. There is nothing to fear tonight, my sweet one."

"I thought I heard an infant when we drew near your tent," Tiryn said.

Suvusa nodded. "This is my son. He is not yet a week old." The infant latched once more to her breast and fell silent, and Suvusa covered her chest once more. "He is the reason we have lingered in this spot for so long. When I am well enough to travel again, we will move to a new place."

"Where will you go?" Nunor asked.

"Wherever the wind will guide us, as the Elori have always done." Suvusa jerked, and the trunk behind her shifted slightly. She gave Nunor and Tiryn an apologetic smile. "I am not used to motherhood just yet, please excuse me."

Nunor muttered a string of words that he hoped conveyed that there was nothing for Suvusa to apologize for, but Tiryn had more questions.

"The Elori, you stay mostly to the desert, correct?"

Suvusa nodded. "My people have walked every inch of these sands, and yet there is always something new to see."

"Then perhaps you can help us?"

"Tiryn, no. It is not our place to ask the Elori for favors."

Suvusa raised an eyebrow. "Help you? How can two wandering Elori help a mighty Vyrisian and a brave Dolduran?"

"We are searching for the Amulet of Earth. We believe it may be in this desert somewhere."

Suvusa jerked again, and the trunk she leaned against rocked softly in the sand. "Forgive me, but I do not understand."

"Your husband didn't understand my request either, or so he said," Tiryn said quietly. "But I think you know exactly what I'm talking about, and perhaps you have even seen the amulet I speak of."

"Tiryn," Nunor barked, but Suvusa interrupted.

"We have seen much of the desert, and we have seen many things, but we have not found this amulet you speak of. If you are in need of a guide, perhaps you can find another Elori to help you cross the sands, but I am in no condition to travel great distances—"

"You may not have found the Amulet of Earth, but you found something else nearly as priceless, didn't you?"

The trunk moved again, and Nunor realized it was moving of its own accord, and not responding to the jerks and shudders of Suvusa as she nursed her child.

Suvusa said nothing.

"What's in the trunk, my lady?" Nunor asked, hoping to

distract Tiryn from the impolite questions he asked the Elori. He cast a dark look at Tiryn, but the elf's lips were pursed together, and his eyes were on the trunk.

Suvusa said nothing, and only held her child closer to her chest.

The trunk rocked again, more violently than ever, and Suvusa was knocked over to her side.

Tiryn took that moment to send a spell flying at the trunk, and the lid fell open.

"Hiriscu!" Suvusa yelled, and before the word was completely from her mouth a towering dark-skinned man burst through the tent's opening, blade in hand. It was a small blade used for cleaning game, and it was wet with blood and offal, but Nunor was sure it could be deadly.

Nunor raised both hands. "Please, this has to be some misunderstanding."

Tiryn fell back, his energy apparently already spent. "I mean no harm, lady Suvusa. But I know what you carry in that trunk, and it seems very eager to come out."

Hiriscu knelt to help Suvusa upright, and they both checked on the infant in her arm before staring between the opened trunk and Tiryn with apprehension.

Nunor could think of nothing to say. *What is Tiryn thinking, acting like some damned fool toward the Elori?*

A small brown creature crawled from the trunk and hopped quietly to the sandy floor. It looked like a small lizard, covered in spines and scales and with a long thin tail. It crawled up Suvusa's arm and settled over her shoulder, and Nunor would not have thought it anything more than a desert reptile if it had not unfolded a wing and shaken sand from its leathery skin before settling back down again.

"A dragon," Nunor muttered.

"It hatched the same day Rushavi was born," Suvusa said. "And you have come to take him from us?"

Tiryn shook his head. "No. I would never dream of separating the child from his parents."

"Not Rushavi," Hiriscu said. His accent was thicker than Suvusa's, and his voice was low and soft. "The dragon. You have come for the dragon."

Tiryn shook his head again.

Nunor knelt in the sand, bowing his head low to the Elori. "We came in search of a dragon, but not to take him away. We need your help, if you are willing to give it."

"The Amulet of Earth," Suvusa said. "What I said to your elf friend was true. We have not seen any such thing."

"Will you help us search the sands for it, then?" Tiryn asked. Color was slowly returning to his pale cheeks, and Nunor wondered how long it would take for the elf to fully heal from his time in the sun.

Suvusa looked to Hiriscu, who looked at the small squirming bundle in Suvusa's arms.

"If we do not find it soon," Nunor said, "I am afraid that the desert will be the site of another great battle the likes of which has not been seen since the Great War."

"Another war?" Suvusa asked.

"The Doldural king is dying. If his son takes the crown before the amulet is found, the dwarfs will march to war."

4 9

LAYLE

Arella was already awake and waiting for her when Layle woke up. She found her granddaughter in their tiny kitchen, dressed in her finest dress with ribbons tied poorly in her long hair.

"You're up and about early."

"We're going to have company this morning," Arella said primly.

Layle counted four bowls and four mugs arranged neatly on the small table they kept against one wall. She raised her eyebrows as Arella carefully set a large kettle in the fireplace to warm. It was heavy, apparently full near to the brim, and it took both of her small hands and a good deal of effort for her to lift it and set it carefully down. "Anyone important?" Layle asked in an amused tone. "Should I dress myself up some as well?" She reached over Arella's shoulder to lift the lid from a pot that also hung over the warm coals of the fire. Inside was the thin beginnings of a porridge.

"It's not ready yet." Arella smacked the back of Layle's hand in much the same way Layle would have done in Arella's place. Layle replaced the lid and retreated. "Our friends are coming today." Arella lifted her chin, taking on the air of

430

someone far older than she was. "If you want to make a good impression, it wouldn't hurt to put on a dress that wasn't flecked with dirt and flour."

Layle dropped all pretense of play. "What friends?"

"The ones I told you about," Arella said carefully. "The ones who would come and ask for our help. Auntie Ishta and the man Nanny Nevina sent."

"They're ... they're coming today?" Layle sat heavily in a chair, feeling suddenly faint.

Arella nodded, her composure still intact. "They'll be here within the hour. Sooner, perhaps."

Layle rose and quickly returned to the bedroom she and Arella shared, but it was not to change.

Instead she sat on the bed, stunned into silence. Arella had never mentioned the two strangers again, not after convincing Layle to remain where they were instead of fleeing. Perhaps it was only to keep Layle from changing her mind about staying, or perhaps her interest had waned until her strange precognition had told her of their imminent arrival. But Layle had secretly hoped that Arella would be wrong. And that they would be safe in their home for years to come.

She may still be wrong. She's been wrong before.

Just as Layle's sister, Arella's namesake, had occasionally been wrong on the rare occasion that her similar Gift had shown itself.

But she is not often wrong about things like this.

Layle paced the bedroom. It was too small to take more than a couple of steps before she had to turn again, especially with the small writing desk that sat in the corner beside the bed, but it was enough to help her dispel some of her agitation.

"Grandmother?" Arella spoke through the door, her voice muffled slightly. "Are you alright?"

Layle took a breath. "No. But I will be in time."

"Can I help?"

Layle smiled, coming to a stop and sitting on the edge of the bed again. "You just keep an eye on that porridge, alright? I'm sure our guests will be hungry."

Arella's footsteps grew quieter, and after a moment Layle could hear the general sounds of kitchen prep. In Arella's case, such work often included a nonsense song or two, and Layle closed her eyes and listened as Arella called out her chores and tasks in a singsong voice.

How would Nevina's plans for Arella change the little girl that sang in a delightful off-key voice in the next room? How would learning more about the Coven, perhaps even finding a way to begin the Coven anew, affect her?

Layle stared at the metal cuffs that still clung to her wrists. It had been years since she'd last used magic, and the heavy bracelets reminded her that she may never use it again.

Will Arella resent me for the life I've asked her to live?

There was a tentative knock at the front door, and Layle opened her eyes once more. The light filtering through the window above the desk had changed, and Layle wondered how long she had sat on the bed, just listening to her granddaughter's singing.

Arella opened the door before Layle could rise from the bed, and her granddaughter happily greeted the company at the door in a cheery voice. She missed the initial introductions, but she caught Arella's greeting to the smaller of the two strangers that stood in her front room when she left the bedroom.

"And you must be Auntie Ishta. Trissa has told me lots about you."

The woman, for it was a woman, Layle realized as the stranger dropped the hood from her cloak, began to answer Arella. The sound of the bedroom door shutting behind Layle silenced them all, and the strangers turned to face her.

Layle sighed. "I should have known it would be you she

sent after me," she said to the red-haired man who stood quietly before her. "You haven't aged at all, have you, Commander Ajax?"

When Ajax replied, it was in the soft baritone she remembered from her childhood. "I don't go by that name any longer. I'm Roland now." He smiled at her, a wan, sad sort of smile. "And it is very nice to see you again, Layle. You look just like your mother."

Layle felt her jaw working, and took a moment to quietly relax. "Arella, please wait in the bedroom."

"Grandmother …" Arella protested feebly.

"Just for a few moments." Layle stepped aside, motioning for Arella to leave. "Please."

Arella went silently, though she gave Layle a dark look as she passed.

Roland waited until the door was shut before speaking again. "You named her after the sister you lost in Etritia."

"It seemed fitting when the moment came," Layle replied, crossing to the fireplace and lifting the lid to the still warm pot that sat on the edge of the hearth. "She and my sister are similar in many ways. But my granddaughter is much more stubborn than my sister ever was." She turned towards them. "Arella has made us some breakfast. Are you hungry?"

"Yes, thank you," the woman said.

Layle filled a bowl and handed it to the woman, gesturing for her to sit. "I recognize you too, though you don't seem to be blessed with agelessness as the commander has been. You were in the castle. You brought us cakes while we passed the day in the library. Before we were kidnapped and taken to the dungeons."

The woman's face paled, and she nodded. "My sisters and I all worked in the castle. My mother was the cook." She sat, leaning back as far as the wall behind her would allow. She swallowed, her hands shaking as she held the sides of the bowl. "She was the one that cared for you in the dungeons."

Layle snorted. "I would not call that caring."

"We are not here to discuss the past, Layle," Roland said firmly. "What has been done can't be fixed."

Layle passed a second bowl to Roland, forcing it roughly into his hands. Porridge slopped over the rim of the bowl and onto his tunic. "Then what shall we discuss? The future?"

"Yes."

"Then tell me, Roland, what does my mother have planned for my granddaughter?"

Roland shook his head. "I don't know. She wanted me to find you. That was all she asked." He motioned towards the chair across from the woman Arella had called Ishta. "May I? It smells delicious, and it has been a long journey to find you."

Layle nodded, and Roland sat, taking care not to further smear porridge on himself or the table.

"Trissa seems to think that you and Arella can help the queen. Or help all of Etritia." Ishta shrugged, not meeting Layle's eyes. "I don't understand a lot of what the princess says, if I'm honest."

Layle crossed her arms, more for her own comfort than for any show of intimidation. "And what did the princess say we were meant to do?"

Ishta shook her head. "I don't know."

The door to the bedroom opened slightly, and Arella called through the crack between door and frame. "Don't forget about the tea! Or it will get cold."

Layle retreated to the fireplace, where the kettle still sat, though Arella had pulled it further from the heat. Layle lifted the heavy kettle and returned to the table, where Ishta and Roland both held out a mug. Roland even set a third one close to the edge for Layle to fill for herself.

"I thought I left that life behind when Martin and Nana took me away from Etritia." Layle sat between the other two, leaving the kettle and the third mug on the table. "But I couldn't stop running away. Not after my son was born. Not after Martin died. Not even after my son told me he was tired of always living life on the road and that he would be staying behind." Layle sniffed at the mug. It was mint and chamomile. Arella had intended for the tea to be relaxing, but Layle was not sure tea alone would be enough. "It wasn't until I held Arella in my arms for the first time that I knew the running had to stop." She squinted over at Roland. "And then Arella told me Nevina was sending someone to find me, and I knew I should have never stopped running if I was going to keep her safe."

"Layle …" Roland took a deep breath, letting it out in a long sigh. "Your mother was working with Areanath on some sort of spell."

"I know. Word has reached even these parts of the missing amulets and the possible return of dragons to Azimar." It took a great deal of effort not to glance over to the mantle, where a certain large white stone rested. "But that was my mother's business, not mine. And certainly not Arella's."

"Please," Roland said earnestly. "Just give me a moment to explain how far we've come. If we had your help, I know we could complete Areanath's quest and find a way to stop Mothlenor."

Layle laughed. "Stop Mothlenor? This isn't a child's game, Roland. He killed his own brother! He killed my mother, my sister, his men killed my son …" She closed her eyes for a brief moment. "I have lost so much in life because of that man, and I would love nothing more than to see him destroyed. But there is nothing the four of us can do."

"There are more of us than that, Layle." Roland reached into a pocket and pulled out a rumpled mess of feather and dropped it inelegantly on the table.

Ishta's face went pale and she looked faintly ill. "Is that a bird? And you've been carrying it around?"

"It's magic, not real," Layle explained. She could feel the arcane energy that held the bird together, though it was nearly spent. "I've never seen one, but I assume you can use it to send messages?"

"Not me personally, but my companions can. This one is from my nephew. It found me only a few days ago. I think it has enough energy for one more listen." The bird perked up at the sound of Roland's voice and began to prune its feathers. "Just ignore the first few seconds. My nephew tries very hard to impress women with his arcane talents."

Layle quirked an eyebrow, but said nothing.

The bird gave itself a good shake, fluffing its wings and tail feathers, then opened its mouth as if to sing.

"I think it likes you, Nieve," a young man's voice said. "Would you like to say hello?"

"Hello, little bird," a woman said in return.

Ishta jerked suddenly, knocking her bowl to the floor and sending porridge rolling across the floor. She murmured an apology and immediately went to retrieve the runaway dish.

Layle continued listening, very aware that Roland was watching her.

"I hope you're doing well, old man. I wish you had let me come with you. Though, all things considered, it was probably for the best that I went on alone. Things are more … delicate than I would otherwise hope for. But we should have the Amulet of Fire in a week, no more. When all is said and done, let's … meet … baaaa …"

The bird crumbled into a pile of feathers, which quickly evaporated into nothing.

"The rest wasn't too important, but if my nephew was right, then we should have the second of the four amulets by now. If we can find the other two before Mothlenor, we can find a way to use them to stop him."

"Roland."

Layle and Roland turned to Ishta, who stood with a

mostly empty bowl in her hands, a trail of porridge leading back to where she'd been sitting. She stared at the mantle above the fireplace, and Layle took in a sharp breath.

"Roland, it's moving."

Layle cursed and rose to her feet. The white dragon's egg was rocking back and forth on the mantle, and when Layle pulled it down before it tumbled from the edge, the shell was hot to the touch.

"No, stop!" Arella rushed from the bedroom and took the egg from Layle.

"Arella, you have to leave it alone!" Layle reached for the egg again, not entirely sure what she meant to do with it. "It's going to hatch."

"No, it's not. I keep telling him it's not time yet, but he's so anxious to come out." Arella held the egg to her chest, both arms cradled around it. She spoke to the egg directly, her mouth an inch away from the hard shell. "I promised I would tell you when the time was right. But you have to stay there for a little while longer."

The egg shivered once and then stilled.

Arella quietly returned the egg to Layle, who was too stunned to speak. "I told him he could come out when we decided to leave and help find the amulets," Arella said softly. "I hope you don't mind."

"It seems fate has pulled us together, Layle," Roland said, placing a hand on the egg. "Nevina was right to ask me to find you, after all."

SYRANI

Syrani rested alone in bed, propped against a large number of pillows. Her right hand was bandaged, but the burn beneath hardly ached and was healing nicely. She didn't even think there would be a scar. And in her injured hand sat the amulet Halcia had helped to retrieve from the Starlit Summit.

It had taken Halcia only moments to do what she had estimated would take them hours upon hours to do on their own, and Halcia had melted the ice that trapped the amulet with two long breaths of fire. When the amulet was finally exposed, Syrani had expected it to be hot to the touch. But when she had reached for it—using the hand she had not injured trying to fight off the demon—it was cool.

Even now she felt a pleasantly cooling sensation, and the color was rich and beautiful.

"May I come in?" Tathiel stood in the entrance to Syrani's bedroom, a soft grin on his face.

Syrani quickly tucked the palm-sized red stone of the Amulet of Fire under her tunic, hoping he had not noticed her staring at it in wonder. "Of course." She uncrossed her legs and slipped from her bed, motioning towards a pair of chairs in the corner closest to the doorway. "I was hoping to have a moment with you, actually."

"Really?" Tathiel sat opposite her, leaning casually to rest his elbows on his knees.

"With you or your sister," Syrani amended with a shrug.

"Ah," Tathiel said. "Eilonwy is busy consoling Jaimes. It seems they still haven't found his fire spirit companion."

Syrani raised an eyebrow. "Is that the jar he's been carrying around?"

Tathiel nodded. "So you only have me to converse with at the moment, I'm afraid."

"I just have a couple of questions." Syrani nervously touched the lump that rested against her chest. "About carrying an amulet."

"Ah, I was here to discuss the same thing." Tathiel grinned again. "I saw you staring at it. It's nothing to be ashamed of. I did much the same after Melonya found the Amulet of Water."

His words did nothing to stop the warmth creeping over Syrani's face and neck. "It just feels so strange, and yet …"

"Not strange at all."

"Yes." Syrani took the amulet out again, looking from it to Tathiel. "Why?"

Tathiel shrugged, removing his own amulet. It was smaller, and the stone was an iridescent blue rather than the deep and slightly transparent red of the one around Syrani's neck. "I don't know. I can tell you that mine feels different since we've found the Amulet of Fire. Stronger, somehow."

"Stronger?" Syrani wrinkled her nose. "It already feels too strong for me to bear. I don't know if I could handle anything more powerful than this."

Syrani could feel a vast amount of energy within the stone, just beneath the gemlike surface. There was nothing in its depths to suggest a source, despite hours spent staring at it, so Syrani's guess was that the stone itself was the source.

But it held more energy than she had ever used before. Even what she had consumed while fighting the demon did not come terribly close to the contents of the Amulet of Fire.

"It will get easier, in time. The amulet will come to learn who you are, and you will find its burden easier to bear."

"Learn who I am?" Syrani asked. "You make it sound as though the thing is alive."

Tathiel laughed. "I am not so sure it isn't." The laughter faded, and his face took on a more serious look. He stared at the stone in his hand. "Sometimes, I think I can hear a voice coming from it. But I can't understand the words or meaning. Or if it is an evil thing or friendly." He laughed again. "Or if perhaps I am imagining it."

Syrani stared at her own amulet, her palm beginning to sweat. "I heard it too. Like … a whisper." She looked up at Tathiel, who had both eyebrows raised in surprise. "Only once, while I was sleeping. I thought perhaps it was a dream. But when I awoke, the amulet was in my hand, and the memory of the voice did not fade."

Tathiel held the Amulet of Water up. "Care to see what happens when fire and water mix?"

Syrani hesitated, then touched the Amulet of Fire to Tathiel's upraised stone. There was the soft clink of stone on stone, but nothing else happened. Syrani shrugged and tucked the amulet away again. "Very little, it seems."

Tathiel seemed disappointed. "I thought something would happen. An exchange of energy. Some sparks or smoke." He shook his head. "Probably for the best. We don't really understand what these things are capable of." Tathiel dropped the amulet beneath his own tunic and stood to leave. "My sister and Jaimes will be returning to Larten soon. I suppose I can follow behind, though I expect I'll be going my own way with Melonya soon after."

"And the arcanist?" Syrani asked.

"He's planning to return with Nieve, and will join his

brother at Larten in the coming weeks." Tathiel's head tilted slightly. "What will you do?"

Syrani sighed. "I don't know."

<hr>

Jaimes and Eilonwy departed later that same day with little fanfare. Jaimes had been reticent for the duration of their stay, and only after asking for an escort back into the depths of the Vyrisian woods at the base of the Starlit Summit did it become clear that he still held out hope that the fire spirit could still be found.

Eilonwy and Tathiel accompanied him, but despite her desire to join them Syrani stayed behind. They returned empty-handed, and Jaimes and Eilonwy climbed into Melonya's saddle and were gone after the briefest of farewells.

Alastor, Syrani noted, was not present for the goodbyes. Instead, she found him sitting at the foot of his father's burial tree, speaking quietly to it.

Syrani waited patiently for a break in the story he was sharing, then sat down beside him. "Do you feel better, knowing where he is?"

Alastor thought for a short moment, then nodded. "I do. I didn't think it bothered me, not knowing what had happened to him. But I suppose it did." He leaned back, bracing his weight against his palms. "And my uncle always wanted to know what became of him."

A silence fell between them. It was a comfortable quiet, and Syrani imagined that they were both listening to the gentle wind that rustled the leaves of the burial trees around them. "My father always told me that you could hear your ancestors speaking to you on the wind, if you knew how to listen."

Alastor frowned. "That's not at all concerning."

Syrani managed to suppress a laugh, but only barely. "Your father had a very similar humor. He was always pleasant to be around."

"If he could speak to us," Alastor asked, his face very serious, "what do you think he would say?"

Syrani listened to the wind again for a moment, wishing very much that she could hear words in the soft whispers of the breeze. "He would say that he was happy we were able to meet, and how sorry he was for forgetting everything about his life before Vyris." She leaned back on her hands in the same way Alastor did. "And he would say that he is very proud of you, I think, for all that you have done for Azimar."

"And would he say that he is proud of you?"

Syrani shook her head. "I don't know."

"I think he would," Alastor said with a sigh. "After all, you came back to the home you fled from. You have also helped to save Azimar. You've stopped running away from what frightens you."

"I haven't stopped running from everything." Syrani squinted at the sky, which was bright and sunny, despite the trees. "Halcia and I have not discussed what we should do next. Whether we should remain here or return to Azimar."

In fact, though she did not want to admit it to Alastor, she had been avoiding Halcia all day. Even their minds were not linked, and she was worried about what might happen when they reforged the connection between them. But the silence had given her time to think about what she wanted. It was too much to hope that Halcia would want to return to their home in Azimar, but Syrani was content to go wherever the dragon wished to, even if it meant remaining in Vyris.

Alastor was looking at her. "Then you better stop running, Syrani. Nieve and I will be leaving in a few hours, and Nieve will never forgive either of us if you choose to stay here and spend the last of that time with me."

Halcia was with Nieve, and at her entrance, Nieve quickly

departed from the empty square that Halcia had claimed for herself. Her excuse was that she was sure Gilaine had forgotten to return some of her belongings and that she wanted to track the elf down, but Syrani knew it was to give Halcia and Syrani some time alone.

"Halcia …"

"Syrani. It is time to sort this out. This stupidity that has fallen between us." Halcia's words were stern, but not overly so, and there was no hint of anger.

"Agreed. I've had a long time to think today, and …" Syrani hesitated, weighing her words.

"And?"

"And I know what I want, more than anything else."

Halcia nodded, her long neck bending slightly as her head dipped. *"You want to return to Azimar."*

"No," Syrani said quickly. "Well, yes." She sighed, then sat on the flagged stone of the courtyard, crossing her legs. "I would like to return to Azimar, but what I want more than anything is to stay with you."

Halcia curled her forelegs beneath her chest, in much the same way a cat would. *"And I want the same. It was foolish of me to let you go to the mountains alone. You could have died, and I chose to remain behind like a coward out of some senseless fear. I would not have forgiven myself if I had lost you like that."*

"Then I want you to be the one to choose where we go. You were miserable in Azimar, and I don't want to leave you like that again. If you are happier here in Vyris, then we can stay in Vyris."

"You would resent me."

"Never," Syrani said with a shake of her head. "I have made my choice of where to go, and I choose to go with you. Wherever you are, I will be beside you."

Halcia's chest rumbled briefly, and her eyes closed slowly. When she opened them again, she fixed them on Syrani. *"I have also had time to think on things today. And I think it is silly to make any choice at all."*

Syrani raised an eyebrow.

"I am a dragon, Great Ones take it. Can't I go wherever the wind will guide me and wherever my wings can carry me? Why must we make a choice at all? Why here or there? Why not both?"

Syrani laughed. "Why limit ourselves to the two choices alone? Why not the whole of the world?"

"Why not, indeed."

"That is your choice, then? To not make a choice? To live where our hearts desire us to be?"

"That is my choice. And I would not ask for it to be any other way," Halcia said solemnly. Then she added, *"I would insist that some changes are made to our home in Azimar, though. Such a small arcane barrier cannot permit me to remain at your side, and I couldn't stand to be apart from you any longer than possible."* She snorted suddenly. *"I won't sleep in some shed like a dog, though. Open air and a soft grassy bed are all I need."*

"Even in winter? And the rainy season?" Syrani asked with a smile.

"Perhaps I will require a little more," Halcia amended.

Syrani lifted a hand, and Halcia pressed her snout against it. With their touch, their minds were one again. Syrani felt the warmth of Halcia's heart consume her, and it brought tears to her cheeks.

"Let's go home."

5 1

FERRAND

Ferrand had not even bothered to bathe or change his clothing once he had entered the walled city of Etritia again. He stank of the road, of sweat and horse shit and all the old gods knew what else. He had paid a hefty price for the small stone in his breast pocket, and every bowel movement since still left fresh blood between his buttocks, but he had returned with a prize for Mothlenor. And a new anger for those that still dwelled in the place he once called his homeland.

"Small wonder Renfrid tried to stab Jorvun in his sleep," Ferrand muttered for perhaps the hundredth time. "It would have far easier on me if he had been successful. Damn the dead man."

The castle was quiet and still, and the only sound Ferrand heard as he made his way through the halls was his own footfalls and the hollow echo they made. He did not make his usual detour to the kitchens to give the younger of the two servant sisters a fierce grope of her ass and a promise to trap her alone in some dark room in a corner of the castle someday. Even the fright in the women's eyes at the sight of him would not make him happier. Not just yet.

He made straight for the king's tower, climbing the steep stone steps and grinding his teeth together as he walked. He did that a lot now, and the teeth on the ruined half of his face ached in constant torment. Several of them had cracked or chipped with the blow to his head that Ajax had given him so many years ago, and now it seemed that even the lesser of the injuries the red-haired heathen had given him were beginning to worsen. The muscles around his empty eye socket twitched.

I will find you, and you will wish I had killed you in the fields outside Etritia that night. You will beg for the simpler torments of our last encounter.

The door to Mothlenor's study was open, and Ferrand paused on the final steps. There was a draft, and it dissipated some of the chill from the tower. He heard faint crying from further inside Mothlenor's chambers, and after a brief listen he could only determine they were the sobs of a child.

The princess? Here?

What had happened while he was away that would warrant Mothlenor bringing the girl all the way to his tower? Was he punishing Anna by separating her from their child?

Ferrand entered the tower quietly, surprised to find Mothlenor standing with his back to the open door.

"My lord?" Ferrand asked, stopping just inside the entrance.

"Ferrand." Mothlenor did not turn his head, but continued to stare out of the window. The glass from the window was shattered, and the books and things that had rested on the floor beneath it were in a disarray.

"What happened, my lord?"

"I thought I had it. One of the Amulets of Power. I had the power to destroy my brother's resistance." Mothlenor turned, his face a stony mask of indifference. His skin was pale, and there was a bloodied bandage wrapped around one of his hands. "But there are two dragons soaring the skies now."

"Two," Ferrand repeated. "How?"

Mothlenor only shook his head.

"There was only one egg."

"Do you think I do not know that?" Mothlenor growled, his face twisting into an ugly grimace. He turned his back on Ferrand, looking through the window again. "Clearly something has changed. Dragons have returned to the world. First, the golden egg that was stolen. Then the sea dragon that destroyed the *Kingfisher*. And now two dragons are in the company of my brother's men." He paused for a moment. "We are doomed," he added in a soft voice.

Ferrand stepped closer and held out the tiny stone Jorvun had given him. "We are not yet doomed, my lord."

Mothlenor stared at the stone for a short moment, his gaze vacant. When he picked it up, Ferrand saw that there was a small vial in his undamaged hand. Eye and vial sat side by side in his palm, and Mothlenor stared at both for a long moment, his eyes slowly sharpening and a gleam returning to them.

"When Azimar and Vyris are yours, my king," Ferrand said, his voice deepening into an angry murmur, "I hope you will turn your attention to the north and help me cleanse that land as well."

THE ARCHIVIST

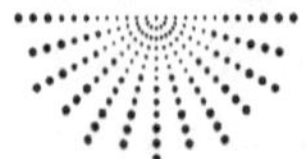

The Archivist shut the book with a heavy sigh. At the sound of both sigh and tome closing, the man in the nearby chair quickly rose to his feet. He already held a tray bearing a single intricate cup. Steam swirled over the surface as he set it down.

"Chamomile and mint, Archivist," Jask said. "To help you relax."

The Archivist smiled. "You have been reading over my shoulder again, Jask." She winked at the man, whose cheeks glowed a faint red. "How else would you know to give me the same concoction that your grand-niece prepared for her guests?"

"It seemed a fitting brew," Jask said stiffly.

"It is a fitting brew," the Archivist admitted, sipping lightly from it. "And I suppose warning you once more of the dangers of trying to emulate your sister and Arella will fall on deaf ears."

"There is no harm in brewing a little tea for you, Archivist." Jask's pale blue eyes were gentle. The familial resemblance was impossible to miss.

"How can you be sure, dear child?"

Jask shrugged. "You would have stopped me before I had even started, otherwise."

The Archivist laughed. "Perhaps, perhaps." She sipped again, then set the cup aside. "Though that is not what the Sight is meant to be used for, Jask."

"I know." Jask sat in the chair across from the Archivist, staring openly at the book on her desk. "Do you know yet what will become of this?"

The Archivist shook her head. "No."

"So there is still nothing that can be done to help them?"

The Archivist sighed. "Jask—"

"I know," Jask repeated. "That is not what the Sight is meant to be used for."

"But you worry for them."

"They are my family."

"Everyone here had family, Jask," the Archivist said with a sad smile. "And they all had to stand by and let events unfold as they were meant to. We are archivists, Jask. Not soldiers."

"I am *an* archivist, yes," Jask said with a nod. "A lost son borne of the Coven and taken where no one would know me. But you," Jask dipped his head in her direction, "you are *the* Archivist. The first of our kind. The true Matriarch of the Coven. And you can save them."

The Archivist closed her eyes, both her natural eye and the arcane eye that granted her and many women of her bloodline the Coven's Gift. "I cannot."

"There must be way," Jask countered.

"There is no way."

Jask laughed. "You are the Archivist," he repeated. "You are closer to the Gift than any other."

"And in this matter, my Sight does not extend any further than that of your relatives," she admitted. "My Sight is failing me, Jask. I cannot See enough to be of any help to the outside world, even if I wanted to forsake my oath and give them counsel."

Jask's eyes were wide. "Your Sight is failing? What will that mean for us? For the Azimar Archives? For the last of the Coven?"

"I don't know," the Archivist said simply. She pushed the now completed record of the finding of the Amulet of Fire closer to Jask. "Bring the next book. And some more tea, if you don't mind."

THANK YOU!

I hope you enjoyed *The Book of Fire*.
If you did, please leave a review on your preferred storefront.

Reviews help other readers like you find my work, and your
support means I can continue doing what I love: Writing.

As always, you can stay up to date on publishing news and
special offers by joining my newsletter at
JacklynHennionAuthor.com.

Thank you!
Jacklyn Hennion

THE STORY CONTINUES...

Coming Soon

The Book of Earth
The Azimar Archives Book Four

ABOUT THE AUTHOR

Jacklyn Hennion is an avid lover of sweets and wine. She enjoys Netflix and video games, and often spends the evenings winding down with a bit of crochet work. She and her husband currently live in Oklahoma. *The Book of Death* is Jacklyn's first published novel.